Film

Sean Condon is the author of *My 'Dam Life, Drive Thru America* and *Sean and David's Long Drive*. His email address is powdermaker@hotmail.com

For more information on Sean Condon visit www.4thestate.com/seancondon

Film

Sean Condon

FOURTH ESTATE • *London*

This paperback edition first published in 2004
First published in Great Britain in 2003 by
Fourth Estate
A Division of HarperCollins*Publishers*
77–85 Fulham Palace Road
London W6 8JB
www.4thestate.com

Copyright © Sean Condon 2003

1 2 3 4 5 6 7 8 9 10

The right of Sean Condon to be identified as the author of
this work has been asserted by him in accordance with the
Copyright, Designs and Patents Act 1988

A catalogue record for this book is available from
the British Library

ISBN 0-00-714317-6

Typeset by Rowland Phototypesetting Ltd,
Bury St Edmunds, Suffolk
Printed in Great Britain by
Clays Ltd, St Ives plc

And now that the tumult was gone, what had the movies been?
A flood of claptrap that had helped bitch up the world.
Screenwriter Ben Hecht, quoting
producer David O. Selznick

Part 1

1

Opening shot. Panning from left to right there is a garden path, new but already worn and wearied by tired footfall, flanked by dirty white pebbles and brown crabgrass, a few young, pale dog-woods and pines, one of which is supported by a stake, and a garage empty but for the simmering shade. A zombie, its face covered in a mixture of self-raising flour and cochineal, stumbles through the side gate and trips over a snake, coiled like a hose on a bed of weeds. As it staggers, a drop of cochineal blood from the creature's forehead drips into its left eye. The zombie begins wink-ing urgently. Its mouth is a slack 'o', its arms are held out straight in front and the oversize boots it wears are heavy, forcing a Karloffian lurch. A dog, a black-and-white border collie named Beau, runs up the driveway, across the lawn and up into the zombie's stiff but welcoming arms. The dog's fat pink tongue licks away all the makeup – the scars and blood and dirt and coffin-pallor – and the zombie is gone, leaving behind a faintly bewildered-looking man in his early forties, his face hot and slick from dog foam.

'We have to do it again now. Beau's wrecked it. And you were winking, Big Dad. It wasn't scary.' The director, the zombie's young son Henry, steps around the Super 8 camera, which is mounted on a tripod. The second-hand Vivitar camera that Henry bought with his own money has a tricky timer – sometimes it goes on before it's supposed to; sometimes hours after, when no one is around. 'Be scary,' he whines. He has a tendency toward whining. 'The hose looks stupid. It looks like a hose. How 'bout we go get a real snake from the pet store in Hallowell, Dad? Please.'

'I'm not sure that's a good idea, Hank. It might eat the dog.' He walks up onto the brick porch, kicks off the boots, then drags his feet across the brown shag-pile of the living room and into the kitchen to reapply his makeup.

On the front lawn Henry rewrites his cardboard clapper board with a felt marker stolen from school. 'Zombie in the Suburbs!!! Scene 1, shot 1, take 2.' Beau the dog runs around back. Somewhere down the street Henry can hear two lawnmowers and the constant roar of a Camaro, which he knows is purple and belongs to Rick Reynolds' stepbrother Carl. Carl has greasy hair like a wet mop and blackheads and drives too fast. Carl is scary.

While he waits for his father to become dead again, Henry wanders over to the driveway and picks up a handful of gravel, letting the cool, rough stones slip through his fist back onto the ground. He used to play on the driveway a lot last summer, when he was a bit younger. Tanks and soldiers and cars. It was easy to have fun with dirt and rocks and a few toys, back then.

'I'm older now,' he says aloud, to the plants, 'I've grown up a bit.' The plants nod in the wind. Henry accidentally steps on a caterpillar, yellowing the underneath of his sneaker. 'Oops,' he says. 'I'm very sorry.' He remembers the morning, not too long ago, when he discovered the uprooted pine tree, wrenched out of its place when Big Dad had driven into it the night before. Henry had hammered in the stake and tied up the limp, nearly flattened tree all by himself. He'd learned in school that Maine's nickname was 'the Pine Tree State' so he felt he should be kind to them.

The front door bangs shut as Big Dad picks up the boots, then sits on the end of the porch to put them on. Henry shouts up to him. 'Act like the hose is really a real snake, okay?'

'Right you are, Mr DeMille,' his father says with a wink.

'Okay,' he says, squinting through the viewfinder, seeing the world in small square sections, the way he likes it. 'You know

4

what to do, Dad. Be scary. Just like the last time, only better. This is gonna be really good.'

Noise. A few days later Henry's mother, Sandra, has made some popcorn and there is a buttery smell coming from the kitchen. She'd said 'goddammit' a few times as she scraped the bottom of the burnt saucepan. Now they are all sitting on the brown velvet couch that Henry loves to rub his hands on, in a secret way, though he is never sure why. He tries not to like the feeling because he is making an effort to be more of a normal kid. Someone who likes sport and likes other kids. Kids whose fathers have normal, proper jobs that last their whole lives.

Jack 'Big Dad' Powdermaker sits on an armchair breathing loudly through his nose and making sucking sounds. He smells of his latest job: miserable, cold and silent, like the green linoleum they have in the foyer of the small theater where he is stage-managing an insignificant production of *A View from a Bridge*. Big Dad doesn't like being a stage manager. 'I could murder that lead,' he'd said one night last week, his voice fat and cold and yellow with anger. Henry can also smell the coffee-chocolate pastilles his father is always popping in his mouth when he is nervous about something.

Big Dad's an actor. Last year he was on a TV show for a few weeks and came home from New York City on weekends talking loudly in funny voices. He played a doctor. Henry was proud of him then. Big Dad used to talk a lot about finding his audience, developing his craft, ad-libbing and other things, but now he is mostly either very quiet or very angry, like in the acting exercises he used to do where he would walk around the bedroom waving his arms and shouting at nobody. Henry would sometimes listen from the hallway or watch from the living-room window, looking across the courtyard into the bedroom. Big Dad could seem very angry, and then later, when he came out from the bedroom, he could be very quiet again, his face soft pink instead of shiny red. 'An actor, unobserved, is merely a man,' Big Dad once told Henry, as the color drained from his father's cheeks.

Henry puts a piece of popcorn in his mouth and rolls it around his tongue, making a 'mmmm' sound. Daniel, who used to keep

Henry awake with his constant crying, lies on the floor pointing at things and making sounds with his raw mouth. Daniel is a mystery to Henry – suddenly one day he was just there, crying and eating all the time. Like a small machine.

'We're ready, Hank. Let's go,' orders Big Dad.

'Don't call me Hank, Dad. You named me Henry, not Hank,' says Henry, trying not to sound sulky.

Daniel murmurs on the carpet.

'It's the same.'

Henry switches off the light and, in the half-light, addresses the family in his best voice, measured pauses between each over-articulated word. 'Ladies and gentlemen and baby. I welcome all of you to the première of *Zombie in the Suburbs*, a film by the very talented young director Henry Powdermaker. I made it with my own money and no lessons or help from anyone except you, Big Dad. I have to make a warning that it is scary and you may be frightened of what you see. But that is just the way of life – and films. And now . . . on with the show!'

Clapping smatters about the dining room, the sharp sounds ruffling Henry's hair and reddening his cheeks. He flicks the switch on the projector, a burning dust smell mixing with the popcorn, and sits down to watch his masterpiece once again.

What was moments before an ordinary wall comes alive. The film's title splashes across the wall in red marker, written on a clear plastic box then filmed against a white background – the 'shirt box credit technique' Henry read about in his manual. Then Henry's name the same way, but only for a few dumb seconds. Next time he'd shoot it longer. There is a quick flash of Henry's back that's not supposed to be there, due to the faulty timer. Then the words 'Starring Jack Powdermaker as the ZOMBIE!!!' appear, bringing with them laughter from Mother and Big Dad. There is a moment of black before the zombie crashes through the side gate, stamps on a hose/snake and begins his unholy rampage of terror in the suburbs of Augusta, Maine by eating Beau the dog – the digested portion of whom is played by a piece of raw lamb that Jack had attacked with an enthusiasm that was, to Henry's mind, disgusting, but truly frightening.

Three minutes and ten seconds later, 'The End ... or is it!!?' chillingly daubs the living-room wall. Big Dad and Daniel are asleep, lightly snoring and moaning respectively. Sandra tells Henry that he is a very, very clever boy with a bright future. 'Thank you,' says Henry humbly, as he winds the film back onto another reel. He stares hard at his sleeping father.

'Don't worry about your father, kid. He's very tired. He's had a hard day.'

'I'm not worried about him,' Henry says.

'What do you think you mean by that?' says Sandra, grabbing at the bowl of popcorn.

'I don't mean anything,' says Henry. 'He's just the father. That's all.'

Henry's father seems to live in a state of constant distraction, only dimly aware of himself and still less aware of his two children. With a series of movements, gestures and stagey mannerisms that appear rehearsed, yet long forgotten, Big Dad Jack never quite hits his marks. He regards Henry and Daniel with a quizzical distance, confused not so much about who they are, but about what role they are supposed to assume in his life. As though they are unknown players, hired hands, bit parts. Henry feels that Big Dad, the out-of-work actor, needs direction.

'Is it hard to be an actor, Dad?'

'When you're not acting, it's very hard.'

On Saturday afternoons, if he doesn't have to work, Big Dad works on a detailed scale model of a lobster boat, a 'Downeaster', while he listens to the horse races, flying into brief but intensely fierce rages when he loses, remaining silent if he wins. These days there are few things that get him excited – the boat, horse racing, Greek food and bouzouki music, and the rich sadness of his own fatherless childhood, hot and Jesuit in a dry, country boarding school somewhere in North Dakota. Henry hates the way his father's face will scrunch up whenever he talks about when he was a boy, crying and making sounds like a blocked sink. Henry often wonders if Jack is sometimes pretending to be dead, like his own father. Big Dad was born on December 7th, 1941 – Pearl

Harbor – and likes to pretend that the Japanese sent his mother into premature labor. But his birth had taken place thousands of miles from Hawaii.

Not too long ago Henry loved his father without question. The bright, sharp smells on his rough face, and the big, broad humor he displayed when things were going well for him: when he would walk around the house practicing his part, pretending to be a prince or a policeman. But most of all, Henry loved the flash and sweep of Big Dad's headlights on his bedroom wall as the car swung into the driveway, back from a theater, or sometimes a television studio. The comforting crunch of tires grinding gravel. 'Dad's home,' Henry would think and finally allow himself to sleep. But Henry had grown a little older, more aware of his father's limited range. And Big Dad hadn't had an acting job in a long while.

'Will I look like you when I finish growing up?' Henry asked one night at the kitchen table.

'I suppose so, yeh.' Big Dad always made 'yeah' sound like 'yeh', as though trying to save time. 'But you'd better hope not. Look at me.' He pointed a stubby finger at his gray waves, then angled it down to the spread of his belly. 'The camera's added ten pounds, permanently.'

Henry looked. 'You're all right. Your eyes are like mud.'

His mother laughed.

'Yes, I suppose I'm all right,' Big Dad said. He slumped a little further on the paisley and cane chair, accentuating the failure of his body.

'Who will Daniel look like?' asked Henry.

'He'll look like all of us. A little bit of everybody.'

'You could call him a mutt,' Big Dad said, leaving the table.

'If you wanted to be a bastard, I suppose you could.'

Mom said that. She'd called Big Dad a bastard. And after that it was quiet, only the murmur of the television creeping in and out of every room in the house. Henry lay awake in bed for a long while, examining the shapes of shadows on the walls. Later Carl's Camaro tore a dark, purple hole in the night, seeping into Henry's dreams.

2

Interior. After school Henry slurps a bowl of cereal as he sits in the living room reading a few pages of a movie book he has selected from his personal library. Before the flakes have had time to sog, he has usually set the bowl down on the marble table and is making careful notes with a green pencil, his milk-caked mouth open, his eyes unblinking. Mostly the notes are of a technical nature ('Show eyes and mouth up big when people are kissing,' he wrote one day, while examining a still from *Chinatown*). However, he sometimes timidly explores the metaphorical: 'Is the spider a disease?' he asked himself in very small handwriting after a scene near the end of *This Sporting Life*.

Lord of the Flies: 'If I was on Lord of the Flies Island, would I be Ralph or Jack? Must be careful not to be Piggy.'

Peeping Tom: 'Camera/tripod can kill.'

Sounder: 'When dogs act they don't know they are acting. They are just doing what somebody tells them. But what happens if the dog thinks that the actor is its new master and it likes him? Are the dogs sad to go back to their old life?'

Psycho: 'Do not watch again by self.'

'How will I get to Hollywood?' he would wonder after just about every film he saw. 'Will they let me in?'

His notebook is full, a lush green field of ideas, observations and plans, because Henry has decided to become a serious person as soon as possible. He has decided exactly what he wants to do with his life ('make films'), when ('as soon as possible') and why ('please discuss this with self later in maturity'). This decision came to him as he watched a 1932 film called *Night World* directed by Hobart Henley. It was on television one Sunday afternoon and Henry was transfixed by the strange story. Boris Karloff as the decayed and corrupt owner of a nightclub, another man – Lew something – as the troubled son of a woman who had murdered her husband. There was a beautiful, wise-cracking chorus girl and George Raft as a Broadway tinhorn – an expression Henry had never heard but quickly adopted and used randomly and wrongly forever after. He loved *Night World* and decided once and for all that Sunday that he wanted to have one of these lives – to be any of these characters, or all of them. Even the troubled son with the dead father.

The only stumble in his development is schoolwork. Henry does not care for it because he is not learning the things he needs to know. Last year they made him do a project about lighthouses, which he hated because they don't even have lighthouses in the *proper* states and he had already made up his mind never to be in one anyway. Another time it was trying to learn the recorder and musical notes. It isn't in his plans to be a recorder player, so why couldn't they just leave him *alone* about that? He would much rather know about other things, the important things. He also isn't very interested in sports and doesn't have a thousand best friends like everyone else, but at least you don't get in *trouble* for that.

Henry can hear other children playing outside, their voices high and wispy, rising like thin clouds. The sounds don't usually bother him; they are merely background noise. However, on this particular day he hears a little boy shrieking, 'Give it back to me! Give it back.' The words ring in Henry's ears. 'Give it back . . . give it back . . .' He wonders what the child is talking about – a red ball, a stolen pet, a piece of sun-greasy cheese on a biscuit? It could be anything. There is a shrill desperation in the boy's voice that makes Henry realize he misses being a child, like he was last summer.

It was Sunday afternoon and unseasonably hot. The rest of the family was out looking at swimming pools, their own backyard being waterless; Big Dad Jack was toying with the idea that he might buy a pool in time for next summer, if he could 'get a half-decent run in a half-decent production', if he could find a builder who wouldn't give him a 'pants-on screwing'. Henry had heard the 'pants-on screwing' business every Sunday for the past month and now preferred to stay at home, chomping as quietly as he could on a peanut-butter roll while he watched a PBS documentary about the director Joseph Losey, occasionally making notes in one of his exercise books. Losey was born in Wisconsin but exiled himself to England after being called upon to testify at HUAC (or 'hewack', as Henry wrote, unaware of the acronym), where, according to the program, he made the best work of his career.

However, in 1947, before the communist witch-hunt, Losey had directed a film called *The Boy With Green Hair*, a parable about an orphan who is ostracized by the community after he wakes up one morning to find that his hair has mysteriously turned green. As soon as he heard the title Henry wanted to be a boy with green hair – no matter that at the end of the film the townsfolk band together and try to shave the boy's head. He imagined himself strutting the streets with a spearmint crewcut, stared at in quiet, curious awe. 'That's the boy with green hair,' people would whisper. They would never laugh. 'Look at him. Look at his beautiful green hair. It's like grass.'

By the time Henry came out of his hair reverie the documentary had moved on to Losey's 1963 film *The Servant*, with James Fox and Dirk Bogarde. They were showing a scene where Bogarde, as the scheming, manipulative servant Barrett, secretly observes his foppish employer Fox through a rounded mirror he is shining, the servant's face freakishly distorted by the mirror's convexity. Henry leaped off the couch, breadcrumbs, books and pens flying from his lap as he dived to the floor, scrabbling on his hands and knees toward the television, thrusting his face right at the screen and staring hard into the mirror which, before he could focus, was replaced by a man in an armchair. Henry slumped to the carpet and let out a deeply disappointed moan. Now he would never know if a mirror on film worked the same way it did in real life. Could you be reflected in it? Could you see a boy's green hair in a mirror on film?

A few hours later the other Powdermakers staggered into the house, limp and tetchy with heat, red-skinned and scratchy red-eyed.

'Can I get green hair?' Henry asked his mother. 'In the foreseeable future?'

She laughed and flapped the collar of her shirt. 'I suppose if you ate too much broccoli. Or peas, perhaps. Why?'

'What's green hair?' asked Jack from the kitchen, where he stood hanging his head in front of the open refrigerator.

'It's hair that's green,' Henry shouted.

'Don't shout, Henry,' Sandra panted. 'It's too hot.'

'I don't mean from vegetables,' Henry said. 'I mean, can I please get my hair turned green?'

'Jesus Christ, it's hot in here!' Big Dad shouted. 'Why do you want your hair turned green, Hank?'

Henry looked over at his father. He seemed to be actually glowing with heat, like a demon. 'I need to for an experiment.'

'Take some pork chops out of the freezer, will you Jaaaack?' Sandra raised her voice as much as she could.

'What!?' Jack shouted.

'Remove pork chops from freezer! What sort of experiment requires you to have green hair?' Sandra asked. 'Is it for school?'

'No. Do mirrors work on TV? Or in a film?'

Henry's mother laughed; hot, fatigued and breathy sounds that came from a dry throat.

'How many!?'

Sandra grabbed the arms of the cane chair and heaved herself up with a quiet 'fuck'.

'I'll do it,' Henry said gathering his pens and notebook. His mother flopped back down. 'Do they?' Henry asked again as he headed to the kitchen.

'Do what?' Sandra asked, her long, perspiring neck stretched over the back of the chair.

'Do mirrors work on television or in a film?'

'I don't know, Henry. It's not the sort of thing that's really very important, is it?'

'I guess not,' Henry muttered. 'But can I get green hair anyway?'

'How many d'you want, Sandra?' Henry's father shouted.

'Not in the *foreseeable* future, Henry.' She giggled again. 'Maybe when you're older.'

'How old?'

'Oh, I don't know . . . fifty-three.'

'*How* many!?'

Documentary techniques. Waiting among the warm smells of the laundry, he would hear a noise and appear suddenly from around a corner, crouching low before he dived into a roll across the padded umber linoleum of the kitchen, staring up at whoever walked in, his right eye a clenched slit and his left contracting and dilating wildly as he tried to focus.

'What on earth are you doing, Henry?' his mother would say.

'Ah, Hank rolling on the floor. What's he up to?' Big Dad would wonder. 'Creating another small-screen role for the old man?'

This technique yielded little more than people looking down at the camera appearing startled, bewildered or annoyed. A fine montage in itself but not exactly what Henry had in mind. He wanted to capture life as it truly was, as it proceeded without the camera. He wanted to know what was going on while he wasn't around.

Nearly everything with the new project was a problem – lighting, shifting focus, turning the camera on, its give-away whir, and having only three minutes and ten seconds of film in each reel. The only thing that wasn't a problem was location. There could be only one. The most mysterious room of all, a place with an atmosphere completely disconnected from the rest of the house, the secret shrine in which Christmas presents were hidden, and muffled arguments colored long, hot nights a steamy gray – his parents' bedroom.

Lying on his side on top of the wardrobe opposite Jack and Sandra's bed, Henry opened the aperture to its widest, rigged the motor to shoot one frame every five seconds, focused long, aimed down and wrapped the camera in a small blanket, a swaddled baby Cyclops. He jumped down onto the carpet, a small thud traveling the length of the empty house like an intruder.

Gradually the afternoon came to life: Mother brought Daniel home from day care, then went to the market to get something for dinner. 'Keep an eye on him while I'm gone, will you Henry? He's making noises,' she'd said, shaking her car keys all over the place. Henry watched Daniel mumbling for a while and wondered what was going on in his brother's mouth and mind. Spit and nothing, he decided. Big Dad arrived home earlier than usual – that evening's small production having been cancelled due to poor box office – and didn't say anything after 'Where's your mother?'

was answered. Sandra came in the back way, through the laundry, and started cooking right away. Crab cakes and potato salad. Steam and starch. Mom and Big Dad ate in competitive silence which Henry had tried to break with a general enquiry.

'Dad?'

'Henry?'

'*Dad.*'

'*Henry.*'

As he lay in bed that night, Henry listened carefully for the sounds of his mother and father preparing for bed – the clicks of lights, the closing of doors, the shutting up and shutting off of the television. As soon as he heard the first sound of the routine – the click of the kitchen light – he jumped out of bed, ran down the hall to his parents' bedroom, stood on a chair in front of the wardrobe and switched on the camera, hoping the timer would work. And was back in bed before the late thunder silenced everything.

3

Sound effects. His mother and father left at seven o'clock the following evening – Mark Antony and Cleopatra climbing into a dark-blue Chrysler, careful not to brush their togas on the gravel in the driveway. Henry waved goodbye from the front porch. 'She'll be here in a minute!' his mother called, poking her laurel-leafed head out the passenger-seat window.

'I know!' Henry shouted back. He'd been told five times in the last half-hour that Madeleine Ford, the girl from two doors down, would be popping in to keep an eye on him and Daniel. 'You told me!'

Madeleine knocked on the door fifteen minutes later, just as Henry's 1950s black-and-white murder marathon was beginning with *Strangers on a Train*. 'Hi Madeleine. Come and have a look at Robert Walker's face,' he called to her as he heard the front door open, letting in the smell of rain. Madeleine crept into the living room on tiptoe, snuck up to the couch on which Henry was sitting, straight-backed and alert. She watched his thin shoulders rise and fall, then pounced, grabbing him and screeching like a wild thing. Henry didn't react. 'I saw you in the television,' he said. 'I knew you were there.'

'Clever, clever.' Madeleine sat down beside him and pulled her long, not-quite-red hair back over her shoulders. 'Where's Daniel?'

'Asleep. Look at that man's face. This is outstanding casting. It's the perfect face of a murderer, isn't it?'

'I don't know, I can't be bothered putting my glasses on.'

'Can't you see without them? Go closer to the TV.'

Madeleine crawled across the floor and sat directly in front of the television. 'He just looks all doughy to me. My eyes are hopeless without glasses. Even with, sometimes.'

'He's bad dough. Have you seen this film? It's called *Strangers on a Train* by Alfred Hitchcock, who they call The Master because of his various techniques. It's about these men who are supposed to do each other's murders. Robert Walker wants the man in the tennis clothes to murder his father. He hates him. And he's supposed to murder the tennis player's wife because the tennis player loves someone else. He keeps saying "Criss-cross! Criss-cross!" and making a sneaky face.'

'I haven't seen it. I don't like black and white. I like it when you can see the blood, like in *Carrie* or like that.'

'Haven't seen that. Not allowed.'

'Just as well. It'd give you nightmares and you'd wet your pants.'

'I would not.'

'You haven't seen it, so how would you know, Henny-Penny?'

'Because I'm not scared of films. They're only films.'

After *Night of the Hunter*, where Robert Mitchum tried to murder two children who stood in the way of him getting some money, Henry began watching *The Bad Seed*. In that film, a young girl who pretends to be too-good-to-be-true murders people – even other children! – when things don't go her way. Gradually the girl's mother realizes that her daughter – her adopted daughter, who turns out to be the child of a homicidal maniac – is a murderer

15

and tries to kill her with sleeping pills before shooting herself. But the little girl doesn't die, except at the very end when she is struck by a bolt of lightning.

> Dream little one, dream.
> Dream my little one, dream.
> Though the hunter in the night,
> Fills your childish heart with fright.
> Fear is only a dream,
> So dream little one, dream.

Henry quietly sang from *Night of the Hunter* to Madeleine, asleep next to him on the couch. During the commercial breaks he watched her face, not sure if it was beautiful, because he felt himself too young to know. But he knew there was something about her eyes. They were green and when they held him in steady, luminous gaze they seemed to calm him, to reduce him to still staring silence – an audience of one in an emerald cinema. If he'd been allowed to have green hair it would have been perfect. Sometimes he took deep breaths and gently stroked her high cheekbones with the back of his shaking index finger. Once, her hand reached up and softly enclosed his own, and all of Henry, except his heart, froze. She *was* beautiful . . .

By the time his parents returned from the fancy-dress party, Henry was asleep on the living-room couch, his face bathed in the sickly gray cast of the television, flashing white noise and softly hissing in the dark room. He half woke but didn't open his eyes when he heard the sharp sound of keys in the front door, the hoarse giggling of his mother, and his father's slow thudding on the hallway carpet, the sound changing to a heavy crack as Big Dad reached the linoleum of the kitchen. They were drunk. Madeleine had left. Henry breathed slowly.

'Left the TV on,' he heard his father say in a thick, sluggish voice. 'Thinks power's free.' Breathing roughly through his nose, like a bull. 'Watches too much TV.'

'It's not TV, Jack, it's movies. All he watches is movies.'

'Guess that's what you get when you conceive a kid in a cinema, yeh? Little cinephile ... phobe, whatever it is. D'you remember the movie?'

'Vaguely. Was it *A Man and a Woman*? I 'member that music.'

Henry heard his father humming a dainty tune, a kitchen drawer graze open, then the sound of rattling cutlery.

'What're you doing?' his mother said. Then, 'Oh, put that away, Jack. What d'you think you're going to do with that?'

'It's the only way.'

Henry heard the sound of a knife against a sharpening steel. He could see the bone handle in his mind and imagine small sparks flying off the blade. He could see his father's eyes, brown like clay you get stuck in.

'Put it back, Jack,' his mother repeated. 'Jack!'

His father sounded breathless. 'Gotta be done. Knife's almost sharp enough.'

His father was going to kill him. Henry struggled to wake further, a cold terror clearing his muddy thoughts. The whooshing of steel on steel abruptly stopped. Henry froze on the couch, listening to his father's strained panting. 'Please, please, please, please,' Henry silently prayed. Images of missing children, vanished children, murdered children, wailing, pleading, bloodied little boys in pajamas crowded his screaming imagination. 'Please don't let him kill me. I haven't done anything wrong. *Please.* I haven't done anything.' The cracking footsteps and steaming bull snorts came closer to the living room.

His mother's voice: 'Jack.' More footsteps and angry breathing. 'Jack! Come back here. There'll be trouble if you do it this way. Big, big trouble.' Henry whimpered. His mother laughed and Henry's mind saw her big, nicotine-stained teeth glaring at him. He clapped his hands over his hot ears and squeezed his eyes shut, imagined himself getting up off the couch and silently running down the hallway, into his bedroom and diving under his bed. Then opened his eyes to the harsh white buzz of the television, and dark silence from the kitchen.

The next morning Henry woke early. Exhausted and tired-eyed he crept out of his bedroom, down to the kitchen and there, on the linoleum floor, he saw a large carving knife lying next to a costume-hire Roman sandal, its knotted leather straps cut and hacked.

4

Première. Big Dad turns up the radio, sending scratchy AM race-calling from the living room into the kitchen, where he is inking and stinking his fingers with raw squid or rolling vine leaves and meatballs. 'Kiftethes,' as he loves to say often, 'is Greek for meatballs, yeh.' In between crushing garlic or squeezing lemons for the dips, he stops and listens to a horse race and begins pounding the bench as a nasal commentator calls his misfortune. 'Holy Christ!' he'll cry as he tears up another ticket. Then he'll storm out to the back yard and check the spiced lamb roasting on a spit underneath a green canvas tarpaulin.

Henry loves it when Mother and Big Dad Jack have a party, the house full of strangers, smoke and music. The night is November 22nd, his parents' tenth wedding anniversary. Henry tries not to get too excited about the after-dinner mints that he knows are hidden in the drawer in the dining room. At five o'clock, Daniel is taken away to be blurrily watched by Madeleine who hates wearing glasses. At six, Henry lies on the floor of his bedroom to watch the cars pull up, ready to run to the front door and breathlessly greet the guests. In a way it is Henry's party too, because he's arranged with his parents to show his latest film, which is in every way a world première, because he has not yet even seen it himself. He hopes it is more than just Jack and Sandra sleeping. He hopes the timer worked.

A few hours later the house is warm with alcohol breath and garlic breath and chat breath. Most of the guests are other actors and actresses. A few people from the doctor's office where Sandra works. There is bouzouki music strangling the speakers, and people seemingly everywhere. Henry notices that the actors all talk much louder than the office people and that they like to tell long stories which end in gales of laughter. He wanders through the sea of legs feeling small and ignored until he claps his hands and announces that everybody has to come to the dining room and watch his film.

'Oh, not now, Hank,' Big Dad says, breathing smoke and meaty smells all over his son.

'But you said,' whines Henry. 'And everything's set up.'

Somewhere up above him an adult cries, 'Yeah Dad, you said!' Henry blushes because the mimic is perfect. It must be an actor.

'All right,' shouts Big Dad. 'Everyone into the screening room! Come on!' Clapping his big hands loudly, or mockingly. Henry cannot tell.

The room is crowded with people, sitting on couches, dragged chairs and cleared table tops, squatting on the floor and falling into each other in the darkness. There are pockets of chatter everywhere. 'You never know, Corinne, little fella could be the next Steven Spielberg.' 'You know I met him when I auditioned for *The Sugarland Express*.' 'Who got the part?' 'Bill Atherton. Almost threw myself in the Kennebec River when I found out.' 'You're hurting my toe, Allan.' 'What, no lobster? I've never been to a party in Maine without lobster.' 'Well *something* was pinching my butt earlier.' Laughter ripples across the floor.

'Excuse me, everybody,' says Henry as loud as he can. 'I am proud to present my new film, called *Mother and Father*. By me, Henry Powdermaker, the son. And starring Jack Powdermaker and Sandra Powdermaker.' There is applause and somebody says, 'I love their work.' Jack says, 'This better be good, Hank. It's the first film job I've had in a long, long while.' The guests laugh at Jack's joke. Henry turns on the projector and hits the 'frame by frame' button. Things happen quickly after that.

Frame by frame
1. An empty bedroom.
2. An empty bedroom.
3. An empty bedroom.
4. A woman – a mother, a wife, a medical secretary, Sandra

Powdermaker – with a green plastic laurel wreath in her hair enters the room.

5. Sandra Powdermaker pulls back the bed covers.
6. Sandra Powdermaker, in a light-blue nightie, lies on the bed.
7. She reaches for a book on her bedside table.
8. A man – the man of the house, Jack Powdermaker – enters the room, walking frozen at an odd angle.
9. Close to the camera, and therefore blurred, he opens the wardrobe door.
10. Jack lies on the bed naked except for a green wreath on his head.
11. Jack kicks the bedclothes off the bed.
12. He begins playing with his dick.
13. His wife turns on her side.
14. Jack reaches for his wife.
15. Sandra pushes Jack's hand off her shoulder.
16. Jack kneels on the bed, facing his wife, still holding his dick.
17. Sandra reaches down for the bedcovers.
18. Jack grabs Sandra by the hair.
19. Sandra has Jack's dick in her mouth. The wreath is gone from her head.
20. Sandra has Jack's dick in her mouth.
21. Sandra tries to push away from Jack, but Jack is holding her down.
22. Jack lies down, still gripping Sandra by the hair.
23. Sandra spits on her husband's stomach.
24. Sandra slides off her side of the bed.
25. Jack gets off the bed from his side.
26. They meet in the middle, in front of the bed.
27. Jack pushes Sandra backward.
28. Sandra stands with her arms folded, saying something to Jack.
29. Jack steps toward Sandra.
30. Jack hits Sandra on the right side of her head.
31. Sandra is on her knees, weeping and shielding her head. Jack's right arm is raised and making a fist.

There is blankness and silence as the projector is switched off and nobody speaks.

Part 2

5

Ext. Night. Two silhouettes – one broad, the other narrow – sitting on a wooden bench overlooking an empty school sports field. Two murmuring shapes cut into the failing light of summer, thin, pale clouds spat out like the labored breath of a pollen-choked sky, the falling dark of Wednesday night just moments away. Behind the shapes is a large red brick building covered with ivy, surrounded by plants. Two or three dim lights cast a yellow glow inside bleak offices. Closer to the silhouettes, the murmuring becomes conversation.

'Well if you're that bored, why don't you come to the game on Saturday and after we'll go do something?' one broad-shouldered outline says, spitting a mandarin seed into a trash can.

The other dark shape, smaller and thinner than the one it sits next to, chomps down on an apple. 'I can't, Charles.'

'Keep it down with that apple. What do you mean you can't? You in detention?'

'No. I just can't.'

'What the fuck, Henry? Why not?'

'Promise you won't laugh?'

'What am I – your girlfriend? If it's funny, of course I'll laugh.'

'It's not funny. It's closer to . . . psychotic,' says Henry. 'And sort of pathetic.' He takes a final bite of his apple and throws it toward the trash can, hitting the rim, skidding across the concrete then rolling down the grassy bank out of sight. 'Damn.'

'Well, get on with it.'

'If I watch you play baseball, it'll remind me of *Bang the Drum Slowly*.'

'What's that?'

'A film about a baseball player. A dying baseball player. Robert De Niro's a catcher and he dies, so watching you'll remind me of it.'

'Apart from the fact that I play first base, so fucking what?'

'I can't watch films anymore. Since my father went. It makes me feel very ... creepy.'

'Don't be such an idiot,' Charlie says with soft contempt.

'I'm not being an idiot, it's just ... it's the way it is.'

'Well get over it. You don't know what you're missing out on – I'm absolutely fantastic.'

'How?'

'A rare combination of speed and size. Makes me practically invincible.'

'No, how am I supposed to get over it?'

Charlie stands then picks up his schoolbag and slings it across his muscular shoulder. The clouds shift and reveal a near-full moon, low and large, silver-bright against the growing darkness. From the side, bent with their bags over their shoulders, the silhouettes look like horror-movie hunchbacks as they walk away from the moonlit outline of the bench, the silver-dusted black grass of the oval, the doused lights of the vacated offices, and fade out into the night. 'Be normal,' Charlie says.

'This is Henry,' he said into the bedroom mirror. 'He's a little worried about his future.' Staring at himself Henry recalled the conversation he'd had with Charlie a few days earlier and tried to decide what he looked like. Normal? Probably not after everything that had happened. Handsome? No – too soft in the cheeks and jowl to be truly handsome, he thought. There was a crinkled concern in his brown, gold-flecked eyes that was probably permanent and might rule out handsomeness for ever. And that, too, was probably because of what had happened that night. He smiled at himself. It was a wrenched, wretched and snaggle-toothed hole of glistening pink, off-white and hot black, lopsided and disconcertingly fake-looking. 'Good Lord,' he gasped. 'You're not normal, you're . . . you're . . . ridiculous.'

By the time he'd turned sixteen, Henry Powdermaker's partial blindness had lasted for more than seven years. He could see but he refused to look, to watch. It was a self-imposed, selective blindness: a condition of both will and instinct; difficult, and at the same time astonishingly easy. He had refused to watch films since he was eight years old. Since that night. Almost everything had changed after that night.

Henry's mother Sandra began to lose her hair, slowly but noticeably; it thinned at first, then disappeared in tufts and clumps that Henry would sometimes find shoved beneath vegetable scraps in the kitchen trash bin. She was completely bald before her fortieth birthday. Sandra also began a long-lasting affair with the back garden, occupying herself out there from early in the morning until far into the evening on weekends, her sweaty scarf clinging to her balding scalp when she finally came back into the house, exhausted and filthy, the dirt from the garden seeming to have worked its way under her skin.

Daniel P. seemed fine. He had taken up golf – actually going out to a golf course and tapping out nine holes on Saturday mornings – at eight years of age. Henry thought that this was almost supernatural in its weirdness. Even odder was the fact that the kid was extremely good at it. Where this ability – let alone the initial urge, the undersized clubs, the size 6 spiked shoes and knowing all that ornithological lingo – came from, Henry had no idea. He was probably a prodigy, like those kids Mendelssohn and Mozart. A few hundred years ago people would have worshiped a child like that. Or burned him at the stake. But hopefully worshiped – his little brother was odd, Henry felt, but really a very nice kid. Quiet and smart and shy and easily embarrassed, especially by the way he sometimes stumbled over words, accidentally Spoonerizing the hell out of things. But a hell of a golfer.

Beau the dog got hit by a newspaper van one weekday morning

two years ago. It was sad and dramatic, but not as dramatic as if Beau had got rabies and Henry had had to shoot him, like that crying kid with the fat face in *Old Yeller*. Something about the combination of tears and bullets appealed to the melodramatic in Henry.

With his dog dead, his little brother out on the green, his mother burying herself in garden, and his father gone, weekends were desolate for Henry. Without films to watch, he was often bored, especially if Madeleine wasn't around. Every so often in the late summer months he would catch a near-empty bus over to Charlie's house on the other side of Augusta and spend an afternoon under water, in a borrowed mask and snorkel, remembering Dustin Hoffman in *The Graduate*. And as soon as an image like that entered his thoughts, Henry would get carried away with the idea of Charlie's mother, the rarely seen but buxomly recalled Mrs Rocket, seducing him. 'Would you like me to seduce you, Henry? Is that what you want?' Or he might think of *Goodbye, Columbus*, Neil meeting Brenda when she asks him to hold her glasses while she swims in the country club pool. Then Henry would want to be Neil and would start to yearn for Ali McGraw. There was no escape.

'This is Henry,' he repeated to the mirror. 'He's a little worried about his future.' The poster of *The Graduate* was reflected in the mirror and Benjamin Braddock (young Dustin Hoffman) stared back, worrying about the same thing. The one part of his face Henry was happy with was his hairline. It was finally beginning to creep back from his forehead, making him if not handsome, then at least adult-looking. It was a long way from his favorite hairline – the 'Jack Nicholson', which he could still recall with absolute clarity from *Five Easy Pieces* and *The King of Marvin Gardens*, a Rafelson double feature he'd seen a long time ago – but, Henry thought, if he continued to worry a lot about everything, his hairline would keep on creeping back and eventually give his face some sort of character. Not leading-man quality, but a memorable bit-player – Billy Green Bush in *Five Easy Pieces* maybe. He snarled at himself, tried to look charming, and told himself to hold an imaginary piece of chicken 'between your knees'. He sounded ridiculous. And he wondered if Jack Nicholson looked foolish in the mirror; whether it was only some strange quality in film that lent Nicholson magnetism and charm and made his smile not ridiculous.

Henry was unable to get *Five Easy Pieces* out of his mind and spent the next few hours lying on his bed, staring at the ceiling as he tried to piece the film together from his distant and fractured memories. He recalled Nicholson sitting on the back of a truck that he's hitched a ride on, lifting a canvas shroud, finding a piano underneath and playing some tunes. He remembered the scene with the waitress, Jack Nicholson ordering a toasted chicken sandwich and telling her to hold the chicken between her knees. Nicholson played some sort of brilliant, concert piano-playing, rich, philandering bastard – Bobby Dupree or something like that – who'd squandered his musical talents out of sheer willfulness, worked on an oil rig somewhere, drifting from job to job, not knowing what the hell he wanted out of life. 'I move around a lot, not because I'm looking for anything really, but because I'm getting away from things that get bad if I stay.' Henry remembered that Nicholson's father is dying and he goes home to see him; there are arguments, the family is all screwed up and alienated. Nicholson treats his pregnant girlfriend badly. 'You love me, Bobby?' she'd ask him. 'What do you think?' he'd answer. And . . . and . . . and that was all – Henry couldn't remember how the film ends.

Wandering into the kitchen, Henry asked his mother whether she had ever seen *Five Easy Pieces*. 'Oh, I wouldn't think so, Henry,' she told him with a peculiar tone of vehemence and derision.

'Why wouldn't you think so? That's a very odd thing to say, you wouldn't *think* so. Like you think it's a porno film or something.'

'Is it?'

'Of course not. It's not *Five Easy Pieces of Ass*. It's a Bob Rafelson film.'

Sandra laughed. 'Is he an actor?'

'No, he's a director. He directed it. Jack Nicholson's the actor. So you haven't seen it?'

'Oh, I wouldn't think so.'

'I hate to tell you this, Mother, but when you say a thing like,

'Oh, I wouldn't think so,' like that, especially *twice*, you sound like a real simpleton.' He said the words trying to give them a Jack Nicholson, between-your-knees quality.

She had her back to him, facing the steam-fogged stove-top, so Henry could not see that she was laughing silently, her slender, bare shoulders shaking and rippling the thin silk scarf on her head.

After dinner he telephoned Charlie Rocket.

'I've come in from a swim for this, Powderkeg, so it better be worth drying off for.'

'Don't you have a cordless phone sitting on the cocktail cart by the pool?'

'I'm shivering. And Vanessa-from-next-door is holding her breath for me in the deep end. I hope this is important.'

'It's important, it really is. I'm sorry to get you all dry under the collar. She wearing a bikini or that one-piece cream job?'

'The cream, but lately she's letting me roll the top down. What do you want?'

'Vanessa the convertible, huh? Nice. Listen, have you ever seen *Five Easy Pieces*?'

'Why?'

'Have you or not?'

'The one with Harvey Keitel and Robert De Niro, right?'

'No, that's *Mean Streets*. God, I'd like to see that, it's meant to be great. *Easy Pieces* is Jack Nicholson. The chicken sandwich.'

'Between your knees!'

'Yeah, that's right. So you've seen it?'

'No.'

'But what about "between your knees"?'

'Everybody knows that line. It's a cult line. What do you wanna know for, anyway?'

'I can't remember how it ends.'

'So get the video.'

'I can't, Charles. You know I can't.' Charlie said nothing, just shivered into the mouthpiece of the telephone. 'I just can't.'

'Jesus, Henry, you got me out of the pool for this . . . idiocy. Be normal.'

'I really need to know how it ends. It's driving me crazy.'

'Well, I can tell you one thing. I can tell you how this conversation ends.'

'How?'

'Like this.' The line went dead.

Henry's 'Vanessa-from-next-door' was Madeleine Margaret Catherine Ford from two doors down and she wasn't a convertible; she and Henry were just friends. (She'd even said to him once, smiling, 'There'll be no panky with Hanky.' Funny, but mildly crushing anyway.) Madeleine was almost eighteen, her rich strawberry-blond hair cut short, her glasses even thicker in the lenses than in the heavy black rims. Henry was completely in love with Madeleine's face – nothing like Ali McGraw's thin, brittle and somehow absent beauty, but generous and soft and warm; literally warm, because it was close and real – and he so looked forward to the nights when the two of them would meet in her back yard to lie on her blue trampoline talking and smoking cigarettes that his mouth would dry with anticipation.

The curves and lines and shapes of Madeleine's face were simple, like a pencil drawing from an old magazine, the sort of thing that Al Hirschfeld guy did of actors and actresses. The thing was, even in a caricature, Maddy would still turn out beautiful. Even if you tried, you couldn't ruin that face. Her lips protruded and she had quite a long nose; not too long, but long enough to want to run your finger along. And she was always pointing that nose upward because she was always throwing her head back in laughter or shock or dismay. Always at some dramatic angle. From the top of her forehead down to her jaw, her face was smooth, protuberant, long and lovely. When she was lying on the trampoline, Madeleine had a way of leaning on her elbow and listening with a thumb pressed against her temple, smiling the whole time. One of those smiles that light not only a person's face, but their soul; a smile that lets you believe they're not just listening to you, they're part of you.

His favorite thing about Maddy Ford was from the year before. They'd been walking along a street in their neighborhood – kids playing in the road; dogs yapping at lawnmowers in back yards; the usual suburban stuff – when out of nowhere, Madeleine asked Henry if he'd ever been to a circus. 'Of course not,' Henry had said. 'They don't even have them anymore, do they?'

'Of course they do,' she'd said to him. 'Where exactly have you been that they don't have circuses? They certainly have circuses, even here in Maine. Anyway, the thing about them is that they always drag some poor fool out of the audience to be teased by a clown, and everybody sits there in all that sawdust and broken peanut shells hoping like hell they're not going to be the one chosen by the clown because they're fat or bald or something. But the thing is, I always want to be chosen by the clown. Always. I sit there actually praying that old Zippo or Zeppo will pick on me.'

'Why?'

'Because I'd love to punch him right in the guts. Right in his fluffy pom-pom. Really hard, not some girl punch he could make comedy stylings out of, but a punch that'd really bring the bastard down. Bam!' Her teeth were gritted and she'd punched the guts of the air between them several times, leaning right into it.

'But why?'

'I hate the way they tease you for cheap laughs. Who the hell do they think they are, anyway?'

Madeleine M. C. Ford giving a little knuckle music to a circus clown – Henry loved that. It curled his toes whenever he thought about it.

Henry drank a long glass of icy orange soda, checked his breath to ensure that it was suitably fresh and spritzy, grabbed his cigarettes, then walked out through the laundry into the back yard. His mother was up in the far corner attacking the vegetable patch with a trowel. Daniel was down the other end practicing putting on a modest-sized green that Sandra had made for him – complete with a hole and flag with '18' sewn onto it. Henry tried to think of something to shout up at his mother, something funny and friendly, maybe that he'd enjoyed dinner, but decided against breaking her fierce concentration on the broad beans and lettuce and whatever else was up there. He wandered down toward Daniel with a quiet 'Hey.'

Without looking at Henry, Daniel held up the index finger of his right hand, keeping hold of the putter with his cotton-gloved left. 'Uht tut-tut,' he said, then resumed his grip, swung back slightly and pocked the golf ball into the hole, a perfectly straight line. 'Oh yes!!' Daniel cried, drawing out the 's' in long, sibilant victory.

'Well done,' Henry said, as his brother held up the putter, made a 'haaahhhhhh' sound of distant applause with his throat and turned to face the crowd, nodding and smiling with what Henry thought was typically golfer-ish phony humility. He even did a casual little wrist-wave to the unseen hordes gathered at the edge of the green.

'Thanks,' Daniel said softly. 'I just became the youngest ever person to win the US PGA Pro-Am and also set a new course record. Sixty-three under par.' He retrieved the ball and slipped it into his pocket in a single fluid move. For someone so young, Daniel was absurdly elegant and confident with his physicality. Henry was jealous, and slightly annoyed with himself for feeling that way. 'Do you know how much the purse is?'

'What's the purse?'

'It's what they call the prize money. Two hundred thousand dollars. I'll invest about eighty-five per cent of it in Swedish tental dechnology and the rest I'll spend on a yacht. Dad and I are going on a cruise.'

'When?'

'After the British Open. I'll buy him a nice car with mum of the sunny. Some of the money.'

'You're a good son. A great golfer and a good son. Will you buy anything for Mom?'

'What d'you think she'd like?'

'Oh, lots of stuff. Nothing you could buy, though.'

'Like what, Henry? Hair?'

'Yeah, hair would be one thing. Other stuff as well. I dunno, maybe we'll talk about it another time, okay Danny?' Henry was suddenly overwhelmed by an urge to ruffle his little brother's sandy hair, making him all tow-headed like some kid out of a Lassie movie. But he couldn't. He was too worried that he might frighten the boy, his brother. 'I gotta go. Over to Madeleine's. I'll see ya later, okay?'

'Say hello to Eileen for me.'

'Who?'

'Madeleine's mother.'

'Oh yeah.' Henry turned back to his brother. 'You call her Eileen?'

'That's her name. The father's name is Tom.' Daniel took off his glove. 'Henry?' he said.

'Yeah?'

'Is our father all right?'

'Of course. Of course he is. Don't worry about him, he's fine.'

'Where is he?'

Henry looked away, over the fence. 'Yeah ... I, uh, I don't know. But he's fine. I promise. Don't worry, okay?'

'Does he hate me?'

'Oh Danny, don't think like that.' Henry's heavy heart pounded and his breath seemed to come in rising bubbles, escaping from his mouth like the gasps of a dying fish. 'Of course he doesn't hate you. Come on now ... He's just ... He's just not too crazy about me, but he loves you, Danny. I promise he does. Come on now. He thinks you need to work on your chip shot is all.'

'All right.' Daniel put his glove back on and dropped the ball at his feet. 'I have to go and win a tunior journament at Pebble Beach now. Junior tournament.'

'Well, good luck,' Henry said. He felt sure that, even in his imagination, Daniel would probably only come second in to-night's tournament. There was too much on the kid's mind. As he walked toward the gate, toes tingling, Henry turned and took a last look at Daniel – down on one knee, aiming the putter at the hole like a rifle – and could almost feel the sensation of his little brother's ruffled hair on his hand. And even as Henry lingered on the phantom touch, a breeze lifted Daniel's fine hair; but his brother barely noticed, absently patting it back down, then resuming his study of the line, the ball and the grass, lemon-green in the falling light.

Dialogue. 'I saw a fantastic film last night, *Stranger in Paradise*.'

'By Jim Jarmusch?'

'I think so.'

'*Stranger* Than *Paradise*.'

'Yeah. What'd I say?'

'In.'

'Well I meant *than*.'

'What's it like?'

'Fantastic. Really odd, you know, but not pretentious. Close, but not. It's more . . . eccentric in such a good, nice way. Funny. Really funny. There's a scene in it, my favorite scene and there's no dialogue in it at all, where the three of them and this guy called Billy who the Hungarian cousin is sort of dating, where they all sit in a theatre and watch a movie, and the camera just sits on them the whole time and shows you them just laughing at what they're watching, but you never see it. But it doesn't matter, because it's like you're seeing it too, through them, because you're laughing when they laugh. You're in a cinema, watching them in a cinema. Everybody's in a cinema. It's just . . . fantastic. I really loved it. I'm going to see it again next week. I wish you'd come with me, Henry. You'd love it. I know you would. I absolutely know it. Absolutely and for certain.'

'I'd like to, Maddy, I really would. But . . .'

'Yeah . . .'

'Yeah, well . . .'

'Don't worry. Pass the matches, will ya. Look at that cloud over to the left, looks like a dwarf squeezing whipped cream through a gas station bowser.'

'Ha! It does too. With a face like he's gonna run away without paying for it. Bad dwarf!'

'With those curly munchkin shoes on. Unfurling now, like . . . eeuuww, like its foot is melting into a big, long club-foot. Bah!'

'Or he's spilling the cream all over himself. I'll take those matches back now, if you don't mind. Tell me another scene from *Stranger Than in Paradise*.'

'Don't be cheeky. Okay, well it's hard because of what I said before, the eccentricity. And it's not as though there's any great plot or anything to string you along. They just go to Cleveland and visit Aunt Lottie, and then Florida. But there's another great bit where they go to visit a lake, Lake Erie, I think and it's freezing cold and snowing and they can't see anything at all. It's all just whiteness but they stand on the end of the pier anyway in all this wind and stare out into it, because it's still the lake, even though they can't see it. And they just kind of chat about nothing much.'

'Who's they?'

'The three of them – the two guys in hats, Willy and Eddie, and Willy's Hungarian cousin, Eva. Then they go to Florida.'

'And that's it?'

'Yeah, that's about it. But you have to see it to understand it properly, Henry. It's a film, for God's sake . . . Looks like some sort of fried egg sandwich up there now. Bits of bacon on the side. But not crisp enough for my liking.'

'You ever see a film called *Five Easy Pieces*?'

'I don't think so. What's it about?'

'You'd remember if you saw it.'

'*Would* I, now?'

'Probably. About Jack Nicholson, he's a concert pianist and he's got this busted family. Drifter, oil rig, busted family and, y'know, like that.'

'Don't think so.'

'If I get it out on video, would you mind watching it for me and telling me how it ends? I like the way you told *Stranger Than Paradise*. Would you mind?'

'Sure.'

'I'll pay.'

'He says, knowing she'd never take the money. Look, the moon's up.'

'Good old moon.'

'My huckleberry friend.'

'That's moon river.'

'I know it is, Henry. Try to *relax* a bit, will you?'

6

Sound. And so Henry began catching up on films that had been lost to his blindness. He made long lists of videos for Maddy to rent on his behalf, scoured the guides for films being shown on television and taped them for her to watch and relate; bought her tickets to films at the cinema, sometimes waiting outside for a couple of hours while she sat in the darkness, wanting to hear about it as soon as she came out, so it was still fresh and vivid for both of them, closing his eyes in a café, sipping on coffee as she transported him to Marseille or the moon. But his favorite venue was lying on Madeleine's trampoline in the dry July air, staring up at the clouds while she spoke, her warm voice like liquid pouring into his mind, somehow matching the color and texture of her hair; lying at Madeleine's side, the raised hairs on his arms sometimes brushing against her arm as he pressed a lighter or a cigarette into her hand without speaking, without breaking the flow of the film, the only disturbance an occasional 'Oh yesss!!!' leaping across the yards if Daniel pulled off a difficult putt at Augusta (the *other* Augusta) or St Andrews. Maddy might pause, Henry would wait for her, and soon they would depart again, bouncing off the trampoline, up into the sky and beyond, to heaven, to Hollywood.

'What would you like to see tonight?' Madeleine asked. She was wearing a dusty yellow shirt, old jeans with thick, turned-up cuffs, and canvas runners with no socks, like a girl in some 1940s farm movie, Henry thought. Walter Brennan as her dad. 'I've got *The Wages of Fear* from two nights ago – original version, as instructed, not the William Friedkin remake, what's it called?'

'*Sorcerer*. I heard it's pretty crappy,' Henry said. 'What else do you have? You look very beautiful tonight, don't you?'

'Shut up. I've got *The Big Heat*, which I saw last night, and *Ghostbusters* from today at the Roxy. It's a big-screen affair, lots of action and effects and comedy, so I've come armed with plenty of funny adjectives. But I'll skip the queuing up for fifteen minutes, okay?'

'Sure. It's hot tonight, why don't we do *The Big Heat*?'

'Not quite the medium meeting the message, but close enough, huh? Okay. Here it is. *The Big Heat*, 1953, directed by Fritz Lang, written by Sydney Boehm, starring Glenn Ford and Gloria Grahame.'

'Mmmm,' said Henry, an uncontrollable response to the mention of Gloria Grahame.

'We fade in on . . .' An hour and a half condensed into twenty minutes passed in a moment. '. . . and that's it. End titles.'

Henry let out a long breath. 'God, that was great. Thanks, Maddy, you were wonderful as everybody. Especially Lee Marvin, when you threw that coffee in Gloria Grahame's face. Shocking. And the way you incorporated the scarring into her character, so she came across all raw and wounded. Boy, that was so great.'

'I love that line about the perfume she's wearing: "Something new, it attracts mosquitoes and repels men." I wish I talked like that.'

'Certainly. Who doesn't?'

'Except without the lisp,' Maddy said, lisping.

'I love her lisp. It's . . . essential. It's the way her mouth goes. She's got a beautiful mouth, that woman. D'you know she married her own former stepson? She was married to Nicholas Ray, but that fell apart while they were making *In a Lonely Place* and she ended up marrying his son. Not straight away, ten years later or something. Around 1960.' Henry sat up and dangled his legs over the edge of the trampoline and put two cigarettes in his mouth. 'This is from *Now, Voyager* with Paul Henreid and Bette Davis,' he murmured as he lit the cigarettes and handed one down to Madeleine, who was still on her back, her shirt pressed softly against the outline of her breasts.

'Thanks,' Madeleine said. 'She really *did* have Bette Davis eyes, y'know.'

Henry laughed. 'Can we do *Ghostbusters* now? I need some comic relief after all that.'

'I'm pretty tired, Henry. Can't you do one for a change? How about something else with Gloria Grahame in it? I like her. You can do the lisp you enjoy so much.'

'I haven't seen a film in years, Maddy. I can't. You know that.'

'More than anyone,' she said, sitting up and looking him in the face. He stared ahead, blowing smoke rings. 'But give it a try, Henry. Concentrate real hard and see what you can remember. Did you ever see that *Lonely Place* you mentioned? Give that a whirl. I'd like to see that one.'

'A long, long time ago. When I was seven or something. But I took a lot of notes as I recall. Maybe I'll go and get my book and –'

'No, don't.' She grabbed his shirt sleeve. 'Do it like I do, Henry. From your memory. Try. You know all that other stuff connected with the films, the gossip and stuff. Try and tell me a film.'

Henry flicked his cigarette into the grass. 'I don't know Maddy, it's been such a long time. I might get the story all confused.'

'That doesn't matter. How would I know anyway? I haven't seen it. And besides, how can you be sure that I haven't been screwing up the films I've been telling you? Leaving out parts that I didn't like or didn't understand. I might've been you know.'

'Have you?'

'Of course not,' Madeleine said. 'Come on, Henry. You sort of owe it to me.'

He knew it was true. Through Maddy he'd seen everything he'd wanted to without going to the cinema once: *Hannah and Her Sisters, Platoon, The Mission* and *Betty Blue.* He'd caught up with dozens more on video: *The Taking of Pelham One Two Three, The Odd Couple* and *Charley Varrick* (all during Walter Matthau Week), *Play Misty for Me* and *Paris, Texas* (which Maddy had summed up: 'Mock-mute guy in a red cap wanders around southwest Texas. Tracks down his wife and through a one-way mirror tells her that he loves her. She says, "I thought you didn't." He says, "Yeah, well I do." The end.'), *The Sterile Cuckoo, Medium Cool, In the Heat of the Night, The Deer Hunter* (a long night), *Reds* (a long and boring night with Diane Keaton's performance described as 'twitchy and shrill'), *Ragtime, The Towering Inferno* (lots of screaming from Maddy), *Rififi, Touchez-Pas au Grisbi* and *Le Samouraï* (all part of a short French gangster film festival, with extra hokey accenting from Madeleine), *The Parallax View*, *All the President's Men*, *Putney Swope*, *I Vitelloni*, *The Seven Ups*, *The French Connection* (the line where Roy Scheider says to a Frenchman, 'You must lead a charming life,' knocked both Henry and Madeleine out, and for a few weeks afterwards they took every slim opportunity to say it to one another) and its sequel, *Saturday Night Fever*, *Equus*, *Newsfront*, five out of six of Eric Rohmer's 'moral tales', *Prince of the City*, *Apocalypse Now*, *Dirty Harry* and three sequels, *The Bad and the Beautiful*, *Two Weeks in Another Town*, *Two-Lane Blacktop*, *Two for the Road* and many, many more, all through the summer. He could hardly say no.

He said, 'I'd really rather not.'

'Well, that's really rather selfish, isn't it?' Madeleine raised her eyebrows and cocked her head. 'Isn't it? Besides which, the darkness is getting darker.'

'Meaning?'

'Meaning that my already bum eyesight is getting worse. I'm not saying it's because of watching all these movies – it's not. But it's degenerating. Dr Burns says perhaps irrevocably.'

'How? I mean . . . Jesus, what's wrong?'

'I have macular degeneration. The dry kind as opposed to the wet kind, so no tears.'

'Does it hurt?'

'No.'

'Can you still see? Can you see me?' Henry sat up to make himself more visible.

Madeleine pulled him back down. 'Yes. Especially if we lie like this and I look at you from the side of my eye. I can see better from the side. Chris – that's Dr Burns – says that the retina works a little like the film in a camera. And the macula is the part of the retina which sort of forms the center of the picture. The sharpest image. Which is getting less sharp. I took an Amsler Grid test thing and the straight lines were wavy. And there were things I should have seen that I couldn't. Basically, it's a blind spot right there in the middle.'

Henry took a deep, shuddering breath. 'Can't they do anything? Operate or something?'

'Vitamins, apparently. Plus I should quit smoking. But who shouldn't? Anyway, it's fine. I can still see and –' She held a hand over her mouth as she coughed drily. 'In some cases it just goes away and everything goes back to normal.'

'Thank God,' Henry said, breathing hot relief into the warm summer air. 'That's what'll happen to you, Maddy. It really will.' He sat up again and looked at her: at her green, glassless eyes; the dusting of freckles across her cheeks and nose; her powdery tan; the soft, slightly curled mouth from which rose the voice that had given him all those films. He knew that he would regret what he was about to not say, probably for the rest of his life. But he didn't say it anyway.

Instead he said, 'All right . . . *In a Lonely Place*, 1950. Directed by Nicholas Ray, written by Andrew Solt. Starring Humphrey Bogart and, as we already know, the very lovely, the very lisping Gloria Grahame.'

'Less jokes, please. More film.' She grabbed his shirt sleeve again and pulled him back down, so that once more they lay side by side, looking up at the stars.

Synopsis. In a Lonely Place is the story of self-loathing Hollywood screenwriter Dixon Steele (Humphrey Bogart), who is plagued by doubt and creative burnout. He's a man who believes that there's no sacrifice too great for a shot at immortality. Steele is hired to adapt a best-selling novel into a screenplay, but rather than read the book he asks Mildred Atkinson (Martha Stewart), the hat-check girl at his favorite nightclub, 'Paul's', to read it for him and retell it. She agrees and breaks a date with her boyfriend, Kesler, in order to do so. At Steele's Santa Monica apartment, dopey chatterbox Mildred drinks Horse's Necks (ginger ale with a twist of lemon) and relates the story. 'It's what I call an epic,' she tells Steele. 'Oh, and what do you call an epic?' he asks. 'You know, lots of people and plenty of things going on.' Tired and bored, Dixon Steele bids Mildred farewell around 12.30 a.m., shortly after spying his beautiful neighbor, Laurel Gray (Gloria Grahame), across the courtyard.

At 5 a.m. Steele is hauled out of bed by Detective Brub Nicolai

(Frank Lovejoy), a former platoon buddy, and taken to the police station for questioning. Mildred Atkinson has been found brutally murdered. Steele, who is quite nonplussed, even somewhat amused by the disturbing news, is the prime suspect; however the would-be starlet, Laurel Gray, provides him with a solid alibi. Out in the hallway following the interrogation, Steele tells a policeman, 'I'll see that Miss Gray gets home all right.' 'Thank you,' she says. 'But I always leave with the man who brought me.'

Despite Laurel's lingering suspicions that the troubled, violent Steele might indeed be the killer, she quickly begins a romance with the writer. For a while everything goes well. Dix is writing more and better than he has in years. Laurel is devoted to him, despite everything she hears: his police record of 'fights, scandals and disruptions'; a former girlfriend of Steele's who withdrew a complaint against him and claimed she'd broken her nose 'walking into a door'; Laurel's masseuse telling her that he's no good and that she'd be better off back with her former boyfriend, a property developer. 'And remember, angel,' the masseuse advises, 'In the beginning was the land. Motion pictures came later.'

At a beach picnic one night, Brub's wife accidentally lets slip that Laurel has been back at the police station for further questioning. Furious that she had not told him, Dix jumps into his car. Laurel follows. He drives speedily, recklessly along the Pacific Coast Highway, sideswiping a roadster driven by a UCLA football star. The college kid verbally abuses Steele, who then severely beats him. He is about to bludgeon the kid with a rock when Laurel begs him to stop. After he has calmed down, Steele tells Laurel some lines he has created for the screenplay: 'I was born when she kissed me. I died when she left me. I lived a few weeks while she loved me.' But he is unsure exactly where to place them.

Laurel's doubts grow stronger and more pernicious, seeping into her dreams. She becomes mistrustful and reserved, relying on pills for sleep. Despite her misgivings, however, Laurel agrees to marry Dix. But moments later, when Steele has rushed off to buy an engagement ring, Laurel breaks down in front of Steele's agent, Mel, confessing that she can't go through with it. 'I don't trust him . . . I'm not even sure he didn't kill Mildred Atkinson . . . Why can't he be like other people?' Mel pleads with Laurel not to break it off until something good happens to Steele. 'If Dix has success, he doesn't need anything else,' Mel says. But while Steele is away, Laurel books a flight to New York City.

That night at Paul's nightclub Dix and Laurel gather with some friends to celebrate. Dix notices that Laurel is a little nervous and, moments later, when he discovers that Mel has secretly given his new script to a producer, he hits out at Mel, breaking his glasses and severing their twenty-year relationship. The evening is a disaster. Laurel disappears and Dixon leaves the nightclub in search of her, just missing a telephone call from Detective Nicolai.

Steele pounds on Laurel's door, insisting she open up. She lets him in and he apologizes for his behavior, assuring her that it will never happen again. But then he notices that she is not wearing her ring and moments later learns that she is planning to leave him and fly to New York. In a rage he pushes her onto her bed, his hands tight around her throat. The telephone rings, bringing him to his senses. Brub tells him that they have an airtight confession from Atkinson's boyfriend. But it is too late; Steele has let go of what matters most and sacrificed his one shot at true happiness – he must walk away and leave Laurel forever . . .

7

At night Henry would lie in bed and sometimes imagine himself and Madeleine as the leads in a film – one shot in black and white and infused with the smoky darkness and tangy jazz of noir – the only swimmers in a sea of two-dimensional and utterly featureless extras. He was a tough, taciturn, moody and edgy but charming guy, who looked smooth yet formidable in his suit, a hint of packed heat about his torso; half cop, half schoolboy. Madeleine was as beautiful as she was in life, only blond. She was also secretly in love with Henry, but afraid to show it. Some tragedy or other brought them together – her aristocratic English parents were killed in a Comet jetliner crash over Malta; Henry investigated, discovered that faulty seals around the oversized windows caused the disaster, flew to Bristol and dispatched the drunken, incompetent engineer who'd given people the panoramic view of their own death. Madeleine would sob into Henry's suit jacket, pressing the gun into his ribs. He would hold her jaw, tilt her face up to his, remove her glasses and kiss her wet, salty cheeks. She would say something like, 'It doesn't matter that you're a few years younger than me. It never mattered. I've loved you since you were sixteen. Do you love me, Henry?' He would say, 'What do you think?' She would know. And then – he could never stop this – her hair would change from Grace Kelly blond back into Madeleine Ford red.

Int. Café – Day
A teenager, HENRY POWDERMAKER, sits in a fluoro-bright, 'Fabulous Fifties' café in downtown Augusta, Maine. On the walls are garish, glossy reprints of period advertising sheets, smiling gas jockeys and car-hops, cigarettes that promote wellbeing and good health. Oh, the irony! Henry is alone in a red vinyl banquette, flicking through the table jukebox and rolling his eyes as he reads the lists of songs. A WAITER, bopping along to the doo-wop that fills the diner, slips a coffee onto the imitation Formica table.

HENRY

Thanks, pal o' mine.

WAITER
(*adjusting his paper fry-boy hat*)
Excuse me?

HENRY

I thought all you cats'd be talking hep jive all the live-long day. Pally.

WAITER

I just work here.

HENRY

You don't say. Thanks for the java. Now amscray, kid, ya bother me.

The waiter scrams, leaving Henry to amuse himself. But not for long – he has barely taken his first tentative sip of the too-hot, too-weak coffee when he is joined by MADELEINE FORD. Henry's face lights up as she slides into the booth. She has red-blond hair and darker, arched eyebrows that lend her face a sexy sardonicism. She picks up a plastic menu and opens it, covering her face completely – from the glimpse we caught earlier, she is panting and flushed, as though she ran here – pretending to read for a while before she drops it onto the table top. Letting out a long breath before she speaks.

MADELEINE

God, what an afternoon! I'll have whatever you're having. What're you having – a coffee, right? And that's all? I'll have a coffee then. What about a whiskey sour? They serve alcohol in this establishment?

HENRY

Probably not to minors. I really don't know why we come to this place. It's absolutely awful.

MADELEINE

I like it – early nothing. That's from–

HENRY

I know where it's from. So how was today's?

MADELEINE

Ehh . . .

HENRY

Ah . . . Well, I didn't expect much.

MADELEINE

There was plenty of drama afterward, though. And there was
a Tom and Jerry cartoon before, but I'll skip the details.
Basically the cat and the mouse were trying to get each other.

HENRY

Yeah, I'm familiar with their work.

MADELEINE

So, the feature presentation then. *Gimme th' Dough, Sucka!*
A title that's trying too hard, if you ask me, because it's not
even a proper blaxploitation film, it just thinks it is. Directed
by an idiot, written by another idiot, based on a novel by a
third idiot. Starring Ron Palillo and Candy Clark.

HENRY

Didn't Ron Palillo play Arnold Horshak in 'Welcome Back
Kotter'?

MADELEINE

Yes. He's back – at last.

Henry laughs, removes a cigarette from his shirt pocket
and slides the packet over to Madeleine. She takes a
cigarette, and as she slips it into her mouth, we see her lips
in extreme close up: the slight cracks in the lipstick; a tiny
drop of moisture left by her tongue as it readied her mouth
for the cigarette; the light flecks in the brown filter paper
ringed by a gold band outside a small, dark hole, a glimpse
of white tooth inside.

MADELEINE (cont'd)

I'm not going into all the detail because it's all far too
stupid, but basically there's a couple of dumb hoods who

44

talk too much trying to set up a scam on this widow who they think is loaded. Horshak plays a rookie cop with a big line in wryly comic asides, especially pop-cultural references, which become painful after about ten seconds. Plus he wears a blue leather tie, which is too much. Anyway, the hoods keep on screwing up and accidentally off a couple of old ladies who live near the main old widow. So stupid Horshak goes . . .

Madeleine's voice begins to fade as we move away from her mouth and turn around. Henry is listening, eyes closed and nodding. The doo-wop grows louder and louder as Madeleine's film replay becomes little more than a murmur. We pull away from the banquette, up over the harsh, bright white-floored and glistening red-seated café. Except for A COOK in back and the waiter out front, adjusting his paper hat using a metal milkshake container for a mirror as he sits slumped with exaggerated boredom at a reproduction chrome 'diner' stool, there is no one else there. Moving along the counter, away from the waiter, we see a row of over-colored hamburgers and ice-cream sundaes. But the hamburgers don't steam and the sundaes don't melt, because they're all made of fabric, soft and lumpy, like miniature Oldenburgs. Yours for $7.50 a pop. We glide up now, past a row of posters on the wall: Marilyn Monroe standing above that pesky subway grate; Humphrey Bogart wearing a trenchcoat, a cigarette and a doleful expression; James Dean walking off into sullen doom with his arms looped over the rifle across his back; and finally, all three of them reunited late one night in some Edward Hopperesque diner, drinking coffee and maybe talking about what it's like to be famously dead, the beginning of a beautiful – and everlasting – friendship.

The music fades and Madeleine's murmuring increases in volume. We linger on the poster of *Heaven's Diner* (or whatever cornball thing it's called), then cut abruptly back to Madeleine and Henry.

. . . and he's pulling and pulling at it, nearly ripping my shoulder off. A coupla people step back, a little frightened, then the guy runs off through the crowd, knocking over some children and screaming the whole time. He's screaming, 'No-no-no! No-no-no!' in groups of three. 'No-no-no!' just like that. Like a chant or something. Or a hysterical child. Then just as he's about to leap through the glass doors at the front, this enormous guy wearing a tiny straw cowboy hat, like he's from a miniature rodeo or something, just thumps the other guy, the purse-snatcher, in the face. BAM! Right in the middle of his face. He goes down and the cowboy sits on top of him, like he's gonna tickle him or something, but instead he starts beating him on the head and neck with a book, a really big book, an atlas or something, while this crowd forms a ring around them, staring and saying nothing. It's like the cowboy-hat guy is gonna kill the other guy and we're all just waiting to watch him die.

Henry looks confused, blinks a few times and jerks his head.

HENRY

And that's how it ends? Like that?

MADELEINE

What?

HENRY

I don't get where the cowboy and the purse-snatcher came from. Where did they come from? Were they at the docks spying on Horshak just before the explosion? Or were they with the Hungarians?

Henry's eyes mist over and he begins talking almost to himself, almost muttering like a madman.

HENRY (cont'd)

I like the 'No-no-no', though. That's kind of a nice touch.

MADELEINE

A nice touch!? Have you been listening to me, Henry? This happened just before I got here. It happened. It wasn't part of that stupid film.

HENRY

How do you mean?

MADELEINE

What do you mean how do I mean? I mean that a guy ran off with my bag, then got whacked in the head by a big cowboy. Bastard might even be brain-damaged the way he was lying there. This happened today. Just now. In the cinema foyer. In real life – the place in which you ought to spend more time.

HENRY

Oh. I see . . . wow . . . really? That just happened to you? That's amazing.

MADELEINE
(*flat, unimpressed*)

Yeah, isn't it?

HENRY

So they weren't with the Hungarians?

It is the wrong thing to say. Madeleine remains stone-faced, so it's hard to tell whether she's looking at her friend with displeasure, pity or despair. Henry realizes his error and does his best to dissolve the self-conscious smirk twisting his face.

HENRY (cont'd)

I was joking, Maddy.

MADELEINE

I know you were. I know you were, but this is . . . all this is becoming too . . . wrong. You're not here, Henry. If a pair of screaming idiots came rushing in here, right into this café, right now, with guns all over the place, yelling at everybody to shut up and hand over their wallets, you'd sit there with this dreamy look on your face, thinking it was all some stupid movie running in your head. They could shoot you right in the arm and you wouldn't even notice. Right in the arm. You wouldn't go to a hospital, you'd just sit and wait and see what happened in the next reel. I don't know where you are, Henry, but you're not here, with me. It's wrong. It's got to stop. I'm stopping it, Henry. Right here and now. It's over.

HENRY

What's over?

MADELEINE

I'm not going to watch any more movies for you. It's too much. You're . . . you're on your own.

Henry is stunned. His face whitens and he looks sick. The only sound we hear is breathing.

MADELEINE (cont'd)

Besides . . .

But she doesn't finish the sentence. Instead she stands and reaches for her handbag, and we see that there is a fine spray of blood across the cream-colored leather.

HENRY

Besides what? Are you getting blinder?

As soon as the words leave his mouth, hanging in the air like insecticide, Henry closes his eyes and slumps with regret and shame. He cannot believe what he has just said.

                    MADELEINE
I have to go.

Madeleine walks quickly toward the door. Just before she leaves, Henry shouts –

                    HENRY
Besides what, Madeleine!?

But she is gone. The waiter walks slowly over to the banquette and leans in close to Henry's face.

                    WAITER
Try to keep it down, will ya? (BEAT) Pal-o-mine.

8

Cut to: The day after Henry made the scene in the diner, he and Charlie Rocket were lying on plastic lounges in Charlie's back yard, a large, kidney-shaped swimming pool rippling and gurgling by their side. Charlie was cheerfully topless, toned and brown; Henry had pulled a fruit-spattered Hawaiian shirt over his paleness immediately after climbing clumsily out of the water. The afternoon sun was directly overhead, making most of Charlie browner and turning Henry a painful pink. Charlie squeezed a bottle of coconut-scented oil into his palm and began rubbing himself, beginning with his feet, leaning into and out of the motion like it was a yogic prayer. The sweet, fake odor of creamed coconuts filled the air; scent mixed almost organically with sound – the low buzz of crickets and hazy zip of mosquitoes.

'Hey,' Charlie said, his deep voice thick and slow, near-narcotic with heat. 'You mind if I slip off my shorts and give the old groinal region a bit of color? It's looking a little sick and white down there. I'd like to be a nice, single tone when I finally unveil my entire gloriousness to Vanessa.'

Henry reached for a towel and covered his head with it. 'Be my guest.'

'So what'd she say after that?'

'Nothing. She left and I haven't spoken to her since.'

'Boy. She's got the old tenterhooks right into you, hasn't she? What do you think it is, this "Besides dot dot dot" business?'

Henry pulled the towel from his face and stood up, his legs striped red and white from the way he'd been lying. 'It's too hot here. I'm going under that tree.' He dragged the plastic lounge over into the shade under an elm tree. 'Can you still hear me?' he shouted.

'Of course I fucking can,' Charlie said. 'This isn't a park, it's somebody's yard. It's *my* yard. Why d'you call the guy "pal o' mine"? You're asking for trouble pulling stunts like that, Henry. It sounds pretty gay.'

'I have no idea what she meant. Maybe she's got a boyfriend or something awful. I don't know.'

'You ever kissed her?'

'Madeleine? Of course not. Not that I don't want to, but y'know . . .'

'Well, there's your problem right there.'

'I'm not glorious like you, Charles freakin' Atlas. I'm regular. I'm a tinhorn. Nobody wants me to kiss them.'

'You've got to make them want to. Be attractive and charming. Try to be a little sexy. These are the kissing years, Henry. At *least* kissing. And you're wasting them lying next to a great-looking older woman on a trampoline talking about movies you haven't seen. A trampoline, for God's sake. You've got pre-made pneumaticness right there. Imagine the thrust power.' Charlie shook his head respectfully. 'You want a drink? I'm going inside and get a soda.'

'You got Coke?'

'Of course.' He said it as though he lived in a supermarket. *Of course we have Coke.* 'Hey,' Charlie went on. 'I wrote a song the other night. Called "Vanessa – I Wanna Undress Ya". Want me to get my guitar and play it for you?'

'Is it lewd?'

'No, it's poetic.' Charlie rolled his eyes. 'Of course it's lewd. D'you wanna hear it?'

'You're teaching yourself the guitar, aren't you, Charles? No lessons?'

'You bet.'

'Maybe next year.'

'Suit yourself, but it's brilliant –' Charlie paused and smirked – 'pal o' mine!' Without bothering to put his shorts back on, he rolled off the plastic lounge laughing and walked across the grass to the rear of the house.

Henry lit a cigarette and watched Charlie's bare butt the whole way, wondering if maybe he was gay. Objectively, he knew that his friend's ass was neat and compact, almost smug the way it sat there all high and proud. But he had no desire whatsoever to touch it or anything. He was only looking at the goddam thing because it was there.

'Nice, isn't it?'

Henry nearly broke his neck, yelping and gagging and snapping his head around all at once. Vanessa was standing behind and above him, her eyes glued firmly to Charlie's buttocks as he mounted the steps and finally disappeared into the kitchen. 'Jesus Christ, Vanessa, you just about gave me a heart attack! Where the hell did you come from?'

'You should smoke less if you don't want a heart attack.' She raised an eyebrow. Vanessa was Italian; they could do stuff like that. She had a mole just to the side of the eyebrow, making her look a lot older (and perhaps sexier) than she was. In fact, Vanessa had many qualities which Henry considered classically Italian, a cultural ideal he'd largely based on Sophia Loren and Gina Lollobrigida: broad hips, a slim waist and a big bust; long, dark hair which gave way to slight curls; full lips, and dark eyes flecked with a menace Henry found highly appealing; light-brown,

Mediterranean skin, a deep, smoky voice and a strong, square jaw which looked like it would give a lot to a kiss and even more to anger. Last of all she had a great name: Vanessa Alessandra LaViola. 'How are you, Henry?' she asked.

Charlie arrived and saved Henry from having to give some dreary response: 'Oh, y'know. Okay.' As though he were discussing a disease. Charlie had put a towel around his waist and Henry tried not to notice his fine collection of abs, but there they were, right above him. Charlie on his right, Vanessa and her breasts on his left, facing each other.

'Is that a rocket in your pocket, Rocket?' Vanessa said, with a salaciousness that almost dripped on Henry's head.

Charlie laughed obscenely and said, 'You two must've been talking about me a lot. Forget the ears, my entire body was burning.'

'That's a combination of sunburn and ego, Cee,' Vanessa told him with her square jaw. She leaned over Henry, then pulled Charlie by the shoulder across to her and gave him a long kiss, Henry lying beneath the smacking sound of the two of them. Charlie spilled soft drink on Henry's head: bubbling black and orange.

Henry slipped off the lounge, out from under them. 'Well, you two'll probably want to get all topless with each other now, so I guess I'll be going.'

'You don't have to leave on account of my chest, Henry,' Vanessa said, fantastically coyly.

'Oh yes, you do,' Charlie said, handing Henry the glass of Coke. 'Sorry, baby.'

'I'll show 'em to you another time,' said Vanessa, her voice breathy, on the verge of laughter. Henry almost choked on the soda.

Charlie laughed into his drink. 'Yeah, when you're old enough.'

'God, what're you two – swingers or something?'

'She's only kidding, Henry,' Charlie said. He looked at Vanessa. 'You're only kidding, aren't you, Vee?'

'I guess so, but they're pretty nice. It seems a shame to keep them so . . . private.' Cee and Vee burst into giggles. One pushed the other onto the ground and they began wrestling, leaves of grass sticking to their brown skin. Henry watched them, deeply envious of the ease his friends enjoyed with one another; confused about where that sort of – was it emotional elegance? – came from; wondering why it wasn't that way with him and Maddy. Him and anybody.

Charlie and Vanessa stopped tussling and sat up in the bright sun. 'How's Madeleine?' asked Vanessa.

'Bad question, baby,' Charlie said, handing her his drink. 'She and the Powderroom are spatting.' Tut-tutting with a teasing tongue, Vanessa tipped some orange fizz over her left arm and held it out to Charlie. Henry couldn't believe it – Charlie actually began licking her right there in front of him.

'Oh come on, you two. Take a shower or something. You're embarrassing the hell out of me. Jeez. Come on now. Really.' Even as he said it, he felt prudish and young. Probably jealous, too, he thought.

Barely lifting his mouth from his girlfriend's taut and sticky forearm, Charlie said, 'We're young and in love, Henry. We've found each other. Teenage suburban love – what could be better?'

'And I think it's just . . . marvelous, but there are other things in life besides love.'

They spoke at the same time. He said, 'Like what?' She said, 'Such as?'

Henry said, 'Well . . .' and wondered about the rest of the sentence all the way home.

Sure, love was nice, probably, maybe even marvelous, if it was real and lasted and didn't develop some sort of tumor. But what about what you actually did with your life besides falling in love? Wasn't that important too? Maybe even more so. Love could fade or die or be killed off, but a person's achievements lasted for ever. That was the important stuff. What did Henry care if Frank Capra had spent his long life alone and miserable, so long as he made *Mr Deeds Goes to Town*? Of course, Capra hadn't spent his life alone, and maybe that meant a loveless person couldn't make a film like *Deeds*, so full of faith and hope and humor. Maybe you had to know about all that sort of stuff before you could share it with strangers in cinemas. Gary Cooper – Mr Deeds himself – had slept with a ton of women, all of them at least as good-looking as he was, but that didn't stop him from coming across all likable and folksy, a little dim and toothy, on-screen. But he was sly and wry too. That was what made him sexy. But who cared what his life was like off-screen? And what did it matter anyway, because what was on-screen was all he left behind. He had cancer, and was apparently in great pain, when he made his last few pictures – you could see it in his face, if you knew to look – and while that was sad and everything, wasn't the important thing not his real-life pain or love, but what he had left behind for ever on film? The other world he helped create and inhabited every time somebody watched *Meet John Doe* or *Sergeant York*? Wasn't that somehow beyond love and death? Even though you knew it was all fakery – acting, reciting lines, hitting marks, doing another take to make it seem more ... real. But what if what you got wasn't all fakery? What if you captured real-life cancer on film, as Henry had done? A sort of cancer, anyway. What then? What was the legacy of something like that? Where was love then? What was the good of licking soft drink off somebody's arm if it ended up like that?

9

'This is for you.' With a dirt-stained, heavy-cotton work glove Sandra handed Henry an envelope with H. P. written on the front.

He sat down on the yellow stool in the kitchen. 'Who from?' he asked.

'M. M. C. F.'

'I see.'

'Okay.' Sandra laughed. 'Ha! We don't even need whole words to communicate with one another anymore. Just letters! Isn't that neat?'

'Mmmm.'

Henry went to his room, lay on his bed and opened the envelope. Inside was a note from Madeleine Margaret Catherine Ford telling Henry Powdermaker that the two of them had to go out that night, 'on a mystery date of my specially prepared and researched itinerary'. She'd underlined 'my' twice and 'specially' three times. Henry tried to stop it – even held his hands over his ribs – but his heart felt as though it was going to beat itself right out of his chest. A smile crept across his face. They were pals again. And she'd used the word 'date'; that really got him. If he had been able to see the smile on his face, he might have considered it not ridiculous.

The afternoon sun and the heat between Charlie and Vanessa had drained him, and as he lay on his bed, his wildly beating heart still rattling his ribcage, Henry fell asleep.

Dream sequence. The dream sequence in Alfred Hitchcock's *Spellbound*, with sets designed, appropriately enough, by Salvador Dali, is a good one, but doesn't add very much to the film's plot. Full of obvious Freudian symbolism, it looks quite interesting, if a little overbaked. Henry dreamed he was in it, Theremin music and all.

The sun was slipping away when Madeleine knocked seven times on the front door of Henry's house. Wearing a pair of plus fours and a matching cap, Daniel answered, a sand wedge sitting rakishly over his shoulder. 'Fadeleine Mord!' he said.

'That's right,' Madeleine said, grinning. 'I've come for your brother Penry Howdermaker.' She wasn't teasing, though, and Daniel knew it.

'Penry's getting dressed. Come in.' Daniel stepped back. 'This is a sand wedge,' he said, hoisting the club. 'For bunkers. Do you want some milk?'

'I just had a bowl, thanks.'

In the kitchen Sandra Powdermaker was sitting with a glass of white wine and a magazine. 'Hi, Madeleine,' she said, waving a knuckly hand but not looking up. 'Glass of semillon?'

'Thanks, Mrs Powdermaker. That'd be great.'

'Call me Sandra, or Ms Fontaine if we're at a funeral. Just not Mrs Powdermaker. Mrs Powdermaker tingles the back of my neck. And not in a pleasant way.' Ms Fontaine rubbed the back of her neck as she opened the refrigerator door.

'Sorry.'

'There's no need to be sorry. Here.' She handed Madeleine a glass of wine. 'Proost! That's European for cheers. You're supposed to roll your tongue on the "r", but who can be bothered?'

'Proost,' Madeleine responded, not bothering. 'How's the garden?'

'That unseasonal rain last Tuesday washed away most of my toppings.'

'It was good for my putting green,' Daniel said. 'It's even lore mush – more lush – now. Can I have a glass of milk?'

'You know where the fridge is, kid,' Sandra said. 'So what are you and Henry up to tonight?'

'It's kind of a secret. If I tell him, he probably won't want to come.'

'Indeed?' Sandra made an 'indeed?' face: stretched and a trifle incredulous. 'How very . . . teeeenage.'

'Well, we're teenagers,' Madeleine said.

'Yes, I suppose you are.'

Henry came into the kitchen. 'Hi everybody,' he said, nervous but trying hard not to show it. 'And I'd like to say a special hello to a very good friend of mine, Madeleine Ford. Hiya there, Maddy.'

'Hi, Henry. And can I just say how wonderful it is to be here tonight?'

'Well, it's great to have you here.' Henry relaxed a little. 'We should do this more often, really.'

Daniel looked at his mother. 'Why are they talking like that?'

Sandra took a sip of wine. 'They're teenagers.'

The two teenagers sat in the back of a taxi heading into the center of Augusta. Madeleine was wearing perfume, something citrusy, fresh and a little masculine – the scent of summer, of holiday. 'I had the craziest dream when I fell asleep this afternoon,' Henry said, closing his eyes and breathing her in: limes and oranges, the salted air of a windy beach. 'There were these –'

'No offence, Henry, but you know how it is with other people's dreams. It's kind of like the political situation in Africa: you know it's sort of interesting and you should care about it, but . . . you just don't.'

Henry laughed. 'Well, I'm not offended, but I'll bet you millions of Africans would be if they heard that.'

'I'll tell 'em I'm sorry if they show up.'

'It had Theremin music. Played by Dr Samuel J. Hoffman.'

'What did?'

'My dream.'

'I told you I don't want to hear about your dream.'

'This is just the soundtrack, not the visuals.'

'All right.' Madeleine lit a cigarette and flicked the match out the window into the whipping wind. 'What's Theremin music?'

'This crazy, whoopy, whiny electronic instrument that makes sounds like . . . well, like from a dream. Or maybe like what insane people hear in their heads all the time.' Henry started whooping and whining, constricting his throat to produce high, ethereal sounds while Maddy smoked and laughed, almost choking at the sight of Henry twisting his head this way and that, wrenching and contorting his mouth. 'Like that,' he said, as happy as he'd ever been.

At the Japanese restaurant Henry told Madeleine that this was his first-ever date. Madeleine said that she was proud to be the one to take his 'date cherry'. She poured him some sake and told him to drink it. She said that it helped people with their Theremin impressions. And that that could only be a good thing.

After they finished eating, Henry and Madeleine, opposite each other, leaned back on their mats and lit cigarettes.

'Do you ever think about what's going to happen to you, Henry?' Madeleine asked. 'What you're going to do?'

'Sure, I do. I'm going to film school. Then Hollywood after that.'

'Simple as that, huh?'

'Well, I certainly hope so. It's all I want to do.'

Madeleine tilted her back. 'You realize, of course, that a necessary component of such a course will be the actual *watching* of films, don't you?'

'Yeah, I'm planning to start being normal pretty soon. Charles keeps telling me to, and it seems to've gotten him places.'

She nodded and did not speak for a moment. 'So about the other day . . .'

'I'm so sorry about the "getting blinder" crack, Maddy. I didn't mean it in a bad way. I mean I really did wonder if that's what was the matter. It just came out wrong. I feel awful. Look at me – I look awful, don't I?'

Madeleine laughed. 'Don't worry about it. And I'm not. Not this week, anyway. Getting blinder, I mean.' She picked up the sake jug and swirled it. 'It's empty,' she said. 'Do you want some more?'

'Are you trying to get me drunk or something, Miss Ford?'

'I think I am, yeah.' She waved small-ly to a waitress in a kimono and ordered another jug. 'There are two reasons why I'm not going to do the films for you anymore, Henry. One because I won't and the other because I can't.' Henry opened his mouth to say something but Madeleine stopped him with a raised finger. 'The first is because of what I said the other day. That you have to . . . this sounds so parental, but I'm sorry, it has to be said. You have to start taking responsibility for yourself and living more . . . directly in the world. Practically everything you experience is vicarious. That's not good, Henry. It's really not. In fact, it's kind of lazy and stupid and dangerous. I mean that business with my being robbed coming out of the cinema and your not even realizing it . . . Don't say anything, this isn't a personal attack, it's just telling you how I think. You have to start facing the world and everything in it.'

'Like what?'

'Like everything. Your family – including your father – what you're going to do, your friends and watching movies again. Everything.'

The waitress placed a fresh jug of sake in the middle of the low table. Madeleine poured a full cup for herself and drank it in a single draught, throwing her head way back. Henry thought of

Joan Crawford taking a belt. 'Well, okay,' he said. 'I can accept that, I really can.'

'I'm glad to hear it.' Madeleine poured them both another cup. 'That was the won't reason. The other reason, the can't reason, is more simple. And maybe worse. I don't know how you're going to take this.'

Henry had raised the cup but stopped now. He was still as he looked at Maddy. 'I'm leaving,' she said.

Henry swallowed drily. Put the cup down. Swallowed again, lifted the cup and drank the sake in a gulp. The hot liquid burned and brought tears to his eyes. 'Where?' he said, his voice small and broken. He quickly cleared his throat. 'That was the sake made me do that.'

'In a way I kind of wish it was like the end of *Love Story* and I could tell you that I had cancer or whatever that silly bitch had and that I was going away to heaven. You might understand it better with a movie as some sort of precedent. Plus I know your feelings for Ali McGraw. But it's not like that. I'm not dying. I'm just going away.'

'Where?' Henry said again.

'College. It may interest you to know that I did very well in my SATs. Insanely well, as a matter of fact.' Madeleine ran her finger around the rim of her cup. 'You have to when you're an only child. All your parents' expectations live in you. And only you.'

'Which college?'

'Tulane.'

'Good Lord, that's way the hell down in . . .'

'Louisiana.'

'That's *right*, Louisiana.' Henry lit another cigarette, shaking his head as he blew out a stream of smoke. 'What are you doing? I mean, what are you majoring in?'

'Communication. Mostly other than visual. For obvious reasons. I'm leaving Monday.'

'I'll never see you again.'

'Oh, don't be so B-movie. Of course you'll see me again.' Madeleine still wasn't looking at Henry. Her finger moved around the cup endlessly. 'Of course you will. It's a college not a hospice.'

Henry wiped his eyes. 'You'll start speaking patois and fall in love with some football star with a roadster.'

Madeleine's finger stopped. She looked up. 'Henry, you're not . . .'

'No, I'm not.' Henry took a few more belts of sake.

'You look gray, Hanky,' Madeleine said. 'Let's get out of here and get some air. Besides, we've got one more thing to do.'

'What is it?'

'You'll see.' Madeleine took Henry's elbow as he struggled upward. She looked into his face. 'Don't get sick. You'll ruin everything.'

'I'm not sick, I'm . . . something else.'

With their arms linked to steady one another, Henry and Madeleine walked a few city blocks. They breathed in and out at the same time, looked at the same things, saw them together. It was a clear, warm night and the trees were hung with lights around which fluttered small groups of moths. The lights and the powdery movement among the leaves made the trees look alive. In silence they passed great, stern banks, glittering windows of jewelry, inching yellow cab ranks and perfumed department stores. They slowed by the entrance to a hotel and Henry stopped breathing, wondering if Madeleine had booked a room. They walked on and heard snatches of lively conversation coming toward them, then passing away. A bicycle with flowers stuck in the spokes rode by. Lights changed and traffic crawled across intersections as they walked in step over black-and-white crosswalks. Somebody sang out of a darkened doorway. The smoke and chatter of intermission seeped from the foyer of a theatre. Henry and Madeleine saw all these things, in silence, together, at the same time.

Madeleine stopped them outside a small repertory cinema. Henry looked up. Big black letters against a diffused white fluorescent box: 'Woody Allen – MANHATTAN, 9:20 p.m.' Madeleine slipped her arm out of Henry's and looked at her watch. 'We're just in time,' she said.

'For what?' Henry asked.

'What do you think?'

'I can't . . . I'm not gonna . . . It's . . .'

'Well I am, Henry. And you have to, too. You can't just leave a date halfway through. It's rude.'

'I'm not ready for this.'

'Monday, Henry. I'm leaving Monday. Come in with me. You're ready.' Madeleine walked toward the entrance. 'I'll spring for the popcorn, too. Come on.' Almost as though she was encouraging a recalcitrant animal. 'Come on, Henry.' He didn't move. Madeleine reached the doors. 'Come on!' Henry looked up at the sign once again. *Manhattan*. He desperately wanted to see the film; he knew all about it and all he knew was good. 'Henry, I'm going in.' Madeleine pushed open the door, then turned to him. 'Well?'

Henry didn't move and Madeleine let the door close softly behind her.

Part 3

10

An Occurrence at Owl Creek Bridge, a French film made in 1962, based on a story by Ambrose Bierce, is a short and complicated but coherent series of memories and flashbacks. In the film, set during the Civil War, an army deserter is condemned to be hanged from a railway bridge, but just as it becomes taut the rope snaps and the deserter plunges into the water far below. He swims downriver and manages to escape through a dense forest, hoping to see his family once more. The man runs and runs, across vast plains and over misty cold mountains, sleeping rough, surviving on wild berries and rainwater. Finally, he reaches his home, his wife flings open the cabin door, and just as he is about to fall exhausted into her arms . . .

Henry Powdermaker, now in his early twenties, thinks about *An Occurrence at Owl Creek Bridge*, likening himself to the condemned man, as he sits on a set of peeling concrete steps – a film projector, still warm from recent use, and ten reels of black-and-white film by his side – out front of the house he has lived in for about a year. It is a house swelling with memories; he thinks about Ethan's broken wrist, Bambi's missing teeth, Godard's theory about the essential elements for a movie, and where it all began to go wrong . . .

Flashbacks. Late in the previous summer, Henry is sitting on a small set of stairs inside the house. Just behind and to his left is a tiny, gloomy kitchen; a grease-coated stuffed blowfish hangs from a hook near his head. Henry nods into a telephone. 'Uh huh . . . uh huh,' he says, rolling his eyes, staring out the grubby, barred window on his right. 'Uh huh.' He puts down the phone and places his head in his hands, his fingers clawing at his scalp. 'Oh God, not again . . .' he says, getting up. In the kitchen he takes a Schlitz from the refrigerator and sinks to the floor, searching for something rueful yet witty to say. Rueful is all he manages. 'Not *again* . . .'

Henry is six feet tall but almost precisely as thin as he was at the age of ten. So thin that from certain angles, and if the lighting is not quite right, he seems not to be there at all. Every so often he has to look in a mirror, just to make sure.

Still on the floor he takes a drink of beer and tries to say, 'Is this something personal, Z?' But the foam and bubbles in his throat catch the words, and all he produces is a strange, pathetic sound like a bird or a dog trying to speak.

From elsewhere in the house, somewhere upstairs or downstairs (it's a split-level place on a busy street-corner above and behind a store, and people can enter from any direction, any height; it's almost like a set), Ethan Vaughan appears. Ethan is around Henry's age, but to Henry he seems older, more completely formed, despite the fact that he is even thinner than Henry. And likes to call himself Ethan Fabulous. And for some reason calls Henry 'Harry'.

'Hi, Harry,' Ethan says, looking down at Henry. 'You're wasting that beer. Is there any left?' He speaks slowly and deeply, with an almost somnambulic drawl as though the words themselves are rising from heavy sleep. But every so often he throws in an over-accented word, like a small, cracking hand grenade.

Henry looks at the bottle, then hands it up to Ethan. 'Here you go.'

Ethan sticks a long index finger into the neck of the bottle. 'Thank you. What's up? Why are you slumping?'

'I didn't make it into film school.'

'Again?'

'Again.'

'Oh. Bad luck,' Ethan says. Then adds, 'I guess.'

'My life is over. Again.'

'Any more beer in the fridge?'

'Take a look.'

'I'll have to step over you. I'm *very!* reluctant to do that. Stepping over another human being is unseemly.'

'Actually I don't think there's any.' Henry gets up off the floor. 'I'll go buy some more.'

Ethan hands Henry a twenty-dollar bill, saying, 'And I *don't!* expect any change.'

Henry weaves in and out of the stream of people on the streets outside – the people he assumes have good jobs and great lives and plenty of money – and directs his stare at the sidewalk. He cannot look anybody in the eye because he is sure that they will see failure in his own eyes. Or that they won't notice him at all. He doesn't like either idea. 'My life is over for another year,' he thinks to himself, as the cracks and gum and dirt and summer-dried leaves pass beneath his stride. It is warm outside and there is a smell to the air that Henry likes despite his unhappiness. It is the smell of summer, of something different, but familiar, about to happen. 'Another year . . .'

Title: One Year Before. Syracuse, NY. It is near the end of summer. Henry puts down the telephone, walks over to his temporary girlfriend, Amelia, and sinks to his knees where she is sitting. She puts her arms around him as he sighs and rubs his back, saying over and over again, 'Oh no, oh no.' Even though Henry appreciates that he is being gently comforted by Amelia, he cannot lose the thought that she is speaking to him and stroking him as though he is some sort of pet.

(Less than a month later, Amelia will dump Henry and tell many of her friends that he has 'a psychotic attachment to dead actresses'. When this news finally reaches Henry some time later, he will shake his head and say, 'God, what a thing to tell people,' even though he knows it is true.)

*

Title: Two Years Before. Syracuse, NY. Summer is ending. Henry is sitting on a dark-purple couch, talking on a telephone. 'Well, they didn't let me in last year or the year before that, so y'know, it's a cliché, but third time lucky. Maybe. Yeah . . . yeah, thanks, Danny . . . You're kidding? Right next to you? Is the guy dead? Good lord . . . Anyway, I'll give you a call later and let you know. Maybe we'll have a drink or something tonight. Say hi to our mother, huh? Bye.' He hangs up, thinks briefly about his brother's unhealthy proximity to doom, looks at his watch, walks to the front door and out to the letterbox, daylight hitting him like a blow. He peers into the letterbox and pulls out a letter with a college stamp in the top corner. 'Well, this is it,' he says to the birds and the sunlight. 'This is my life I'm holding in my hands.' He tears open his life and reads what it has to say to him. He absorbs the news, walks back into the flat and calls his girlfriend, the woman he lives with. 'Jeanne, you've got to come home right away. There's a slim, but very real chance I might kill myself.'

(But the closest Henry comes to suicide that night is when, while carelessly chopping an onion, he slices open his thumb. 'This doesn't hurt anywhere near as much as you'd think,' he tells Jeanne, holding up his extravagantly bloody hand. He looks at it and briefly considers fainting, for impact.)

Title: Three Years Before. Waterville, ME. Late summer. A Thursday afternoon. Henry behind a large, ergonomically unsound plastic desk. Sifting through a sheaf of papers. Hating the crackly feeling of the paper on his fingers. Smudges of carbon ink on his chin. Hidden beneath a pink manila folder, a telephone rings. Henry answers: 'Administrative Clerk Grade One Henry Powdermaker speaking.' With each silent nod of his head, Henry's bony shoulders slump a little further beneath his brown jacket. It's a short call, but he nods a lot; when he hangs up his neck and shoulders are level with the desk. His face lies flat on a pile of paper, faded blue ink bruising his nose, lips, cheeks and forehead.

(Six weeks later the place where he works elects not to extend Henry's three-month contract, citing reasons such as 'being barefoot in the office environment; reading comics at desk; sliding down stair banister; wearing a hat indoors'.)

Title: Four Years Before. Augusta, ME. It is just about the end of summer and Henry has graduated from high school. He plans to move to Syracuse, New York once he's accepted into the film course he's applied to. Maybe share a dorm with other film geeks, whiling away long nights talking about Hal Ashby, Ring Lardner Junior, Garson Kanin and Ben Hecht. If, somehow, he fails to get in to film school, he has told his mother, he will 'bum around and sleep in a lot'. 'Not in my house, you won't,' she's advised him. 'You'll get a job.'

But he's confident that he won't fail.

A few days later he calls the film school, eager for news of his future, and is told that he has been unsuccessful. Sitting at the kitchen table, over a cup of coffee and a cigarette he has borrowed from her, Henry tells his mother the news. 'They didn't let me in,' he says, confusion and bewilderment tainting the simple words.

'Oh well,' his mother says, rubbing at a spot on her head. 'Maybe next year.' Henry nods. But his mother has not finished speaking. 'And would you pleeeease give up smoking? You look absolutely ridiculous.'

Daniel comes home from school and reports that geography lessons have been suspended for a while, due to what he calls 'highly unforeseeable circumstances'. At fourteen he's an unusually self-contained boy, but carries with him a heavy air, as though the blues songs he has developed a great fondness for have taken root inside him, nourishing him even as they prematurely age and tire him. He looks his mother in the eye and then his brother and says, 'You two wouldn't believe some of the things that are happening to me. And I'm not palking about tuberty, which has passed and seems to have gone quite well, by the way.' After an uncertain pause Henry and Sandra burst into laughter, as sharp and shocking as two claps of thunder.

(Henry quits neither smoking nor sleeping in. He moves out of his mother's house in order to further develop both habits, but sorely misses his little brother's ability to make him smile.)

11

Henry takes a cigarette from a pack and lights it as he struggles back up the hill with a carton of beer and a bottle of cheap whiskey. The walk back home takes a while and when he finally gets there, the sun has fallen behind the house, silhouetting it and making it look like a big ship moored at the intersection of two great seas of tar. He kicks open the door on the port side and puts the bottles down on the kitchen bench. Sylvia Moriarty, a newspaper photographer who shares the house with Ethan and Henry, says, 'Oh hi, Henry, did you get the onion?' Henry vaguely recalls something about an onion. Clearly his face betrays a distinct dimness because Sylvia huffs and says, 'I rang before. For the risotto, don't you remember?'

'Things have changed since then, Sylvia,' calls Ethan from another room. 'Harry don't buy onions for *no-one!* no more.'

'I'll go back,' offers Henry, willing Sylvia to say 'Don't worry about it.'

'Don't worry about it,' she says. 'I'll use a stock cube, it'll do.'

'I don't put a lot of stock in stock cubes,' say Ethan, in the kitchen, ripping open the carton of beer.

'You cook then,' says Sylvia.

'My religion prevents me from touching food with anything other than a knife and *fork!* You know that, Sylvia.'

'Actually, I didn't know that. And I suspect it's not true.'

Ethan hands a beer to Henry. 'Harry failed to get into film school for the *fifth!* year in a row today, Sylv. Why don't you give him a roll in the hay and make him feel better?'

Sylvia glares at Ethan and blushes. She has jet-black hair worn in a neat bob, and her red lips and make-up reddened cheeks make her look like a pretty, petulant doll, like Evans Evans in *Bonnie and Clyde*. 'Oh, what a shame,' she says. 'By the way, fuck you, Ethan, you idiot.' Ethan laughs loudly.

'Oh well,' Henry says, looking at his feet. 'I probably would have been a poor student. Unpopular, too. Maybe my life will turn out better this way. Although I can't really see how. But, y'know, you never know.' The words are rueful, he thinks, but not very witty.

Sylvia gives Henry a quick kiss and a wink then goes upstairs to her room. Henry knows her well enough to realize that it is not an invitation, although he cannot help wishing it was. He finds winking very attractive, although unusual, in a woman. But it's the unusualness of it that makes it so sexy, he decides. That and saying 'fuck you' to Ethan. He pours two glasses of beer and hands one to Ethan.

'I have some advice for you, Harry,' says Ethan, lighting a cigarette. 'And *this!* I do mean. If you want to be a film maker, all you have to do is head on over to Poland and change your name to Andrzej or Jerzy.'

Henry laughs. 'They didn't let Roman Polanski into the film school at Lodz about fifty times. Or Krakow or wherever it was.'

'Because he had the wrong first name. Change your name, Henry. It's completely unsuitable.'

Many hours later there are four people in the lamp-lit living room: Ethan, Henry, Sylvia and her friend, Klaus, a highly-strung actor with a face like a rusty hatchet and a bad temper which Henry sometimes fears. Ethan is sitting on a green vinyl armchair. 'Hey, Harry, why don't you become a junkie? It's a very popular vocation and it's got respect. Practically everybody's a junkie these days. People are even *pretending!* they're junkies just for credibility. It's the new cool.'

'The thing about Ethan,' Sylvia tells everyone. 'Is that he's an idiot.'

'I couldn't,' says Henry. 'I don't really think I have the constitution to be an addict. Or the character.'

Ethan says, 'I may be an idiot, Sylv. But at least I'm not a *fucking!* idiot.' Everybody laughs, except Ethan, who likes to pretend that he has said something unremarkable when he makes a joke. 'D'you have any boo?' Ethan asks Sylvia. This is not a joke. Sylvia often smokes hash or marijuana for her back pain. There is something mysteriously wrong with her spine. Something that makes her face look permanently white and tired. Ethan, Sylvia and Klaus pass the small, oily joint between them. Henry declines because being stoned makes him anxious and failure-conscious.

'So what are you going to do now, Henry?' Sylvia asks in a dark breath of dope.

'I'm not sure.'

'Why don't you crew up on a lobster boat. Greet the dawn as you notch V's in the tails of shorts and eggers with your bone-handled fisherman's knife. You miss the lobsters back home, don't you Harry?' Ethan says.

'No, I don't, Ethan.' Henry turns to Sylvia. 'I really don't know what to do. Stay in my stupid job, I guess. I'm sure as hell not applying to that damn film school ever again, though. Good God. I think they see my name on the envelope and immediately fire up the shredder.' Henry looks at Ethan, puzzled, wondering how he knows about the practice of marking undersized and roe-heavy lobster with a V and throwing them back into the ocean, especially considering that Ethan grew up in . . .

'Where are you actually from, Ethan?' Henry asks.

'Where am I *actually* from? What does that mean?'

'It means where are you from, Ethan,' Sylvia explains, crushing the wrinkled white worm between her fingers in a glass ashtray. 'Don't be such an asshole. It's a fairly simple question.'

'Kentucky.'

Sylvia shakes her head and her hair swishes like shiny curtains on either side of her head. 'No, you're not.'

Ethan sighs. 'Right, right. I forgot. I sometimes feel *highly!* Kentuckian. It confuses me. Am I from Indiana?'

'No.'

'Alaska?'

'No!'

Forty-seven guesses later Ethan still hasn't worked out where he is from, by which time Henry is no longer interested – although he is convinced, for some reason, that Ethan was born in Utah.

Charlie calls to tell Henry that the following night's cine-matheque screening has been cancelled and that since this is the third week in succession that this has happened, maybe they should quit being members and demand their money back. 'Apart from which, when they *do* manage to show a film, it's usually some piece of weirdness from Romania featuring marionette dwarfs waddling around sets that give you nightmares. Also, you owe me twenty-five bucks. Sorry, but I need it for my date with umm ... Vanessa.' Charlie is in law school at Syracuse, 'ole S.U.,' as he likes to call it, giving it a Southern twang. His band, between names at the moment, is building up a steady and loyal following, despite the fact that the fans don't know when, where or as whom the band will be playing. But they are very very loud and people seem to like that. Vanessa has nearly finished studying to be a nurse. ('God I envy that Rocket's sex life,' Ethan once remarked. 'He went *straight!* from the schoolgirl fantasy to the nurse fantasy. I hate to think what's next.') She and Charlie remain the happiest people Henry has ever known. 'And we owe it all to each other,' Charlie has said.

It is late now. Sylvia and Klaus are long gone. Ethan and Henry sit in the living room in front of the television, waiting for a documentary about German war crimes to come on. An announcement informs them that the show has been replaced by coverage of a golf game.

'Six million over par,' mutters Ethan. 'This is completely unacceptable. How are we expected to examine the sins of the Nazis without footage!?'

Still searching for that elusive witty-but-rueful remark, Henry says goodnight to Ethan and walks down the long hallway, down to his bedroom, down into sleep and the stark footage of his dreams.

12

Daylight. Henry has two jobs. During the day he does something he tells people is 'indescribably clerical' at a small firm which prints legal stationery; and three nights a week he is an usher at a failing repertory cinema. Monday to Friday he sits at a desk, blue pen in hand, wearing a nylon shirt, a little damp and discolored at the armpits but reeking of purpose. There is the smudge of carbon, the scar and scratch of streaks of printer's ink, and his lower lip, chewed and raw as he wonders, 'Where am I?', 'What the hell am I doing here?', 'What tragic style of sandwich will I have for lunch?' He sits near Mrs Harston, a sixty-year-old woman whom he is convinced is a frottagist because she is always pressing her heavy, powder-gray breasts into his back while she admonishes him for some error or other. Her breath smells of dry biscuits even though her lunch, which she always takes at her desk and which is always the same, is a plate of sliced meat and half an apple. Henry's work is maddeningly detailed, repetitive, very poorly paid and without even the smallest perk; but the thing that upsets him most of all about his job is Mrs Harston's unchanging, miserable lunch. It depresses him so much because, while not a big fan of apples – or fruit in general – he has a weakness for thinly sliced processed meat himself and it makes him terribly sad to think of Mrs Harston choosing meat at a counter, her mouth perhaps watering in anticipation of the taste, as his own often does.

The morning after his fifth film school failure, even though it's only a short walk from his home, Henry arrives a half-hour late at the printer's, a little bleary with sleeplessness. He can tell that everyone can tell he's slightly hung over, too. Four of them share the small office: Mrs Harston, the depressing luncheonist; Mr Partridge, the boss, a big man whose facial ruddiness is permanently exacerbated by the garish, strangling ties he favors; reedy, lopsided Lenny Niehaus, the accounts department with a sneaky nose, a glass eye and a permanent smirk; and hungover Henry, who is more or less everybody's assistant.

There is a head-turning silence as Henry stands in the entrance, his left hand clutching a battered brown briefcase, which is empty – nothing more than a prop that he thinks will make him more convincing in the role of employee. He holds it loosely, like a detachable limb. The rest of him, clothed in stained, hand-me-down brown and cream and beige, looks like it too might slip away leprously at any moment. His mouth is open and he is gulping air like food. 'Morning folks,' he pants, the words falling like dropped balls.

'I'm glad you could join us, Mr Powdermaker,' Partridge says lugubriously. Henry has heard this tone and this very same expression many times before and wonders if people like Mr Partridge attend some sort of Boss School to learn sarcastic clichés like that.

'Sorry,' Henry says. 'I . . . I . . .' But there is nothing more he can say. He thinks of the lines from Tod Browning's *Freaks*, when the dwarves and bearded ladies and frog-men are imploring the stranger to join them: 'One of us, one of us,' the freaks chant. 'One of us, one of us.' He tries not to laugh because he knows it would be wrong. Well, not wrong exactly, but definitely not right.

Mr Partridge nods to his left and to his right. 'Mrs Harston, Mr Niehaus, would you leave Mr Powdermaker and me for a moment?' In Mr Partridge's mouth, 'Powdermaker' is a long word, rising and falling over the course of its unpleasantly attenuated length. *Pow* is a blow. *Der* a simpleton's dribble. *Make* an ancient curse. The protracted *rrrrr* a creepy caress – James Mason's mouth cunnilingually tickling Lolita's luscious consonants.

The others leave and Partridge points to a chair. Henry sits. He wants a Coke. 'Oh damn, damn, damn, damn,' his mind mutters. It's not the loss of the job that distresses him, it's the being fired. 'Damn!'

'Mr Powdermaker,' begins Mr Partridge, blinking slowly and laboring every syllable. 'You came to us many months ago, a young man full of assurances that you were serious about a career here. That you were . . . willing. That you were . . . prepared. It seems abundantly clear that, in fact, you are neither of those things.' Partridge changes to a delightedly mordant tone, reminding Henry of Charles Laughton in *Witness for the Prosecution*, all spit and puffed, purple lips. This strikes Henry as appropriate. 'Your work is, at best, merely terrible. At worst, appalling.' He switches back to rich sincerity. 'Have you anything to say for yourself?'

'Well . . . no. Not really. Well, actually . . .' Henry thinks for a long moment, mainly about Coca-Cola and the fantastic trick ending of *Witness for the Prosecution*. And about how Charles Laughton was married to Elsa Lanchester, the Bride of Franken-stein. Who was actually pretty good-looking underneath that crazy hairstyle. 'Oh, not really, no,' he says. 'Nothing. I *wish* I did, you understand, but . . . well, I think you're having a pretty good time firing me, Mr Partridge, so, y'know, I won't spoil it for you.'

Partridge nods, the folds of flesh around his neck flapping like chicken skin. 'You may collect your final payment and leave. There will be no farewell cake.'

'No . . .' Henry looks around the dull, cramped office and tries to imagine the other 'farewell cakes' that have been eaten there. Hard icing and dry sponge. 'Well,' he says, picking up his briefcase. 'Well . . . I don't blame you for firing me. I really don't.'

'I would think not.'

'No, I guess not. But I'm just saying . . .' Henry sighs. He wants to tell Mr Partridge about film school, either the truth or a lie, but he says nothing. Just picks up his briefcase and piles in the things that are his from his desk: a pen and a crinkled picture of Joseph Mankiewicz from an old newspaper obituary. Mrs Harston the Bearded Lady and Lenny the Frog-Man come back in, knowing that it is over, as though they have been listening behind the door. Neither says a word to Henry, chatting pleasantly with Partridge as if Henry isn't there at all.

Henry murmurs, 'One of us,' all the way home.

'Who goes there?' shouts Ethan's deep, disembodied voice as Henry shuts the front door of the house.

'Me,' Henry says. 'Harry. I got fired.'

'You *certainly!* did.'

'What do you mean?'

'I mean that the *malignant!* Metro called and asked you never to darken their sweeping staircase again. They also want the purple waistcoat back.'

'Oh man! Fired from two jobs in one day. God, I must be a terrible employee.'

'Why did they fire you?'

'Which?'

'Either.'

'I suppose it's the same for both. But I don't know. Do we have any Coke?'

'-Aine or -acola?'

'Yeah, cocaine, Mr Fabulous. I just lost both my jobs and now I'm gonna donate money to some Colombian in a tracksuit.'

'*Hey!* Come and look at this. The space between my big toe and the toe next to it is an almost perfect paisley shape.'

Ethan Vaughan looks a lot like James Coburn would look if the sides of James Coburn's head were pushed together: a high forehead and high cheekbones, a large, garishly toothy smile, although one that appears rarely in either man. Sometimes he even moves like Coburn doing the goofy, paranoid antics of *The President's Analyst* or *Our Man Flint* – sudden ducks and swoops and dives and changes of direction, his head going one way while his knees trick off in another. It is nearly midday and Ethan is almost naked, almost asleep on the couch: his chest is sunken and he looks like a mummy, unwrapped and undead. Henry genuinely likes Ethan but finds him exasperating, his apparent happiness with doing absolutely nothing. With not having a job. With appearing not to study whatever it is he purports to study, or reading or even watching much television. His great satisfaction with investigating the curious shapes between his toes. At this moment Henry envies Ethan; he is envious, repulsed and awed – not so much by Ethan himself, but by the way he acts. The way he mutters sometimes and always does as he pleases, almost as if he believes he is the only rational man living in a nursing home and knows that, surrounded by the frail, ancient and derelict, nobody will notice his own strange behavior. Ethan's character belongs in a film, but Henry cannot think who might make it.

'This is quite the life you've got, being a student, isn't it?' Henry says. 'A real challenge.'

'I *happen!* to be between semesters at the moment.'

'Some difference. What is it exactly that you study anyway?'

'History. The lives that make history.'

'Whose lives?'

'Anybody's. Everybody's. De Gaulle, de Kooning, DeLillo –'

'De Witt,' offers Henry.

'Who?'

'George Sanders in *All About Eve*. Addison De Witt.'

'It could be anyone, although *usually!* not the utterly fictional.'

'DeMille then. And De Witt wasn't all that fictional. He was based on–'

'Whoever. At the moment I'm particularly interested in Salvador Dali's muse-slash-girlfriend, Amanda Lear. She's a complete *boob!*, but very fascinating.'

Henry thinks for a moment, then says quietly, 'Jesus.'

'Certainly,' says Ethan, misunderstanding Henry's whisper. 'But He's been pretty well covered.

'So what are you gonna do now, Harry? Now that you're a twice unemployed five-time film school entry failure?'

And before he knew it, Henry said, 'I'm going to make a film.'

13

Starlet. Ethan had a girlfriend named Bambi who seemed to be moving into the house by osmosis. She was there almost all the time. Apart from the fact that she wore leather trousers exclusively and very well, Henry couldn't see what Ethan saw in her. She was without doubt the most guileless person Henry had ever met in his life and consequently he found her quite entertaining. He loved the way she spoke in exquisitely enunciated bursts that arrived uninvited from nowhere; brief monologues which sounded formal and rehearsed, yet inspired. Although by what, Henry was never certain.

'I believe in a combination of success and spirituality,' Bambi had told Henry the first time they met. 'I find Deepak Chopper an inspiration, although I do wish he would write some books with recipes in them. I feel sure they would sell well. And taste good.'

Henry also loved Bambi's name. She had been christened Amber Yesson, but when she turned eighteen had decided that she was more Bambi than Amber and had her name legally changed. Unfortunately, she was mildly dyslexic and misspelled her surname, becoming, in the slip of a shaky pen and a swift deed poll stamp, Bambi Yessno.

'Many people did not take Madonna seriously at first because of her name, which some thought a blasphemation against the church and the memory of the Madonna. But look at Madonna now,' Bambi explained for absolutely no reason to a pensively nodding Henry the second time they met. 'She is a very powerful figure ... I am talking about the singer – not the other one.'

Bambi Yessno played a nylon-stringed acoustic guitar and fancied herself as a singer-songwriter and/or actress, convinced that the big break which would bring her international stardom was just a screen test or demo tape away. She was pretty in a folky, hippy kind of way – all batting blue eyes, tangled, dirty-blond hair and halter tops that showed off her perky breasts and flat, brown midriff, where there was some sort of eastern sun tattooed around her navel. Henry loved her navel.

'Not to gild the lily of the field, but my friend Darla van Popje says I have a certain *je ne sais pas*,' Bambi announced to Henry and Sylvia one morning while Ethan was upstairs in the shower. 'Darla is from theater. They talk like that in theater. Other languages. She has an unusual name because her parents are Netherland ... ish.' Henry had covered his smiling mouth with his hand. Sylvia said, 'Really?'; about precisely what, Henry was not sure.

Why Ethan, a dour skeleton who dressed in coffin-dusty burial suits, appealed to a girl who sometimes brushed her cheeks with glitter and wore a plastic yellow daffodil clip in her hair, was a mystery to Sylvia and Henry. Why the showily erudite Ethan tolerated Bambi's dull-wittedness and frequent urges to sit cross-legged on the floor and sing her own poor poetry was less mysterious, at least to Henry, who concluded that Bambi was probably a nymphomaniac. And pretty sexy. Thick-headed and ingenuous, but a sexy nympho.

'She is *not!* a nymphomaniac,' Ethan told Henry firmly on the first night of Henry's double unemployment. They were spread around the living room: Sylvia lying on the couch, Henry sitting at the table staring out the window, Ethan standing in front of the television with his hands on his hips. 'I would never go out with any kind of maniac.'

'Except a dipsomaniac,' Sylvia said. 'Move.'

Ethan took a step aside. 'Especially not a dipsomaniac.'

'Or a brainiac,' Henry muttered. 'Is she coming over tonight?'

'Yes, Harry, she is,' Ethan said. 'She jonesing for another instalment of your snideness and sarcasm.'

'I like her, Ethan. She's what I believe they used to call "a sweet kid".'

'Back when everybody was patronizing the hell out of each other.'

'Yeah, back then,' Henry said, imagining himself as Burt Lancaster in *The Sweet Smell of Success* – ruthless, smart-mouthed J. J. Hunsecker, always ready with a crushing remark. Match me, Sidney! 'They were some good times back then, Ethan, I'm telling you.'

There was a knock at the front door. Sylvia said, 'Before you answer that, Ethan, could you change the channel to the news, please? I think a CBS crew shot me in a media pack outside the car bomb site this morning.'

'Who said I was going to answer it?'

'Well, isn't it Bambi?' asked Sylvia.

'Probably.'

Henry leaped up, crying, 'I'll get it. Tape it if you're on, Sylvia.'

Sylvia said, 'Please change the channel, Ethan. Please,' as Henry bounded up the three stairs and yanked open the heavy door. Behind him he heard a click, a stab of fuzz, then a newsreader's voice. On the front steps stood a man in a charcoal-gray suit, wearing wire-rimmed glasses. The man opened his mouth in what was meant to be a smile but looked merely like a stretch. His teeth were small and pointed. There was a neat, scalp-revealing part in his damp red hair. Dusk had slipped away and the sky was growing dark and cold.

'Good evening,' the man said, nasally.

'Good evening. Are you a Witness?' Henry asked.

'No, I'm—'

'Amway?'

'No, sir, I'm—'

'Encyclopedias?'

'If you'll just let—'

Down in the living room, Ethan shouted, 'Let her in, Henry, you *Mongoloid!*'

'Just a second,' Henry said to the man. Then he partially closed the door and shouted into the living room, 'It's not her! It's . . . someone else!' He opened the door and took a step forward, forcing the stranger back down a step. 'Who are you?'

'My name is Michael Mulcahy and I'm just visiting people in the neighborhood on behalf of Tandec Cinemas and if you're a movie fan then you might be very interested in a very special offer that Tandec has at the moment which you won't see advertised in any newspapers or magazines are you a movie fan, Mr . . . ?' Mulcahy said breathlessly. He had an Irish accent, lilting all over the place.

'Powdermaker. Yes, I am.'

'Well, if I may just quickly show you what we're offering today, it'll only take a minute or two and you could end up saving up to fifty dollars on cinema tickets as well as Pepsi Cola and popcorn upgrades in the next six months.'

'Product placement-wise, I have to tell you I'm more of a Coke man, Mr Mulcahy.' Henry looked above the man's head. 'The next six months, you say?'

'Yes, the offer is valid for six months from date of sign.'

Henry made a disappointed sucking sound with his tongue. 'Six months from date of sign, huh? That's too bad.' In the grim, dark sky he saw a star.

'Why is that, may I ask?'

'Because I'm going overseas next week. To Ireland, as a matter of fact.' A little bit of bullshitting to pass the time.

'Oh!' Michael Mulcahy said excitedly. 'Business or pleasure, may I ask, although you'll love it either way, I'm sure.'

'Business. I'm shooting a film in . . . uh, London . . . *derry*.'

'Oh marvelous. Marvelous.'

'So I can't really use cinema discounts in the near future.'

'What about the other people in the house? Might they be interested, do you think?'

Trying to have fun with the guy, Henry said, 'There's nobody else here. They're only actors. And actors, unobserved, don't exist.' It came out wrong; smug and snide, precisely as Ethan had described Henry's tone toward Bambi.

Mulcahy looked confused and raised his eyebrows behind the rims of his glasses. 'I . . . I see. Well, goodnight to you then.' He stepped backwards, down to the pavement, and looked up at Henry, nodding silently and slowly. Henry felt uncomfortable, as though Mulcahy knew that he had been lied to. He sighed and looked upward. There were a few more stars.

'Hey, they're not really actors,' Henry said heavily. 'They're just people I live with.'

'Oh. Goodnight to you then.' Mulcahy nodded once more and walked away, the heavy briefcase pulling at his shoulder.

Henry walked wordlessly through the silence between Sylvia and Ethan, past the television's blather and straight down the hall to his bedroom where he threw some clothes into a valise and grabbed his car keys. The hollowness of the lie he'd told the Irishman had already worked its way deep inside him, leaving him gnawingly empty. Shooting a film in Londonderry . . . He felt like such a dick.

The drive from Syracuse to Augusta, via Utica, Troy, the gloomy outskirts of Boston, Portsmouth and Portland took about eight hours and by the time he arrived at his mother's house Henry was shaking with exhaustion and nerves. Twice he'd had to skid to a stop and wait for a head-lit deer to move off the road. His clothes felt like a clammy second skin. He let himself in the front door and dragged his feet toward the kitchen, thinking sleepily about eggs and coffee, deers and lies.

'Hello,' Sandra said. 'You look awful.' She was fully dressed, chopping things and boiling things. 'Really quite awful.'

'Ah, but underneath I *feel* terrific,' Henry said, shuddering. 'Hello to you, too, Mother.' He gave her a peck on the cheek. 'What are you doing?'

'Preparing dinner.'

Henry glanced at his watch – it was 6:10 a.m. He raised his eyebrows.

'It's a big dinner. I'm having some women over.'

The word 'lesbians' flashed into his head. He shook it away. 'Is Daniel around?'

'He's out on a links somewhere. Then he goes straight to school. He'll be back at five.'

'Can you wake me around four?'

Sandra looked at her son. 'Why are you here, Henry? Is something wrong? You seem to be convulsing.'

'Not really,' he said. 'I almost hit a deer on the way here and I told some lies to an Irishman last night, so y'know, I'm a little . . . worried.'

'About what?'

'Things.'

'In general?'

'That's right.'

'Will you be staying for dinner?'

'Is it a lesbian dinner party?'

'Yes, Henry, it is. The house will be full of lesbians this evening.'

Henry smiled at his mother. She grinned back and told him to go to sleep.

Daniel Powdermaker had grown up to be a tall, good-looking boy with broad shoulders and the quick, alert eyes of a fox, and when he was thirteen he had his first kiss. The following day the girl with whom he'd shared the kiss, a plump, pretty girl who claimed Narragansett blood somewhere in her lineage and who had whispered 'Don't get any big ideas' to Daniel as her lips left his, drowned in the flash-flooded waters of the Kennebec River. For her funeral, the young girl's parents had selected a Robert Johnson song, 'If I Had Possession Over Judgement Day'. Daniel had never heard such music and it changed his life. But there was more to come. During the next few years his biology lab partner lost a foot when he was run down by a ride-on mower, his geography teacher vanished, a golf pro standing just ten feet from Daniel was put into a coma after being struck in the temple by a wildly sliced Titleist, a female quarter of a double date broke her wrist hastily removing her own bra when the Pontiac wagon she and Danny were sprawled in back of drove over a fallen branch, and, just a few months earlier, a college freshman he was dating was killed in a 'mishap' involving a parachute, the problem being that she apparently leaped out of a plane without wearing one.

'I'm afraid that if I ever choose my lerry the poor girl's entire family'll be wiped out,' he told Henry as they shared a pitcher of beer in a tavern popular with fishing boat crews, big hulks of men covered in flannel and beards, Cimmerian holes for eyes. 'Mother even said that I'll have to stay a virgin or risk being prosecuted for reckless endangerment.'

'She would.' Henry told Daniel to ignore what Mother said, that losing his cherry would definitely be worth it, but he might consider doing it somewhere out of town. They both laughed uneasily; Daniel because he suspected that what he said might actually be true; Henry because he, too, feared the same thing, and that it was his fault. That due to some egregious cosmic misalignment he had cursed his younger brother and that people all around the boy, but completely unknown to Henry, were paying for Henry's sins, one in particular. Then it occurred to Henry that Daniel might not be aware of why his father had suddenly left his wife and children; certainly Henry himself had never said anything about it to his brother, and he very much doubted that Sandra would have willingly brought the subject up with him either . . .

'It's because of that film, isn't it?' Daniel said, looking down at the pitcher of beer.

'You know?' A solid roar of laughter rose from a table directly behind Henry. 'You *know?*'

Daniel knew. He had known since he was twelve and had stumbled across the reel stuffed inside a sock and hidden in a box in the garage. When he'd first played the film Daniel had thought it was a deleted scene from one of Henry's projects, that his mother and a man who looked like the few photographs of his father he'd seen were just acting. But at the same time he'd known enough not to mention it to Sandra; that there was something wrong about it. Although he had only ever run the film once and returned it to the box where he'd found it, the images lingered and it wasn't very long before Daniel realized that what he had seen was from life rather than some poisoned fantasy. He had, he told Henry, ruined the shafts of three irons smashing them against trees. He'd wanted desperately to ask his mother about it but every time he'd said 'Mom?' and she'd turned to him with a bright, expectant smile, ready perhaps to help with his homework or to tell him what they were having for dinner, Daniel choked.

'God Danny, why didn't you ever ask me about it?' Henry said. 'Though, of course, I'd probably have lied to you about it.' He laughed drily, then quickly swallowed a mouthful of beer.

'Because I didn't know if you knew about it. And I sure as hell didn't want to have to tell you about it. I mean, why would they even want to film something so horrible?' Daniel finally looked up. 'So how did you discover it?'

Henry's heart cooled, his thoughts slowed. Daniel knew almost everything – more than enough to infect his feelings for the world – but he didn't know the most awful thing of all . . .

When Henry finished explaining that it was in fact he who had made the film and then shown it to all of Jack and Sandra's friends, but that it was a mistake, an accident, he saw a tear fall onto the wooden table top. Then another and another. Daniel wiped his eyes with the back of his sleeve. With each silent sob Daniel's stomach heaved sharply, as though a fist inside was trying to punch its way out. Henry reached over and placed a hand on his brother's shoulder, knowing that he need not say another word. That this, at least for now, would be enough.

A shadow loomed. 'Whatsamatter ladies? Having a little man trouble?'

Henry told the dark mixture of hair, flannel and sour smells to please mind its own business.

'Got yer period there, sister?' the shadow growled.

'Come on, get lost, will you? This is really none of your business. Really.'

A hand leapt from the shadow and grabbed Henry's hair, yanking his head back. The words 'fuck off' had barely left Henry's contorted mouth when his head filled with stars and he felt the floor fly up to meet him. He rammed the chair he'd been sitting on at the shadow's legs and immediately heard a cry and the sounds of heavy, fleshy tumbling. He pulled himself up in time to see Daniel square off against the shadow's two companions, both big, wide men, but probably drunk and without Daniel's youth, build and the righteous anger that was at this moment filling his eyes with a furious light. On the floor to Henry's right, the shadow was on its knees, reaching into its back pocket. Henry took a step forward and kicked the glinting steel that suddenly appeared into a dark corner. 'Well come on,' Daniel said to the two men. Then everything went to hell.

There were fists, elbows and ashtrays slammed into faces, guts and ribs; knees and feet and shoulders ground into backs, necks, arms, cheekbones and noses. There were shouts and yelps and roars, smashing glasses, harsh slaps, the crunching of bone and gristle, and something that sounded like a sped-up rush of applause from an old movie newsreel. There was light and dark; vibrant, dizzying color draining to blacks and whites so deep and complete they seemed like whole universes. At one point the shadow had its hands around Henry's throat. Then suddenly didn't. Daniel was standing there instead. Then he wasn't. Henry punched wildly and hit the chest of one of the shadow's friends, who made an 'oof!' sound, just like a comic book sound effect. The shadow himself was back in the fray, pinning Daniel against a wall, pulling back a beefy arm. Henry hit him over the head with a chair, precisely as he'd seen done in a hundred Westerns. Only the chair didn't break into pieces and the shadow didn't slump to the ground. Instead it howled, clutching its bleeding head as it turned and looked at Henry with a look of truly murderous intent. For the first time, Henry felt frightened. The shadow had eyes. It sent its right fist at Henry's face. Henry sidestepped and fell over one of the shadow's flattened companions straight to the floor. The shadow showed a terrible mouth as it brought its face close to Henry's and once again pulled back its right arm, ready to kill him with a single blow. Daniel brought two hands clutching a pitcher down on the shadow's head then threw the crumpling, moaning shape to one side. He reached down and grabbed Henry's hand, pulling him upright. Then Daniel drew back his own fist. 'Hey! Hey! Wait! It's me,' Henry said.

Daniel said, 'I know,' before punching his brother hard in the stomach, looking him squarely in the eyes all the way down to the ground.

Make up. 'What'll we tell Mother?'

'About what?'

'What do you mean about what? About why we look like we've just been in a barroom brawl. Which we have.'

'Right. And she's got all her friends over, too.'

'Okay, what we'll do is go straight to her bathroom, clean ourselves up the best we can and hide the bruises and whatever with her blusher and foundation and stuff. What do you think?'

'Could work.'

'I think it's our only chance. She'll kill us if we come in looking like we've been fighting.'

'Yeah, she'd rather have drag queens for sons than a coupla thugs.'

'Probably.'

'She's an unusual woman.'

'Yes, yes she is.'

'Y'know, I know I shouldn't even be thinking about something like this, but ... d'you think Mother's gay?'

'I don't know. It's ... it's really hard to tell one way or the other, isn't it?'

'It certainly is ... It wouldn't bother me, of course.'

'Me either ... Listen I'm sorry about before. Everything, I mean.'

'Yeah, of course ... me too. Don't worry, things'll be all right.'

'Do you think?'

14

Biopic. Henry hated not having a job. He wished he had breakfast meetings in the Polo Lounge at the Beverly Hills Hotel, where he could be tired and scowl at his colleagues over a croissant, wallowing in early-morning resentment over a soaring budget they had to discuss urgently and dailies that looked unpromising. *Goddammit Eisner, you tinhorn! I told you to attach Grazer and Howard to this project or there'd be trouble!* He wanted a job he could tell other people about with pride. *So then Eisner started crying – because I fired him!* Something in the film industry – Hollywood preferably – was the obvious first choice: studio head or script-reader, he didn't mind which. Weeks passed. He wrote letters by the dozen, usually along these lines.

> *Dear——*
> *I read your autobiography and you seem like a pretty nice, smart person, full of terrific ideas and enthusiasms and wry reflections on yourself and your film career. I myself am sort of nice, pretty smart, full of fine ideas, plenty of enthusiasm and given to the occasional wry reflection on myself – my film career is going through something of a non-existent phase at the moment, so when I can bear to think about it, I needn't bother.*
>
> *I was wondering if you needed an assistant of any description. I'll do absolutely anything and do it to the very best of my ability. And for minimal dough. Also, I'll take a reasonable amount of personal abuse, which I realize is necessary to obtain and keep any job in the industry.*
>
> *I have close to no qualifications of any kind apart from the fact*

that I am not a complete moron. But if you'd give me a chance,
you really wouldn't be sorry. Really. Seriously.

Yours sincerely,
H. Powdermaker

P.S. Really.

And he applied to other film schools: the American Film Institute, Columbia (NYC), Columbia College (Chicago), Florida State, NYU, Savannah College of Art and Design, Temple University, UCLA, Northwestern, U of T in Austin and many, many more. His applications were short, simple and sober; the envelopes licked with a tongue dried and dancing with nerves.

He wrote short stories, short scripts, long screenplays, treatments, outlines, lines of dialogue, character profiles, brief edit/camera sequences for features that would never be made; he made budgets, both realistic and absurd; he sketched marketing plans for films that existed as titles only; he watched films three, four, five times in succession; he watched particular sections of films dozens of times over; he closed his eyes and just *listened* to entire films – sound only; he mentally recast films, re-cut them, re-scored them and re-named them; he read theory, biography and criticism; he read screenplays, memoirs, how to's, what to's and what not to's; the hell with college and the hell with a job – he lived and breathed film without them.

Henry dreamed. Henry wrote. Henry worked.

Monologue. The things that brought Henry, Ethan and Sylvia together were television, during which they were sensibly silent, or alcohol, in which case they made a lot of noise but little sense.

Bambi was over and they were all watching television and drinking tequila, pushing small cups of the yellowy poison to each other on a wooden skateboard. A still photograph of a dark, intense but strangely silly-looking man flashed on the screen. Henry leaped on it. 'I hate that Philip Roth. I mean he's a pretty good writer and everything, and the casting of *Goodbye, Columbus* – Richard

Benjamin and Ali McGraw – is spot-on, but what a bastard cheating on Claire Bloom and then writing about it. And boy, she's so beautiful. How could he do it?'

'Yeah, Henry,' Sylvia said, her face darkening with sarcasm. 'It's far worse to cheat on your wife if she's good-looking.'

'She's a Muslim now,' Ethan said. 'Changed her name to Mohammed Ali McGraw.'

Everybody – except Ethan – laughed. Henry continued, 'I'm not saying it's worse, it's just . . . Do you know what Claire Bloom looks like?'

'Not really.'

'You have to see her. Then you'll get it. And he's not exactly a handsome man himself, y'know. Richard Benjamin was probably too good-looking a choice, actually.'

'But he wasn't playing Philip Roth, was he? He was playing the character in the story.'

'Yeah, Neil – but what's the difference?'

'It's a film, not real life. That's the difference.'

'It all comes from the same source.'

'Which is?'

'Life.'

Sylvia said, 'Uh-huh,' leaning hard on the 'huh'.

The skateboard was covered in spilled tequila.

Sometime later Henry said, 'Those people on television who say, "Oh, I never thought anything like this would ever happen to me. You always think these sorts of things happen to other people." What they don't understand is that *they're* the people. The *other* people, I mean. They don't even realize it: *they're* the ones stuff happens to. Those things don't happen to us.'

'Things like what?'

'Like winning the lottery or a light plane crashing into your house. Stuff that gets you on the news. Discovering human bones in the yard.'

'And what if something like that does happen to you? I mean, they do happen. You see it on television,' Bambi slurred, pointing over at the dead screen. 'Oh. When did that go off?'

'It won't. But if it did, then you'd become one of them.'

'One of who?'

'Other people. The sort of person that things happen to. As it is, we're just like everybody else. We'll never win the lottery or be in a plane crash or marry an actress or whatever. We'll never have to say –' Henry put his hands to his face in silent-era shock – '"Gosh, I never thought anything like this would ever happen to me." Thank God. The thing is, when a film tries to tackle something like the surviving-a-plane-crash issue, nobody even says that, they just grow their hair long and become all spiritual and holy. I find it very unconvincing. Real plane-crash survivors, the first thing they always say is, "I never thought this'd happen to me."'

'But that's because they're in a film, not out here in real life,' Sylvia said.

'Same source though, Sylvia. I thought we agreed on that.'

'You agreed on it. With yourself.'

'Where are you from, Ethan?' Henry asked.

'I'm from around. Around the traps. Around the neighborhood. Around and about.'

'Isn't there a movie where a man wins a lottery ticket and says, "I never thought that this would happen to me"?' asked Bambi. 'I'm sure I have seen something like that. Maybe it was the news.'

'Well, whatever it was it'd be another morality tale full of phony spirituality and general bullshit.'

'And long hair?'

'Probably. Movie characters always let their hair grow after a spiritual awakening.'

'So what's your point with all this?' Ethan said.

'Oh, y'know ... I don't know. I'm just babbling.'

'You *certainly!* are. You've contradicted yourself about fifty times in the last ten minutes.'

'God, I don't know what I think about anything anymore.'

'You miss the lobsters back home, don't you, Harry?'

'Shut up.'

There was a small rapping at the door. At first, Henry was not sure if it was real. 'Is there someone at the door?' he asked of no one in particular.

'How do I know?' Sylvia replied. 'Go and see.'

'I'll go and see,' Henry said, and weaved up the stairs, taking a shot of tequila with him.

Standing on the front steps was a small pink rabbit holding a plastic bag in its left paw. 'Oh,' Henry said, and downed the tequila shot. 'Hi.' The rabbit said nothing. Henry shouted down into the living room, 'Is it Halloween tonight!?' There was no response from the babble below and he turned back to the rabbit. 'Is it Halloween?' The rabbit held out the bag. Henry could see candy-colored paper inside. 'I guess it is,' he said. 'Come on in.' Henry stepped back and the rabbit walked inside, and downstairs to the living room, where it stopped and stood still in the center of an almost mystical silence.

'I think it's Halloween,' Henry announced.

'I *certainly!* hope it is,' Ethan said.

The rabbit didn't move.

'Do we have any candy?' Sylvia asked.

'I'll grab something,' Henry said a little too loudly, and went back to the kitchen. He heard Sylvia introducing herself and Bambi and Ethan (as Ethan Fabulous) to the rabbit. 'What's your name?' The rabbit said nothing. Henry returned with a large banana and handed it to the rabbit. The rabbit put down the plastic bag and held the banana in its right paw.

'A banana?' Bambi said incredulously. 'You can't give fruit for Halloween, Henry, it's . . . I'll get her something else.' Suddenly Bambi was out of the room and running upstairs.

'Do you know this . . . person?' Ethan asked Henry.

'No. How would I?' Henry said. He turned to the rabbit. 'What's your name, bunny? Is it Harvey?' The rabbit gripped the sword-sized yellow banana in its pink paw and said nothing.

Bambi jumped into the living room and handed the rabbit a small piece of brightly colored plastic. 'Here you are, sweetheart,' she said, bending down to rabbit level. 'This is a very nice hairclip.' The rabbit took the clip in its left paw and still refused to comment.

Henry sat down on the steps and stared at the small, pink polyester rabbit holding a long banana and a shiny blue hairclip.

Nobody spoke for a while until Ethan said, 'Bambi, what makes you think it's a girl?'

Later, after the rabbit had left and all the tequila was gone and somebody had found a bottle of whiskey among the paint tins in the dank hallway, Henry began his joke-marathon, vowing not to stop until his material dried up or he passed out. 'Have you seen Stevie Wonder's new car?'

Ethan rolled his eyes. 'Oh come on.'

'Everybody knows this one,' Bambi said. 'And it's stupid.'

But Henry would not be stopped. 'Have you seen Stevie Wonder's new car?'

'No,' huffed Bambi.

'It's an Aston-Martin in a lovely shade of blue. Almost, but not quite, green,' Henry said.

Ethan chuckled. Bambi said, 'Oh.'

'Where did Sergei Eisenstein buy his liquor?' As a comedian, Henry sounded as unnatural as he looked. There was something dry and dusty about his deep voice, which seemed almost to creep out of his loose, mismatched suit pants and jacket. It was a seductive, transporting voice, but one that took you nowhere. Henry told his jokes with his long arms outstretched, his palms out flat, reminding himself of one of those fake preachers who often showed up in Westerns. 'At the Bottleshop Potemkin. How long did it take to make *Apocalypse Now*?' Nobody said anything. 'A Coppola years. Why can't elephants fly planes? Because they're just big, dumb animals. What time is it when an elephant sits on your fence? How the hell would I know? It could happen anytime. How do you make a hormone? Ask a biochemist – it's very complicated and I'm pretty drunk.'

'You can stop now, Henry,' said Sylvia. 'You've established your hilariousness.'

'Keep going,' urged Ethan. 'Hilarity is boundless.'

'My wife's going on holiday,' Henry said, pouring another straight whiskey.

'Jamaica?' Ethan offered.

'I think I know this one too,' Bambi said, almost asleep at the end of the couch.

'No, she bought an accordion,' Henry said, wincing as he spied an empty bottle on the floor. 'Ugh, tequila. *Tequila Mockingbird* by Harper Lee. And speaking of lady writers – George Eliot. What do you call a hatmaker addicted to dental care? A milliner on the floss! When is a door not a door? When a door is a duncan.'

'Oh please, Henry,' Sylvia said, but she was smiling. 'That hurt.'

'A horse walks into a bar. Barman says, "You can't come in here." The horse doesn't say anything because it's a horse. And even if it could talk, what would it say? "Oh yes, I can"? The fact is, horses really *aren't* allowed in bars. Bear gets thrown out for having bare feet. A boxer walks into the same bar, barman says, "Why the flat face?" The boxer punches the barman for being a smartass. There's blood everywhere and most people leave. Bar closes early.'

Ethan rolled his head from side to side. 'That one kind of lost it.'

'It's not finished. On the way home, the barman slips on a banana peel because he's such a big fan of slapstick. He'll do anything to make himself laugh. Fall off things, make people throw cream pies at him, walk with an exaggerated limp, talk with a lisp or a funny accent, drive his jalopy straight into a river, get tied up on train tracks by villains with curly black moustaches – anything. The only problem is, he never has much of an audience, just a few cream-pie throwers and sometimes the odd villain. He does it all just for his own amusement. He's insane. And an utter genius at the same time. Then one day, there is a turning point in the life of this lonely, brilliant master of the pratfall and the close-call. A moment of such profound and catastrophic insight that life will never be the same for him again. He will know that every stunt he pulled, every utterance he made, every breath he ever drew was wasted and wrong. The elements of his gags will now take on an eerie, almost religious sense, and he will look back on everything he used to say and do in a completely different light. And all this will happen because . . . all bec –' Henry stopped, breathed in, closed his mouth and clutched his stomach. He looked green. His brown eyes seemed to fade and fall deeper into their sockets, the gold flecks lost their lustre. Ethan thought it was an excellent touch of authenticity until Henry staggered over to the dank hallway door, pushed it open and vomited loudly onto the concrete. Sylvia stopped rubbing Bambi's feet as they both stared at Henry's bent back. He coughed and spat, then settled on his haunches, remaining still.

15

Odorama. Henry stepped over the skeleton of a pram filled with something that looked, in the weak torchlight, like hundreds of blackened hands of rotting bananas. A fetid odor washed over him and he retched a little.

A few feet away Charlie laughed. 'Disgusting, isn't it?' he said. 'And yet strangely invigorating. Makes you realize how very alive you are, being among all this decay.' Charlie picked up some sort of rod and used it as a walking stick. The terrain was treacherous – soft then hard then sharp then squishy.

'In many ways, I think I'd rather be dead.' Henry no longer saw as much of Charlie as he used to – or as he'd have liked – now that his friend's band had decided on a name and become even more popular. So he had to settle for occasions like this, trawling through a huge garbage dump with Charlie, looking for stage props. 'You probably can't smell stuff when you're dead.' Henry poked at a throbbing plastic bag.

'Ideally I'd like to find some sort of throne. I'd like to be lowered onto the stage in a throne. Look for anything throne-like,' Charlie advised. His band, Biff (named after the son in *Death of a Salesman*), played a kind of thunderous power-Glam rock, not at all what Henry had expected given Charlie's definite and narrow taste in music. The band all wore platform shoes, blonde wigs and thick makeup. The choruses of Biff's songs sounded like the chants you heard at sporting events. The audience sang along and sometimes dressed up like the band, a sea of yellow hair and clenched, punching fists.

'You know Screamin' Jay Hawkins?' Charlie asked, picking up the spoked hubcap of an old Cadillac.

Henry nodded. '"I Put a Spell on You" was all through *Stranger Than Paradise*.'

'You know how he liked to appear on stage in a tiger-striped coffin and wave that skull on a stick all over the place? Guess what that skull's name was.'

'Yorick?'

'Henry.'

'What?'

'Its name was Henry. How about that?' Charlie said, tossing the hubcap away.

In his own skull, Henry rolled his eyes. 'Astonishing. Truly astonishing. I'm astonished. So how come you don't play all those old funky tunes you love so much, Charles?' he asked. 'Or at least stuff that sounds like it? Something with a bit of sex and blood and oomph.'

'Well, I'd like to, Pacemaker, but there are two reasons why not.' Charlie leaped across a small, dark trash chasm. 'First of all, I'm white – as funky as a white man can be, but white nevertheless. Second, and this is an even sadder fact than the first, but unfortunately that sort of music just isn't very popular at the moment. What we do, is. Plus it's very white.'

'So what, though? You don't love it.'

'Doing what you love and being successful are not necessarily two sides of the same coin.' Charlie tucked the walking stick under his arm and lit a cigarette. 'In fact, they might even be different currencies.'

'Therefore you play that anthemic, rockist garbage.'

'Quality garbage, babe. First class. We're very good at it and people eat it up. We're starting to get the sort of reaction you see in people in Syria or Iran grieving for some dead leader. Lots of wailing and sobbing and face-clutching. It's very cool.' Charlie stood on the top of a rusted washing machine. 'We're bigger than Allah.'

Henry clambered over some sort of bundled-up stink. 'You can corner the market for state funerals.'

Charlie laughed. 'Maybe do the Pope's wake if he ever croaks.' He flipped his torch around and held the handle to his mouth. 'Hello Rome!!' he screamed as Henry fell to the patch of light on the ground and pretended to be thousands of mourning Catholics. 'Are you ready to rock!!?'

Bambi and Ethan were side by side on the couch in the living room when Henry got home very late after the garbage trip, which had yielded nothing throne-like. Ethan was rubbing Bambi's back and whispering quiet, soothing noises into her hair. Henry wished that he could sneak through the room unnoticed, but he knew that even if he was as quiet as a cartoon mouse, his trashy smell would give him away. So he jumped down the stairs into the living room.

'Hello, Henry,' Ethan said stiffly. Henry heard a muffled greeting from Bambi. 'Grab me a beer, would you? Do you want one?'

'Yes, thanks,' Henry said, as Bambi muffled a 'No'.

Henry got two beers, gave one to Ethan, then sat on the floor beneath the shelf which held the record player. He took a long drink from the mouth of the bottle. 'The one good thing about spending an evening in a garbage dump is that it makes you feel like you really deserve a drink when it's over,' Henry said. 'I'm telling you.' Bambi nestled further into Ethan's shoulder, as though she was trying to bury herself. 'What's up Bambi?'

Bambi dug herself out of Ethan's jacket, patted the yellow plastic daffodil clip in her hair and sniffled. There was glitter dusted across her cheeks and glinting brightly around her right eye, swollen black and purple. 'Oh ... what happened?' Unable to help himself, Henry looked at Ethan.

'I had an accident.'

'What sort?'

'Car.'

'Car with other car or car versus lamppost?'

'Car and person crossing road.'

'Oh right,' Henry said, a little shocked. 'The serious sort.'

Ethan continued to stare levelly at Henry while Bambi, gradually regaining her composure and syntax, explained what had happened. Earlier that night she had been driving along a busy road, 'trying to think of a good rhyme for orange', when she heard a thud at the front of her car. She jammed on the brakes and looked up to see 'a man falling off my hood, who looked like he was waving. And then there was some screaming'. After which, in a panic, Bambi had sped off home through back streets, 'at the speed of lightning'. 'I was really scared of policemen coming after me,' she said.

'What about the guy you hit?'

'He could not come after me, Henry. He was lying on the road.' She gave Henry a look. 'When I got home I did not know what to do. Not at all. I was really, really scared like never before, except one time when I lost my spare locker key in high school and I thought the vice-principal was going to expel me. I got teased mercifully for that sort of thing in school. It was a difficult time for me. I knew I would have to go to the police, so I called my friend Bobbi Kackowski to come with me. She plays police officer Annabelle Cherry on NBC's *Country Cops*. So she–'

'Wait a minute,' Henry interrupted, ignoring Ethan's glare. 'Don't you share a house with two law students?'

'Yes,' Bambi said.

'So couldn't they have helped you?'

'Only one was at home. And I did not think of asking him. Anyway, Annabelle – I mean Bobbi – came with me to the police station to help me give my statement. She knows all that police language. And the other police look up to her as a TV role model. She has won two awards, you know. Bobbi is a popular favorite among many viewers.'

'But she's just an actress. You hit a real person.'

'What is that yucky smell?' Bambi said, crinkling her nose. 'I smell a smell.'

'It's me,' Henry said. 'Why did you take a television actress with you to the cops, Bambi?'

'I could not just give myself up like a ham to the slaughter,' Bambi told Henry, then turned to Ethan. 'How can you live in the same house as him, Eth? He smells.'

'You think your friend Bobbi is really a policewoman, don't you?' Henry began to laugh. 'Don't you, Bambi? And you thought the real cops would be intimidated by her!' He started to convulse with laughter. 'If you were sick, Bambi, and you knew Richard,' – he swallowed and tried to get his breath – 'Richard Chamberlain, would you ask him to come over and pretend to be Dr Kildare?'

Ethan loomed over Henry. 'You miss the lobsters back home, don't you Harry?'

'I really don't know what you mean by that, Ethan.'

16

Henry was alone in the house one morning before work late in November. It was raining outside. Even though he had three rooms – virtually a wing of his own – he liked having the entire house to himself. He could scream if he wanted to and no one would worry and come running; he could strut around naked and no one would be appalled; he could shout, intrude, explore, laugh or cry and no one would know. Usually he just made himself a cup of coffee and wondered where the others were. Sylvia would be off photographing car wrecks or white-collar criminals leaving court with briefcases over their faces. Ethan would be . . . wherever he went doing whatever it was that he did as a student.

There was a noise up near the front door as the mail fell through the slot. Henry took a slurp of coffee then checked it out: a pile of advertising junk, a wad of bills, a doctor's reminder for Sylvia, a Fortean Society magazine for Ethan, *Premiere* and *Variety* magazines for Henry as well as a letter from a post-production facility telling him they had no available positions. There was a knock at the door. Henry opened it. 'And this,' the shivering postman said, handing over a package for Henry.

There were no sender details on it and the postmark was smudged. It was the size of a hardback but weighed only as much as a paperback. His name and address were typed onto a white label and stuck on the front. There was a slight, plastic-sounding rattle when he shook it. It didn't smell or leak or tick. After about fifteen minutes he opened it. Inside was a commercial videotape of the film *JFK*. Henry's only thought was 'Hmmm . . .' He'd seen the film and thought it okay (although Jim Garrison was probably a crackpot) but couldn't think why anybody would want to send it to him. Most likely a very late birthday gift from a dippy aunt or something. Someone who knew he liked films and had heard that this was a controversial number which might appeal to a young, slightly paranoid fellow. He spent the next few hours watching *JFK*, and this time round liked it more and thought Jim Garrison less of a crackpot. But he still didn't know to whom he should send a thank-you note.

17

Cinema. Christmas was near and as they shopped half-heartedly in the bump and grind of a busy mall, Ethan and Henry talked about how much they weren't looking forward to it – unwrapping all that tissue paper and grief – before moving on to a discussion of more general unpleasantries.

'What's the worst thing that's happened so far in your willfully miserable life?' asked Ethan, dropping a quarter as he passed a bell-ringing charity Santa.

A single frame of fuzzy, saturated color flashed behind Henry's eyes: pink, naked Jack Powdermaker with an olive halo, his blurred, frozen fist a wash of orange about to hit his gray-faced and shrinking wife, Sandra. Henry blinked and the image disappeared, leaving flat white. 'The worst thing I've done?' he said. 'Or the worst thing that's happened to me?'

'I don't care either way. As long as it's really bad.'

'Why do you want to know?'

'It's research – I'm trying to discover whether you actually have a soul.'

Henry laughed, as soulfully as he could. 'White Christmas' segued into 'The Little Drummer Boy'. 'Do you think a person's soul is revealed more truly through trauma rather than joy?'

'As a matter of fact I do. Consider "the method".' Ethan said the words as though he was swallowing sour milk. 'Every exercise which that *freakish!* cult-leader-in-disguise Lee Strasberg made his disciples do – exercises which were all about getting to "the truth" of the moment – resulted in the actor-slash-disciple crawling around the floor moaning and crying and tearing at his or her hair.' Ethan pretended to tear at his own thin, brown hair. 'Stras was always at them to dredge up their pasts to give power and meaning to their acting. And it was *always!* about horror and trauma and misery. You never saw anybody walk out of a class at The Actor's Studio beaming with hope and joy.'

Henry nodded, admiring and envious of the way Ethan thought. Maybe college really *did* make you smart. He glanced at three little kids smiling and holding hands on a wooden bench, all of them wearing red woolen caps. 'Do you know about James Dean and the ice? That's classic "method" madness.' Ethan shook his head. 'When Jimmy was doing *East of Eden* he made them shut down filming for two whole days while he went to work at an ice factory, so that he could learn to hate the ice – that's what he called it, hating the ice – for this one particular scene which required convincing ice-hatred.'

'Actors. They're *preposterous!*'

'Yeah. He was pretty good in *The Godfather II*, though, Lee Strasberg. Nominated for an Academy Award.'

'So dredge up some misery of your own, Harry. What's the secret, hated ice at your core?'

Henry stopped. He'd thought about this more than he cared to remember, but he was still surprised at the way that the words spewed out of him: blunt, immediate and fully formed.

'I had a friend,' he told Ethan, 'until I was sixteen. I didn't really realize it at the time, I mean I had some inklings and clues, but I wasn't completely aware until after she'd gone that I was in love with her. Her name was Madeleine Ford. She was a few years older than me, and at that age a couple of years between a boy and a girl may as well be twenty. Your sense of history is ridiculously stretched when you're a teenager. The summer she finished high school we spent a lot of time together doing different stuff. It was wonderful, the best summer I ever had. One night she took me out for dinner and then wanted me to see a film with her. *Manhattan*, the Woody Allen film. I'd had this problem with films for quite a while by then – watching them made me sick because . . . Anyway, I just couldn't go in. Madeleine pleaded with me for a little while then just gave up while I stood there, not saying or doing anything. Just paralyzed. The door closed and she was gone from my sight. I stood there for a few minutes staring at the word "Manhattan" and imagining what the film might be like, imagining Maddy inside looking up at the screen. I went into the foyer and after a while I could hear all that Gershwin music coming through the doors, the piano skittering under the cracks and filling the place with music you could almost see, like motes. And hearing that music seemed to release me. Suddenly I was filled with a strange, thrilling energy; the idea of actually going inside and watching the film was still impossible, so I just paced up and down the carpet listening. When the music stopped I heard the audience laughing. There was such joy – such *shared* joy – in that wonderful sound that I knew I wanted to be part of it, so I bought a ticket and ran through the door into the cinema. Those first few moments in the dark, before I could see anything apart from the images on the screen, were the happiest of my life. It was that scene where the four of them – Woody Allen, Mariel Hemingway, Michael Murphy and Anne Byrne – are having dinner at Elaine's restaurant. It's an absolutely brilliant scene, warm and convivial and very real. I wished I could've been at that restaurant with them, eating and drinking and making witty comments. Or that I'd invented those characters – directed them and written those lines. I found a seat at the front of the balcony, overlooking the seats below. And that's where the trouble started. I was loving the film, but naturally I couldn't forget that Madeleine was somewhere down there, seeing and hearing the same things as me, at the same time. I leaned over the balustrade and found her sitting far to the right – she could see things better if she looked at them from the corner of her eye. She looked beautiful. She wasn't all slouched over the chair; she didn't have a hand diving into a bucket of popcorn; she wasn't sipping soda through a straw. She sat poised and attentive, laughing when the film was funny, but not ostentatiously, not throwing her head back and barking at the ceiling. So now my attention was divided between watching the film and watching Madeleine watch the film. I listened to the dialogue and watched her reactions, the way she'd sometimes press her index finger against her mouth to try and stop laughing, and how she nodded at certain things. And only at the end of the film, when there's a close-up of Woody Allen's face, stunned and drained as he realizes that Mariel Hemingway really is going to go away to London to study and that he may never see her again, only then did I realize that I had been sitting there crying a little and . . . and that I was in love with her and also . . . that it was too late.'

Henry had finished speaking for a while before Ethan lit a cigarette, cleared his throat and said, 'I understand.'

Henry looked over at the bench; the kids were gone, replaced by a perspiring fat man looking for something – water, his wife – with tiny, darting eyes.

'But it's still no excuse,' Ethan said.

'For what?'

The fat man stopped searching, closed his eyes and slumped. Ethan and Henry began to move on through the hot, damp, excited crowd.

'For anything.'

18

Henry lay on the green vinyl couch in the living room complaining at the news on television – lurid reports of new year's eve violence and how a family of eagles had made a nest on a city skyscraper. The telephone rang. Henry ignored it. Ethan, seated at the desk and staring out the living-room window, perhaps looking for a perfect paisley shape in the clouds, ignored it. Sylvia, in the kitchen, closest to the phone and in a bad, silent mood because of her ruined back, sucked hard on a joint and ignored it. The front door opened. Bambi walked in. The telephone rang once more, and she answered it brightly and immediately.

'Henry,' she called out. 'Are you here? It's for you.'

'Who is it?'

'Someone who says she is your mother.'

Henry picked up the phone. His mother said, 'Hi. I thought I'd better just call and let you know that your paternal grandfather died yesterday.'

'Oh,' Henry said in confusion, certain that his father's father had in fact been killed in a rail accident many years before Henry was born.

'I only just found out,' his mother continued. 'I'm going to send some flowers.'

'Paternal?' Henry said. 'You said paternal. Don't you mean maternal?'

His mother started laughing, but not in a hysterical, hollow, hacking way informed by shock and grief; this laughter was hearty. 'Yes, maternal.' This was joyful laughter. She was greatly amused, delighted even, by her own mix-up. 'Did I really say paternal?'

'Yes. And . . . Who exactly was he to you?' Henry had to ask, family history on his mother's side being somewhat shadowy. 'Father or stepfather?'

'My father,' she told her son, unable to stop laughing.

'Your father? And you're laughing?'

'Well, I didn't know him very well. I certainly didn't know he had a stroke last fall! I'm going to send some flowers. That's all right, isn't it? I don't want to have to send a letter.'

'Yeah, I guess that's okay,' Henry said, glancing outside at the gathering dusk. 'You should send something.' There was a brief silence. 'How's Daniel?'

'Oh fine. And so are the Fords, who I presume will be the subject of the next enquiry. Except that Madeleine's having an operation next week.'

Henry swallowed his next words. 'What for?'

'Pardon!?' Sandra said shortly.

'What's the operation for?' Henry said, squeezing the telephone tightly, briefly imagining it was his mother's neck.

'Oh, I don't know, a laser treatment for her eyes. She's got some muscular problem.'

He took two deep breaths and relaxed his grip on the telephone. 'Macular. Do you happen to know which hospital she'll be at, Mom?'

Sandra told her son that she did not, that she was no longer a secretary keeping other people's appointments and why didn't he call Madeleine's parents – or better still, Madeleine herself – and find out? Henry told his mother that he might just do that; even though he knew he would not.

'It's been a pleasure,' he said in conclusion.

'Don't be sarcastic, Henry, it doesn't suit you. You're too nice.'

'I am not.'

'Oh listen to yourself – you're too sweet to even sound properly indignant. Bye honey!'

Voice-over. An hour later, Henry is sitting at his large wooden desk writing furiously, beneath the shelves of film books and film magazines he subscribes to. There is the sound of pen scratching paper, huffing breaths and low, involuntary sighs.

Dear Maddy,

By the time you read this letter, I may be alive. Did you ever see the film Letter from an Unknown Woman? *Joan Fontaine plays this woman called Lisa who falls in love with a concert pianist named Stefan. It's set in Vienna around the turn of the century, a time and place when people did stuff like that and had names like Stefan. Anyway, it's full of all these flashbacks which begin with Stefan about to flee Vienna (not leave, flee; people back then always fled from things) to avoid fighting a duel. He's just about to flee when this letter arrives. It begins, rather dramatically, 'By the time you read this letter, I may be dead.' It's from Lisa and it's all about how much in love with Stefan she is, since when she was fourteen and Stefan was her neighbor. As she grows older, the romance gets*

*more serious and they have a brief affair. Stefan leaves on a concert
tour, promising to come back, but of course he never does. Mean-
while Lisa marries some other guy, after she discovers that she's
pregnant by Stefan. Years later she runs into Stefan, who doesn't
have a clue who the hell she is and tries to seduce her. Anyway,
after Stefan reads the letter he wants to rush off and see her immediately, but by now poor old Lisa is just about dead from typhus.
The end. Not bad, huh?*

   *Anyway, the only reason I mention it is because this letter is
kind of like the opposite to that film – it's a letter to an unknown
woman. Nobody plays piano, nobody's in Vienna and nobody dies
of typhus, hopefully. On the other hand, there are a few parallels,
mostly about unrequited love, but I don't feel like going into them
right now. Except to say this – I love you, Margarita Catarina, and
I think of you constantly, and of what might have been between
us if things had been different. If I had been just a few of the good
things I thought I might one day be.*

Good luck with the operation.
Love,
Henry P. (owdermaker)

Henry then puts down the pen, leans back in his chair, yawns,
rubs his eyes, glances at the digital clock, lights a cigarette and
says aloud to himself, 'Now, if this was the voice-over for a short
film, what images would accompany it? Hmmm . . . Establishing
shot of a blank piece of paper, maybe a pen. Then we see a guy
pick up the pen and start writing. The voice-over begins. I hate
letter voice-overs in films, people reading out what they're writing
or reading. Nobody does that in real life. But . . . but if I make
myself do it now, then it is what's happening in life. Maybe have
the camera wander around the rooms while I talk. Make it a
character-developing piece. Show my tatty clothes, rows of books,
and the poster of God's finger reaching out to Adam. Then a
photograph of Madeleine – And I say something extra-cornball
like, "Aaah, sweet Madeleine." '

Laughing, Henry neatly folds the letter twice and slips it into an envelope with 'Madeleine M. C. Ford' on the front. He gets up from the desk and lies on his bed, his head twittering with schemes and fantasies which keep him from sleep and never join him in dreams.

If a camera was cruising the room it would move from his desktop, where the letter lies, and up to a wooden shelf above, where there is a neat row of envelopes – maybe fifty or sixty – all of them bulging with paper and sentiment, all of them stamped and addressed to Madeleine Ford, not one of them mailed.

19

Pre-production. After seven or eight weeks of solid work Henry had almost finished a film script called *Three Kinds o' Headache*, vaguely based on a comic book he'd read somewhere in which two jazz musicians chat absently about nothing much and in which nothing much happens. Henry thought it was a fine idea and spent hours thinking of ways he could make the film on what little money was available to a young man with no job, especially not two.

There are ways. The film must be shot at almost a 1:1 shooting ratio on black-and-white Tri-X Super 8. It must be shot by a non-professional with a cheap camera, using friends instead of actors in a room lit with bright household lamps rather than a proper set properly lit. Costumes come from personal wardrobes and makeup consists of whatever is in the upstairs bathroom. The local supermarket is employed as caterer during the demanding six-hour shoot. By lending the dedicated young writer/director/editor/actor two hundred dollars to pay for the film stock, Sylvia Moriarty is given the title of Executive Producer. The processed film must be edited by cotton-gloved hand with scissors and transparent tape, while the entire soundtrack has to be created from scratch using a cassette deck and a crude mixer. The title sequence can be made by employing the old 'shirt box' technique. There can be no work print and no special effects. There will be no distribution deal. There will be no trip to Cannes and no awards. But there will be a film.

The dedicated young film maker must at no point during his struggle think about the fact that Orson Welles was just twenty-five when he began work on *Citizen Kane*. If, even for a moment, he recalls this fact, he will very probably give up.

Henry blocked out all Wellesian thoughts as he sat down at his desk and decided that this would be the day that the final draft of *Three Kinds o' Headache* would be completed. He opened the top drawer and didn't think about Gregg Toland. He chose a pen while giving no consideration to Herman Mankiewicz. He sucked on the pen for a short while and never once pictured Joseph Cotten, Ray Collins or Agnes Moorehead. His mental landscape was mercifully Kane-less. But then, just as he was about to simplify a camera move, one hoarsely whispered word slipped from his mouth. Two other words quickly followed: 'Oh hell!' he said angrily, as he threw down the pen. He made his way to the kitchen, where Sylvia was grinding coffee beans.

'D'you want a coffee?' Sylvia said. 'I put some French vanilla beans in with the espresso. It's a very nice mixture.'

'Thanks,' muttered Henry. 'Goddam that Orson Welles.'

'Oh not this again,' Sylvia said. 'Why do you do this to yourself? It's so pointless. You just use it as an excuse for giving up.'

'I'm a failure and he was a genius.'

'He was more unhappy than you'll ever be in your life.'

'I'm well on the way, believe me. And I never got to sleep with Rita Hayworth.'

'Your condition is self-pity, not real unhappiness.' She handed Henry a cup of coffee and sat down on the steps just outside the kitchen, chopping the middle of her light cotton skirt to create an underwear-obscuring valley of fabric. 'And if you think sleeping with a redhead is the answer to your problems, you deserve every one of them.'

'Thanks. For the coffee, not the appraisal.'

'It's true though, isn't it?'

'Yes, I guess it is,' he sighed. 'Which?'

Sylvia gave him a long look, hardening her eyes: an inscrutable doll. 'Anyway, you can't afford to wallow any longer.'

'Why not? I kind of like wallowing. It's good for the skin.'

'That depends on what you're wallowing in.' She let herself smile faintly. 'But your wallowing days are over, mainly because it's pathetic. But also because I have, as of ten o'clock this morning, secured you a camera, a camera operator, ten rolls of Tri-X and a location that we can use this Saturday. Provided you get off your ass and finish the script. And I can convince Ethan to act in it. You sure you won't ask my friend Klaus?'

'Professional actors, Sylvia . . .' Henry winced and crinkled. 'Y'know, they're . . . they just get in the way.'

'What's Ethan's problem with it?'

'He thinks the script is, I think he said, "hollow and dull".' Henry rolled his eyes. 'He read it, then sort of tossed it away and starts telling me that Godard said all you needed to make a film were two things. Then he points at me and says, "And you're only *half!* way there." It was kind of humiliating and annoying. But maybe he's right . . . Maybe the whole thing really is half-assed. Anyway, I still want old Fabulous to do it. He'll be able to pull it off. He's got the ego for it, I'm sure. And he looks right.'

'All right then, I'll see if I can get him to cooperate.'

'You wonderful person!' Henry cried. 'You'll get me to Hollywood yet. I love you!' With sticky, coffee-caked lips, he kissed Sylvia, leaving a brown smudge on her cheek. 'Tell Ethan I'll write a small part for Bambi – as a singing call girl or something. Maybe that'll sweeten the deal.' He raised his brows at her as Sylvia rolled her eyes back at him.

'All right,' she said.

'You're very good to me, Sylvia. You're one of the only good things in my life. I mean it. In a way, you're my –' Henry lowered his voice to a hoarse whisper – 'Rosebud.'

Sylvia laughed. 'By the way, what are the two Godard things?'

'For the life of me, Sylv, I can't remember.'

The screenplay. We open on the front door to an old-style apartment. We can make out the wood grain and then, as the shot opens up, a fly buzzing in a shaft of sunlight that falls across the number 12 on the door. A hand comes into frame and raps on the door. Cut to reverse angle. We see a thin-faced man, WALLACE, standing in a dark hallway. He is wearing a ragged suit and a fedora. He has a brief moustache in the Errol Flynn style and baleful eyes in a mournful face. Under his arm he carries a bottle of booze in a paper bag.

Cut to a different angle – a shot over Wallace's shoulder. The door opens and we see a small person in a rabbit costume holding a banana and a hairclip walk out in poised silence. Wallace watches the rabbit leave and says nothing. He looks up again and we see another man, FRANK, standing in the light of a living room. Frank is a sallow, depressed-looking man, who moves and speaks slowly, somewhat theatrically carrying the weight of the world on his sloped shoulders. He wears an open-necked shirt, loose pants and suspenders. Wallace nods a greeting.

WALLACE

Well, hiya there, Frank. How goes it?

Frank shows Wallace into the small living room.

FRANK

Oh, well as can be expected, thanks pal o' mine.

Wallace removes a bottle of brown spirits from the paper bag and, by way of offer, holds it up to Frank. As he pours a couple of glasses, Frank speaks.

FRANK (cont'd)

Don't mind if I do, Wally boy. You're the very kind kind, ain'tcha? So how's it been? Your life and such?

They are both seated now. Between them is a small, round table on which sits an ashtray, their glasses, the bottle of booze and a wireless. Throughout the following exchange, the camera picks up the backs of their heads, the props on the table, etc.

WALLACE

Not so bad. You know how life goes.

FRANK

I know how it's going. But I'm not so sure I know how it goes.

WALLACE

It just goes. That's all you can ever hope to know. Anyways, enough of this dime-store philosophizing, it's givin' me three kinds o' headache. Say, isn't Spider Murphy's outfit about due to come on WBLS about now?

We see Wallace's hand twiddling the wireless dial.

FRANK

Spider's joined Beiderbecke. The old outfit's ixnayed.

WALLACE

Shame. He was foot-stompin' good. Not a bit sweet. What about yourself, Frankie? You playing?

FRANK

Not so much any more, pal. I've lost the urge. And when you–

WALLACE

Yeah, yeah. When you lose the urge, you lose the feel. I know how it goes. Be nicer if it rhymed, though. Urge, purge – something like that. But c'mon, Frankie boy. You've still got the gift. You've still got those dancing fingers . . . Surge, maybe.

We see a mid-shot of Wallace miming playing the guitar. Next to him, Frank shakes his head.

FRANK

No, Wally, I faked the gift. All I ever really had was the urge, the desire to be good. But I was never really much. And now I don't even want to pretend.

WALLACE

Some funeral we're having tonight.

FRANK

I feel like I'm dying, Wal . . . I am dying. I haven't got a disease or like that. But I'm dying, sure enough.

WALLACE

Everybody's dying. And everybody knows everybody else is dying. That's why people are as good as they are.

FRANK

But people aren't very good to each other, Wallace.

WALLACE

They could be worse.

FRANK

We got murder, war, abuse, abandonment. The popularization of inferior art. Humanity is terrible – how could it be worse?

WALLACE

There are ways.

FRANK

What ways, Wal? What ways?

WALLACE

A person gives up hope. And without hope a person doesn't care what happens to them. Or what they do to someone else. Living like that is the worst possible way to live.

FRANK

Oh, what a bunch of horseshit. Living without money or talent or love is far worse. Living with bad history in your own blood is worse.

WALLACE

Bad history like what?

FRANK

Where you know you're gonna turn out bad because it's in your flesh and your blood. In your history. You're doomed because you're connected to your past, maybe even cursed by it. You could curse your own brother if you weren't careful. And you gotta be careful 'cause every little thing is connected to everything else.

WALLACE

Only a very weak person believes in inevitability like that.

Frank takes a long pull on his filterless cigarette, then blows out a stream of smoke. The camera follows the smoke as long as it can before it disappears. Frank sighs.

FRANK

Yeah, I guess you're onto something there. You gotta force the hand of your own destiny, right? Well, maybe it'll turn out all right. Or all different. We'll see, huh . . .

There is a knock at the door. After the sound is heard, we cut to outside the apartment and see a young woman with dirty-blond hair standing in the doorway. She is SUNNY, a part-time hooker. Frank makes his way to the door and opens it.

SUNNY
        (perhaps chewing gum but definitely smiling)
Evenin'.

FRANK

Evenin'. You a Witness?

SUNNY

Nope.

FRANK

'Cyclopedia salesman? Travellin' tinhorn? Fuller Brush girl?

SUNNY

Funny. Ease up on the wise, mister. Time's money, and
besides you're breakin' my funny bone. Like it says in the
Bible, 'Gild not the lilies of the field.' So, you call up for a
little . . . company?

FRANK

Uh-uh. (He turns to Wallace and shouts.) You expecting a
lady friend, Wally?

WALLACE

I ain't, but ask her in for a drink anyways. She drink rye?

FRANK

You drink rye?

SUNNY

Not on duty. So it's an ixnay on me?

FRANK

Yes.

SUNNY

Yes no, or yes yes?

FRANK

Yes no.

Sunny leaves and Frank returns to sitting with Wallace.

WALLACE

What'd she look like?

FRANK

Like a sweet kid. But sort of a nympho as well.

WALLACE

A nympho, huh? That can be nice . . . Say Francis, lemme
ask you somethin'. I'm wondering, what would you think
if a coupla screaming gunsels burst in here demanding our
wallets and such?

FRANK

What would I think?

WALLACE

Gun in your face, maybe one of 'em shoots you in the arm
or somewheres. What would you think of that?

FRANK

Here? Right in this room? In my house?

WALLACE

Uh huh.

FRANK

I'd think I was in some sorta picture wit' Edward G or
Jimmy C. Either that or I was dreamin'.

20

Action. Although the script was somewhat cheerless (Henry had even lifted a line from *Bang the Drum Slowly*, the film in which De Niro dies of Hodgkin's Disease), the day of the shoot was bristling with fun. There was laughter and enthusiasm, a great sense of involvement and purpose from everybody, even from Ethan, who was ordinarily a little removed from the activities in which he was engaged, as though he was somewhere above, watching someone very much like himself doing the things he was doing. He had a small wooden box with him which he said contained 'the key to this whole cock-eyed production', and which he refused to let anybody open. Bambi asked dozens of questions about her character's motivation, backstory and the pronunciation of the word 'ixnay'. Cole, the cameraman, was constantly busy lighting and planning and rehearsing his shots, creating an irresistible energy and humor that pulled everybody along in its wake. Sylvia had made a detailed shooting schedule which allowed just enough time to get everything they needed before they had to leave the turn-of-the-century mansion which contained the ballroom and stage they were using as a set. Henry saw that she was not merely an executive producer; that she was in fact a very real and capable actual producer. It was clear that without her none of this would have happened. Henry was so excited and proud and happy that he very nearly could not stand it.

Late in the day, while Cole blocked a complicated shot, Henry took a walk around the grounds of the rambling property. The enormous house, in the center of a leafy inner suburb, was once the home of a judge. As well as the formal ballroom there were twenty-two other rooms, an empty, in-ground swimming pool and a tennis court in that Xanadu. He remembered a line from *Sunset Boulevard*: 'A decrepit house has an unhappy look and this one had it in spades.' The mansion was now owned by the Catholic Church and occupied by a group of college students who were, incredibly, paid to live here as long as they tended to the garden every so often. The garden was wildly overgrown; the concrete at the bottom of the pool covered in dirt and leaves; the netless tennis court – 'or rather the ghost of a tennis court, with faded markings and a sagging net', again from *Sunset Boulevard* – was scuffed, an abandoned roller lying in the middle; but the stern beauty of the property was not in the least diminished by the lack of attention. It was the physical despair of the place which gave it so much character. Henry was saddened, almost grief-stricken by the knowledge that he would never live in a home like that, that he did not grow up in one, that he would not grow old in one.

He walked out onto the diving board, a wooden tongue poking out over an empty mouth. It was cold standing above the memory of water and Henry shivered. Clouds passed over the sun and a gust of wind sent more leaves into the bottom of the pool. Henry thought of screenwriter Joe Gillis, played by William Holden, narrating *Sunset Boulevard* as he lies face down, dead in the swimming pool, fished out at the end of the film by policemen with hooked poles. 'If I jumped off, I'd probably break both my ankles,' Henry thought to himself. 'I have never broken a bone in my body. Am I careful or just frightened?' He jumped up and down a little bit, bending the wooden board beneath him. It creaked quietly under the strain and Henry jumped higher, his heart racing as he bounced up and down; higher and higher until suddenly he bent his knees and absorbed the upward thrust in a single, smooth motion. The board was still and quiet. Frightened and careful, Henry turned and walked slowly back onto the concrete edge. Then, because he was trying not to let them, his thoughts turned to the last film he made, many, many years ago. 'Ma and Pa in the sack. A snuff piece by Henry Powdermaker.' He laughed and headed back to the house as snow fell, ducking his head to avoid the branch of an oak dipping in the rough wind.

21

Cut. Five days later, five long days slowed and stretched by anxiety, anticipation and silence, Henry is sitting on the floor in what used to be his bedroom, a film projector mounted on a cardboard box by his side, pointed toward a white wall, ready to run the film he has shot. He switches on the projector, runs the leader down into the clacketing mouth and rolls it into the feeder reel at the back. Then, smoking in the dark, ashing onto the floor of the empty room because it doesn't matter anymore – because he knows what will soon be revealed to him in the bright square of light – he watches.

The film looks great. Cole has done a beautiful job. The many tones of impure black create a wonderful, rich depth, ranging from strange, chiaroscuric close-ups to large swathes of darkness that are like falling into a void. The soft whites and grays and creams are like breaths of light.

There is mostly only one take of each shot, sometimes two if the camera bumped or if Henry or Ethan laughed. Once, Sylvia's hand, holding a reflector, drifted into the frame and that had to be done over. But for the most part it is without repetition. Up until the tenth reel. At the beginning of the tenth reel is a shot of a silver ashtray in the shape of a boat, a wraithlike trail of smoke curling and weaving upward from the end of a cigarette. The camera picks up the smoke and follows its path, almost dancing with it as it sways and rises against the dark background. It is gorgeous, hypnotic, elegant, and it is the last planned shot of the day. After that is improvisation.

Henry had wanted to shoot this particular thing himself; his way of putting the misery and mess of his previous film behind him. So he took the camera, still mounted on the tripod, from Cole and went in search of Ethan and Bambi, who had gone to a small room behind the stage to rehearse her lines.

The picture wobbles down a hallway and stops at a wooden door. The door is kicked open and there is Bambi, on the floor, on her knees in front of Ethan, who is sitting in a chair, the velvet-lined wooden box lying open at his feet. His right arm is extended, a shiny/dull black lump at the end. Bambi's cheeks glisten. There is a gun barrel in her puffed mouth. Ethan turns to the camera, smiles and winks then disappears as the wall and roof lurch and loom downward, then back up again swiftly, blurred black and white crashing down on Ethan's wrist, ripping the gun from Bambi's mouth, two shining white squares flying out and disappearing before the film cuts to black.

That is all there is to see. Henry switches off the projector. 'Well, I guess old Godard was on to something,' he says. 'All you *do* need is a girl and a gun.'

Moments later, no more than a blink in time, Henry has packed up the projector and is sitting on the steps out front of the house, waiting for a moving van to arrive. He is thinking about the end of *An Occurrence at Owl Creek Bridge*, how just as the deserter reaches his cabin and the open arms of his wife, the film cuts back to the hanging rope, precisely at the moment that it goes taut once again and snaps the neck of the doomed man, who has, during that lifetime of seconds, been plummeting to his fate.

Part 4

22

Point of view. A handsome man with sparkling white teeth and startling blue eyes lies next to a beautiful sleeping woman tangled in sunlit cotton sheets beneath an open bedroom window. His eyes are open, but he's not seeing – thinking, perhaps. He nudges the woman.

'What?' she says, muffled with sleep.

'You're making that lipping sound with your mouth.'

'I was asleep . . . Henry.' She sits up, catching a slab of light on her broad back, and rubs her eyes with the heel of her hands then looks at him and smiles.

He reaches under his pillow and slides out a ten-franc piece, rolling it across his knuckles like a cardsharp before making it disappear, swallowed by his hungry hand. Her mouth drops with genuine delight and surprise. 'Welcome back, Aud,' he says, before leaning over and giving her a long, deep kiss. Her fingernails dance on the back of his neck. The pillow beneath his elbow shifts and reveals a sprinkling of silver, copper and gold coins – pesetas, escudos, pfennigs and lire – glittering in the early morning sunlight.

Audrey and Henry are in a bright bathroom, quiet and tired. The thin towel around his waist is almost falling off his flat, brown stomach, partially revealing a taut groin. He is saying in a nasal whine that he is worried about what to wear. Looking at herself in the large bathroom mirror as she puts lipstick on, she says to him, 'We're just going for a drive in the country. It's no big deal.'

Now they are leaning out of a window, leaning into the day outside, smoking, and staring at one another. Outside it is cold and sunny – a far-reaching crispness both of them can feel on their cheeks. Henry takes a long drag and blows rings as he speaks. 'I know it's stupid, Aud. But I can't help getting like that. My mind's so slow on Saturday mornings. It's that shock of not having to go to work. The horror of freedom. And Charles always looks good, even if it's just for a drive. That rock-star ethic. It makes me insecure as hell.'

Charlie walks through the gate and shouts. 'Gillespie! Powder-monkey! The limo's here!' Audrey removes the cigarette from Henry's mouth, takes a drag and flicks it out the window. 'Let's go,' she says. 'He's here.'

They are driving through the outskirts of a city in an old white Chevrolet. The red seats are deep, rich, comfortable. Audrey is in the back reading a newspaper. The men are in the front. Charlie rubs his eyes as he steers. There is a map spread across Henry's knees.

'Pass me that tape, Henry.'

'What's on it?'

'Curtis Mayfield. A song called "Move On Up" about black consciousness and self-esteem. Probably my favorite song of all time. Do you know it?'

Henry shakes his head.

'That's a shame. It's wonderful. There's a line where he says to take nothing less than the second best. That's genius. It could be "supreme best" but I like second best better. He's paralyzed now, from the neck down, like Christopher Reeve. It outrages me that some B-grade film dude gets all the sympathy and attention, becomes the poster-boy for paralysis, while a true artist like Mayfield is practically ignored. But that's fucking movies for you, acting superior to everything else in life.'

They are silent for a while, reading, driving or staring out at the dreary trailer-home parks, gas stations and concrete-gardened churches. Aerodynamic white almost flying down a low green and snow-white hilltop and across a bridge over a dribbling river, thundering and shuddering the wooden planks. As a cloud of dirt and exhaust fumes obscures the speeding car, Charlie pats the dashboard and says, 'The old girl loves the open road.'

'Hey, Charles, why do people always refer to cars in the feminine, do you think?'

'No idea. But I'll tell you one thing, I wish like hell you'd stop referring to me as Charles. I much prefer Charlie. It's more . . . raffish.'

'Really? God, I had no idea. What about Chuck?'

'Absolutely not. Too louche. Didn't you ever notice on all the Biff CDs I'm listed as Charlie Rocket?'

'I thought that was just a rock thing,' Henry says. 'I really had no idea.'

The Chevrolet, mud-spattered now, is parked in a lot behind a small, dreary restaurant. Inside, the three of them sit at a long wooden table littered with mismatching cutlery and dishwasher-spotted goblets. The two men are staring dolefully at their pale food, as if it has somehow betrayed them: small overcooked hamburger patties on long, wrong-shaped buns with hunks of dry cheese and no-color salad. There is a whole brown trout in front of Audrey. A bottle of red wine warming by the fire. Audrey sniffs at a forkful of fish flesh then quickly puts it into her mouth and chews slowly.

'What's it like?' asks Henry.

Her face is briefly gray, almost translucent for a moment. She says, 'Absolutely freezing.' And once again, for no reason, smiles at her boyfriend.

They are still at the table, in the same positions as a moment ago, but the food is gone and they are drinking from old mugs. In the middle of the table there is a cheap, cut-glass vase containing a wilted rose and a drowned mosquito.

'I think this coffee is instant,' says Henry unhappily. 'Does it taste instant to you?'

Audrey points to the blackboard menu and speaks in haiku:

'A bottomless cup.
That's what this brown muck tastes like.
But it's paid for – cheers!'

The Chevy is shaking and bumping. Audrey hits her head on the roof and the newspaper slides to her feet. Shadow and sunlight shoot through the trees, close and blinding on either side of the rough track, thick snow creeping up into the hills beside them. Underneath, rocks thud against the chassis. The Chevrolet rounds a tight corner too fast, the brakes lock and the rear spins wide before acceleration pulls the car away from the plunging cliff. On and on it winds, heading down the mountain, hot inside from all the panting and fear.

The Chevy is parked by a wide river, near some other cars – a four-wheel-drive and a pick-up truck. Henry is pouring wine into a plastic cup, tasting it and making a sharp face. He is trying not to, but he still looks handsome. Charlie stares across the river, while Audrey tilts her face to the sky, a long, long way past the top of the mountain, looking for whatever is there.

'Look at those idiots,' says Henry, surreptitiously pointing across the river. Three thickly bearded men in flannel jackets are picking up fist-sized rocks and throwing them into the water where they land close to a madly yapping dog.

'Stone-tossing Neanderthals,' says Charlie.

'They're gonna hit that dog,' says Henry. 'I should do something about it. I wish I was brave. But it's their dog, I guess. Good Lord, what's the purpose of people like that?'

'Manual labor,' answers Charlie, lighting another cigarette. 'Cold enough for you guys?'

Audrey says, 'They probably have a club. A rock-throwing club. They visit rivers with their pets and throw stones at them. It's probably even fun, but we're all too bourgeois to know it.'

The rock-throwing goes on for a while longer, regarded in contemptuous silence by Charlie, Audrey and Henry. The rocks never hit the dog.

The three of them take a short walk to a cemetery on a hillside, the sun sinking now to a warm color, making cool shadows of stone angels and crucifixes. A gardener wearing tartan earmuffs carves a path on a snowmobile.

'Look,' says Audrey, pointing, grabbing Henry's arm and leaning in against him. 'Little Doaty's Grave. Look.' There is a small, picketed plot with an almost-black headstone that reads 'Little Doaty's Grave'. Nothing else.

'Sounds like something from Dickens,' says Charlie.

'Can a fictional character have a real grave?' asks Audrey. 'Is that allowed?'

Nobody answers. Henry and Audrey head off in one direction, Charlie wanders off in another. They spend some time walking, being alive, looking at graves, while the snowmobile growls in the near distance. The gardener does not seem to notice them. Far, far away Henry and Audrey sit on a bench outside a small cottage, holding hands.

They are back by Little Doaty's Grave, its shadow longer than before. Audrey is staring at Henry as though she doesn't know him. 'I hate cemeteries,' says Henry. 'I mean I hate headstones. They're so inadequate. A few dates and some predictable bits of scripture. And maybe the person's age when they died so you don't have to be bothered doing the math, but that's all. There's nothing about their lives – who they actually were, what they did. Nothing. It's such a shame, because it's the last thing most of us have and it just says so little.'

'There was one back there that said "Musicians" under the names, did you see that?' asks Charlie. The snowmobile noise stops.

'Yeah, but what sort of musicians – jazz, classical, circus? It's just never enough.'

'I guess . . .' says Charlie. 'Got a cigarette? I've run out.'

Audrey has not taken her eyes from Henry. In a low voice, almost a whisper, she says, 'Did you really mean what you said back there by the cottage?' Henry smiles and nods. 'As you or as him?' Her glance hits the camera momentarily as she says the word 'him'.

'Me.'

As the buttery light falls on her face, Audrey beams bright white, her eyes glaze as though consumed by ecstatic trance. Then the image solarizes and she is gone, as though faded into the snow at her feet or the sky above.

23

Stills. In the years that Henry lived with his girlfriend Audrey, he was photographed many, many times – at parties, barbecues, a wedding, several birthdays, on vacation and sometimes for no reason at all. He can vividly recall standing in large groups with his arm around Audrey, or late nights in somebody's kitchen waiting for the sharp flash as he grinned stiffly into the middle distance. He can remember: actually saying 'Cheese' once and thinking it very funny; clamping a cigar between his teeth as he sat next to Charlie, both of them in leather armchairs clutching glasses of cognac and toasting Vanessa, who was winking through a Pentax. Henry can remember all these and a great many more. And it is just as well that he can, because in every one of these photographs he does not appear.

Sometimes there is a blur, as though Henry pulled himself out of the frame just as the shutter came down, leaving a wash of bland color where he had stood. Or sometimes there is a person standing directly in front of Henry, obscuring him almost completely, except for a shirt collar or errant spike of black hair. Sometimes there is a fog that has appeared from nowhere, and sometimes there is simply nothing at all.

Naturally, this odd phenomenon gave rise to lots of joking between Henry and Charlie Rocket, who insisted that Henry's body as well as his soul was being stolen by the camera. That he was a figment of everybody's imagination. That his character needed proper development. That, like a Czechoslovakian communist, he was being air-brushed out of history. He was the un-Henry. The ghost.

When it all started, Henry had been living alone for a little over a year in a small apartment not far from the mansion where he'd shot *Three Kinds o' Headache* and broken Ethan's wrist. He was working quietly and conscientiously in a job he didn't enjoy, crossing a river twice a day, and dispassionately watching his life slip into a haze of alcohol and ennui, television and films.

When he could stand to, he thought a lot about why he was still so enraptured with the idea of film. Film was everywhere and reached everyone; it was as omnipresent as God. And in the notion of himself as a film maker, Henry could project the person that he wanted to be, or perhaps see himself as he truly was. In the dark, he could imagine himself up there on the screen, or toiling unknown behind the camera – the director, the auteur, the creator of imagined lives; and in this role, Henry himself could become the small god he felt no presence of in his own life. He wanted people to see things the way he saw them.

At first Henry had enjoyed the long periods of intoxication and nightly seven- or eight-hour orgies of network-broadcast rubbish or semi-drunken video marathons. He even enjoyed the weakness and powerlessness that frequently being either drunk or hung over reduced him to. And despite everything, he thought he was having a fine time. Then the business with the clocks began.

There were two digital clocks in Henry's apartment. One with a red face on a radio alarm clock in his bedroom and another, with a dull blue face, on the front of his VCR, which sat on top of his huge television in the living room. For a long time, for as long as he'd had them, they were merely clocks, simply telling the time with a reliable dependability which can only come from the inanimate. Then one Tuesday evening after work, Henry was carrying his carton of takeout food from the kitchenette over to the couch in front of the television when he happened to glance at the VCR clock and then away from it in less than a fraction of a second, and at that precise moment he saw the time change – from 8:12 to 8:13. It was an odd experience, but nothing shattering. Then later that same night, in his bedroom this time and with a mouthful of foaming toothpaste, he flashed a look at his clock radio. Once again, in that infinitesimal moment, the time leaped from 1:43 to 1:44. This occasion unsettled him a little but he soon gave it no more thought. Then it happened on his computer at work the next day. And again after work, on the video recorder. Every time he glanced at a digital clock, it would jump from one time to another; most often from one minute to the next, but there were occasions when whole hours would evaporate in an instant. This was not the same as staring numbly at a flashing timer, watching the inevitable plodding progress of the seconds, minutes and hours. This was entirely different. These were jump cuts. There was no doubt about it, Henry decided, he was seeing time move.

Other things started happening. A few nights after the clocks had turned on him (a problem he solved by simply covering them with masking tape and keeping to his schedule by following the TV guide), he was halfway through a bottle of red wine and watching something ridiculous on television when the telephone rang. Henry turned and looked at it, heard it ring once more and then . . . and then . . . He just didn't know what to do. He was aware that he was required to do something, but precisely what, he could not remember. He stared at the telephone and could almost see the demands of the sound it was making, but what these messages were, he did not know. It was as though mentally he was paralyzed. He stared at the telephone until it fell silent. In the sudden, noiseless calm, Henry was frightened and began wondering if he had had some sort of mini-stroke. He got up off the couch, picked up the telephone and dialed his mother.

'Hello,' Sandra said, looping the 'o' upward in that distinctive way she had.

'Hi, it's me,' Henry said. 'Did you just call me?'

'Noooo. Should I have?' she asked, faintly sarcastic. 'Have you done something call-worthy?'

'No. I only . . . What did you do just now when your telephone rang?'

'I was grilling some ciabata. Why?'

'No, I mean when you heard the phone ringing, what did you do?'

'What sort of a question is that? Are you smoking pot or something?'

'Please just tell me, Mother,' Henry said.

'I picked up the stupid thing and answered it! If there's nothing else, Daniel's here and my bread's burning.'

'No. Thanks. Say hi to Danny. Bye.'

'Bye then,' his mother said. 'Don't smoke drugs, Henry. You're too sensitive and they'll rot your brain.'

How could he have not known that when a telephone rings, you simply answer it? He turned the television back on, wondering only briefly when he'd turned it off.

There was more. Over the next few weeks, he sometimes found himself staring in wonderment at the mirror, certain that another person was staring back at him, someone who regarded him with a queasy mixture of distance and contempt. While reading a book or a magazine he might stop at a word and look at it for a long time, gravely and suspiciously trying to tease out its meaning before being able to continue with the sentence. Light seemed to become slower. Somebody sent him a pink, blood-spattered lady's pill-box hat in the mail late in November. The refrigerator sometimes acted sexy. Daniel's face materialized on Henry's pillow. He slipped a key into the door of the flat next to his own and was confronted by a man in a dressing gown. 'Grandpa?' Kitchen faucets were left on. He offered cups of coffee to people on television and was slightly offended that the beverages were never consumed.

Finally there was a breakthrough – comical in a certain way, given the right direction, but serious enough, perhaps even disturbing, in another – which made Henry seek help. He was at work, feeling a little faint from listening to the sea-blue murmur of the paint on his cubicle wall, staring at his computer terminal and waiting to remember exactly what the relationship between it and him was supposed to be. These synaptic lapses happened each morning, the inert periods lengthening gradually every day – three, five, nine minutes of dedicated concentration – but the snap into action would always come eventually and he would gratefully begin work. But on this particular morning, Henry could not get Cary Grant out of his mind. Cary Grant and Irene Dunne. Cary Grant and Rosalind Russell. Cary Grant and Katharine

Hepburn. Henry decided that the relationship between him and his computer was going nowhere; that he didn't want to be in this pale life in a murmuring cubicle any longer. He needed to be in a screwball comedy, running around cracking wise with some broad while they chased after a lost panther and ended up in a country house somewhere upstate, getting married or having breakfast. He wanted a whimsical life fueled by the energy of laughter in the face of chaos. He needed a hard-bitten but leggy dame with a dazzling smile by his side. He needed a tweed suit and a pipe.

As he walked past the office receptionist, he said in a strange staccato, 'I'm going out, Hildy! If I'm not back in fifteen years, have my life and things sent on to Mother's and I'll pick them up there. See ya, kid, it's been perpendicular!' And that was the beginning of Henry's brief, new life.

24

In character. Henry bought an auburn-colored tweed suit and a meerschaum pipe with small, sharp bird claws under the fat bowl. He began addressing people with a snappy, italicized enthusiasm that had been very much absent in his previously flat speech. He would never say more than three or four lines in succession because, although he was most definitely the leading man, the star of every scene, he didn't want his new life to be overly talky. Of course, given that he was the only person aware of the script, much of what he said came across as bizarre non sequitur.

'I tell ya, kid, I'd positively worship myself if only I could get enough distance from me!'

'Say, fella, you don't by any chance have a spare watch on ya, do ya? C'mon, gimme a look at your other wrist!'

'You know the comedy business, bub. You try to get out, they threaten you with donuts!'

'Pardon me, officer, which is the next exit to Hollywoodland?'

'Now listen here, kid, just because I'm mad doesn't mean I'm crazy. If you want a second opinion, talk to my psychiatrist!'

'Y'know somethin', Joe – you don't mind if I call ya Joe, do ya, Joe? Y'know, I sometimes get the distinct impression that this ain't the way things were supposed to turn out. That things were meant to be a little more . . . Technicolor than this. You ever get that impression, Joe?'

And he insisted on referring to everybody as kid, bub, Joe or fella, which nobody much liked – except for kids, people named Joe, and a certain type of fellow. There simply were no bubs.

One night Henry put on a tuxedo he didn't know he owned and went out looking for Ralph Bellamy. He needed a sidekick, some big, stupid-but-lovable yokel type to bounce witticisms off. Some fella from out of town who owned a Bugatti and a couple of oil wells; someone who called his mother 'Maw'.

Out on the street, Henry hailed a cab and told the driver to take him to the Stork Club.

'Where?' the driver, a large-headed man named Mac asked. 'The where'd you say?'

'The Stork, Mac. First day in the checkered racket, is it? Surely you've made deposits and withdrawals at the Stork Club. Just follow the trail of minks!'

'It'd help me no end if you had an address, mister. I can't tell ya.'

Henry tapped his gloves on his neatly crossed knee. 'Okay, old girl, here's what we'll do – just drop me off when I squeal, whaddaya say?'

'Whatever you like, mister. It's your dough.'

'*Ain't* it though?'

They drove off, Mac anxiously awaiting Henry's squeal. The night streets were bright and busy. Henry felt good, a little tight from the pitcher of martinis he'd mixed before he left, but alert and ready for action, ready for fun. Buildings were tall, solid and beautiful. Policemen waved and children played stickball or hoops. Trios of sailors linked arms and skipped daintily along the sidewalk. There were pretty girls everywhere.

The caper really took off when the taxicab was hit by an asteroid the size of a fist just as they pulled up outside the El Maroc. The thing made the most godawful noise as it plowed into the trunk. Henry and Mac got out and shook their heads at the smoking hole. Henry squealed and handed the cabby a few bucks.

'Well, I'll be!' said Mac, scratching his big head in wonderment. 'I never in all my years . . .'

A geophysicist with a trim moustache stepped out of the small crowd that had gathered and pulled Henry aside. 'D'you know what you've got here?' he whispered.

'A lulu of an insurance case!' Henry said. 'And a good reason for another drink. C'mon, professor, let's slip away before this drizzle turns into a meteor shower!'

The geophysicist plucked the still-smoking asteroid from the trunk and accompanied Henry into the El Maroc. Antoine the maître d' showed them to a table, where they were soon joined by Blond Betty and Madge, a woman of no fixed hair color. The four of them got on famously, swapping jokes about space-dust over bottle after bottle of champagne sent to their table by various asteroid admirers. It turned out that Madge and the professor were going through a very clean divorce, due to become final on the stroke of midnight, but their love was sparked anew by the asteroid, which they decided to adopt and call Junior. Betty was a showgirl, starring at the moment in the chorus of *Feldman's Follies*, and even had a number of her own, 'The Star-Spangled Banana'. 'Featuwing some vewy impwessive fwuit.'

'You never happened to run into a fella named Ralph Bellamy while you were hoofing around the traps, did you?' Henry asked. 'Looks like that actor fella, er . . . Ralph Bellamy.'

Betty said she'd eyeballed William Powell and Harry Langdon, and that once she even saw Henry Fonda being sick into an ashcan outside the mayor's house. But no Ralph Bellamy or anyone fitting the description of either 'Ralph' or 'Bellamy'. Henry almost gave up his search for an appropriately chuckle-headed buffoon, but then asked the prof what he called his mother.

'Why, that's none of your business, Powdermaker!'

'I'm not trying to ruffle your mortarboard, bub, I only meant

. . . Oh, never mind. Let's have another drink! I feel like we're in a Noel Coward play. Someone should be making martinis.'

A waiter leaned in close. They drank, they danced, they laughed and sometime before 2 a.m. they climbed into an oyster-colored Stutz-Bearcat roadster and headed for the professor's cabin up by the lake. There they all put on striped pajamas and drank eggnog by an open fire, chatting gaily.

'You folks ever get the feeling that you're – how can I put this? – not quite here?' Henry asked.

Without a moment's hesitation, Madge said, 'Sure do.'

'Why d'you think that is?'

'Because we're not.'

Madge was right. She, Blond Betty, the professor, the smoking, fateful asteroid, large-headed Mac, all the champagne they'd drunk, the striped pajamas and the entire El Maroc – none of it was quite there. And especially not Ralph Bellamy.

Henry's scenery-chewing at work came to the attention of his boss, a patient and kind woman in her early forties named Jean, who was unfortunately given to a peculiarly corporate verbosity. Jean popped by Henry's desk late in the second week of Henry's new life and asked if they might have a 'quick chat about some workplace-related behavioral issues'.

'Why I'd be delighted, kid. Lemme just file this piece on the missing millionaire and I'll be right with you,' Henry said, through a pipe-clenching jaw as he entered a warehouse stock list into his computer.

'Actually, I think we'd better talk more or less right now, Henry,' Jean said. 'End of play today we'd want to come to some sort of result, I think.'

'Right you are. No time like the present. Old man Wheeler'll still be gone while I am, huh?' Henry spun around in his chair and beamed up at Jean.

'Yes, I'm sure he will.' Jean brushed at her sculpted curls nervously.

'Don't move a follicle, kid. You look simply marvelous as you are!'

'Thanks . . . Shall we?' She motioned toward her office.

'Lead on Macduff and I'll lend you my ears – but I must have them back by eight for the opera! Say, you haven't seen that Bellamy character around lately, have you? When I get my hands on him, I'll positively kiss him!'

Jean lowered the blinds in her glass-walled office before she sat down.

'Well, don't keep me in the dark, kid. What's on your mind?'

'Look, I'll get straight to the point without preamble, Henry. There's been a lot of concern around the office lately as to your . . . emotional wellbeing. Maybe you're working too hard or maybe you've got some issues outside work, but you seem to be having some problems with – I don't know how to put this exactly – some problems with . . . reality. Would you agree with this assessment?'

'Well, covering the Wheeler scandal sure took it out of me, kid. I can't deny that. But I'm back and raring to go.'

'That's the sort of thing we mean. What exactly is the Wheeler scandal? Or these missing millions you keep talking about?'

'Millionaire, boss. *Millionaire*. Old Whitlock Wheeler. It's right there on the front page.'

'Would you like some time off? Perhaps some sort of vacation situation might be what you need.'

'I'll take a vacation when the news does, kid. Me and current events'll work on our tans over piña coladas on the beach in Bermuda!'

Jean took in a breath and let out a sigh. 'But . . . but this isn't a newspaper, Henry. We're a sporting goods wholesaler. I think you know that, don't you?'

Henry said nothing.

'Don't you, Henry?'

Henry looked over to his left and, to a director whom only he could see, he said, 'I'm sorry. What's my line? I've lost my place.'

In the car park behind the warehouse, Jean asked Henry if he wanted somebody to drive his car home for him.

'No thanks,' he said flatly, without italic or exclamation. 'I'll be all right.'

'Are you sure?' Jean said, with gentle insistence. 'It's no trouble.'

'No, I'm . . . I'm . . . here.' Henry got into his car. Jean stepped back, folded her arms and watched him reverse out of the space. She watched the car long enough to see it safely enter the flow of traffic and then walked back to the office, carefully avoiding the small patches of oil on the asphalt.

From start to finish, the bridge back to Henry's side of town was about a quarter mile long. Henry had driven across the bridge hundreds of times without ever giving it much thought, rarely even absorbing the view of the jagged cityscape from the top. But on this day, shortly after his chat with Jean, just as he began the incline, Henry started to feel a little nauseous and slowed down. Further up and along the great concrete sweep, he felt bilious and wondered how he could possibly make it across to the other side. His stomach rolled as he reached the peak and the other side of the city rose into view. Suddenly his mouth was full and he spat hot, thick water onto his tweed trousers. He pulled over to the emergency lane, wild skidding and bleating horns behind him. An accidental glimpse of the skyscrapers ahead induced more nausea and he vomited between his knees. He thought of how far away he was, how high up, how removed. Home seemed an impossible distance and the earth beneath him rushed away. He began heaving and sobbing, a great hyperventilation that felt as if his very soul was being expunged.

The tapping at his window grew loud and more rapid. Henry turned and saw a crinkle-eyed woman rapping on the glass, mouthing words he could not hear. He wound down the window.

'Are you all right?' the woman said, her voice high and airy with concern. 'What's the matter?'

The smell of vomit hit Henry sharply. He looked down and saw awful lumps covering his tweed suit. His right hand was still clutching his pipe. He turned back to the woman in the window.

'What's the matter?' she asked again.

'I'm . . . I'm . . . not Cary Grant,' he panted.

And if Audrey had not laughed discreetly, things might have been very different.

25

Treatment. 'I suppose you were expecting a couch and a picture of Sigmund Freud,' Dr Wagner said, without smiling. He spoke quietly and pleasantly, but Henry thought he could detect a practiced wry note in the remark. A well-rehearsed doctor-patient ice-breaker wafting in the dim light and conditioned air.

'Well, you *are* a psychiatrist and this *is* your office, so yes, I was.' Henry tried to keep his voice down, but found speaking that softly to another man a little creepy. A little post-coital. Henry had also expected the psychiatrist to be older, grayer, bearded, addled-yet-cunning, wise, obscure and European. But this Dr Felix X. Wagner had short, precisely cut dark hair salted with the merest hint of gray, and wore thick-rimmed black glasses. He had a barrel chest, muscular biceps beneath his white, short-sleeved shirt, and he moved with grace, confidence and ease. He looked like Clark Kent, but stronger. Perhaps he even practiced a kind of Nietzschean Superman type of therapy.

'Are you reassured by clichés, Henry?'

Henry settled into a Berber armchair in front of the desk, opposite the doctor. 'If I give the wrong answers, will you give me electrotherapy? Are you gonna make a McMurphy out of me?'

'A what?' the doctor asked.

'Jack Nicholson in *One Flew Over the Cuckoo's Nest*. He was called McMurphy. Randle Patrick McMurphy. They wired him up. "They was giving me ten thousand watts a day, you know, and I'm hot to trot! The next woman takes me on's gonna light up like a pinball machine and pay off in silver dollars!"'

Dr Wagner laughed perfunctorily, then leaned across the desk, his elbows cracking on the wood. 'When were you happiest?'

'Now,' Henry answered.

'And when were you saddest?'

'Now,' Henry said.

There was a long silence. Both men breathed loudly through their noses, not looking at each other. Henry thought about cigarettes and looked for an ashtray on the desk.

Finally Dr Wagner spoke. 'Forgive me, Henry, and correct me if I'm wrong, but aren't those answers from *The English Patient*?'

'Yes,' Henry said. 'But so were the questions.'

'True enough,' Dr Wagner said, with the irritatingly imperturbable sangfroid so common to people of his profession, at least all the ones Henry knew: implacable Judd Hirsch in *Ordinary People*; immovable Lee J. Cobb in *The Three Faces of Eve*; removed, unwilling Natalie Wood in *Sex and the Single Girl*. 'So tell me, using your own life as the source, when you were happiest.'

Henry breathed in and out a bit. 'Well, okay. Well, there was this time once when me and this girl, um . . . God, I can't even remember her name – Anna, Allie, Millie, I don't know. My memory's all . . . soupy. Anyway, I do remember that she was thin, and kind of seventies-looking. Wore this horrible, floppy brown hat all the time but I liked her anyway. We went away for the weekend, up to some coastal shack with tinny water and weird heating and bad TV reception. We'd only been going out for not that long, and everything was fun and tinged with hilarity, that feeling where you could burst, I mean really burst, out laughing at any time. It's like a gas inside you, that feeling. And I was breaking every damn bone and organ in my body trying to make her laugh – cracks, gags, pratfalls, close-calls, the works. I seriously thought I was gonna die from being hilarious. Either her or me. Anyway, one night we bought a couple of lobsters to cook for dinner. The thing was, the bastards were still alive and we had the most terrible and funny time trying to get them into the pot of boiling water. A couple of them escaped and hid behind the refrigerator, and I was running around with a broom trying to sweep them somewhere safe and cracking jokes every two seconds, and she was laughing her head off and almost crying. I remember saying something about scaring a lobster out from behind the fridge by placing some butter sauce and a nutcracker at one end. It was pretty funny and nice, the whole thing. I was very happy then. God, I can't believe I can't remember her name.'

'Perhaps her name is not very important,' Felix Wagner murmured. 'It's you we want to discuss today. Now, when were you saddest?'

'Saddest? Or will very sad suffice?'

'Very sad will be fine.'

'Well, it's funny you should ask that, even though you already did. Because, as a matter of fact, I was pretty sad another time at the exact same place with a different girl, whose name I also can't remember, but it may have been Louise. This was a few months after me and the other girl – Diane, was her name maybe, or Anne – broke up. I don't know why I went back up to the holiday house, probably because I'd had such a good time before, I guess. But anyway, there we were at the same place, and all the same stuff with the lobsters happened, they escaped, ran around the kitchen like before. Only this time the girl was just leaning against the kitchen door smoking a cigarette and telling me to act like a man, or grow up or something, and just pick up the damned lobsters. She didn't laugh at the butter sauce crack. It was pretty depressing, the comparison and the reality itself.' Dr Wagner scribbled and after a pause, Henry asked, 'Are you writing "butter sauce"?'

Wagner didn't answer. 'What about the recent afternoon on the bridge, Henry?' he asked. 'Were you sad then?'

'Well, not really. I wasn't feeling a million bucks, of course, but I wasn't sad, exactly. I was more upset. In despair. It's quite a different feeling from being sad, isn't it?'

'Is it?' Dr Wagner cleaned his lenses with a handkerchief. 'In what way?'

'Well, sad is like when your cat gets accidentally run over and despair is when you kill it yourself.'

'Interesting.' Henry was pleased with this response; it felt reassuringly psychiatric. 'And why were you in despair on the bridge?'

'Shouldn't you tell me?' Henry asked, trying not to sound antagonistic.

The doctor put his glasses back on, did several test-blinks and said, 'There is nothing inside you that you do not know yourself.'

'Then why am I here?' Henry sounded dense and hostile. 'I mean,' he whispered gently, 'why am I here?'

'Why are you whispering?' Dr Wagner whispered.

'My life is a great disappointment to me.'

'That's why you're whispering?'

'No, that's why I was upset on the bridge.'

'I see. And in what way is your life a disappointment?'

'In every way it possibly could be, but basically because I wanted it to turn out one way and it turned out another. The same goes for me too, actually. I mean myself. I thought I'd turn out different than how I am. I'm very disappointed in myself, too.'

'And that's why you were pretending to be Cary Grant?'

'Well, I wasn't being strictly him 'cause I don't really have the looks for it. I was being a kind of melange of general screwball types. But it was mostly him, I guess. Even though I'm not particularly handsome or anything.'

'So you feel that your life would be better if you were Cary Grant, or one of the characters he played.'

'Yeah, either way,' Henry sighed. 'It'd be a whole lot more interesting. If you were in film, I mean. Or in *a* film. Things happen. They don't seem to happen much in my life. Basically, I wish like hell that I was somebody else.'

'I find it interesting that you use Cary Grant as your exemplar.'

'Why? You think I'm more of a Ronald Colman type? I haven't got the face for a moustache. Or the hormones.'

'No, it's because there's a famous quote by Grant along the lines of "Everybody wants to be Cary Grant – even me".'

'You too?'

'No, he said that. Grant did. That even he wanted to be Cary Grant.'

Henry thought for a moment. 'God, that'd be tough, not even being who you were ... I guess underneath everything he was stuck being Archie Leach. That was his real name.'

'Yes. But I'm sure you realize, Henry, that a person, any person, must make things happen for him- or herself, whoever they are. Or wish to be.'

'I've heard that. Actually, I've heard it a hell of a lot, but I don't really think it's always true. I think it's more a matter of luck than will. And being good-looking always helps. You can try your head off and never get anywhere in life. You've gotta have good luck and good looks, otherwise you can pretty much forget it.'

'I don't believe that you really believe that, Henry.'

'Well, I really believe that I really believe it.' Henry shook his head once very quickly. 'Did that sound too glib? Do you want me to do it again? I can try to come across more sympathetically if you want me to.'

Dr Wagner made a brief 'hmph' noise, then said, 'I'm afraid that's all we have time for today.'

'It's a wrap!' Henry stood up, brushing balls of brown Berber from his corduroy trousers. 'When's my next call?'

Dr Wagner consulted a sheet of paper. 'Thursday at three.'

'Okay. I guess I'll be in my trailer until then. Send over a case of Evian and a masseuse, will you?'

Dr Wagner nodded, then said, 'Don't worry, Henry, you have a very normal collection of symptoms.' The very normal collection of symptoms was diagnosed as depression, and Henry was given a prescription for Xanax and Zoloft. 'The Zoloft will take time to gather effect, but the Xanax will alleviate your anxiety almost immediately. And remember to keep breathing,' the psychiatrist said. 'It's most important. Now you really must go, I have other analysands.'

Henry cocked his head in one direction and his mouth in another. 'Other what?'

'Patients, Henry,' Dr Wagner said. 'Patients.'

And for the rest of the day Henry wondered whether the psychiatrist had said 'patients' or 'patience'. Or maybe even one of each. It drove him nuts.

The pills helped – Henry's neurotic and endogenous reactions were chemically sedated – but initially it was his relationship with Audrey that exerted the more powerful influence. While the pills relieved his feelings of confusion and panic, and forced long, deep, dream-ridden sleep upon him, it was being with Audrey that made him want to recover, to try to keep breathing.

Over the following weeks Henry thought about Audrey constantly. He became tired and even somehow breathless (despite his doctor's orders) in his wild, swirling obsession with Audrey and her loveliness. She was his savior. He left flowers on her doorstep and pinned notes to her door. He called and delivered monologues into her answering machine. He met her for lunch, always with some sort of gift, even if it was just a small story to tell her. He asked many questions about her job as a homewares buyer for a department store, about her friends, her family, her past. He was careful not to be too eccentric in his behavior or unctuous in his gratitude toward her. He smiled a lot and wore himself out trying to be interesting and well balanced.

Audrey agreed to go out with him one night – Henry considered it their first proper 'date', because it happened in the evening – to see a movie and have dinner. After Henry had showered, shaved, aftershaved, combed his hair, shined his shoes, cleaned his teeth, combed his hair again, climbed into a suit, changed his tie five or six times and put on a record that put him in a good mood (the screaming, bossy horns of 'Ice Pick Mike' from Lalo Schifrin's soundtrack to *Bullitt*), he poured himself a large vodka and tonic to lubricate his thoughts and silver his tongue. The telephone rang.

'Hello, Henry, it's Audrey,' she said. 'I'm just checking – this is not an actual date, is it? It's just two people hanging around together, right?'

Henry's heart tumbled as she said the words, but he affected a light tone. 'A date!? Of course not. It's just two pals passing time. I probably should have warned you before – no matter how hard you might try, I won't be lured to your bed.'

Audrey laughed. 'Just checking.'

'On the other hand . . .'

'On the other hand, what?'

'Um . . . nothing. I'll see you in half an hour.'

'On the other hand what?'

Half an hour later, lit by flashing headlights and a pool of red neon, he kissed her lightly and drily on the lips on a damp street-corner. 'Hi, it's me,' he said. 'Henry Powdermaker, pleased to meet you.'

'You too,' Audrey said. 'My name's Audrey Gael Gillespie.' They began walking down the street, flanked by dark, candle-lit restaurants, bright book stores and clothing boutiques. 'How are you feeling?'

'Vodka and platonic.'

'Funny. I'm feeling quite . . . gin and orange you glad to see me?'

'Yes, I am. I always am. And I'm beginning to wonder if I should be. Especially because of how beautiful you look. It's breaking my heart.' Gray-eyed Audrey was wearing a gray woolen skirt suit with quiet yellow and red checks. Underneath the open jacket was a bra-hugging white t-shirt. Her chunky black high heels put her at head height with Henry. He looked into her eyes for a moment, then buried his gaze in the curls of her long, dark hair. 'Not really,' he said. 'My heart is just fine.'

'But why didn't you just stop trying to be Cary Grant?' Audrey asked Henry a short time later, as they walked in the light rain.

'Because I didn't want to. I'm sick of my regular life. It was fun wearing tweed and smoking a pipe.'

'But you didn't even smoke it. You just had it poking out of your mouth.'

'It was a prop.'

'It looked very silly.'

'Would it have looked better with smoke pouring out of it?'

'It would have looked real,' she said.

'If it looked real, then people would have thought I was *really* insane.'

Stunts. Henry almost sprained his ankle clowning around on the cinema stairs, staggering near the bottom and missing the brass handrail. Then he cut his eyebrow by deliberately walking into a door in the restaurant. He spilled white wine on his shirt. He looped a strand of spaghetti over his ear when Audrey wasn't looking, then carried on with the conversation as though he didn't know it was there. He burned his fingers lighting cigarettes. Poked

144

out his tongue with a black piece of star anise on it. Back out on the wet street, he could not resist slipping on an imaginary banana peel, falling onto his back, winding himself and tearing a hole in the back of his suit jacket. It was seduction by slapstick. Henry knew that the very Chaplinesque mixture of humor and pathos was a cheap, dishonest trick, but he also knew that it worked.

'Back to my place for coffee and Band-Aids?' Audrey said, as they reached the intersection where they would normally go their separate ways.

'Gee, I don't know if I should, Ms Gillespie. It's getting late and I think I've broken my leg.'

'Suit yourself,' Audrey said, briskly walking away.

'On the other hand . . .' he shouted, limping after her.

26

On Thursday at three o'clock, Henry sat down opposite Dr Felix Wagner, settling comfortably into the Berber armchair he was already beginning to think of as his. It was his fifth or sixth session and he was enjoying them.

Wagner was scribbling with a fountain pen. He glanced up briefly and said, 'I'll just be a moment, Henry.'

'No problem. You trying to save money by making your own Rorschach blots, Doc?' The psychiatrist laughed quietly. Henry smiled, a little surprised that the doctor had a sense of humor. 'What'll we talk about today? You got any flashcards you want to flash at me? A bit of the old word association, maybe?'

'No, but how about we employ another cliché? Tell me about your childhood.'

'Well, my father tried to kill me with a knife when I was a kid.'

'Really?'

'Actually, no. It turned out that he was just trying to cut off a sandal strap, but still. It was completely terrifying. The funny thing is, it's not all that uncommon an experience. I know other kids – well, they're not kids any more, but when they were kids – who thought their parents were trying to knock 'em off.'

'Really?'

'Oh, sure. I vaguely remember a girl in grade school, a real goody-two-shoes of a kid, whose mother tried to kill her with sleeping tablets.'

'But the little girl didn't die, obviously?'

'No. Not right then, anyway. I think she got hit by lightning soon afterward, though. What a way to go, huh? Straight from God. It happens, though, doesn't it? There's that park ranger in Virginia or North Carolina or somewhere who's been hit something like fourteen times and all he's got from it is no eyebrows.' There was a pause. Henry said, 'I think I'd like to be struck by lightning. It could be interesting.'

Dr Wagner said with his eyes closed, 'Why do you think that you thought your father might have wanted to kill you?'

'I'm not sure. You know what it's like when you're young, you think crazy thoughts. The world's a strange and horrible place. The funny thing is, I hadn't even done the thing yet, which would have been the only reason he might've wanted to slit my throat. But that was like a week later or something.'

'Which thing is that?'

'The film thing which I've already told you about.' Henry looked away. 'Which I'd really rather not talk about.'

'The film of your parents in the bedroom.'

'Yes, that one. Which I don't want to talk about.'

'Of your father forcing himself upon your mother.'

'Yes! That one!' Henry snapped, bringing his eyes up from the floor to look at Dr Wagner. 'Of my father raping my mother. Which was then shown to all my parents' friends, somewhat abruptly ending the party and my parents' marriage. And putting something of a dent in my own life.'

'Good.' Dr Wagner opened his eyes and nodded keenly. 'Good.'

'Yes, terrific,' said Henry, leaning sarcastically on the two 'r's. 'What's good about it?'

'I think it's important that you acknowledge the incident. Get it out. It would be even better if you could speak with your mother, possibly even your brother, about it as well.'

'I don't. In fact I think it would be very bad. And I'm sure that they all feel the same way, too. I know they do. We're not the sort of family that's keen on self-examination, particularly of our own personal Zapruder film.'

'Why is that, do you think?'

'Are you serious?' Henry began scratching at his leg. 'Does that really need an answer? I ended my parents' marriage. My father left and probably wants to kill me – for real this time. My mother lost her hair, for God's sake. She's bald because of me. Bald and alone.'

'You ended their marriage? Surely it was a doomed relationship whether you made the film or not, whether the film was shown or not.'

'Probably. I guess so, but the film, and the *screening* of the film, certainly added another dimension to the . . . to the doom, wouldn't you say?'

'No doubt, no doubt,' the doctor said, incorporating his shoulders and upper body into his nodding. 'But the essential fact – the essential fact, Henry – is that you did not end their relationship. Your father did.'

'I don't know about that. They were still together, being married, being a mother and father to Daniel and me for a while after he . . . did that to her. If he was to blame, he would've been gone before the film was shown, wouldn't he?'

'Perhaps.'

'Not perhaps – if my mother had've wanted it over, he would have been gone before.'

'Maybe, Henry. Things don't always happen as swiftly or immediately as we might wish. Many things in life are difficult. They take time. Courage, for instance. Courage that perhaps your mother needed to develop in order to act. You're not a fool, Henry, I'm sure you know what I mean. But what I find most acute here is that you seem quite determined to blame yourself for your parents' break-up and your father's departure. That you very much want to be responsible for it.'

Still rhythmically scratching his leg, Henry began shaking his head and said, 'And why would that be?'

'It's your revenge upon your father.'

Henry was still. A while passed before he spoke. 'Really?'

'Boy, have I got some issues,' he told Audrey that night. 'Some sort of reverse Oedipus complex where my *father*'s the one who wants to sleep with my mother and kill *me*.'

As time passed Henry got better, gradually accepting the fact that things were as they were. Added to the Zoloft and Xanax were various combinations of Wellbutrin, Navane, BuSpar and Paxil, which helped smooth out the edges, clear the air. He did his best to hide the side-effects – irritability, headaches and a kind of mental indigestion where certain ideas would sometimes sit in the middle of his head for days, considered but never entirely understood – from Audrey. They slept together two or three times a week. Her friends became his, and his – Charlie and Vanessa, mainly – gradually became hers. They moved in together, into a house in a neighborhood of small, close streets and dense trees near a river.

Among other things Audrey greatly disliked: the smells and stains created by wet towels left hanging over doors; the noises people made when they were cracking the pimpled claws and hot orange bellies of cooked crab (phoney moans of pleasure, usually followed by meaty but nervous laughter. 'Plus having to wear a bib when you're eating – it's so wrong. So very wrong.'); the physical shape of Great Britain, which she felt was too jagged and sharp; the word 'panties', particularly when said by men; men who went by the nickname Bunny – she'd met far too many at college; Moog synthesizer sounds; almost all hats, but especially pith helmets; being told that she could pass for Winona Ryder's sister; models of the male, female and super variety; the gradual but noticeable synonymization of 'reticent' and 'reluctant'; being reminded, through the unexpected meeting of an alumnus on the street or the unwanted arrival of an invitation to a reunion, that she went to Bennington College; being mistaken for Winona Ryder; the notion of the universe being either finite *or* infinite; crème de menthe; and Larry King's spectacles. 'I don't much care for his suspenders, either,' she told Henry one early fall night as they drove up to her parents' house in Oswego. 'But if I had to choose one accessory for him to lose, I'd choose the glasses. They're hideous.'

Audrey never enumerated in apposition the things that she *did* like but Henry assumed it was just about everything else; Audrey Gillespie was extremely accepting of the world as she reckoned it to be. The world had been good to her and she treated it in kind. But it was the odd collection of things that she held in disfavor which gave Henry the biggest kick; he loved that she hated so randomly and with such fervor.

Audrey's mother, Taylor, was an award-winning glassblower and competition target shooter whose fingers were so long and soft and delicate that Henry's favorite part of every visit was the shaking of her hand, a formality he tried to engage at every possible turn – congratulating her on her latest prize, for the fine dinner she cooked, the spectacular view of Lake Ontario. 'Why thank you, Henry,' she would say, trying not to look shocked as he pumped her hand yet again. 'You're very sweet. Isn't that sweet of Henry to mention, Rex?'

'Yes, the boy's brimming with compliments . . .' Rex Gillespie was a small, almost gnomic man with a carefully manicured beard of such tidy whiteness it sometimes seemed to emit an audible buzzing. He had left the advertising business in Manhattan and now owned a micro-brewery called Empyreal which, he never tired of telling Henry, produced a range of outstanding beers the subtleties of which were entirely wasted on the American palate. 'People either don't understand or won't accept a hint of cilantro in their alcohol,' he often groused. 'If only they knew . . .' If only they knew *what*? Henry wanted to ask but never did because he was loath to appear ignorant; he simply nodded as though he, too, appreciated something profound yet elusive about beer, cilantro and popular American tastes. On his third or fourth visit Henry joined Rex for an afternoon on the lake in Rex's sloop, *The Something*, so called because Audrey's father did not much care for boat names but cared even less for unnamed boats. *The Something* reminded Henry very much of the 'Downeaster' model his father used to tinker with on afternoons when the air was heavy with salt and the sound of a crackling radio broadcasting horse races. Henry told Rex that his was a fine boat – sturdy, sleek and easy in the water. Rex nodded sagely and asked whether Henry had spent much time 'on deck', given that he'd grown up so close to the Atlantic. Henry said no, that his had been a largely land-based upbringing as his father had not had much facility with boats, except in miniature. The small talk continued for a while as the two men gently rose and fell on the lake's frothy waves until Rex grew silent and began rubbing his snowy beard with the outside of both hands. Henry wondered if he and Rex ought to be fishing or sharing nips of whiskey, something that would create the appearance of a bond between them. After a time Rex suddenly announced that it was about marketing. That it was *all* about marketing. Henry made sounds meant to indicate that he understood and most certainly agreed with Audrey's father – that in fact to his ears at least truer words were never spoken. 'That's very wise, Sir,' he said. 'You're very wise.'

'. . . positively brimming,' Rex told his wife.

'Well it's nice that somebody occasionally gives me a compliment, Rex, for God's sake . . . You can let go now, Henry.'

Henry enjoyed the monthly overnight visits to Audrey's parents, mostly because of the lunatic idea that her gravel-voiced, elegant-fingered mother might corner him somewhere upstairs (Audrey's old bedroom, probably) and ask Henry if he wanted her to seduce him, arching one heavy eyebrow, slowly blinking Cleopatra lashes at him. He planned to say no, of course, but was very keen to be asked; perhaps to place a shaking hand on her black bra-ed breast before coming to his senses and stumbling away, urgently trying to suppress the erection he imagined would be visible from miles away.

'What's so funny, Henry?' Audrey asked on their way back to Syracuse one late fall morning.

'I was just imagining, umm . . . your mother trying to, aah, trying to teach me about . . . y'know, glass-blowing.'

Audrey nodded. 'Well try not to,' she said then turned to him, her mouth caught somewhere between a smile and a knowing smirk. 'That's another thing I don't like – the way men stare at my mother's hands.' Henry blushed, swallowed and looked at his girlfriend's hands as they gripped the steering wheel, a spot of creamy white paling each smooth knuckle.

Sex scene. Henry walked into the kitchen, reached into a paper bag, held out a long green vegetable and asked, 'Is this right?'

Audrey shook her head and smiled. 'That's a cucumber, you dummy.'

Henry plucked out something else long and green. 'How 'bout this?'

'Marrow.' She laughed. Henry offered another choice, one that even he knew was a long shot. 'Eggplant.'

'Okay,' Henry said, 'this is the last one. I've blown close to five dollars on after-five o'clock Saturday vegetable extortion prices, so I hope it's right.'

'Now *that's* a zucchini,' Audrey said.

'Phew. Y'know, I first went to a florist and asked for zucchini flowers and the guy just started laughing at me.' Henry poured two glasses of wine and lit himself a cigarette. 'After that I became too embarrassed to ask the fella in the market which thing was a zucchini.'

'How can a person be so vegetable ignorant? I don't understand it.'

'Despite my mother's best efforts, I'm a meat man, Aud. I can tell different sorts of bacon with a mere glance. Streaky. Canadian. Back. Makin'. I know and love them all. What I don't understand is how a person can enjoy cooking.'

Audrey took her glass of wine into the living room and sat on the candy-striped couch. Henry followed and sat on a chair opposite her, balancing an ashtray on his knee because he knew that if he spilled ash on the chair she'd be upset, but then expend too much energy trying not to show it (possibly because she didn't want Henry reciprocally upset by feeling guilty for his drug-induced clumsiness, of which she knew him to be ashamed); after which he'd have to apologize, even though she was pretending it didn't bother her.

'Do you ever think about having your own restaurant?'

'No, never,' Audrey replied simply. 'I like what I do for a living. Running a restaurant would be hell on wheels.'

'But if you enjoy cooking so much, don't you want to do it all the time? Make it your life? Employ someone who knows the difference between a zucchini and . . . whatever those other things are.'

'No. I think if I did it professionally I'd stop loving it.' Audrey leaned forward and took a sip of wine, careful not to bring the glass over the couch. 'I'd have to shout at people, most likely, and I'm not quite cut out for that. I prefer my confrontations in the form of memos. Or nasty haiku.'

'I think I'm the opposite. Every time I see a film, I hate the fact that I'm not a film maker. Even the crappy ones. It depresses the hell out of me.' Audrey's eyes were closed and her head was swaying softly in time to the music, her long hair brushing her neck, teasing her cleavage. Henry hurriedly quit his cigarette and joined her on the couch. '*Especially* the crappy ones.'

'You should stop watching them then,' she said.

He laughed. 'That'd be like me saying you should stop cooking.' He moved closer to Audrey, put his arms around her and with a single, fluid motion unhooked her bra through her shirt. She giggled. 'Or eating. Then where would we be?'

She opened her eyes. 'Hungry,' she said, giving him a look and laughing into a kiss.

'Hmmm . . . Remember that scene with the strawberries in *9½ Weeks*?' Henry said.

'Forget it, Henry,' Audrey said, removing his t-shirt. 'The fruit's for tomorrow.'

27

Film. Henry and Audrey were invited to a large Sunday lunch at some friends of Audrey's – Terry, who had a white moustache, and his wife Teri, who had white hair. The meal was a celebration

of food itself, a lavish spread of home-made pies, colorful, complicated salads, juicy roast meats, marinated vegetables, fresh cakes,
pastries, Audrey's fruit concoction and dozens of bottles of wine.

The small, crumbling house in which the lunch was held backed
onto a shady, verdant park, where later in the afternoon the group
went to play some game or other to work off the bloated laziness
that had devoured it. Ten of them, happy, drunk and shouting in
the dappled light of the park. There were people walking dogs,
other people playing games or sitting on benches kissing or reading. And there was, Henry noticed, a little blond boy about three
years old standing with his father, who looked to be some sad,
nondescript age between twenty-eight and forty. The kid had the
same color hair as Daniel had had when he was young, that time
Henry had wanted to ruffle it, give his brother some reassuring
touch. Just the two of them, Henry thought as he stared. No
mother or brothers or sisters or anything. He saw that the little
boy was kind of dirty, dressed in second-hand clothing that hadn't
been washed in a while, and he wondered if perhaps the mother
was dead. At first the boy stood close to his father, fearful of
everything too far away. The father had lank hair of no real color
or cut and was wearing old runners and a pair of grimy jeans
slung low over his hips. He wore glasses and bent down often,
whispering things to his son. It seemed to Henry that every time
the man opened his mouth, he was infecting the boy with the same
hollow hopelessness that had followed the father for his whole
life. Secret words that coated the little boy in a clinging film of
warm grime and milky despair. Henry couldn't take his eyes off
the two of them – troubled son and troubling father.

As the games wore on and the sunlight dimmed, the little boy
became more drawn and unhappy-looking, slumping toward the
ground, almost disappearing. Eventually he moved away from his
father and stood between Henry and some of the other players,
who paid the kid no attention. The game finished and the others
went back to the house, leaving Henry, the boy and his father
standing in a near-triangle, a few yards apart from one another.
The boy stared into the ground as though willing it to consume
him. The father shifted his thick gaze from Henry to the boy and

back. Henry thought that in some way the son and father were faintly embarrassed by one another; uncomfortable and unhappy that this grimy lineage, this contamination, was being passed from father to son. Henry's eyes filled with tears. When he couldn't stand watching any more, he went back inside to join the others, who, he felt sure, had had clean and happy childhoods.

28

First of all I'd, uh, I'd like to thank the Academy . . . *First* of all, I must thank the Academy for this award . . . This very *shiny* award . . . Henry sat in the warm underlit waiting room, finger-ironing the lapels of his jacket and trying to think of new and different ways to thank the Academy; unusual angles at which he might proudly-yet-self-effacingly hold aloft his Oscar; methods of ingratiating himself with a billion people around the world in under sixty seconds. Thank you, thank you all *so* much, *merci beaucoup, grazie, hartelijk bedankt, doh je*, and to everybody watching in Micronesia, *kili so chapur* . . . He'd grown to love his Thursday appointments by now, never missing a session, often arriving up to an hour early, tapping his feet in eager anticipation of being inside the large, well-smelling psychiatrist's office. Gosh, there are just so many people I have to credit, but first of all, before I go any further and thank my wife Madeleine and our many happy, well-adjusted children and my dear friend and psychiatrist Felix Wagner – you're the greatest, Felix! You made me sane again, buddy! – my tuxedo designer, and the non-interfering studio who believed in me and my vision as an artist and made it possible for my dream to come true, I have to thank the Academy . . .

'How about I kick things off today?' Henry said. 'I feel I'm not doing enough in this relationship. You're always leading. I feel lazy.'

Felix Wagner rubbed his huge left bicep with his big and hairy right hand. 'That's fine.'

'I mean, I don't know a damned thing about you and your life. All I know is you're a muscley bastard. D'you start off as a psychiatric nurse and work your way up, or what?' The doctor unleashed a deep, rumbling laugh which perturbed Henry slightly. He decided to act a bit more serious. 'So, uh, what made you become a psychiatrist?'

'I read a book.'

'*The Psychopathology of Everyday Life* by Sigmund Freud?' Henry rushed out the sentence so quickly he almost fell out of his chair.

'Actually, it was *The Dice Man* by–'

'Luke Rinehart.'

'You've read it?'

'Not really, but John Schlesinger was set to direct a film of it for Paramount in '72. I guess the project must've fallen apart, though, because they never made it. Things were pretty chaotic at Paramount back then. That crazy Charlie Bluhdorn, eh?'

Wagner scribbled something on a pad. 'Yes, well that was the book that put me on this path. Primarily because the main character's looks reminded me very much of me. I was quite young and easily influenced by myself.'

'Good Lord,' Henry said with alarm. 'That seems rather . . . precarious. What if they'd actually made the film and cast someone who doesn't look anything like you? Ernest Borgnine or someone. Then what?'

'Then I might've become something else. However, our sense of personal destiny isn't quite that easily pinpointed. I think it's imprudent to be too certain of exactly who or what you are. A person should always be prepared to become someone – or something – else. How do you account for the person you've become, thus far?'

'Well,' Henry said. 'For a start, it's a question of who, not how. And I prefer to use the word "blame", rather than "account". Blame is important and healthy, I think. Which is just as well because I like to do a lot of blaming. And apart from the self-directed stuff, I have a large portion left over for a fella called Z. Barry Robertson.'

'And who was he?'

'The guy who refused to let me into his film school five years in succession, Z. Barry Robertson. Imagine leaving a Z just hanging there like that. It's kinda dickish, don't you think? Anyway, it's his fault. Everything is his fault.'

'Everything is his fault?'

'Well, except for the stuff which is my fault or my father's fault.' Henry shifted in his armchair. 'And no, of course it's not Robertson's fault. But at the same time there's no doubt in my mind that my stupid life would be a whole lot different if he'd said yes one of those times.'

'Why don't you apply again?'

'Because the bastard's dead now. It wouldn't be worth it if I did get in – no revenge factor.'

'You're being facetious, Henry.'

'Yes I am, but even if I wasn't, the simple truth is that my life is pretty much finished anyway.'

'You're how old?'

'Over twenty-five.'

'Yes, I see what you mean.'

'Now you're being a tad facetious yourself, Doc. Hangin' a little sarcasm out there, because you're like forty-three or something, but the fact is, at my age being over twenty-five is old. To begin with the incredibly obvious and most disheartening fact, Orson Welles wrote, directed and starred in *Citizen Kane* when he was twenty-five. Steven Spielberg whipped up *Jaws* when he was twenty-eight. Owen Wilson wrote and put in a genius performance in *Bottle Rocket* well before thirty. Jon Favreau wrote and starred in the very brilliant *Swingers* at the age of twenty-nine. Truffaut made *The 400 Blows* when he was twenty-seven; and won best director at Cannes in 1959, for God's sake. Spike Lee did his first feature when he was twenty-nine. *Sex, Lies and* Soderbergh – twenty-six. John Singleton wrote and directed *Boyz N the Hood* when he was twenty-three. Peter Bogdanovich – same age when he made *Targets*. I don't know exactly how old Christopher

McQuarrie was when he won the Academy Award for best screenplay for *The Usual Suspects*, but he *looked* pretty damn young. Shane Black sold his script for *Lethal* goddam *Weapon* when he was, like twenty-one or something insane. For a million bucks! The Coens, Hal Hartley . . .'

'Yes, all right, Henry. I get the picture – no pun intended.'

'You can't imagine how much all of this knowledge, goddam useless as it is, how much it crushes me. It crushes me.'

'Well, you have to try and un-know it. Relieve yourself of it.'

'Un-know it? What kind of Zen story is that? Un-know it.' Henry's mouth twisted around the words. 'That's like trying to tell someone to un-cancer themselves – it's impossible. And . . . and kind of insulting. Once you know stuff like this, it's impossible to un-know it. You're stuck with it. I virtually never stop thinking about it. Never. All those guys are having wonderful, exciting lives – the ones that are still alive at least. Tom di Cillo. Jim Jarmusch. Kevin Smith. But old Henry Powdermaker works in a sporting goods warehouse. You can't imagine how much that makes me hate myself – and Z. Barry Robertson. And that's just a few film makers. I could do artists and writers if you want. They can make me feel inferior as hell, too. Whenever I go to a gallery, which because of all this garbage is not too often, I take a quick look at the painting and then my eyes slip straight over to the little card beside it with the artist's details, his date of birth and stuff. And I work out how old he was when he did the painting, and if it works out he was younger than me, I can't look at it anymore. I hate the guy. I walk away. It's just too depressing. And obviously, the older I get, the more it happens. By the time I'm seventy I'm gonna be completely culturally illiterate. When teenagers start directing films, I'm gonna kill myself, I really am.'

'You can't just appreciate art or beauty or achievement for its own sake?'

'Sadly, no. I want to be one of the people who *creates* the beauty or achieves something before I can start to relax and enjoy other people's work.' Henry calmed down a little. 'It's a very big stumbling block, though, I know. It's not very healthy.'

'And you feel that if you can't make films you won't be happy?'

'How can I be happy when I compare myself to somebody like Woody Allen or Orson Welles? I mean, it'd be just so great to be lauded and needed and . . . in demand all the time. Busy doing things and being worthwhile instead of just wasting your life, like I do. And it's not like I'm not trying to be funny and talented all over the place – I do it all the time. I try all the time. It just never works out very well. Which leads me to the conclusion that I'm not funny or talented. Except if you have really low standards about these things. Which I don't. So the truth is, people aren't calling me up and asking me to do things all the time – write this, direct that, doctor this script. There's no heat around me. I'm not in demand.'

'A lot of this sounds like substitution for love, Henry. That you want only to be loved.'

'I'm already loved, and it's fine. What I want is different. What I want is to be . . .' Henry paused and thought. 'I want an Oscar.'

Dr Wagner laughed, the involuntary sound coming out of his nose. 'What for?' He covered his mouth, but Henry knew he was still smiling.

'Whatever. I don't care. I just want one. I want to be in among that crowd. The statuette crowd, clutching and thanking and grinning. I want to be envied by other poor idiots like me. Seriously, I do. I think it'd be good.'

'I thought you wanted to make films. What you just told me sounds like the sort of superficial longing of somebody flicking through *People* magazine, somebody who –'

'I *used* to want to make films, when I was young enough to want to. Now I'd take anything I could get. I'd be happy enough being a measly actor. But I work in a sporting goods warehouse. Which, as if it wasn't pathetic enough, is also horrifically ironic in that I pretty much hate sport.'

'Let's say some talent scouts were out scouring sporting goods warehouses and did happen to chance upon you, Henry, what exactly might they expect to discover?'

'What do you mean?'

'What would you have to offer them?'

'Desire,' Henry said. 'Great desire, not just an urge or an inclination, but a great, passionate desire to be in film.'

'And do you think that's enough?'

'Well, it *ought* to be. It ought to be enough to at least get you started. Get you into film school. It should at least get you that far and give you the chance to go further.'

'Perhaps you just weren't cut out for film school at that time.'

'*Times*. Five times. So what does that mean? That the way that my life has turned out is what I'm cut out for?'

'If you're unhappy with your life, Henry, you must make appropriate changes.'

'I agree but it's a hell of a word, isn't it, "appropriate"?'

29

Jump cuts: #1. Henry heard from a friend who still remained in touch with her that Jeanne, Henry's favorite ex-girlfriend, was moving to New Mexico to paint rocks and cactuses. In his memory, Jeanne looked like Jane Russell in the poster of Howard Hughes's 'daring' production of *The Outlaw*, arched eyebrows above a stretched, unsmiling mouth, relaxed and gorgeously sensuous. Brown curls and a hay bale for a pillow, her legendary, fabulous bust inviting all who stared to dive in. Henry began to wonder if it was Jeanne he quietly yearned for, or Jane.

#2. Biff made the cover of a glossy music magazine which hailed Charlie as 'the greatest lawyer/guitarist in rock today'. To his great surprise, Henry was only amazingly jealous. He'd expected to find himself suicidal. Or homicidal. 'And I owe it all to myself,' Charlie was quoted regarding the band's success. Henry had laughed out loud, spitting cornflakes and milk all over the table.

#3. Through one of his mother's vague, disordered reports, Henry learned that Madeleine Ford was in Washington – state or D.C., Sandra had been unable to remember. 'Or perhaps I didn't ask.'

Sandra had used the word 'glamorous' several times in the conversation and Henry could picture her mouth twisting around the word, which she lengthened because, Henry was sure, she enjoyed the bitter taste of it. 'I think I was meant to get the impression from Eileen that Madeleine was having quite the glamorous life.' What Henry really wanted to know was whether Madeleine was happy and safe; whether she was living the life she desired; whether she thought of him often or at all.

#4. About once a month he was woken in the middle of the night by long skids followed by the hollow, boxy sound of a car hitting another car on the road just outside his bedroom. The first few times he thought he was dreaming, until the next day, when he would find small pools of crushed orange or red plastic from a smashed rear light.

#5. One night after chicken fried steak at a diner in the deep, mossy south of Mississippi, Daniel Powdermaker was knifed in the arm during a mugging. He was in a place called Purvis on what he called a 'blues excursion' with his girlfriend Shirley, the first woman Daniel had dated since the parachute-less parachutist (he'd waited several years before becoming, he said, 'recklessly horny'), and because she'd remained safe and well throughout their courtship – not so much as a sprained ankle – Danny planned to marry her. Henry was very happy for his brother: on the one occasion he'd met Shirley she had struck him as very much like Judy Holliday, a combination of buxom wise-ass and peroxide-blonde ingenue, and he felt these were fine – possibly even necessary – qualities in a prospective sister-in-law.

The injury was fatal to Danny's golf game but, somewhat improbably, cured him of his speech problem. 'And you know what else, Henry? You know what else?' Daniel had told his brother. 'I miss them. I miss both those things terribly. I'm not sure who I am without them.'

Henry assured Daniel that he would always be somebody and that he didn't need a handicap – of either variety – to be so. 'You're my brother,' Henry had said.

'Yeah but I practically never see you, Henry. You may as well be . . .'

'I know,' Henry said. And I'm sorry, he'd meant to add, but although he felt the sentiment keenly, he could not bring himself to say the words. Rightly or wrongly (and he suspected the latter) Henry had always felt that the less said – especially to his mother and brother – about his father the better, as though in applied silence he might somehow make everything right. Or, like film run repeatedly through a projector, crack, fade and eventually disappear.

#6. Henry, Charlie and a small woman called Gina were at a clean, bright restaurant full of blond-wood furniture and blond, wooden staff. Charlie and Vanessa had broken up while he was on tour. Through Gina, Charlie's sudden new girlfriend who worked as a sub-editor on the same newspaper where Sylvia was a photographer, Henry learned that Sylvia Moriarty and her actor friend-then-boyfriend-then-fiancée-then-husband, Klaus, had bought a house together. That she updated her car every year and continued to expand upon her large wardrobe. And that she was very content and comfortable. To Henry, it all seemed to fit. Sylvia had always been good at life.

'Good at life! What's the holy hell's that supposed to mean?' Gina snapped at him. Henry noticed Charlie rolling his contact-blue eyes, and wondered how long Charlie and Gina would last. Rocket appreciated flippancy.

'You don't happen to recall if Sylvia ever mentioned a guy called Ethan, do you?' Henry asked Gina. 'A guy called Ethan Vaughan? Thin, enigmatic type? Maybe you know him as Ethan Fabulous? Looks a little like James Coburn with his head in a vice?'

'No,' Gina clipped.

'You're lucky that Ethan and his Bambi never sued, y'know Henry,' Charlie said.

'Yeah, me with all my millions.'

'Nevertheless.'

'These people,' Gina said. 'Why would they have sued you?'

'Oh . . . you know,' Henry sighed. 'For being annoying.'

'Actually, Henry attacked this Ethan fellow with camera equipment.' Charlie leaned back in his chair and started chuckling. Henry blushed and smiled. 'Broke the poor bastard's wrist!'

'Well,' Gina said. 'Why would you do a thing like that?'

'Oh ... y'know. It was kind of an ... impulse. I apologized afterward,' Henry said. 'A lot.'

With one hand Charlie patted Henry's shoulder and with the other took a cigarette from Henry's pack. 'The Powderkeg here sometimes has a little trouble distinguishing the real world from its celluloid counterpart, don't you Henry? And that was a classic case.'

'At times, I have to admit, yes, things can get ... a little muddy.' His face was on fire. He crumbled a bread roll onto the white tablecloth.

'Henry was shooting a little independent production starring himself and his former-buddy Ethan, and he somehow came under the great misapprehension that Ethan was physically threatening his girlfriend Bambi.'

'He had a gun in her mouth, Charles.'

'It was a *starter's pistol*!' Charlie shouted, slapping the table.

'Calm down,' Gina said.

'They're guns,' Henry said. 'Sort of.'

'Took out two of the distressed damsel's teeth as well!'

'I didn't mean to hurt her,' Henry said. 'Or him.'

'This Ethan,' Gina said, pointing a finger at Henry. 'Why did he have a pistol in this Bambi's mouth? Was it sex-related?'

Charlie roared and slapped the table again. 'Sex-related! Gina, you tiger!'

'Calm down,' Gina said.

'Uh, no, it wasn't,' Henry explained to Gina's finger. 'He was just rehearsing an improvised scene for this film I was trying to make. He and Jean-Luc Godard felt that my script was missing a crucial element, and Ethan was, uh, he was trying to provide that element. Which was a gun.'

'Well,' Gina said with a loud and hungry finality. 'What a charming story. Can we order now?'

#7. In the last week of November Henry received a tattered old booklet in the mail. It was the owner's manual for a Mannlicher carbine and the cover was stained and rotted at the edges. There was a rust-colored thumbprint on page four, which showed how to clean the rifle. The postmark on the envelope was smudged. He had no idea who'd sent it to him, or why. He was tickled and intrigued for a while, then forgot about it.

#8. Audrey began to travel to Europe for work. Henry often became convinced that he was going to be killed somehow while she was away and that there would be no opportunity to do the right thing by his girlfriend, the precise nature of which he was not sure. She returned from these trips tired, occasionally sunburned, her suitcase rattling with small foreign coins she placed in jars and planned to take back with her next time, but never remembered to. Henry was glad of Audrey's absent-mindedness, for while she was away he would remove from the jar a coin from whatever country Audrey happened to be in and sleep with it under his pillow: a silver-banded 500-lire piece if Audrey was at a furniture show in Milan; when she went back to Copenhagen for a trade fair, he chose a Danish one-krone coin, in the middle of which there was a hole, and on both sides two tiny hearts. The coins made Henry feel closer to his girlfriend and at the same time reminded him tangibly, with a sour hint of relief, how far away she was.

#9. Gradually, Henry began to lower the dosages of his pills and worked on finding more effective combinations of the drugs, based at first on complementary colors, then on relative size, on alphabetical and/or numerological factors and, finally, on his psychiatrist's quite insistent recommendations.

'You simply cannot treat these drugs like that, Henry,' Felix Wagner warned sternly. 'They're very strong. Even the side-effects have side-effects, you know. You'll lose yourself if you're not careful. If it's not too late already.'

'How would it be too late already?'

The doctor cracked a thick and crunchy knuckle, as though he was preparing to punch Henry in the head. Henry slowly moved his head back. 'I know the name of that girl you spoke about during our first session, the one whose name you couldn't remember.'

'From the beach house? With the lobsters? *Her*?'

'That's right.'

Henry's voice went up a notch with disbelief. 'How?' He physically followed the note by straightening up in his armchair. 'How could you know her name?'

'Well, it's quite interesting as a matter of fact. Over the weekend I happened to watch a movie called *Annie Hall*–'

'I love that film.'

'I'm quite sure you do.'

'Best Picture, Best Director, Best Screenplay and Best Actress in 1978. That final scene where he talks to the camera and compares his relationships to this joke about a guy whose brother thinks he's a chicken, and he says, "I need the eggs." It's brilliant. The whole thing is brilliant.'

'So you've seen the film a number of times.'

'Oh, yeah. Not for a while, but I've seen it plenty of times. I love it.'

'Your girlfriend's name –' Dr Wagner waggled two fingers apostrophically over "girlfriend's" '– is Annie, Annie Hall. Or Diane Keaton, depending on how one views these things.'

Henry looked to his left, then his right. 'What do you mean?'

'The entire scene of the couple at the beach house trying to boil the live lobsters is directly from *Annie Hall*. Even the joke about placing some butter sauce and a nutcracker at the back of the refrigerator to frighten the lobster out. It's a movie. It didn't happen to you, Henry. At first I thought that perhaps it was coincidence, that maybe a similar lobster-boiling incident had in fact been part of your emotional makeup and that you merely borrowed the butter sauce quip. But then later in the film, to illustrate the difference between Annie and his subsequent lovers, Woody Allen – or Alvy Singer, depending on how one views these things – inserts a montage, part of which incorporates a second lobster-boiling scene with another woman who watches him scurry about the kitchen. She is nonplussed by his antics and tells him to –' Wagner bent his head and flicked through some papers. 'She tells him, "You're a grown man." This, all of this, is almost precisely the description you gave me in our initial session of your own happiest and saddest moments. These images – the very idea itself – is taken entirely from the movie.'

'Well, la-di-da,' Henry said slowly. 'La-di-da, la la . . .'

'And so is that!' Dr Wagner exclaimed. Then immediately shifted down, clearing his throat as though it was a gearbox. 'As I presume you're aware.'

Henry let out a long breath. 'I guess so. I'm still shocked, though. Obviously.'

'Because you're aware of the fiction?'

'No, because somebody cashed my check for the beach house rental.'

'Really?'

'No. I'm joking. Trying to, anyway. I'm in shock. I mean, I was really upset when Annie and I broke up. She was a terrific girl and it was fun knowing her.'

'That seems inappropriate to me. And emotionally wasteful.'

'She wasn't your girlfriend, Doc.'

'Nor yours, Henry. Come on now, she's a fictional character.'

'Not entirely. A lot of her character was based on Diane Keaton, who's real. So, y'know, she almost exists out here with the rest of us.'

'Nevertheless, it's simply not possible for you to have gone to a beach house – or anywhere else, for that matter – with Annie Hall.' Dr Wagner raised his eyebrows. 'And I assume that you and Diane Keaton were never . . . an item.'

Henry recoiled slightly. 'God, no. Did you ever see her in *Reds*? She was so twitchy and shrill.' He lowered his voice slightly and said to himself, 'Although I wonder how much of that was Beatty's fault. He directed her.'

'But your confusion of some scenes in a movie with your own experience is at the very heart of your trouble, Henry. It's the essence of your problem. And I think it would be dangerous, very dangerous, for you to continue to live like this, outside reality.'

'Well, yeah, I guess you're right, but in a way I suppose it's a bit like the joke I mentioned before. The one that Woody tells at the end of the film, about this guy who goes to a psychiatrist and says, "Doc, uh, my brother's crazy. He thinks he's a chicken." And, uh, the doctor says, "Well, why don't you turn him in?" And the guy says, "I would, but I need the eggs." So even though Annie and I never actually dated or anything, I guess that's how I feel about my relationship with her, and films generally – y'know, it's totally irrational and crazy and absurd . . . but I guess I keep going through it because I need the eggs.'

Henry's egg discovery marked the end of his sessions with Dr Felix X. Wagner, which Henry missed for several reasons – he liked the way the man had listened so vividly, the pleasantly medicinal air of the office, and the way the Berber armchair had seemed to mold itself to fit him – but mostly because he'd always meant to ask the psychiatrist about his resemblance to Clark Kent, and whether when he took off his shirt and tie there was a skintight blue-and-red body suit underneath. Henry doubted it, of course, but he'd always wanted to make sure.

30

Henry and Audrey were at a small independent cinema, watching a Japanese film by Kitano Takeshi called *Hana-Bi* ('Flower-Fire' or 'Fireworks'). It was a strange, almost narcotically poetic, yet quite violent film about guilt and love and loyalty. There was a scene in which the main character's former partner, a police detective, sitting in a wheelchair on a sandy beach, discussed what he would do with his life now that he had been shot in the spine and crippled. He considered taking up painting or perhaps haiku. Moments after he spoke these lines, Audrey leaned into Henry's ear and whispered:

'Rolling right along,
In this rotten steel wheelchair,
Because I got shot.'

Unable to help himself, Henry laughed loudly through his mouth and nose and eyes, Audrey shuddering with silent glee by his side, until a person in front turned around and harshly told him to be quiet.

Afterwards, in the foyer, Henry started laughing again. 'God, Aud,' he said, wiping dried tears from his eyes. 'I didn't know you could do that. That was hilarious.'

'I make them up all the time. I'm addicted to it,' she explained, smiling. 'That just seemed like the right moment to tell you one.'

'Really?' Henry asked. 'All the time? God, I had no idea.'

'How 'bout some sushi?' Looking to one side of Henry, her lips moving quickly and silently in time with the fluttering fingers of her right hand, Audrey continued:

'In a small tatami room.
I just love raw fish.'

Heat. Somewhere nearby, in the same neighborhood as Henry and Audrey, lived a young film maker named Darla van Popje. Henry saw her from time to time, in the supermarket, strolling on the opposite side of the street with her face tilted up toward the sun, or sitting alone in a café. A year or so earlier Darla had had a great and wholly unexpected international success with a low-budget feature she'd written and directed, about a child actress in the 1930s who had to pretend that her pet Mexican hairless was actually her baby brother because she couldn't afford a three-dollar dog license. The film was called *The Magic Cocktail* and starred 'the discovery of the year', Bambi Yessno, as a pushy but lovable stage mother (who had all her teeth, Henry was relieved to note when he first saw Bambi smiling at him on the film's poster). And for a short, bright while, Darla, even more than Bambi, was everywhere: nodding and smiling eagerly on television; attaching herself to her handsome hairdresser boyfriend's strong arm; earnestly quoting film theory in newspaper interviews; look-ing successful and elfin in glossy magazine pages. Darla was a very pretty girl – perfect white skin, a broad smile and alert, engaging eyes beneath lovely arrow-head eyebrows. She favored bright clothing, dazzling washes of color under a leopardskin coat which she seemed to wear all the time. Even in still photographs she exuded a vibrant and irresistible energy.

Henry had, of course, been hot and sick with jealousy, steadfastly refusing to see *The Magic Cocktail* – even when it was eventually released on video and later became available at a weekly rate. By that time, he'd had more than enough of gamine little Darla van P. And by that time, apart from infrequent reports of Hollywood's mysteriously enduring interest in the young talent and what her next project might be, most of the fuss had finally died down.

Darla had changed. When Henry saw her these days, she was always hurrying, and carried with her a palpable nervousness, glancing over her shoulder as though she was being followed. She draped herself in anonymous black clothing. Strangest of all, she had taken to wearing an enormous pair of square, black plastic sunglasses which covered half her small, white face. She seemed to be in disguise – but why? and as what? Henry often felt a strong impulse to stop her in the street as she rushed toward him, stop her and ask if she wanted to have a coffee and tell him what went wrong. Ask her if this was what happened when you made films – did half of you disappear, or wish to?

'I shot a film of my father,' he imagined telling his tiny, pale confi-dante. 'And it made him disappear.' Whenever he let himself think about saying something like that his breath would become short and constricted, his neck and face growing so red and hot that he had to head straight to the nearest faucet and douse his burning face. And as he scooped handfuls of water onto his forehead and cheeks, Henry always wondered if he was, at the same time, diluting or disguising tears that may or may not have been falling from his eyes. Sometimes he would wipe a finger across a cheek and lick the tip to see if it was salty, remembering Rutger Hauer's line in *Blade Runner*. 'All those moments will be lost in time, like tears in rain.' God, he hoped so.

*

The method. Henry took a couple of weeks off work over Christmas and, both inspired by and bitterly envious of Darla van Popje's success, decided to have another shot at making a film. He would hire a digital video camera and shoot it over a weekend. It would be a film about nothing much in particular – his favorite subject. The narrative would be whatever took place on the day. A simple exercise in realism, with long takes, few cuts and absolutely no script. It would be difficult to get Charlie and Audrey (both in the born-to-play roles of themselves) to ignore the camera, but he'd edit out the parts that seemed unnatural. Henry liked the idea of a personal take on the dynamic between three friends. And before he'd shot a second of footage – a moment, a breath, a glance – he had decided he would call his film *Point of View*.

There was one problem – his persistent photographic absences led Henry to suspect that he might not appear on the videotape. He had to find somebody to play himself. He supposed it would have to be an actor . . .

The only guy who answered the ad ('Wanted – Me' was the first line, which Henry thought was intriguing and rather catchy) that Henry posted on the noticeboard of an arts college a few days later was a freshman with the unlikely name of Alec Name. Name, a drama student, was far too handsome for the part, especially his eyes, which were a bright watery blue; still, Henry thought, directors can't be choosers. He spent several afternoons coaching Name in Henry's mannerisms, idiosyncrasies, tics, tricks, inclinations, frailties, anxieties and vanities; his moods, tempers, tones, facial expressions, vocal expressions, instincts, sensations, sentiments, gaps and particular tastes in just about everything. Name took copious notes, and Henry found the experience of sharing his self-obsession sublime.

'Will there be any nudity?' Name asked once. 'Do you sleep in the nude?'

'I sleep in *a* nude,' Henry had replied, blushing slightly. 'I wouldn't call it *the* nude. Not with my body.'

Early one evening, soon after new year, Name came over to the house to meet Audrey. 'Call me Henry,' Name said, with an outstretched (but limp) hand and as sullen a look as he could manage with his excellent teeth, rosy cheeks and bright eyes.

'I'd really rather not, if you don't mind,' Audrey said.

Name looked at Henry. 'Do I mind?' he asked, as he sat down on a chair in the opposite corner of the room.

'Of course you do,' Henry answered firmly. 'It's my name.'

'Please call me Henry, Aud,' Name said.

Audrey's face twisted with distaste. 'Do you have to call me Aud?'

'He does,' Henry said. He turned to Alec Name, who was awaiting his cue in the corner. 'You do.'

'I do,' Name told Audrey, his eyes never having left her face.

Audrey sighed slightly and her face relaxed back to normal. 'All right. But it's making me very uncomfortable. Those are your clothes he's wearing, aren't they?' she said to Henry, waggling a long, red fingernail at Name. Audrey looked thinner and more tired these days. Henry wondered if being with him was ageing her prematurely.

'I prefer to think of them as ours,' Henry said. 'His and mine.'

Audrey's finger still waggled at Name's chest. 'I bought you that shirt.'

'For my birthday on . . . September 1st. And I'm still very grateful,' Alec Name said. 'Thank you, Aud.'

'So what do you do for a living, Alec?' she asked. Name said nothing. Audrey huffed. 'I mean, Henry.'

'I left a sporting equipment company a few months ago and now I'm a supervisor at a telemarketing firm. Mostly in market research, as opposed to cold-calling sales, which I find a little . . .' Name looked over at Henry with neat, raised eyebrows.

'"Grimy" would probably be the word I'd use,' Henry told him.

'Grimy,' said Name.

Henry made a decision. 'Listen, Alec – I'm speaking to you as Alec Name now, not as your character, Henry Powdermaker – I think I should leave you to try and be me without my assistance for a while. You're going to have to get used to making it up as you go along and you should begin as soon as possible.'

On the couch, Audrey was giving Henry a steaming, sharp look which he knew meant that he should absolutely not leave her alone with the actor. But in the interest of his film, he elected to ignore it. 'So see you later, and good luck being me. It's not easy, and the rewards are few, except for living with this wonderful woman.'

Audrey caught up with Henry just as he reached the front door. 'You're not really going to leave me with this complete stranger, are you Henry?'

Henry smiled. 'What stranger? He's me – you'll love him.'

Charlie was far more interested in his chicken, fries, orange soda and an *L.A. Law* re-run than in discussing Henry's film. Henry didn't blame him. It was growing increasingly clear, even to Henry himself, that he was becoming more boring as he got older.

'Audrey's very patient with you, y'know,' Charlie said, his mouth and chin glistening with chicken fat. 'Very patient.'

'I know.'

'I hate to use a daytime-TV expression on you, but you're really "not there" for her.'

'I know.'

'You should be – and don't say "I know". It's obnoxious.' Charlie burped thinly.

'That's why you're not showing up in all those photos. I believe in the power of metaphor. You're just literally not there.'

'And you should be a fat bastard from all the junk you talk and eat.'

'Nah, I believe in the power of metabolism even more than that of metaphor.'

Henry laughed. 'So where's old Gina?'

'Gone.'

'Gone where?'

'Gone, baby.' Mr Rocket waved his hand vaguely. 'She just wasn't ... flippant enough. Not only that, she was always getting near me and eating very crisp apples right in my ear. I can't stand that sound. It's disgusting. And the crisper the fruit the worse the sound – and this broad was practically pulling 'em straight off of trees.'

'I had an idea that superficiality'd be the end of you two.' Henry clapped his friend on the back. 'I'm proud of you, Charles.'

'And if she couldn't find an apple she'd whip a carrot out of her bag and start munching away on that. Or a stick of celery. She was a walking market, this kid. And you shoulda heard her with M&M's – like a fucking pinball machine.' Charlie took a long sip of soda. 'So anyway, Vanessa and I are –' he paused to release another burp – 'getting married. I want you to be my best man.'

'Good God!' Henry slid to the floor. 'When did this happen? When did you two. . . .? I mean, you're going out for half your life, then you break up for twenty minutes and now all of a sudden you're getting married?'

'Breaking up was the worst mistake either of us ever made, but we had to give it a try. We'd only ever slept with each other. We were practically virgins.' Charlie paused and looked at Henry. 'I mean, you'd slept with more women than me. *You*. Anyway, you gonna do it or not, babe?'

'Of course. Of course I am. But why did–'

'We've found each other again, Powdercase. It's love. Also, she's pretty pregnant. What could be better?'

Henry thought for a minute. 'Nothing, I guess. Congratulations. Twice.' He held out a hand.

Charlie shook it. 'Thanks. You want a Coke?' Like they were sixteen again.

Henry wanted to give Alec plenty of time to get to know Audrey, so an hour after his elevation to best man, he and Charlie were still sitting side by side, watching *The Manchurian Candidate* – Laurence Harvey as a brainwashed Russian agent programed to neutralize the president. 'I wonder if I'll ever be assassinated,' Henry said.

'Assassinated? Who the hell would want to assassinate you, baby?' Charlie turned. 'Besides, don't you have to have done something worthy in public life to warrant assassination?'

'Yeah, you're right, I think you do.' Henry kicked off his shoes and balled up his toes, a tension-relieving trick he'd learned from Bruce Willis in *Die Hard*. 'I mean even if somebody shot, say, Tom Cruise, even he'd only be considered killed rather than assassinated. Assassination seems to apply only to political figures. Lucky bastards.'

'Like those Gandhis. They're always being assassinated. It's practically in the family contract. Get born, be political, get assassinated.'

'They're the Kennedys of India, but without the overbite.'

'All pretty big, important people. Not just regular Joes like you and me – especially you.' Charlie thrust a thumb at Henry.

'Sal Mineo got knifed in an alley. But he was just an actor – and a homosexual, to boot – so it was only a murder.'

'Harvey Milk was gay. That was still an assassination.'

'I'm not saying it doesn't count if you're gay. But there does often seem to be an element of sanctimonious blamelessness about the life of the assassinated person. They're all pretty . . . angelic or something to begin with.'

'That's true. On the way up even while earthbound.'

'There was that attempt on Reagan, and he was an actor once, but they always referred to it as an attempted assassination, not attempted murder.'

'Yeah, but he was the president at the time, not just a former actor. There's a big difference – not so much in his case, obviously, but usually.'

'I guess once you make it to president, no matter what you've done before, you're guaranteed assassination material.'

'It's a comforting thought.'

'If you're the president. What about executions? I wonder if I'll ever be executed. I suppose I'd have to commit a serious crime . . .'

'An assassination, maybe.'

'Yeah. Then I could be executed. Hanged, gassed, electrocuted, injected or shot through the heart by men in hoods.'

'And what about this – why do they call it "an execution-style killing" when some Mafia guy gets two bullets in the back of the head? That's not how the state does it when it executes people by firing squad. They should call the Mafia jobs murder-style killings.'

'Tommy Lee Jones, or, if you prefer, Gary Gilmore, got it in the chest. That was a proper execution. A classic.'

'And what if a president committed a capital crime and was sentenced to death? Would he be "executed" or "assassinated by the state"?'

'Very interesting. Very interesting indeed.' Henry nodded

interestedly. 'I have no idea. Overall, I think it works like this – important people are assassinated, criminals are executed and the rest of us just get murdered.'

When he finally finished eating, Charlie went into the kitchen and returned with two large glass ashtrays. 'One each,' he said. 'I'm planning on doing a lot of smoking tonight. It's been a bad week.'

'In which field?'

'Legal. Band's off for three months. We're "emotionally exhaus-ted".' Charlie rolled his eyes. 'So what's brought all this assassina-tion business on, anyway? Apart from the movie. You seem very preoccupied with it.'

'I think somebody's trying to kill me.'

Charlie nodded his head equivocally and eagerly.

'I mean it, Charles.'

'I know you do. And I think you may be right.'

'Why would you think I think somebody is trying to kill me?'

'Well, come on, Henry, take a look at yourself. You've annoyed a hell of a lot of people in your life.'

'Enough for them to want to kill me?'

'You said it, sister, not me.'

'Yeah, but it's the kind of thing people say. They don't mean it. Unless they're in the mob or something. To tell you the truth, it kind of offends me how readily you believe me.'

'You're my friend. You tell me you think somebody might be trying to kill you, I agree with you. I'm trying to support you.'

'Thanks.'

'So who do you think it is? Ethan the gunslinger?'

'No, he certainly doesn't like me, but he's too . . . unmotivated to commit murder. Plus, as I've told you before, it was a misunder-standing. Anyway, I'm not sure they're actually trying to literally kill me, it's more like somebody's trying to scare me into having a heart-attack or something.'

'How?'

'I got a bullet in the mail.'

'Ouch!'

'This is very b-comedy you're doing, Charles. Very Buddy

Hackett. I'm serious. Some bastard sent me a bullet. And I'm telling you, it's really not a pleasant thing to unwrap, a bullet.'

'And you're not even a lawyer.'

'Exactly. That's the kind of mail you should be receiving. Is it against the law?'

'Probably.'

'You don't know?'

'No, I'd have to look in one of those big leather books on the shelf behind my desk. But probably. Was there a note or anything? An inscription on the casing – "To Henry, from your number one fan"?'

'Just the bullet. The odd thing is that something bizarre like this happens to me almost every year around late November.'

'Gimme another one of your cigarettes, will you? Mine are too mild.' Henry handed Charlie a cigarette. 'So what's the pattern?'

'It's always toward the end of November. I get something creepy and death-oriented in the mail. The bullet, a sort of 1960s lady's hat with blood all over it, stuff like that.'

'What else?'

'Well, it's hard to remember because I only realized it was a pattern after quite a few years, so I've forgotten some of them. Or I guess I have. All those prescription drugs I was taking. One year there were some blown-up stills from the Zapruder film, the parts where you can see Kennedy's head coming apart, all pink and spongy.' Henry paused and tapped his fingers against his forehead. 'Oh, and an instruction manual for a rifle, a Mannlicher carbine.'

Charlie laughed and coughed. 'Fuck!'

'I know.'

'Fuck!'

'Yeah.'

'Wow . . . fuck.'

'I agree.'

Charlie moved away from Henry slightly, and turned his thin neck around to look his friend square in the face. 'You're being punished, Powderburn,' he said confidently. 'And there's a definite theme developing.'

'Oh, I know I'm being punished, Charles, but for what?'

*

Audrey and Alec were sitting together at the dining table, bright food stains on their napkins and plates, spattered palettes of yellow, brown and green, an empty wine bottle between them. Neither of them appeared to notice Henry as he walked back into the room.

'So if that story is true, Name's not your real name, is it?' Audrey's cheeks were hot and red with laughter and she was grinning widely.

'No, it is indeed not. I had it changed,' Name said. 'My real name is Alec Amen, but nobody took it seriously.' He leaned over the table, holding out a firm hand; his voice was deeper and tawnier, and he suddenly seemed far more charismatic than before. Henry didn't like it – after watching the guy pretending to be Henry, the real Alec didn't seem real. Too handsome, too charming.

Holding her eyes with his own, Alec encased Audrey's proffered hand in both of his. 'I'm very pleased to meet you, Audrey.'

Henry watched as Audrey smiled – comfortable, enchanted and happy – for real. She took a mouthful of wine, paused as her fingers danced on the bell of the glass, then spat the red back out as a haiku suddenly leaped from her.

'Alec the actor,
Pretending to be Henry.
Free to call me Aud.'

Motivation. The next night Henry took Alec to a nearby bar, where they drank whiskey and Alec practiced being Henry in public for a few hours. The barman seemed to like him and Henry couldn't help noticing that Alec received a heart-breaking number of lingering looks from the women in the bar. Lingering looks and eager smiles. 'A final question,' Alec said, as he and Henry pulled on their coats and embraced the chilly night air. 'What's my motivation?'

They began walking down a wide street lined with tall, leafless trees clawing at street lamps and the sky. 'For taking this role? How would I know? You need the money, I guess,' Henry said. On the pavement outside every third or fourth house was a discarded

Christmas tree – a small fir, cypress, pine or spruce – lying on its side, awaiting collection the next morning by a garbage truck.

'You're not paying me anything.' Name breathed enthusiastically into his hands a couple of times, then thrust them into his coat pockets. 'And in any case, that's not what I mean. What I'm talking about, what I'm getting at is, what's my – by which I mean me as Henry Powdermaker, so your – what's your motivation?'

'For what?'

'Anything,' Name said, and after a moment added, 'Everything. Getting out of bed in the morning. Going to work. Frying an egg. Walking the dog. Kissing Audrey, rubbing her toes, watching the way she subtly sniffs at each mouthful of food on her fork, trying not to let you notice before she slips it into her mouth. The way her left eye closes just a moment before her right when she blinks. Running outside to catch a snowflake, reading poetry, wishing a friend luck, eating a cookie, smoking, drinking, laughing – everything.'

'Catching a snowflake? Eating a cookie? What am I, a character in a children's book?' Henry said, stopping and staring down at a miniature pine tree lying by a trash can, two planks nailed into its trunk. 'I can't stand the way people just dump these things,' he muttered to himself, then continued loudly, 'What's my motivation for frying an egg? I don't want to sound uncomplicated, Alec, but on the rare occasions that I find myself frying an egg, it's because I don't want to eat it raw. Or poached, which I find nauseating.' In a foggy pool of light, Alec scribbled hurriedly in his notebook. Henry bent down and picked up the Christmas tree, placing it upright next to the road, wondering if Alec was writing the words 'glib' and 'obnoxious'. Perhaps 'nauseating'. 'I haven't walked a dog since I was ten, poetry unnerves me and I never rub Audrey's toes. Ever.' Henry stood back from the tree, pleased. 'That's better.'

'God, I'd love to swallow a strand of your DNA.'

A picture of himself standing at a stove and frying up a batch of his own DNA popped into Henry's head. Wearing a gingham apron, serving fried DNA, garnished with a zucchini flower, to Alec Name. 'You really wouldn't.' He shook away the image and crossed to the other side of the street, where there were three or four more Christmas trees lying on their sides. 'Come on, give me a hand,' he called.

Alec crossed the street. 'I find you fascinating.'

'Well,' Henry said nervously. 'That's, uh, well, I'm very flattered, but you really shouldn't. Actually *being* me is not fascinating, it's more . . . irritating.'

'Either way, I have to know what drives you, what keeps you going, for my performance to ring true. To have any substance.' Name uprighted two trees at once, slamming them firmly onto the cold ground. 'They do look better this way,' he said. 'Let me ask you, Henry, why exactly are you making this movie? What's it for?'

'To see if I can make it,' Henry answered, looking down the street for more sleeping trees. They continued walking, stopping to replant a tree whenever they came to one. Henry remembered that he'd done this tree thing before, when he was a kid back in the Pine Tree state. The state whose motto, he suddenly remembered, was 'I direct'. He laughed.

'*Make it* make it, or literally, physically make it?' Alec asked.

'What do you mean?'

'Henry, by now I know you well enough to know that you know what I mean. Stop being so coy and answer me.' Name brushed green needles from his coat. 'Although I know what you're going to say.'

'No, you don't.' Name's insistent intimacy in the area of Henry's psychology made Henry feel as though he was trying to keep a secret from himself, so he didn't even attempt to blur his answer. 'I applied to film school five years in a row after I left school – at least that's what I tell everybody. Audrey, Charles Rocket, my mother and brother, everybody. They all think that I gave up after those first five years. But the truth is that I've put in an application, a whole new execution of the assignment they require, every single year since I left high school. And, needless to say, been rejected every time. Although I should point out, in the interest of not coming across as an unmitigated loser, that I was wait-listed twice. Not that that really counts for much. But still.'

'That's fascinating!' exclaimed Name, showing many of his very nice teeth. 'I *knew* you were fascinating!'

'Thanks. You're very kind,' said Henry, drily. 'So that's why I'm making this film. To prove that even though I'm a film school reject, I'm not a hopeless failure. I've also saved a fortune in unspent school fees, which I've stashed away in case they do ever let me in.'

'You can still be a film maker, Henry, a director, producer, writer, whatever you want.' Alec's words came in cold white puffs that disappeared as soon as they were spoken. 'But there's one thing you need, one rule above all others, like they're always telling us at drama school. The secret of success, Hollywood success, anyway. And they keep dredging up failed relationships, broken marriages, ruined lives and spectacular careers, all of them the result of living by this secret rule.'

'Which is?'

Alec paused dramatically, a small cypress in his right hand. 'No attachments. You have to live for no one – and with no one – but yourself. Your world must consist only of you and your dreams.' He placed the tree on its base and draped some muddy tinsel over it.

Henry lifted the top off a trash can and peered in. 'Do you believe in that?'

'As you I believe it and will remain committed to the idea for the duration of the project,' Name said, watching Henry remove a foil pie dish from the bin 'Personally, I think it's a crock, but you're a whole other matter. I think it'd work for you.' Name seemed convinced; he seemed to believe in Henry.

Henry was quiet for a long time, thinking about giving up his life for a dream. He ripped out the centre of the pie dish and, as his gloved hands manipulated the silver ring, he thought about some of his favorite film makers. Over the years, he'd read enormous amounts about the directors, screenwriters and producers responsible for his most cherished films. And he was always disappointed to learn that in one way or another, virtually every key person involved with these films was an egomaniac, a lunatic, a greedy bastard or, in many cases, simply an idiot. And every single successful film maker that Henry admired had put their careers –

their dreams – ahead of everything else in their lives. It seemed an awfully big sacrifice to make. But even as he had the thought, something inside him stirred. He turned and looked back down the street, now lined with battered and drooping but erect Christmas trees that nobody wanted. As he placed the silver wreath he'd made on top of the last tree, he asked, 'Does Audrey really sniff her food?'

Scene stealing. 'Are you an actress?' Ray Milland asks.

Theresa Russell is perched on the edge of a desk, legs crossed, wearing a short-sleeved shirt and a white chiffon bubble skirt, an outfit that looks more fifties rather than authentically thirties (which it should) even though the film – *The Last Tycoon* – was made in 1976. She giggles and answers. 'No, I'm just Daddy's little daughter. What're you?'

'Oh, I'm just a lawyer from New York.'

Removing a ruffle of smooth green notes from a billfold, studio boss Robert Mitchum tells Ray Milland that his daughter is too intelligent to be an actress. 'She's graduating from Bennington in June – with honors.'

Theresa Russell swings her leg and smiles at Ray Milland. 'I love actors, though.'

Watching this scene in his darkened living room, with the television volume turned conspiratorially low, Henry is inspired.

31

Wardrobe. Henry pulled a pair of black pants over his plaid boxer shorts and stepped out of the tiny changing room. 'So I've saved about sixteen thousand dollars in unpaid tuition fees,' he said, concluding his 'Film School Confidential' confession.

'Unpaid?' asked Charlie, slipping on a tuxedo and stroking the dark-olive lapels.

'Well, I guess "unrequired" would be more accurate.'

'In fact, completely accurate.'

Henry reached behind his neck and fiddled with a bow tie. 'I figure I need another five or ten thousand to see me through what may well be a very, um . . . lean period in Hollywood.'

'If not actually skeletal.' Charlie laughed and shot his shirt sleeves, revealing a pair of Masonic cufflinks. He shook his head slowly in wrist-appreciative awe. 'These look superb.' His eyes returned to Henry. 'So how does Audrey fit into your California plans?'

Henry looked away from the hard blue gaze. 'I don't know,' he said, his voice low because, thanks to the film he saw the previous night, he knew very well. 'She'll have to break up with me, I guess. After we make the movie.' He swallowed and forced his tone back up. 'So what do you think?'

'What do I think about what? Your tie's crooked. Are you asking me for a loan? I really hope you're not because–'

Henry turned to a mirror and adjusted the black wings of his tie. 'Of course I'm not – I know about Vanessa's terms. I'm just asking if you have any brilliant ideas about where I might scare up a few grand.'

'Rob a bank. If you don't go in armed . . . First offense . . . I could probably get you off with around three to five. It *would* be your first offense, wouldn't it, Henry?'

'Yes, it would. But I don't think I've really got the cojones for a bank job. We're not wearing cummerbunds, are we?'

'Don't be ridiculous. How about a gas station, then? Or a convenience store? Work your way up.'

'You ever see *Papillon* or *Midnight Express*? They leave quite an impression, I can tell you. I really don't think I have the stones for a prison jolt.'

'If you got caught.'

'Oh, I'd get caught.'

'All right. You got any healthy organs left? Not counting your stones.' Charlie pointed at Henry's feet. 'Shoes.'

'Not too many,' Henry said, slipping into a pair of black wingtips. 'I don't use my spleen as much as I used to – that could be worth something. But I was really thinking more along the lines of stocks and portfolios and insider-trading type stuff. You got any of that in your office?'

'I work for a law firm Henry, not a brokerage. Or an investment bank. Or a "sanitation" interest.' Charlie stretched his eyebrows archly over the word 'sanitation'. 'You want a mob contact? Is that it? Because that I can actually help you with.'

'Really?'

Charlie nodded. 'They're actually pretty nice people, the Costellos. They have a laundry interest. Some concrete as well.'

'Are they like the Corleones?'

'Not at all. Except for they're kind of . . . the modern Mafia.'

'So more like Henry Hill's crew from *Goodfellas*?'

'No, they're actual, real people. Businessmen.'

'Who are gangsters.'

'I suppose so, yes.'

'Are you surprised, Charles?'

'About what?'

'About the fact that your life has turned out where you're a mob lawyer?'

'I am not a mob lawyer. The firm I work for does some work for the Costellos. Not me personally.'

Henry laughed. 'And you've got an Italian fiancée! Good God. Should I start calling you Carlo from now on? Wait.' Henry pointed up at the ceiling. 'Do I hear Nino Rota coming through those speakers?'

Charlie shook his head slowly at Henry and stared, saying nothing. Then, very gradually, he raised his right hand, finally holding it over his heart and beginning a cold smile. Standing there in the antichromatic black and white of shirts, ties and tuxedos, it occurred to Henry that he and his friend looked a lot like Sonny and Michael in the opening wedding scenes of *The Godfather*. 'You're a good lawyer,' Henry told Charlie, recalling Michael Corleone's words about Tom Hagen. 'Not a Sicilian but I think you're gonna be *consigliere*.'

In the end Henry chose robbery. Two days after Charlie and Vanessa's wedding, which was when his hangover finally began to recede, Henry sat down and began writing a long and pointlessly violent hold-up scene for a movie. 'Two men, CARLO and FRANKIE, need money to pay for Carlo's wedding. Wearing pink rabbit masks, they hop into a crowded diner waving slick silver pistols and large yellow bananas . . .'

When it was finished, he sold it for a few thousand dollars to a guy who produced television commercials. Through a former colleague of Rex Gillespie's, Henry was put in touch with a hot young commercial director looking for something 'bold and original, yet violent and highly personal' to shoot for his showreel. Henry had seen some of his commercials and was eager to help the guy pursue his overhyped, underlit vision.

'Not a bad haul for a few days' work, huh?' he told Charlie over the telephone.

'You call that work, sitting at a desk typing up stories?' Charlie said. 'You love doing that. It's not work if you love it. There have to be equal elements of boredom, despair and self-loathing for an undertaking to be work.'

'Is that a fact,' Henry said dully.

'It's a fact here in the real world, babe.'

'You all set for the shoot tomorrow?'

'The gun's cleaned and oiled. And my dentures are packed.' Charlie put down the phone laughing loudly.

Henry hung up then immediately dialed Alec Name's number.

'Henry Powdermaker speaking,' Name said.

'Hi Alec, it's me.'

'Who?'

Henry sighed into a smile. 'You. Me – Henry. The *real* Henry.' The real Henry shook his head and stifled a laugh with the thought of what he was about to do. 'Listen, I know I told you that the whole film was gonna be improvised but there's one small change I'd like to make. Just one line I want you to deliver, on or off-camera I don't really care just so long as you make it convincing.'

'Okay, what is it?'

Henry told Alec the line.

'Good lord, are you serious?'

'Yes, Henry, I am,' Henry said. 'And I hope you will be too.'

32

Criticism. Despite the faults with his film – poor sound quality in parts; wild variations of exposure; some rough, jarring edits – Henry was very pleased with it. It was a strange but likable film. On the other hand, he had several complaints about Alec Name's performance as Henry Powdermaker. Although Name managed to capture a certain authentic whining quality he seemed overenthusiastic about other things. There was too much scenerychewing, and giving Audrey the European coin, Henry would never have done that; he'd told Alec about it only as research, not for him to use as some bit of romantic trickery. Which, of course, Audrey now believed to have been born in Alec's heart, not Henry's, and would never know otherwise. Learning that he'd been calling his best friend the wrong name all these years was quite a shock, too. But for the most part, Alec did seem to come across as actually quite a lot like Henry. Which was very interesting, but sort of horrible.

Dissolve. There was a moment early on in the film which bothered Henry more than anything else, but he couldn't put his finger on exactly why. It was when Alec/Henry and Audrey were in the bathroom, just as the camera moved from Audrey's face and over to the mirror as she applied her lipstick. Henry played the brief scene over and over again, wondering what it was that unsettled him so much. It wasn't that Alec Name was standing there fully tanned and half naked pretending to be Audrey's handsome, flat-stomached boyfriend. It wasn't the visual cliché in reverse of moving from Audrey's face to the mirror. He rewound and watched the scene again. The focus was right, the light was good, the sound clear, the acting fine, the cuts in and out were smooth, and there was a nice, clear depth of field, except for when the whole frame was occupied by the mirror just before Audrey's reflection came into it . . .

And suddenly Henry knew exactly what it was. He remembered

the mirror in *The Servant*, how when he was a kid he'd wondered whether or not a person could be reflected in a mirror on film. He grabbed the VCR remote, leaped off the striped couch, sat close to the television and rolled the tape backward frame by frame until the screen was full of the shimmering silver-white of the bathroom mirror. He froze the image and crawled across the carpet closer to the television, praying that he would come face to face with himself. When he did not, he was neither surprised nor discouraged, and continued staring into the frozen white, as though by will alone he could project himself into the image. And eventually he did see himself, not in the mirror, but reflected in the distended glass of the television, small and dim and opaque, but there nonetheless. It was close enough, he decided.

'Alec's very good at being you,' Audrey said later that evening. She was in her customary position, lying on the candy-striped couch, happy and comfortable in the living room.

Henry said, 'Let's hope he uses that power for good instead of pointlessness.'

'So what will you do with it, now that it's finished?' Audrey asked. Henry looked over at her. She seemed nervous, her gray eyes wide, pale and skittish with guilt.

'I really don't know,' he confessed, absently tucking in his shirt. 'I'd like to try and get it into some film festivals. Except it's shot on video and your better class of film festival tends to sneer at that. Unless you're one of those Dogme guys. It makes me sick, but I can see why. Once you start embracing video at a film festival, any idiot with a Handycam starts to think they're Alfred Hitchcock.'

'Why don't you use it to try and get into film school?'

'I'm too old. It's too late for me.'

'Don't be so silly. You're not even thirty.'

Henry stood up and began to pace about nervously, but sat down again when he thought that it might look too stagey. 'Well, I feel too old. And you know, five attempts. I don't think I could stand the humiliation of another failure.' He blushed slightly at the lie.

'You won't necessarily fail.'

'Look at the odds.'

'Well you've got no one to blame but yourself if you don't even try.'

'But I have tried. They don't want me. I'm probably really bad at this whole thing but too stupid to realize it. Or maybe the reason it's all gone so wrong is because of the lack of the presence of God in my life. Or even a god. Some obscure, lower-case figure who demands sacrifices or something.'

'But it's not God's, or a god's, fault.'

'Well, whose is it? *I* don't want to have to take the blame. I hate the way things have turned out for me. I tried to make it different. I tried and tried and tried, but everything failed. It's much better to have absolutely no ambition. To not care.'

After some time Audrey said, 'You really mean that, don't you Henry?' She sounded exhausted, defeated.

'Yes.' Henry was firm. 'Yes, I do.'

Audrey said nothing. Henry retreated into tight silence, hating himself for being so calculating. He could feel Audrey staring at him as she made a tooth-cleaning noise with her tongue. 'Henry . . .' she said, and in the pause he knew what was coming. 'Alec . . . Alec is in love with me. He told me that day by the cottage in the cemetery.' *I know*, Henry thought, *I asked him to*. 'I didn't want this to happen, I really didn't, but . . . I have to be honest with you . . . I think I'm in love with him, too.' She sat up and put her head in her hands. Henry could see tears and spit falling through her fingers and onto the carpet. He felt his throat tighten and the corners of his mouth pulling downward, beyond his control. Audrey was sobbing rhythmically now. It was awful and heart-breaking and he wanted to help, to tell her that it was okay and that she'd be happier with a better version of himself but when he said her name she covered her ears with her hands.

Part 5

Part 3

33

Fade in. Ext. Los Angeles – Day. A cold, litter-lifting wind skids along the pavement near the corner of La Brea and Sunset. Nestled in the brown-green hills behind and above are the homes of Lew Wasserman and Sid Sheinberg, enormous palaces with pools, patios and private screening rooms. There is a crack of thunder as the sky clouds over. From an upstairs apartment window, Mexican rock from a fuzzy AM radio drifts down to the street; mixing with the wind is a chorus of throaty males urging a woman named Dolores to wake up. Henry turns up the collar of his jacket, hunches his shoulders and slopes along the dull street. He is on the wrong side of the warm, steamy windows, affecting a soulful, brooding menace as he paces the mouth of an alleyway. He hears a cry.

'Hey! Jimmy Dean!'

Henry slows and turns. Freshwater-blue eyes look up at him, shining through the dirty shadow of too much hair. A young man dressed in shreds of black and gray is sitting on a wooden vegetable crate, his legs kicked out to show that he doesn't care about anything, or much. He is younger than Henry – on the desperate side of twenty – and cancer-thin; a junkie probably, or maybe just sick and hungry.

'Yeah?' says Henry, flatly.

The young man asks, 'You got money?'

'A little.'

'You got spare? I'll tell you the story of my life for five bucks. It's useless but interesting, and not a word of a lie. All one hundred per cent verifiable. Five bucks'll get you a whole generation and change.'

Henry is intrigued by the neat spin on straight panhandling and takes a few steps into the alley toward the guy. 'Okay, go ahead.'

'You better get comfortable, Jack. I've led a long and rich life.' With a flap-tongue boot that shows nails, the young man kicks a crate toward Henry, who sits down and holds out a pack of cigarettes. The guy takes two and swiftly tucks them inside himself, like a magician working backward. His eyes cloud over and his smile fades. Everything loses focus. Even the street sounds blur into fading mesh. Rain begins to fall.

Beneath a torn and faded poster of a red clown whose smile he seems to have borrowed or stolen, in a dry monotone with a voice from far away, the young man speaks.

'They were both slipping around the wooden floor in their socks. Everybody was in their socks. All the shoes were piled in another room. If you stood in that other room it must have seemed like something from a concentration camp. A room full of warm, empty shoes. But there was music nearby. Dancing music. And the sounds of laughter and clumsy seduction. My father was not much of a dancer but he loved crowds and noise and I believe he mistook these simple things for joy. He was Polish. Over from after the war. He saw a young woman up to her elbows in her handbag and thought he knew what she was looking for, so he slipped across the floor and offered her some gum. Chocolate, chewing gum and pantyhose. Maybe he thought he was a G.I. She took the gum with a promise and a smile. It snapped and broke her nail. It was a small town – Caliente, near Bakersfield – and they'd never seen snapping gum before. She laughed so hard she fell over. He tried to pick her up but the floor was so polished you could see up dresses. They slipped around in their socks, falling over one another. Everybody was in their socks. It wasn't unusual. They danced the jitterbug and they got married and my father forgot the ring. Everybody thought it was another of his pranks. But he wasn't kidding. Every pocket was patted but the ring was nowhere. Somebody had a tin of washers in their truck, so they used one of those instead of a ring. The priest blushed and chuckled and my father laughed with his sharp, Polish jaw. But my mother never took him or their relationship seriously after that. She should have known right from the start with the gum that broke her nail.

'I was born a little while later. Seven, eight months. I had a train set with a light on the engine and I used to sit in the dark hallway watching it go around and around. It was nice. I was alone. Maybe there was a dog outside, barking at nothing. That's all I remember until I was around fifteen when my mother had another baby. A girl. My sister. But my father was too old. The baby's eyes were too close together and the ears were bigger than looked right. She was another thing to add to the weight of my father's guilty life. After the baby he walked close to the walls and the small jokes stopped. I gave the train set to my sister but the light had gone out and she wasn't interested. My mother was distant, distracted, moody. She talked to the baby in whispers, as though they were sharing secrets. But what can a baby know? Our house became dirty and the food always tasted a little old. A year later it was dusk. We went to a carnival and my mother dropped the baby from the top of a Ferris wheel. A bundle of blood and blankets in the center of strangers' screams. I won a porcelain horse at a coconut shy. It was rearing up, frightened or angry. My mother spent the rest of her life at an institution in Camarillo. Even though it wasn't far away, my father and I visited her no more than every couple of months. Each time we went, my father wore a different style of hair on his face. A moustache, a beard, sideburns, a goatee. It changed every time. My mother was distressed and uneasy during the visits. She made most of her conversation at me. But I had pimples and was ashamed. Later she died with a few others in a fire that they had made from sheets and heating oil. At her funeral my father was clean-shaven for the first time since the Ferris wheel. I threw down a tight handful of dirt and chipped the casket with a stone by accident.

'I fell in love with a tall, skinny girl who was an artist in her heart but a hairdresser in her hands. We drank ourselves into sexless stupors to ease the boredom. It worked for a while but then became routine. She was beautiful and felt sorry for me. I felt sorry for myself. She was raped and murdered and found buried under a door in a field two hundred miles away, both her hands stuck pushing up, a pair of her own scissors in the side of her throat. I didn't kill her, but her brothers beat a limp into me for life. I didn't want anything more to happen to me so I took a bus out of town forever. A blond cowboy listened to a small radio and offered mints to children and nuns. He cried out for his grandmother in his sleep. This great city was the end of the line. I got off deep in the morning and wondered what I would let happen to me. Back then my ass was fresh, white and clean, and it sold for good money. My first pimp, Pedro, was straight, which was lucky for me but I didn't know it then. He took money from me but left me alone. No beatings and no angry sex. And he knew people. I've been fucked by some pretty important people. TV people. Movie people. Not lately, but when I was ripe. I was a pretty hot date for a while. These days I'll spit for twenty and drink for twenty more. Things got fucked up after Pedro died. He got leukemia. Surrounded by fucking murderers and dope dealers, all kinds of assholes, and the stupid spic dies of some lame fucking blood cell disease. I started to ride the horse after he kicked. I'd never touched the stuff before because I was high on cash money and being star-fucked. Things were as interesting as they were ever gonna get. Like I never imagined. But then, just like everyone I've ever known except my poor father, Pedro bade me adios.

'I was bored with it all, but once you're in this game it's not so easy to get out. You just get out of your mind 'cause it's almost the same. There was all sorts of vermin after me for their little stables. So I shot junk to shoot the boredom and the pain. I hung with other jockeys. We did all the usual crimes and got all diseased up from sharing or fucking or being fucked or whatever. Some jail time, some public hospital, a lot of unconscious and the years go by. Things go on and on, around and around. You look for the light but the light's gone out and everything's the same, only some days are worse than others. Some things you remember, most of it just passes by.

'My last trick I'll probably remember for the rest of the week. He wasn't right. Crazy from something worse than drugs. Life crazy. His name was Adam and he had a wrong face. Not hinkey or anything, but wrong for the way he acted. He was car-wreck handsome. Fucked up, but straight somewhere underneath. His smile was the only thing that wasn't shattered. I take him to my place and cop his wad, a hundred, before he shoots it. He sits on the edge of my bed and looks around like he's casing it, but I know the look and this isn't it exactly. But similar. "What's your pleasure, Adam?" I ask him. I'd shoved the bills up the faucet, so now I owed him. I don't rip people off, you see. It's my ethics. Adam tells me to do whatever I do. I tell him I do everything. And it's true. These days it's the only way to get by. So I have a gun and a couple of knives in some spots around my house for getting by. "Everything's good," Adam says and laughs this laugh that freaks me, but I laugh too, to make him at his ease. That way they come quicker and get out of your life. For a while anyway. I kneel down by the bed and unzip him and start the work. He runs his fingers through my hair and it's all normal until I feel him on the way and he starts moaning words about how Van Gogh cut his ears off and would Charlie Parker be any good if he was thin and straight and white and didn't laugh himself to death in front of a rolling black-and-white TV juggler. Then Adam pulls my head away and stands up and kicks me onto my back and tears open my pants and starts going at me like I'm a fucking trombone or something. My hairs catching in his teeth and all tearing out. He's going crazy with all these jazzed sound effects and it's freaking me pretty bad so I reach around under the bed, pull out a blade, put it at his throat and tell him to get the fuck out. "Cut me," he says with a mouth full of my pubes. "Keep my fingers, I don't use them," he says. "Take my ears off and I'll paint you a pretty picture." The smile is way gone and he's scaring the Christ faith out of me as my veins ice up and I get the junk jag right away in my guts but I step away from him and keep the knife flashing in his eyes, he's looking at it like he's gonna take it and stick me when all of a sudden he starts crying like a kid, rolls into a little ball and I don't know what the fuck, the pain's reached up into my throat so I leave him balled up and bawling and go to the refrigerator and shoot some iced water to cool my blood and when I go back to my bedroom and the guy's gone, Adam's gone, like he was never even there.'

The guy's stopped a while before Henry realizes it, his mind still transported by the story. He feels awful for the fellow, his miserable life. He shakes himself out of the young man's past and reaches for his wallet. 'Here, you can have everything I've got on me.'

The storyteller smiles and adopts a bright, warm, sunny tone. 'Ah, don't worry about it, Jack. A five'll do nicely. Thanks for listening. Tell you the truth, I'm not really that fucked-up kid. That's just a rehearsal piece I do for auditions and stuff. I'm an actor – Toby Strong. How are ya?' He stands up grinning and thrusts out his hand.

Henry refuses to shake. 'Well, Jesus . . . you . . . you . . . complete fucking . . . tinhorn!'

'It's a tough town, Jack. You get ahead any way you can,' Toby tells him.

34

Henry had been in Los Angeles less than ten days when he'd encountered Toby Strong that unusually wet afternoon. At first he had been appalled, even oddly insulted by the incident. But gradually he felt less sick and cheated and burned, more amused and callused. He'd even gone past the alley again and heard Toby delivering his monologue in precisely the same tone with precisely the same stutters and pauses to other five-dollar audiences. Henry laughed about it now – a little forcedly, he had to admit – after all, L.A. was a tough town and you really did have to get ahead any way you could.

But what, Henry wondered often, did all the rich, happy, creative, successful, fulfilled people he knew of do before they took that first step? Who were they before they got ahead and became what they were?

After a lot of thought, and with Woody Allen and Mike Nichols as vague examples and inspirations, Henry decided to become a comedian and screenwriter. To try, anyway. Screenwriter tapping away at a keyboard by day; comedian with a uniquely skewed take on modern life, dazzling and amusing and provoking large, grateful audiences by night. Alone in his small west Hollywood flat on the second story of the Alameda Apartments, a pink stucco mission-style block of six near the Paramount lot, Henry tapped. He tapped his life for material, then tapped it into a second-hand computer he'd bought from a pawn shop on Melrose. The 'p' on the keyboard was tricky, sometimes producing dozens of 'p's and sometimes none at all. Sitting at a desk beneath a picture of Preston Sturges, staring down at a chopped and cropped, purple 1950 Ford with lime-green hubcaps, Henry tapped.

He had plenty of ideas for films. *Man or Superman?* was about a hero who assumed the disguise of a mild-mannered but muscular psychiatrist, but who was in reality a superman who constantly saved the world using a combination of Freudian therapy and the lime-green death ray which shot out of his purple eyes. In *Titanic – Part II*, DNA scrapings are taken from Leonardo DiCaprio's frozen body and he is resurrected in the twenty-first century, only to be tragically killed once again when he takes the first commercial flight to the moon and the spaceship is struck by the *Titanic*, which has somehow ended up in space. *Zombie in the Suburbs*, a big-budget remake of the eight-millimeter original, was about a zombie in the suburbs. A one-line idea was a shot-for-shot remake of *Casablanca* with an entire cast of ten-year-old children. There was a treatment of an untitled film about the true-life horror visited upon the crew of the USS *Indianapolis* after the ship was torpedoed by a Japanese submarine in 1945. Another lengthy treatment for a film called *each other's lullaby*

outlining the extraordinary experiences of the Boston blueblood/
dilettante/libertine/poet/publisher/pilot/photographer Henry Grew
Crosby who committed murder-suicide in 1929. A screwball
comedy called *Ralph?* concerned a guy in a tuxedo who gets hit
on the head by a small asteroid and begins a crazy search for
Ralph Bellamy. *The Big House* was about three people – two
young men and a young woman – who lived in a large house
which was also a kind of prison. One of the young men did
something awful (by accident) to the other young man but was
forgiven and allowed to stay in the big house. But was it a home
or a prison? *Bases Loaded*, the story of a ball player trying to
make a comeback, he lifted wholesale from a pitch in *Sunset
Boulevard*. Henry's favorite title was *35 mm – My Life as a Complete Idiot* (Harry Pennyspender fails to get into film school five-
to-ten years in a row and ends up as a failed comedian/screenwriter
in Hollywood), but he didn't much care for the plot.

Henry's best film idea was vaguely inspired by his encounter
with Toby Strong. It began as a short story called 'Falling for
Holden.'

35

Story. I don't even know what the hell I was doing in New York
anyway, if you want to know the truth. I don't even like the place
that much. It's too big and confusing and often you never know
who the hell you are. All I know for sure is that I fell in love with
her right away and pretty soon after that I ended up in here.

I'm gonna skip all that David Copperfield kind of crap about
where I was born and what my lousy childhood was like and all.
In the first place it's just not that interesting and in the second
place, there's already a whole bunch of other goddam embarrassing stuff that I have to admit to anyway. I wish like hell I didn't,
but I do. I really do.

You've probably guessed by now that I've read *The Catcher in the Rye*. I've read it about two thousand times in fact. I just keep on reading it. I can't help it – the goddam thing just keeps on showing up and I keep on reading it. I was even reading it just recently when I was in New York that day when I met this girl. It was right in my back pocket.

It was cold that day. Not snowing-cold, but breath-cold. You could see your breath if you breathed out real hard. I was breathing like a goddam asthmatic, partly because I'm a pretty heavy smoker and partly because I'd been running around Madison and 75th Street all over the place looking for the Whitney Museum, which I couldn't find anywhere. I could've sworn they'd moved it since last time I was here. That's the thing with New York – it's simple blocks and straight grids everywhere but it seems different every time you go there. Like they've changed it around a little bit while you weren't looking. If you start out from just slightly the wrong place you can end up getting lost forever. Anyway, I'd just about given up and was lighting my millionth cigarette of the day when out of nowhere this big stupid St Bernard leaped up on me and knocked me flat on my back. All of a sudden I was lying on the sidewalk looking up at the sky. I was pretty surprised. You don't see too many unleashed dogs in the city, especially ones as big as that goddam St Bernard. But I didn't really mind, because he was a pretty friendly bastard and was slobbering all over me in that dog way while I lay there only pretending to fend him off. If I really wanted to I could've fended him off easily. I'm a pretty good fender, if you want to know the truth. And in a way, I think that crazy St Bernard knew that.

Anyway, a minute later I heard a voice crying, 'Laddy! Laddy!' and some very rapid footsteps clacking and echoing all over the place. And before I had time to get up and brush myself off, this girl was standing right over me with an empty leash in one hand and a Styrofoam skull in the other. And boy, she was beautiful.

She was the kind of beautiful where you can't speak because you wouldn't know what the hell to say to a girl like that if you had a million years to think about it. Two million even. And at the same time you knew you had to think of something to say or you'd never see her again and you didn't even want to think about what your life would be like if you never saw her again. It's not a great situation to find yourself in ever, let alone with a big dog lying right on top of you.

So there we were, Laddy and me lying on the sidewalk and her looking down at us. Everybody was silent except for old Laddy's hot, noisy slobbering. It felt like we could stay that way for years, when all of a sudden she broke the spell by smiling this gorgeous smile. I was free. I could speak.

I pushed the dog off me and stood up. And right away, because she'd smiled that terrific smile, I could think of hundreds of things to say. Unfortunately, I said just about the stupidest thing anybody could say right at that moment. I pointed to the goddam foam skull she was carrying and said, 'So did ya know Yorick well, or did ya just know him?' Boy, I was really showing off with that crack. Even to tell you exactly how I was showing off sounds like showing off but unfortunately I have to or it doesn't make any sense. What it is, in the play *Hamlet* everybody thinks it's, 'Alas, poor Yorick. I knew him well.' But it's not. It's actually, 'Alas! Poor Yorick. I knew him, Horatio.' So that was how I was showing off. I hate having to remember it and tell you about it, but that was the way it happened.

It didn't matter anyway, because she began laughing her head off as though it was the funniest goddam thing she'd ever heard. She may have even been laughing at me for being such a show-off. I'm not sure because I forgot to ask her about it later. She had a beautiful laugh too. Some people have terrible laughs, all loud and horsey, or it sounds like it comes from their nose or something. But not her. Hers was like music. I know that's a terrible cliché, but it's true. When she laughed on the corner that day, it was like beautiful music and light fog rising from her mouth into the cold.

After that I didn't waste too much time before finding out her name and if she lacked a boyfriend and seeing whether she might be interested in meeting me for a cocktail that evening. I was pouring on the charm. I can be quite charming when I'm in the right mood and I was really pouring it on. Frances said she'd be delighted. Delighted. It kills me when somebody says they'd be delighted to do something. Especially if it's something I've suggested. Even more if I've suggested a date with me.

Boy, I was so excited I could hardly stand it. As soon as I got back to my crummy little room at the Edmont Hotel, I started calling up all my friends back in Montreal, where I live, and telling them that they should start packing and come to New York right away because I was going to get married in a day or two. I actually told them I was getting married. That's how excited I was. I even called my mother to tell her the big news. The thing was, all of them had heard that kind of stuff from me a number of times before, so mostly they just kind of laughed and said, 'Yeah, sure. See you soon.' They said it in a nice way, of course, but it still depressed the hell out of me that everybody found me so unreliable. Or predictable.

I wore my best suit. The only suit I had with me to be completely accurate, but it was still a hell of a nice suit. I always travel with a good suit because you never know if you're going to meet somebody where you need to wear a suit. It's terrible if you can't represent yourself properly in the right clothes. I'm not particularly handsome, but I do like to make the best of things by wearing nice clothes. I have to admit that I had a pretty nice tie and shoes as well.

The fact is I pass myself off as a bigshot quite frequently, if you want to know the truth. Old moneybags. I just can't help it. I get a big kick out of spending money on other people and pretending that I don't have a financial care in the world. I'm practically broke almost all the time but I can't stand admitting it to myself or anybody I'm with. It's a problem, I know it.

Anyway, we met that night at this little hole-in-the-wall type bar on Houston Street called Milano's. It's not particularly swanky or anything but they have this terrific jukebox there, and I always feel a whole lot more comfortable if I'm surrounded by music I like. Some people don't mind what they listen to, no matter how awful it might be. I have to have the right music around me – usually just so I don't have to hear other people's idiotic conversations.

Frances arrived right on time and waved at me when she walked in. She actually waved to me in a bar. I damn near fell off my chair when she did that. It was so corny and sweet. She sat down opposite me and put her face so close to mine I thought she was gonna kiss me. But all she did was say, 'Well, hello.' Then she said something that really threw me. She said, 'You know, I don't even know your name.'

Right away I knew I was in trouble. I mean she looked absolutely terrific in this fur hat and one of those furry hand-warmer things. Not too many people could get away with stuff like that but old Frances pulled it off like a pro. So I didn't really know what to say because of how great she looked. And I have a really bad name. Not like a criminal record name but one that just sounds dumb. Like it doesn't really belong to me.

'Uh . . . Holden. Pleased to meetcha,' I said and shook her hand like a real cornball. I didn't want her to say anything about the name, so right away I asked her what she was in the mood to drink. I got up from the table in such a hurry that I almost knocked the goddam thing over. 'I'm gonna have a scotch and soda, you want one of those?' I said. 'They're really very good. If you like them and all. I'll get us a coupla those, whaddaya say?' She nodded and I got the hell away from her as fast as I could.

I calmed down after a few more drinks and quit acting like such a madman. Not that she seemed to mind me hyperventilating all over the place. I was talking about a hundred miles an hour too. All 'goddam this' and 'phony that'. It was quite a feat, I can tell you. I even asked her if she knew where the goddam ducks from Central Park go in winter. I really did. And I have to tell you, she loved it. God, she was a nice kid though. And interesting as hell too.

She lived with her folks in Manhattan and was studying medicine and psychiatry, which was why she was carrying that crazy skull. Before that she'd attended Dana Hall, which in case you never heard of it, is a very exclusive school. But she wasn't all snooty about it either. She didn't think it was the biggest deal on earth that she went to this very exclusive school. You take most people who go to a school like that, they think the rest of us have to start worshiping them right away. She didn't though. I don't even know why she mentioned it in the first place. I probably asked.

Somewhere in our conversation way up the back in the dark of old Milano's, Frances told me this great story from when she was little. How she'd gone to this kind of holiday camp at her school for the day where they just had fun playing games and all. This was when she was about seven or eight years old. That crazy age where you don't know what's going on – the bad stuff at least. Anyway, they spent the first morning inside a classroom and all the kids had to take their shoes off to save the floor or something. When they got let out at lunchtime old Frances left her shoes inside and the teacher had locked the door to the classroom. So she just wandered around the playground in her white socks doing laps of the concrete ring that circled the grassy oval, all crying and miserable and too scared to ask to get her shoes back. Her socks became all dirty because she didn't even take them off. That story damn near broke my heart, I can tell you. I was laughing when she told me but sort of crying in my mind at the same time. It killed me. It really did.

So then I started telling her some stories from when I was a kid. Only they weren't my stories. They were straight out of *The Catcher in the Goddam Rye*. I told her about me and Jane Gallagher playing checkers that summer in Maine and my little brother Allie's baseball mitt and how I went crazy after he died and all sorts of other stuff. Fighting with Ward Stradlater in the dorm and pretending my name was Rudolf Schmidt to this lady I'd met on a train. Boy, I was on fire. I gave her the works. She just sat there listening to me in the most beautiful way you could imagine. Her eyes were on me the whole time. I could tell that she really liked me. But it wasn't just that she was watching me – you could tell that she could see in her imagination everything I was telling her about. I could too, to tell you the truth. It was all pretty vivid and believable.

Then all the really bad stuff happened. I'd just finished telling Frances about my little sister Phoebe and this record I'd bought for her and how I broke it, and I guess I must have looked kind of teary, because although I don't even have a little sister called

Phoebe and it didn't actually happen to me, it was still pretty upsetting. Anyway, I must have looked upset because right then Frances put her hand over mine and said, 'Oh Holden, please don't cry.' Boy, I was finished after she said that.

I started bawling like a madman – the real kind, not the kind you get in literature – and trying to explain that my name wasn't really Holden and that none of the stuff I'd told her about was real. That I was just some regular idiot on a stupid holiday going crazy from being all alone in a city the size of New York. I could tell that she was quite confused and bothered by all of it. In fact, it probably annoyed the hell out of her, but I had to confess. I liked her way too much to go on pretending. I still wanted to marry her, for Christ's sake. I guess I must've been shouting by that time because she kept telling me to keep my voice down. But I can't remember too well.

Anyway, by the time I'd finished telling her about all that David Copperfield kind of crap – the real David Copperfield kind of crap about who I really was and what my not-particularly-lousy childhood was actually like – Frances looked kind of exhausted. And a little bored. She just shook her head and said, 'It's such a shame. I liked you so much. The other you.' It was terrible. I could've died.

But I didn't die, I just sort of disappeared. As though I'd fallen off the edge of a great field where I'd been playing and there was no one around to catch me.

36

Henry worked hard on turning these few scenes and characters into a screenplay – three acts, tension, drama, laughs and a happy ending, the whole bit. It wasn't easy.

As a comedian too, Henry was having a tough time. The main problem was that he wasn't very funny and in addition to being not very funny, he was somewhat shifty and nervous, lacking charisma and presence on stage. But he exclaimed a lot and he dressed unusually (gray suit, black tie, spectacles), and a comedian who looked like a near-sighted FBI agent who thought it was 1962 was enough of a novelty to get him in the door of most club amateur nights at least once. But no more.

Actor/comedian Richard Belzer (*Scarface*), someone Henry greatly admired and who happened to be hosting a try-out night at! in Glendale, told him, 'I'm not saying you're not good, kid, but when and if we ever need a comedy undertaker, we'll call you. Interesting tie, by the way, come with a matching psychosis?'

Actor/comedian Rodney Dangerfield (*Natural Born Killers*), a surprise guest at the Ha Ha Hole in Santa Monica, said, 'You're a funny guy, but not in the amusing sense of the word. More like how mental patients are funny. You ever think about a lobotomy? They can do wonders for your hairline. That tie's ridiculous. Looks good on you, though.'

Actor/comedian Jackie Gayle (*Tin Men*) stopped Henry before he left Hysterica in Culver City and said, 'You gotta find your comedic voice, son. Find that voice, then give it laryngitis, I'm begging you. Maybe tighten that tie a little more.'

Actor/comedian Chris Rock (*New Jack City*) sat down with Henry at the bar of the Comedy Shack and told him, 'Brother, you ain't funny. But you dress nice. That's all I got to say.'

Actor/comedian Janeane Garofalo (*Dogma*), the featured performer at The Bunny Fone, shoved a drink into Henry's sweaty hands and said, 'Lose the tie and drink this. It'll be good for your career – it's a hemlock cocktail. I'm from New Jersey.'

Actor/comedian Denis Leary (*Wag the Dog*) said simply, 'You're an asshole.'

Naturally, Henry was hurt and discouraged by these comments, but at the same time he was utterly thrilled to meet every one of his detractors. That was the thing he loved about living in Los Angeles – he could be walking along the street or having a coffee somewhere and he might see James Woods waiting for a cab outside the Chateau Marmont or sweaty Linda Hamilton skulking out of a gym; William Forsythe tossing a blackened match into the gutter or Ed Pressman handing his car keys to a parking attendant, who had no idea who the producer was; Vincent D'Onofrio buying a carton of Camels in a Rite Aid (Henry was absurdly excited to see that there was at least one other L.A. resident who smoked cigarettes); Tobey Maguire emanating an almost visible aura of niceness and decency and fresh-scrubbed goodness when a dog-walker's web of seven leash-bucking whippets became tangled in the actor's legs. Henry was pleased to the point of gratitude that some of the depth as well as the sheen of Maguire's Maguireness wasn't – or at least seemed not to be – an entirely celluloid construct; that he could see the man from up on the screen down here out in the world. Once, when Henry was hanging around the lobby of the Beverly Hills Hotel for no reason, pinch-eyed and scraggle-haired Dyan Cannon asked him for the time. 'It's just a little before two-thirty,' he said in his best voice. She cracked a foundation-flaking smile by way of appreciation, then walked away. When, after a few blank seconds, Henry remembered that she had been married to Cary Grant, he fainted quietly onto an overstuffed pink-and-green armchair.

He might have also seen: Peter Bogdanovich drunkenly staring down Heather Graham's loose shirtfront outside Morton's, the backs of his gold-ringed fingers constantly brushing against the top of her firm, faintly twitching thigh; Robert Downey Jr, Martin Sheen Jr (Charlie) and Jack Nicholson Jr (Christian Slater) sitting hunched in a smoky circle in a downtown bar, pumping raw blues music from a jukebox to make themselves seem like hard men while swapping stories about doing time, guns and hookers; Quentin Tarantino failing to convince a fellow diner in a café that he'd never read Elmore Leonard before he made *Pulp Fiction*; Courtney Love using her lawyer's briefcase to belt an autograph-seeking female fan in the teeth; Paul Schrader stabbing his brother Leonard in the back with either a plastic knife or a pen; Val Kilmer (not doing anything much, but Henry was still horrified because he'd always secretly hoped that Kilmer didn't actually exist); Bambi and Ethan speeding along Slauson Avenue in a convertible, their heads thrown back in joyous laughter . . . However, all these particular sightings occurred late at night, in dim light, and Henry was never completely sure whether or not the parties involved were actually themselves, or merely people who looked like them. There was, after all, thanks to sunshine and surgery, a certain homogeneous aesthetic to the denizens of Los Angeles.

But it was more than just star-spotting (or telling them the time) that made Henry almost nauseated with excitement about being in L.A.: it was the fact that all around him, day after day, films were being written, pitched, developed, green-lit, produced, distributed and consumed. He was living right in the heart of his dream, gratefully overwhelmed by it even as he realized that most of what went on all around him was just so much bullshit pursuant to creating further bullshit in the form of atrocious films. But while this tainted thrill would sustain him for a while, Henry knew that sooner or later he would have to make the difficult dream a potentially bruising reality. And he also knew that his comedy routine, at least in its present form, was not going to help.

'It seems that I'm just not funny,' Henry said to Charlie. He had his feet up on the steel railing of his first-floor balcony, his preferred place to talk on the telephone. Reclining in the middle of bright white concrete. 'In fact, I'm quite unfunny.'

'I've always said that.'

'Ha-ha.'

'I really have. Seriously. You've made me laugh less than seven times in my entire life. I mean even your funny bone isn't. What made you think you could get by as a comedian anyway?'

'Well most comedians aren't funny. So I thought it wouldn't be all that hard. But it turns out it is. I need a gag writer or a stylist or something. Maybe a trainer or a dietician might help. Can I use that funny bone line?'

'It's yours. But it's not very funny. So how's it going apart from that?' Charlie asked. Henry heard a child's cry in the background. 'Spencer says hello.'

'How could you give a kid a name like Spencer Rocket?' said Henry.

'He'll grow up, fella, and when he does the little bastard'll be so grateful he won't believe it. That's a name headed straight for greatness, Powdermaker. Straight to the top, from kindergarten onward. So how're you making money? You a script doctor yet? Got a stethoscope?'

'I'm more of a script midwife, Charles – I mean, uh, Charlie. Trying to assist with the difficult birth of my own offspring. It's hard, though. I can't seem to find the right . . . inspiration. To tell you the truth, I sit around doing nothing quite a bit.' Henry reached for his sunglasses. 'It's hard to work much in this weather. They really do have pretty good weather here, it's not just in the movies.' Down on the street the purple Ford rumbled, shook and took off. Sunlight tightened Henry's face. He heard Spencer squawking, or maybe laughing – it was hard to tell over the telephone. 'How's Vanessa?'

'Good. Her tits are enormous. She says she loves the kid so much that she literally wants to eat him. I'm constantly on guard, hiding the cutlery and stuff. The baby marinades.' Henry could hear Charlie lighting a cigarette.

'How's Biff? I haven't seen you guys too much everywhere lately.'

'I think it might be all over soon. I'm getting too old for sustained success. Rock belongs to the young.' Charlie sounded serious. 'I'm thinking of trading in my amplifier for a foot bath.'

'Really?'

'The senior partners are urging me to become . . . more like them.'

Henry thought for a moment, then said, 'D'you ever worry about who you are?'

'No, I always keep my birth certificate handy.'

'God, you're glib. What I mean is who you are in the world, in the scheme of things. It's like, how would you feel if you were Sam Elliott compared to Clint Eastwood? Or Scott Glenn even? It just doesn't make sense. Scott Glenn's a fine actor, terrific even, but where was his chance to really star? Then direct? Get all ubiquitous, then become an icon? Was it denied him because he decided not to get involved with films where he had to deliver cornball lines like, "Go ahead, make my day?" Or mess around with a fucking orangutan. It's just not right.' Henry sighed sadly. 'I wonder how he feels about it, Scott Glenn, I mean. I wonder if it keeps him awake. I bet it does. It'd have to. Sam Elliott I wouldn't know for sure, but probably.'

'Jesus Christ, Henry, haven't you got more important things to think about? Like for instance whether you're going insane? What the hell are you worrying about if Scott Glenn feels culturally hijacked by Clint Eastwood for? It's crazy.' Charlie exhaled a lungful of smoke. 'And who the hell is Sam Elliott?'

'Never mind. An actor. He's got quite an impressive moustache. Don't you ever worry that you won't be like Clarence Darrow or F. Lee Bailey?'

'I'm just glad I'm not Marcia Clark, babe. Not being her gets me through the night. Anyway, is this conversation about me or Scott Glenn?'

'Actually, I think it's about me,' Henry said, not too enthusiastically. 'As usual.'

'So who're you – Clint, Scott or the other guy?'

'Well, that's the thing. I don't know. I really don't know what I should be doing. Could be anything, but that's the thing, I guess, isn't it?'

'I guess it is.' Charlie spoke quickly and Henry knew he was wrapping up the conversation. 'You ever hear the Brooklyn Funk Essentials song "The Revolution Was Postponed Because of Rain"?'

'As with all the songs you ever ask me about, Charles, no.'

'You should find it and listen to it. There's a message in it for you.'

'What's the message?'

'Stop talking about it and do it. Get off your ass and do something!' Charlie shouted.

'Do what, though? Become a cowboy actor? I couldn't grow a moustache to save my life.'

37

Ever since he'd arrived in L.A., Henry had had trouble sleeping. Night after night he found himself suddenly awake at odd hours consumed by the startling and horrifying – but not entirely unjustified – feeling of profound and complete failure of both his body and his soul. He felt as though every organ was shutting down, that his already feeble musculature was liquescing into mush as he lay in bed, that his bones were calcifying, each vertebra in his spine fusing with the next until he would soon no longer be able to stretch, bend, reach or move at all. It seemed, too, that his thoughts were growing weaker or moving off in directions so pointless and obscure that he wondered if he was becoming a whole other, even more irrelevant person than he used to be. He wrote notes to himself which he looked at with dis-ease and embarrassment the next morning, like waking up next to a whore: 'The wonderful thing about ambition and a sense of who you might become, rather than who or what you are, is that it will never be satisfied. And nor should it be.' Just what the hell do I mean by *that*, he would wonder.

A great deal of Henry's daydream life was spent bumping into Madeleine Ford – on street-corners, at cinemas, in diners. In his slapstick comedy dream life he literally bumped into her and broke his ankle and she tended to him, Grace Kelly to his Jimmy Stewart in *Rear Window*. In his romantic comedy they met chasing after the same leaf in Central Park one dusty fall afternoon, then kept on almost-but-not-quite getting together until they were caught in a rainstorm back in Central Park, huddling under the very same tree which had lost the leaf that had brought them together in the first place. In his action-thriller scenario he appeared barechested, except for twin bandoliers slung across his torso, and rescued her from a bunch of ruthless terrorists who'd taken her hostage. In his classic Western fantasy he was the mysterious stranger who rode into town, drank some whiskey, played some cards, got in a couple of gunfights, ran some rustlers out of town and finally captured the heart of the pretty young widow with reddish hair who was always anxiously wiping her hands on her apron. In his actual, inescapable life, however, Henry continued to write letters to Madeleine which he continued not to send. It seemed easier that way because life, even when you lived it in Hollywood, was never like film.

Written and directed by. Even though Henry worked beneath a photograph of Preston Sturges, he had never seen a single one of the writer/director's films. They were never shown on television, virtually impossible to get on video or DVD, and no longer screened in small, shabby cinemas filled with wheezily chuckling buffs. Henry had never seen *The Palm Beach Story* or *Sullivan's Travels* or *The Miracle of Morgan's Creek* or *The Lady Eve*. He knew all about them – the stories, the famous lines, what made each of them great. He knew that they were smart, sharp, literate, funny, unsentimental, personal pictures. That Sturges was a pioneer. That before Woody Allen, Billy Wilder, Paul Mazursky and the sudden rash of suspect 'auteurism' that spread like a plague through film-making in the eighties, there was Preston Sturges.

Incredibly, but also somehow inevitably, square-faced, moustachioed Sturges had actually led the kind of knockabout, screwball life deftly depicted in his films. The sort of life that only happened to men with square faces and moustaches. A life almost wrenched with tightly plotted destiny: born in 1898, which was perfect timing to be raring to go in the Roaring Twenties; classically educated in France; a glamorous mother who was a close friend of Isadora Duncan; sent to Deauville at fifteen to run a branch of his mother's beauty product empire; drinking at places with names like Delmonico's and the Knickerbocker Grill in New York City; joining the Aviation Section of the Signal Corps; inventing a popular, 'kiss-proof' lipstick called Desti's Red Red Rouge; getting married four times (once to a breakfast cereal heiress); writing some hit plays; going to Hollywood; working; winning the first-ever Oscar in the new category of Best Original Screenplay (for *The Great McGinty*); opening the Players restaurant/club on Sunset Boulevard; making eleven great films in eight short years; quitting

Hollywood; writing for television; falling into debt and dying alone in a room at the Algonquin in New York, twenty minutes after a last big meal and last big drink.

This was the heavy gaze under which Henry worked – a man whose life and art he envied and admired; whose work he'd never seen. 'It's pretty ironic, isn't it?' Henry often said aloud, looking into that big, square face, the eyes twinkling above the thin moustache. 'Isn't it?'

A month or so after he finished the story 'Falling for Holden', Henry completed the first draft of the script version, which he named *Holen Cawffle* because he didn't care for film titles with verbs as the first word. *Leaving Normal. Falling in Love. Being Human. Killing Zoë.* They were all awful titles and pretty awful films. Perhaps even cursed. He finished the draft late one afternoon and, limp-fingered but high on achievement and the stark southern California light streaming into his apartment, decided to go out and get good and drunk.

Henry didn't have too many friends in Los Angeles. There was the guy downstairs, a graphic artist from Oklahoma called Shaker Townsend, and his girlfriend, Rainey O'Leary, a tall, busty blonde from Chicago who sometimes worked as a bondage mistress. Shaker owned the purple hot rod. Rainey owned some guns and liked to get around in a tight green Beverly Hills Gun Club t-shirt. Henry knew them a little bit, but not well enough to latch onto as drinking buddies.

Toby Strong was just finishing up his monologue for two delicately teared women in the alley near La Brea and Sunset. Henry stood a few feet away, waiting for the conclusion and possibly some sobbing from the audience. Moments later the two women brushed by him, dabbing at their eyes. 'God, you're shameless,' Henry said to the young actor, who was sitting on the vegetable crate in his gray rags. 'Is that it for today or are you planning some evening shows?'

'People tend to be somewhat reluctant to venture into alleyways after six,' Toby said. 'What're you doing here, man?'

'Have you by any chance ever heard of Preston Sturges?' Henry asked.

'Trudy Kockenlocker,' Toby said immediately. 'John D. Hackensacker. Harold Diddlebock. E. J. Waggleberry. Algernon McNiff. Woodrow Lafayette Pershing Truesmith. The golden age of film character names. I mean Jerry MacGuire, could they be more bread-and-milk Everyman?'

Henry's smile grew wide and spread into his eyes. 'Fantastic! You want to go get a drink?'

'Sure. Lemme just get changed.' Toby Strong disappeared behind a garbage container for a minute, then returned dressed Gaply. 'You know Sturges's mother gave the fatal scarf to Isadora Duncan?'

'I know,' Henry said as they walked out onto La Brea. He looked up into the hills and wondered which of the white concrete houses belonged to Sid Sheinberg or Lew Wasserman.

'You know what I hate?' Toby said as he opened a cab door for Henry. 'I hate how people are always saying what a sensitive intellectual Don Simpson was. He produced *Days of Thunder* and *Flashdance*. He was obviously an idiot.'

'Don't forget *Thief of Hearts*.'

Henry and Toby ended up at a tiny bar called Chez Jay's over in Santa Monica. Henry had heard that Warren Beatty used to hang around Chez Jay's back in the late sixties. Dr Kissinger too, he seemed to recall, so he liked the pedigree. The room was dark, lit only by a string of red Christmas lights over the bar, and decorated with ocean-themed brass and wood: an oar, a ship's bell, a porthole. The top half of the Dutch door was always left open, and if it was quiet you could hear the hush of the surf rolling in on the beach. In a dim corner up the back was a jukebox featuring Curtis Mayfield, the Jackson Sisters, Eddie Kendricks, Sly Stone, the Wild Magnolias, William deVaughn and more. Charlie would have loved it.

Henry and Toby Strong sat at the bar and drank Coors Banquet straight from the bottles. 'So where exactly are you from?' Toby asked, tapping his soft fingers on the bar top in time to the song Henry had selected.

'Not L.A.,' Henry answered.

'Yeah, well, that's pretty obvious. The way you walk around

all wide-eyed with that smile on your face. Anybody can tell you're not from L.A. Anybody from L.A., I mean. And let's be honest, who else matters? So where?'

'I grew up in Augusta, Maine.'

'That's the other side of the world.'

'I know. It's beautiful, small and boring.' Henry took a big drink. 'I think I belong here. I like it here.'

'It's a tough town, Henry.'

'Yeah, you mentioned when we first met. How do you get by, apart from your performance-begging?'

'Any way I can. Except drugs and prostitution, that's strictly for the act. I do anything I can. Television, commercials, walk-ons, walk-offs, extra work, anything. Hell, I'd be happy ending up like Jack the Body. I once even went on that fucking "Family Feud" wearing a pink tuxedo and a hideous flouncy shirt, hoping that some casting director'd see and think about me for one of those seventies retro slacker comedies they were doing every ten minutes a few years back.' Toby shook his head at the memory and began laughing. 'They made us name three famous Rudolfs, me and my brothers. Three famous Rudolfs for five thousand bucks, in the bag. Geoffrey says, "Rudolf the red-nosed reindeer." I say, "Rudolf Nureyev" and then my idiot brother Thomas says to the host, Richard Whatsisname–'

'Dawson.'

'He says, "I got it, Richard. I got it in the bag – Rudolf Hitler"!' Toby shouted, drowning out the music, slapping the bar, beer suds spilling over the back of his hand. 'Rudolf Hitler!! For five thousand bucks. Can you fucking believe it?'

Through his own laughter, Henry said, 'Should I?'

'I'm not making this up, man. I've got the tape at home. Rudolf fucking Hitler!'

The barman lolled over. 'Enough with the Hitler, all right boys? I got sensitivities.'

'So, Henry, you an alcoholic or drinking for pleasure?' Toby asked.

'I just felt like it. I finished a script today.'

'You and every other dishwasher in L.A.'

'But mine's really good . . . Boy, I wish I didn't say that.'

Toby touched Henry's arm lightly. 'I'm not trying to bring you down, it's just the way it is.'

'I know.' Henry ordered another round from the Hitler-sensitive bartender. 'I really do. And even if it was the best script in L.A., I probably wouldn't be able to sell it anyway.'

'Why not?'

'It's riddled with typos. The letter "p" sticks on my computer, so even the cover reads "Holen Cawffle by Henry PPPPPPPPPPPPowdermaker".'

Toby suddenly straightened up on his stool. 'Henry who?' he asked.

'Powdermaker – with one "p".'

'Are you related to Jack the Body?'

'Who's Jack the Body?'

'Jack "the Body" Powdermaker, also with one "p".'

'I'm related to *a* Jack Powdermaker who's my father, but I haven't seen or heard from him in around twenty years. He's a barely employed actor. Or was, anyway.'

'How old is he? I mean, it's an unusual name, Powdermaker, right? There couldn't be too many of you.'

'I dunno. He'd be around fifty-five, sixty, I guess.'

Toby nodded. 'Jack the Body's right there.'

'What's this guy do, exactly?'

'A lot of things, but mostly plays dead.' Toby slipped off the barstool and fished around the back pocket of his chinos. 'Here, I have his card.'

Henry went over to the jukebox and dropped in a quarter. For a moment he could hear the quiet crash of waves behind him. 'One more time,' he said, and the Jackson Sisters began to sing once again: 'I believe in miracles . . .'

After drinking with Toby for six more hours, Henry arrived home, very tired and very drunk. But even through the thick boozy haze, the card inside his wallet and the wallet inside his coat pocket felt heavy and hot. As he made his way stiffly through thick, balmy air along the path toward his apartment block, Henry saw Shaker Townsend and Rainey O'Leary sitting on their front porch. Shaker was smoking a long, black cigar and drinking something brown from a big glass. Rainey was cleaning a tiny pistol.

'Evenin',' they both said at the same time.

'Hey, you Okie.' Henry's voice was a muddy mixture of speech, song and slur. 'I believe in miracles, I believe in miracles, baby. Oh, I believe in miracles, don't you?'

Shaker and Rainey both laughed. Rainey said, 'I believe in the good people at the Derringer company.'

Shaker puffed lovingly on his cigar and said, 'Ah mahself believe in the firm, golden thighs of the women of Cuba.'

Henry laughed. 'You're an Okie.' Henry swayed. 'I believe I'm gonna pass out.' And his faith was not in vain.

38

The next morning Henry's head hurt, both from the hangover and from where he'd hit it on the path out front. Moving around the hot, still air of his apartment was slow and difficult. In the bathroom mirror he saw that there was a plaster over what he assumed was a cut on his forehead. His slept-in clothes were rumpled. His tongue was fat and dry. The thick air stuck in his throat; it was like trying to breathe cotton wool. With a cringing shudder he realized that after he passed out Shaker and Rainey must have carried him upstairs, searched for his keys, carried him inside and put him on his bed.

Henry took Jack the Body's card out of his wallet and wondered if it could really be his father's. And if it was, did he really want to see him? What would he say? He poured himself a Coke, drank it in a single stinging gulp that brought tears to his eyes and dialed the number on the card.

After three rings the telephone was answered. 'Jack the Body.' The voice sounded distantly familiar. Henry hung up and felt a quick rush of fear, panic and horror as it hit him that perhaps his father was in the city. A 310 area code. He could be just a few miles away. Henry sat still.

There was a knock on his front door. Slowly, full of sugar and dread, Henry walked over to it and opened up. Shaker and Rainey stood in the hallway, grinning. 'Afternoon,' they said together.

'Hi.' Henry raised a hand limply. 'I'm sorry for calling you an Okie, Shaker.'

'Why?' Shaker said, stroking his long jet of chin hair. He looked tiny next to his girlfriend. 'It ain't no kinda insult. Say listen, we're headed over to Bob's Big Boy in Toluca Lake tomorrow night to check out the rods. You wanna come with? They make the greatest cheeseburger in the Valley. You look like you could use some grease.'

Henry's bare feet shuffled on the floorboards. 'Yeah, probably not. But thanks, anyway. And thanks for, uh, for putting me . . . to bed.'

'We had to bring you up and make sure you didn't choke on your own vomit!!' Rainey said, then began laughing keenly: 'Hyekhyackhyukhyock!' She sounded like a hysterical chicken. A hysterical chicken from Chicago. 'A death in the building makes the property value absolutely dive!'

'Thanks for the plaster on my cut, too,' Henry added. 'D'you wanna come in? For a coffee or something?'

They both caught the reluctance in his tone and declined. 'Fact is, you don't look like you could even boil water right,' Shaker said.

To his surprise, Henry found that he only thought of the fact that his father might be in the city when he remembered that he was trying to forget it. Three or four times an hour he forgot to forget it and remembered. Big Dad.

After a few hours Henry couldn't stand it. He wished he was a proper, serious man and could take his mind off things by grimly cleaning a barbecue or changing the spark plugs on his car. Some guy with thick sideburns and strong hands who'd feel happy and comfortable drenched in sweat. One of those silent, capable types who looked as though they just suddenly popped into the world fully grown, fatherless.

He picked up the telephone and dialed the number on the card once more.

'Jack the Body.'

'Hello,' Henry began. 'Hi. Hello, I, uh . . . Is this Jack the Body?'

'Yeah. Who's this?'

'It's, um . . . I'm . . . My name is, uh, Henry Puh . . . Puh . . .' Oh, hell. He couldn't give Jack his real name. 'It's, um . . . Harry Gondorf here, I . . . I have a job for you.'

'What sorta job?'

'It's in a . . . for a film. A feature.'

'How many days?'

'How many days?'

'Work. How many days' work? What'd you say your name was?'

'Gondorf. H. Gondorf.'

'Who're you with?'

'Um . . . Gondorf Productions. We're new in town.' Henry began feeling sick all over again. Sick and sugary. 'It's a good picture. I'm sure you'll like it.'

'I could care less if I liked the picture, Mr Gondorf. I do the work, I get paid, I leave. I'm not gunning for an Academy Award here.' Jack the Body laid down the facts bluntly. 'It's a job.'

There's the old Powdermaker charm at work, Henry thought. 'Okay. That's fine. So, ah, I wonder if we could meet.'

'Yeah. Where?'

'Um . . . My office is . . .' Henry's mind wandered through the few parts of sprawling L.A. that he knew. 'My office is –' he plucked a street-corner from nowhere – 'at the corner of Wilshire and Fairfax.' He swallowed.

'You in the Petersen Building? Top of the museum?'

'Ah no, diagonally opposite there.'

'Diagonally opposite is Johnie's Coffee Shop. That's your office?'

'No. Of course not. I thought we could, uh . . . We could have lunch there.'

'Swanky. Okay, what day and what time, Mr Gondorf?'

'Say, Monday, midday?'

'Fine. How will I know you?'

'Oh, don't worry, I know you. I'm very familiar with your work.'

Henry hung up, taking great deep breaths that thinned his thoughts.

The nearest copy center charged three cents a page. Henry did some sluggish calculations. One hundred and twenty pages times three cents per page times seventy-five copies, plus binding plus tax would cost him . . . he had no idea. Somewhere around fifty bucks, he concluded. Probably. He began copying his script.

Three hours later he was completely surrounded by stacks of paper. And he realized that more alarming than the cost of his scripts was the matter of their weight. His car was parked outside his apartment – how would he get them home? He turned to a clerk behind the counter and said, 'Do you by any chance deliver?'

The clerk rolled his eyes, dropped his jaw and tiredly nodded his head. The move made Henry a little dizzy. 'Yes, we deliver. It says we deliver on the sign out front, so it's a pretty good bet that we deliver, wouldn't you say?'

The copying, plus binding, plus delivery, plus tax cost him close to four hundred dollars; Henry thought his credit card was going to disintegrate right before his eyes as the clerk swiped it.

He sat in the front of the delivery van chatting absently with the driver, a Mexican guy with a club foot, giving him vague directions, feeling stunned and hollowed by the unexpectedly large financial outlay.

'You in the movie business, huh?' the driver asked. The name 'Sammy' was stitched in yellow onto his green shirt pocket.

'No,' Henry said. He wondered how he'd feel about having a job where you had to wear a shirt with your name on it. Or a hairnet. 'Not really.'

'What all this about then, man?' Sammy asked, jerking his thumb over his shoulder to the back of the van, where Henry's seventy-five white bricks lay.

'I don't know, Sammy,' Henry said. 'My grand delusion, I guess.'

'I'm not Sammy, man. I'm Reyes. Sammy my brother. This his shirt.'

'I have a brother,' Henry said. 'But according to his shirt his name's Ralph Lauren.' Sammy laughed a little. It made Henry feel good.

'I saw the bill, man. Lotta money to spend on an illusion.'

Henry half said, half sang, 'Believe in dreams as if they're real.'

Reyes turned to Henry and smiled. 'I know that song. The Jackson Sisters, right, man?' Henry nodded, feeling better than he had all day, a kind of carbonated joy rising from his stomach. 'That a great song.' Pointing his thumb to the rear again, Reyes said, 'What the movie about?'

'About a guy who thinks his life would be better if he pretends to be somebody else.'

'He right, this guy?'

'I dunno.'

'He get the girl at the end?'

'How'd you know that there's a girl at the end?'

'All the good stories got a girl at the end, man. Everybody know that. So he get her, the pretender?'

'Well . . . in a way, he does. I guess so.' Henry began nodding, as if to convince himself. 'Yeah, he does. Of course he does.'

'Good.'

'Make a right here, can you?' Reyes turned, and Henry craned his neck to hang onto the view of the Paramount gates, wondering what it would be like to have the guard nod a familiar greeting at him each morning. 'Hello, Mr Powdermaker. That's a lovely hairnet you're wearing today.' He laughed aloud as the van made its way down his street. 'You live around here, Reyes?' Henry asked.

'No, man. I live over to Monterey Park. People like me not too welcome around here, 'cept as maids or gardeners.'

Even though Reyes seemed unconcerned by it, Henry wished like hell he hadn't asked the question. 'Okay, this is it, up here on the left.'

'The pink building? Where the Ford is?'

'Yep.'

'Nice ride, man. Yours?'

'No,' Henry said. 'I've got a . . .' He stopped himself. 'I don't have a car.'

Reyes pulled up, almost touching bumpers with Shaker's Ford. 'My mala suerte tells me you don't live on the ground floor, right man?' Reyes said, opening the van's rear door.

'Yeah, second floor.' Henry made himself not look at the Mexican's oversized left boot. 'But you don't have to help me carry all this stuff up. Especially not on a day like today.' He looked up at the sun and searched for something banal to say about the heat. When he brought himself back to earth, Reyes was halfway to the front door with a stack of scripts. Henry shouted, 'Right there'll be fine!'

When they finished unloading the van, Henry handed Reyes a ten-dollar bill. 'Thanks for your help,' he said. 'I really appreciate it.'

'No problem,' Reyes said, and limped off down the concrete path that divided the grass lawn in front of the apartment. Responding to an urge whose source and reason was unknown to him, Henry followed, wondering what he was doing, what he was going to say. 'Wanna come in for a drink? Which do you like better – sky or earth? How much they pay you an hour? Is your life better when you're wearing your brother's shirt?'

Reyes turned around. 'What is it, man? What you want?'

'It's not that great around here,' Henry said, the words coming out like they'd been forced by a shot of ipecac. 'To live, I mean. It's not all that great.'

Reyes smiled, a glint in his dark-brown eyes. 'It's okay, man. I understand. You don't gotta tell me how it is.'

Caught somewhere between strange tears and even stranger laughter, Henry nodded and Reyes drove away. Henry turned back toward the apartment block, then stopped and stared at his scripts, sitting by the entrance in three neat stacks, tall and bright and white, like a group of pillars arranged in support of nothing.

39

Dear Madeleine,

It's hot and thirty-six hours after my last drink I'm still hung over. Hot like the heat in every frame of Do the Right Thing *(except this is L.A.; so maybe* Heat *is a more appropriate film) and hung over like Ray Milland in* The Lost Weekend. *Or maybe Meg Ryan in that awful* When a Man Loves a Woman, *except my hair is not as nice and neat as hers was. Actually, neither of those last two 'cinelies' (an original H. P. neologism combining cinema and simile; this singular gift has really gotten me places in this town. They just love words here, and the newer the better.) is quite right because the fact is they never, ever get hangovers exactly right in films: the condition only lasts about ten minutes; nobody vomits or rolls around thinking they're about to die; there's never any Coke in sight; and the actors never look gray and bloated and depressed. (Which, in at least some cases, is rather odd – I'm pretty sure Meg Ryan was an actual, real-life alcoholic for a while. But maintained nice, neat hair throughout.) Out here in the real world, even L.A., hangovers kill you.*

I like Los Angeles very much. I'm intimidated by the place, I'm quite lonely, it's far too big and mostly full of idiots, but I still like it. I feel as though I belong here. (I realize that a remark like that leaves me wide open to mockery and ridicule, but since you don't actually receive these letters, I'm leaving it in. But in the part of my imagination in which you live, you're mercilessly mocking away.)

Anyway, enough blathering, I'll get to the point – I think about you all the time, Maddy. I think about what you're doing, where you might be, whether or not you're happy or engaged or married or pregnant or even a mother. (If you are any of those things, congratulations.) And I often wonder if you think about me. I'm sure you do; I'm just not sure whether it's pleasant or unpleasant.

I wish you were here, Maddy. Right here, right now. I wish that we were together, hungover and hot and happy. My saying that probably sounds selfish, maybe even shocking, but it's not meant to be. I have loved you since that summer on the trampoline, I just never had the courage to recognize it, or to tell you. And I'll probably never have the courage to tell you, except in this way – writing it all down in a letter I'll never send. How poetic. And pathetic.

I love you. That's all I have left to say, and all I've ever wanted to say.

Henry

P.S. If you have typhus and are in love with some guy called Stefan, please forgive my intrusion. How's Vienna?

As he'd done hundreds of times over the years, Henry folded the letter in three, slipped it into an envelope addressed to the house where Madeleine had grown up and sealed it. He leaned back in his chair and looked at the pillars of scripts he'd hauled up from out front, now arranged in a rough half-circle around him like the ruins of an ancient palace. He wondered if one of the copies of his script, one small part of one of these piles of words and paper, might somehow change his life. Then he leaned forward and, with his head resting on the letter to Madeleine, fell asleep.

40

Henry woke up to hear Shaker's rumbling rod out on the street. He grabbed his wallet and keys, ran out the front door, jumped down the stairs and sprinted up the concrete path toward the shuddering purple car. Rainey wound down the window and screamed, 'Change your mind, honey?'

Above the engine roar Honey shouted that he had. Rainey opened the passenger door using the outside handle and got out. 'There's no back seat, you'll have to sit on the shaft housing. There's a cushion.'

'Is there a seatbelt?'

'Seatbelts are for fairies!' she yelled.

Reluctantly, Henry climbed into the hollowed-out shell of the car, sat on the floor in the back and held on to anything he could. There wasn't much of anything in the car – no door handles, no radio, no air-conditioning, no glove compartment, no dashboard. And especially no seatbelts. It was as though the car had been stripped by a gang of car thieves working from the inside.

Shaker drove like a madman: in and out of the tiniest gaps in freeway lanes; overtaking at 120 miles an hour; shooting through amber lights at enormous death-intersections; sneaking into the whining slipstream of speeding ambulances; slamming Henry's untethered body against the back and side panels with every wild, sudden turn; sending him nose-breakingly forward with each harsh slam of brake. On the few occasions when they were stopped and idling at a million decibels, Shaker tapped his hands on the large paintbrush which served as a gear-stick, while Rainey turned around and, with her sharply plucked eyebrows almost touching her pointed hairline, screamed 'rod lore' at Henry, explaining why there were no 'unnecessary' elements like seatbelts in the coupe. 'Ed Roth said, "If it doesn't make it go, it's gone!!"'

As they drove, Henry thought about the quintessentially 'L.A. driving' films – the bleached, dusty backroads of *Chinatown*; the cross-town convoys in search of parties and diners and booze and love in *Swingers*; the easy despair of Altman's updated *Long Goodbye*, Elliot Gould chasing after a Mustang along Ventura; the running machine-gun battles in the wide downtown streets of *Heat*; William Holden's fateful turn off Mulholland in *Sunset Boulevard*; Woody Allen in *Annie Hall* calling L.A. a city where the only cultural advantage is that you can make a right turn on a red light. And he thought about another film about two men and a woman in a car – his own – *Point of View*.

When they finally arrived at Bob's Big Boy in Toluca Lake, Henry was a boneless wreck. 'I'll just be a minute,' he told Shaker and Rainey, as he flopped on the bonnet of the Ford. Rainey combed her hair with quick, wrenching brushstrokes that looked to Henry like punishment. Shaker extracted a large cigar from a leather case and lit it with a Zippo on which was enameled one of his own designs, a semi-nude Devil Girl who was herself sucking on a very phallic stogie. 'See-gar?' Shaker said, offering the case. 'It's a Cohiba.'

Henry declined, then stood up and looked around. He could barely believe what he saw. It was straight out of *American Graffiti*: the car park was filled with classic cars that looked like they'd just rolled off the production line and chopped, channeled, cropped, shaved and Frenched rods, most with their hoods up for inspection like so many mouths at a dentist; strolling and posing up and down the asphalt lanes were men wearing oily jeans and leather jackets, red-lipped women in twin-sets with breasts like missile heads clutching glossy handbags; wax-slick hair on the guys and beehives on the gals; Louis Prima shaking and wailing out of car stereos; hanging above it all, the roar of engines and the smell of grilled, greasy meat and exhaust fumes. The only thing missing, Henry thought, was a female car-hop on white roller-skates. A female car-hop on white roller-skates glided by. Henry felt happy. He wondered whether if he thought about Ron Howard and Charlie Martin Smith, they too would suddenly appear.

He spent a while looking at the Chevys and Buicks and Fords and Mercurys and Oldsmobiles and Dodges and Cadillacs. He stared admiringly at a '53 Ford Edsel with a push-button gear selector in the middle of the steering wheel. He stopped in awe in front of a pearl-red 1949 Mercury with, Shaker pointed out, a four-inch top chop, tilted steering wheel, electric suicide doors, Frenched headlights and a long chrome tail-pipe snaking out from beneath the side panels. Henry had never thought that steel could be so beautiful and so . . . arousing. Soon, however, the smell of frying burger became more of an arousal, and he told Shaker and Rainey that he'd see them inside Bob's. With a watering mouth he headed indoors and grabbed a slippery-seated booth all to himself.

Pitch. Henry, once more overcome with *American Graffiti*-ness, ordered a cheeseburger, fries and a chocolate malted from a perky waitress, raising his voice slightly above the rumble outside. It wasn't actually being in a film, but it was close. And it was . . .

neat, he decided, trying to remain true to the mood with his choice of adjective. He waited for two gun-toting bandits to burst in and demand valuables, then shoot him in the arm . . .

Gradually, Henry became aware of the conversation taking place in the booth directly behind him. 'I asked for a rewrite in three weeks,' a piercing, nasal voice said. 'And the fucker tells me no less than six can he have it repolished and retooled and retyped and re-whatever those pussy jerk-offs do. Fuckin' writers, huh? Every one of 'em thinks they're a whaddayacall, a Hemingworth.'

'So what do you have?' a deeper voice asked.

'I got dick. I got nuthin', nada, zip. Sweet Fanny Brice. And if I don't get something soon, my whole deal with Universal's gonna fall through. I'd kill for the next *Pulp Fiction*. Even the next *Jackie Brown* I'd probably maim for.'

Henry's heart started pounding and he clearly saw himself standing up, clearly heard himself speak the words, before he'd moved or spoken. It was as though he was watching a film of the next few seconds, then enacting it. He slid off the banquette and turned to the two people in the next booth. One was a thin, sharp-faced man with a pointed nose and very short hair – the nasal voice, Henry assumed. The other, a broad-faced and tanned man who could have been George Hamilton's stand-in, was wearing a suit and an open-necked shirt.

'Pardon my interruption, gentlemen,' Henry said, his voice flat but oddly confident. 'I couldn't help overhearing your conversation and I'm wondering if I can't be of some assistance.'

'How?' the nasal voice asked, then held up a hand. 'No, don't tell me – you're a writer and you got this hot script you want me to take a look at. Right?'

Henry nodded. The nasal voice nodded. The tan nodded. 'I am and I do,' Henry said.

'Who's your agent?' the tan asked.

'Harry Gondorf,' Henry said quickly.

'Never heard of him.'

'He's new in town.'

'Wasn't Gondorf a character in *The Sting*?' said the tan.

Dammit, I knew I knew that name from somewhere, Henry

thought. 'Yes,' he said. 'But this one's real, not a character. Well, he's a bit of a character, but he's real. Heh-heh. Anyway, he encourages me to pursue my own leads.'

'But still takes fifteen per cent, right? Or did he make you cop twenty?' sharp face said. 'Don't tell me it's twenty-five!' He turned to his companion. 'You believe this guy, Guy?'

'You know agents,' Henry said. 'Sharks on land, aren't they? Lousy bastards. Heh-heh!'

'Guy's an agent,' sharp face said, pointing across the table.

Henry should have known – every agent he'd ever heard of was named Guy. He stuck out his hand. 'Pleased to meet you, Guy. I'm Henry Powdermaker.'

Guy shook hands and Henry sat down. 'Henry Powdermaker,' he said to the other man.

'H. M. Swansong,' said H. M. Swansong, without offering his hand. 'Do not ask what the "H" stands for. Ever. I'll give you two minutes. C'mon, quit wasting my time.'

'Well, okay, all right. Okay, um . . . Well, basically it's about this kid who pretends to be Holden Caulfield from *The Catcher in the Rye* and he goes to New York and . . .'

When Henry was through, H. M. Swansong handed him a card and said, 'Have this Bergdorf send me a copy of the script Monday. I'll see you in two weeks, when I've had someone read it. But over the next fourteen days, I want you to consider one word of advice: nudity. You can go now. Get lost.'

Henry thanked his head off and slipped back to his own booth, where his sagging hamburger, softening fries and melting malted awaited him. He stared at the food, but was too busy mentally casting *Holen Cawffle* to eat. Ten years ago John Cusack or Matthew Broderick might have been perfect for the lead. Maybe Adam Horovitz from the Beastie Boys could still pull it off; the character he played in *Roadside Prophets* was already halfway there, all anxious and screwy like that. Probably too old by now, though. Probably too funky as well. Damn. And all the young male actors around these days were too muscley and healthy-looking. The idiots. That Adrien Brody could perhaps do it – he even looked like Salinger did when he was young. Or maybe Jason

Schwartzman – he was excellent in *Rushmore*. They'd have to find someone just right. It wouldn't be easy, but . . .

Henry suddenly decided that he absolutely had to have casting approval. He turned around to ask what his chances were, but H. M. and Guy the Very Brown Agent had gone. Probably the noise was too much, Henry thought. It certainly was getting loud in there. It even felt like the restaurant was shaking from all those thundering engines, it really did.

It really was. The burger slid off Henry's table, followed by the malted. There was a scream from somewhere nearby. Outside, the roar grew much louder and much lower. The lights flickered on and off. A dreamy swaying coming from the floor traveled straight up into Henry's body. Why were the walls wavering like that? A plate-glass window a few booths down shattered, spilling shards all over the group sitting below it. There were more screams and some strange, inhuman moaning sounds. As Henry stood up, the floor beneath him seemed to swell and he fell down. The lights went off again. Another window shattered and there were booms outside.

Henry managed to get up and ran for the exit, slipping momentarily in a pool of blood next to the booth where the first window had come down. He glanced to his left and saw a finger on the table. Up ahead, the exit was blocked by people shouting and shrieking and pushing at each other, their livid faces stretched with horror and panic. He climbed onto the seat next to the table with the finger on it and jumped through the window frame. From a sickeningly skewed angle, he looked up at the huge Bob's sign towering over the restaurant and saw the great, grinning burger boy topple. They hit the quaking ground hard at the same time, an explosion of light and glass from the burger boy and a dull black moan from Henry.

When he came to, Henry was covered in the gingham that had once been the burger boy's apron, a treacherous puddle of red and white glass. He saw Riverside Drive, spinning blue and red and orange light; white jets of steam shooting through jagged cracks in the sidewalk; the flattening wind of a helicopter pouring still white light onto the tableau; a ring of police cars surrounding an ambulance, open-backed and sterile, which was gingerly reversing toward the center of a five-car pile-up while dumb, beefy towtrucks slobbered at the edge; half a sedan, the front of the car disappearing somewhere inside a ripped-open and written-off hatchback, the first of three interments for the open-eyed driver – car, body bag, casket; a trailer and small boat flipped and smashed into thousands of white-varnished wood chips, small and hard as frozen snowflakes; a broken-backed black dog lying among pulverized wood, wide-eyed with fear; a cop walking over to the dog and putting a bullet into its head while a news crew stood by and filmed.

Still sitting stunned on the ground, his back against the restaurant wall, Henry looked around and saw dozens more cameras operated by both professionals and amateurs: Bolexes, old Super 8s, hand-held digital video cameras and big broadcast jobs. He thought of *Medium Cool* as he watched cameras swarm, trained on the sharply buckled road; the great dark hole at the intersection of Riverside and Alameda; an empty silver Buick falling into the hole at forty-five degrees on a slab of asphalt and concrete, slick and dark from a water-spewing underground pipe; three long lumps with shoes, covered by yellow plastic held down by pieces of rubble, lined up outside a Starbucks; thousands of oranges spilled from an overturned truck, the strong, sweet smell a strange counterpoint to the bodies nearby; the bucking blue light from a downed power line; emergency teams running ropes and cables across rooftops; paramedics bent over the injured, whispering and bandaging. Henry thought of the crane shot from *Gone With the Wind*, gently rising over the scattered bodies of soldiers in Atlanta. He saw storefront fires and baton-wielding cops belting booze-laden looters, the incident shot from four different angles by camera-clutching hopefuls. He thought of *Rashomon*. Handfuls of rubbernecks pointing and laughing made Henry remember the crazed, wild mob at the end of *The Day of the Locust*. His eyes moved to a young woman in blood-covered white Capri pants and a flame-singed shirt who was standing by a crumpled Dodge and screaming, but making no sound. Then Henry realized that there were no sounds at all – the bullet the policeman had fired moments ago had issued a puff of smoke but no sharp crack; the helicopter forty feet above hovered in silence; the screaming woman's mouth was wide open but there was nothing coming out.

A paramedic, showing a tough mouth but frightened eyes, picked his way over concrete rubble and steel toward where Henry sat. He could see the guy mouthing the words, 'Are you okay?' Henry nodded and as the man grew closer said, 'I can't hear.'

The ambulance man mouthed, 'I said, are you okay?'

Henry nodded again and said – or at least believed he said – 'I can't hear.'

'Are you hurt?' Henry saw the ambulance officer say.

Henry shook his head emphatically. 'But I can't hear!!' It was like being stuck in an Abbot and Costello routine with David Lynch and Irwin Allen in charge. Who's on triage? Henry felt himself chuckle.

The guy clapped his hands together in front of Henry's face and mouthed, 'Can you hear me?'

Henry shook his head. The ambulance man kneeled in front of Henry and held up his forefinger. Henry mimicked the gesture, the simplest way of answering the question he knew would follow: 'How many fingers do you see?' Thirty feet behind the ambulance guy, Henry saw the silver Buick slip into the hole, rupturing another water pipe and sending up a geyser. Squashing oranges under their feet, the people nearby darted back, as though in the middle of all this destruction, the most immediate danger was getting wet. Henry smiled, then began laughing; silently or aloud, he didn't know. The ambulance officer gave him a look of undiluted contempt and walked away; presumably to tend to more seriously injured – and serious – people.

Henry stood up woozily and clambered over smashed burger-boy glass and plastic, slowly making his way to the parking lot on the other side of the restaurant. The lot and all the vintage vehicles in it were untouched, except for a row of three low-riders flattened by a fallen tree. Henry looked for Shaker and Rainey in the pale, stunned groups attempting to calm themselves with belts from hip-flasks or tokes on joints. He saw other people like himself, wandering alone, stuporous and dazed, in slack-jawed silence – straight from *Night of the Living Dead*.

The ride back was long, slow and circuitous; roads were blocked by cops and sawhorses, cops and cop cars, cops and firetrucks; diversionary routes were choked with traffic; sidewalks were teeming with people trying to get back to their homes and others out for a look at the injured, the looters, the police and the other rubbernecks. Every so often, Rainey would turn around and say something to Henry, her red-lipped mouth so big and busy that Henry felt as though it was a hole he might fall into if he looked at it for too long, like a silver Buick slipping slowly into the earth. The scent of citrus, from the bursting bag of oranges in the back of the car, was heavy, sticky, sickening, as if the oils and juices were seeping into Henry's pores. The smell reminded him, for some reason he couldn't immediately pinpoint, of *The Godfather* trilogy. Then it clicked: Coppola had equated oranges with death. Every time there were oranges, somebody died. Didn't Vito Corleone die with an orange in his mouth? The side of Henry's head began to throb and his body slumped.

He woke when the car stopped. It was almost dawn, and they were parked on a thin and dusty ridgeback. Shaker and Rainey got out of the car. Henry followed, lagging behind so that he wouldn't have to talk. Something that felt like wet sand shifted inside his head.

They reached a sagebrush-bordered bluff and stood at the edge. Way down below them, the Valley was almost throbbing with red and orange light from fires and emergency vehicles. Plumes of light-gray and heavy-black smoke rose high into the pinkish-blue sky. Henry turned and walked to the other side of the ridge, wondering what he might see from there. A line of scrub pines blocked the view west, up toward Mount Lee. More sand moved in his skull as he headed toward the trees. He wondered how many people were dead. He hoped that H. M. Swansong had survived, then wondered if the noisy producer would hire a deaf screenwriter. Henry emerged from the trees and before him was a perfect view of Mount Lee.

The earthquake had hit the great white letters that spelled HOLLYWOOD so hard that only three and a half were left standing. WOOD was completely gone. There was no Y and only half of the first O, which was split right down the middle. What remained was HCLL. Henry stood transfixed, the muscles in his mouth and throat twitching. Then something in his head popped sharply, and he heard the clear sound of his own laughter, deep, rich and very, very loud.

41

Henry's piles of scripts were a white spill on the wooden floor of his apartment, whether as a result of the earthquake or mere instability, he didn't know. He gathered them all up and then, with a yellow phone book by his side, laboriously addressed seventy-four envelopes to seventy-four production companies: from American Zoetrope (Francis Coppola's company) and Barwood Films (Barbra Streisand's) to Yablans Entertainment Co. (a father and son outfit run by Eddie and Frank) and Zanuck Inck (absolutely no relation to Darryl or Dick but the management kept that pretty quiet).

In between restless bouts of dreamless sleep, Henry spent the weekend drinking iced coffee and sitting on his couch, glued to the television news, eager for reports of celebrity-related tragedy. Jim Carrey broke his ankle when he went outside to investigate the crack in his large, empty swimming pool and fell in the deep end. ('Where was my stand-in when I needed him?' he quipped, pulling a face and making a humorous noise. 'Or my mother-in-law?') Goldie Hawn's house was flattened; she, however, was in New York City at the time and only her housekeeper was killed. ('I don't know exactly who was on duty at the time,' Ms Hawn said, in a prepared statement. 'But whoever it was, she or he was a nice lady or man and I loved her or him very much. They were like family to me.') Arnold Schwarzenegger was saved from death when the roof of his twelve-car garage fell on the Humvee in which he was allegedly sleeping. (While unscathed, Mr Schwarzenegger was deeply shaken by the loss of several prestige Bentleys, Ferraris, Bugattis and a 1959 Austin-Healy. 'They were like children to me,' he said. Hummer sales rose sharply the following week.) Actor James Gandolfini broke his left wrist when a heavy copper saucepan fell on his arm as he was cooking black satin duck with egg noodles and bok choi for guests, including fellow actor Jim Metzler, former SPY columnist Celia Brady and writer John Gregory Dunne. (Detail is character, screen gurus were always saying, and evidently L.A.'s news fraternity agreed.) William Friedkin's nose was broken, but popular speculation had it that a right hook rather than tectonic realignment was responsible. Henry's favorite film composer, Lalo Schifrin, had three stitches put in his eyebrow when he was rolled out of bed onto the slate floor in Clara Bow's former home, which he was renting. One of Meryl Streep's Oscars broke; she would be sent a replacement. And, finally, while nobody actually mourned the death of 'promising' 'young' 'director' James Merendino from 'cardiac arrest' some seventeen hours after the 'event', there was a rush on pre-paid 'sites' at Forest Lawn 'memorial park'.

Apart from Merendino and Goldie Hawn's housekeeper (an Ecuadorian woman, it turned out), seventeen non-industry people were killed: fifteen of them in the Valley, very close to where Henry had been at the time of the tremor; the other two, a young couple from San Bernadino apparently picnicking on Mount Lee, were decapitated by the thirty-foot Y. Their names were never mentioned.

The earthquake measured a comparatively mild 6.5, but on most network stations rated in the high 30s. The news media had a visual field day with the shattered sign and Henry couldn't get enough of it: the shaky, lingering helicopter shots of HCLI; long zooms from down in the L.A. basin up to Mount Lee, an all-too-obvious message; packs of souvenir-hunters scavenging at the fallen remains; hot dog and soda carts crawling across the mountainside, an ant-like caravan feeding and extorting the souvenir-hunters and news-gatherers.

A special committee comprising representatives from all the major studios and talent agencies was assembled to plan the rebuilding of HOLLYWOOD. Dozens of stars volunteered their precious time and sweat. Somebody suggested that the letter Y be painted black in memory of the luckless, headless picnickers. Production designer Richard Sylbert lobbied vigorously against the idea, claiming that it would be 'visually unsound'. Religious-right groups insisted that the earthquake was a direct communication from God and that the sign be left alone, perhaps even declared the Lourdes of Los Angeles. The president called it a national disaster comparable only to the notional disaster of Mount Rushmore losing Lincoln's chin. *Variety* called it 'the industry's biggest shake up since Sony choked down Columbia'.

Close to the HOLLYWOOD sign, the Griffith Park Observatory, which Henry had never visited but knew well from its prominence in *Rebel Without a Cause*, was badly damaged but received far less media coverage than the neighboring destruction; after all, the observatory, like the public, merely gazed at the stars; it did not, unlike the mutilated icon, represent them.

On Saturday afternoon Henry's mother called, ostensibly to ask whether he had her Francis Lai record, but Henry suspected that she was really trying to find out if he was all right. 'I'm fine, don't worry,' he said. 'How are you, Mom?'

'Marvelous. D'you know where the record is?' she asked, and began breathily humming its signature tune, the Oscar-winning theme from *A Man and a Woman*. He told her that he did not and asked again how she was. 'Seriously, I want to know. Just in case you've got Lupus or something.'

Sandra, a little suspicious of her son's enquiry (why on earth would he think she had Lupus? she wondered), told him that she was fine then hung up before he'd had time to even think about mentioning Jack the Body.

On Sunday, Charlie was more direct. 'Are you dead?' he asked as soon as Henry picked up the telephone.

'Only spiritually,' Henry replied.

'Somehow I knew you were going to say that.'

'It's nice to be well known.'

'Known well is not the same as well known.'

'I know.' There was silence between them for a moment. Henry massaged his temple. 'Hey, you remember that conversation we had a while back about being assassinated?'

'Yeah, what about it?'

'I've been thinking some more along those lines – listen to this.' Henry leaned back on his chair and closed his eyes. 'Phillip Seymour Hoffman, Sarah Jessica Parker, Sarah Michelle Gellar, Neil Patrick Harris, Melissa Joan Hart, Jennifer Love Hewitt, James Earl Ray, Lee Harvey Oswald, Mark David Chapman, John Wilkes Boothe, Sirhan Sirhan Sirhan. You see how easily you can go from actors to assassins? It's no accident, and you know why?'

'Why?'

'Because actors hate the audience. They want to kill us, to destroy us.'

'And why would they want to do that?' Charlie asked. He'd emptied his voice but Henry could tell that he was smiling.

'Because they need us and they can't stand the idea of needing anything other than themselves,' Henry explained. 'And their assistants.'

'Uh-huh,' Charlie said, unimpressed. 'I guess the whole three-name thing started with Mary Tyler Moore, didn't it? And she was a killer, wasn't she? A real destroyer.'

'I know you're being sarcastic, Charlie, but you go and watch *Ordinary People*. She could kill you in that, believe me.' Henry drank some iced coffee and shivered. 'So you don't buy it, what I'm saying about the names?'

'To tell you the truth, Henry, you sound like a crackpot. D'you have lots of pictures cut out of newspapers and magazines pasted up all over your walls? Notebooks full of tiny writing in different colored inks? Bags packed ready for a quick flight from the law?' Charlie laughed and Henry could almost see his small, sharp teeth. 'Son of Samsonite.'

'I can live with sounding like a crackpot. They said McMurphy was a crackpot and look at him.'

'He's not real, Henry.'

'He's real enough. Anyway, what I really dislike about it is that it leaves a no-middle-name guy like me completely out in the cold. If I wanted to be an actor, I mean,' Henry said. 'Or an assassin.'

'Yeah, that's a really tough break – apart from having no acting skills to speak of.'

'I'm saying if, Charlie. *If.* Which I never would, anyway, because I hate actors right back – probably even more than they hate me, as a matter of fact – and it would be the ultimate hypocrisy for me to become one.'

'If you could act.'

'Yeah, if! So why do you think directors never seem to do that three-name thing?'

'I have no idea and I don't care. You added an extra Sirhan before. Don't think I didn't notice because I did.'

'Had to keep the theory going. Anyway –' Henry began smiling and speaking very rapidly. Talking with Charlie had made him more excited and happy than he'd realized. 'Anyway, the thing is, what they all really want, actors I mean, what they all really aspire to is having just one name – like Arnold, Tom, Bruce, Sigourney, Uma, Harrison, etc. Although I suppose with those last few it's unlikely there'll ever be more than one.'

'There's more than one Tom. There's Cruise and Hanks.'

'Stop trying to wreck my theories, will you? They're good theories.'

'And what happens when an actor's name is a composite of two already-taken first names?'

'Like . . . um . . . Tom Arnold?'

'Exactly.'

'It simply means that he can never make it to the A-list. Besides which, he's a crappy actor, anyway. And, no doubt, a very annoying person.'

'Mel's a crappy actor and he's A-list. A-plus. Your theories need work, Henry, they'd never hold up in the courtroom. They don't even hold up in the living room. Do you have any other theories you need to run by me? You got some big ideas about salaries or budgets or marketing?'

'None right now, but thanks for listening.'

'No problem, Powderpuff. It's been pointless and . . . well, just pointless.'

'No song recommendations today?' Henry asked, surprised to find himself a little disappointed. 'Which reminds me, there's a jukebox here with your name all over it. You should come out and listen some time.'

'I don't holiday on fault lines, my friend.'

'Well, it's your loss.'

'Yeah, not visiting L.A. My loss. Right,' Charlie said, then added, 'Forget it, Hank, it's tryna town. I'm tryna get a production deal. I'm tryna get a part. I'm tryna get Sid or Jake or Bert to return my—'

'Yeah, I get it, Charlie. Don't be so sarcastic – this place really isn't that bad . . .' But after he put the phone down, Henry wondered if he'd lied to his best friend, and to himself.

42

Music. The heat woke Henry early on Monday morning. The air in his bedroom was a little rank, as though somebody garlicky or rotten-toothed had spent the night with him. He opened a window and let in a rolling wave of heat and sharp Cuban music, all horns and darting percussion, from a transistor radio somewhere downstairs. He liked the music; it gave life and a kind of odd, jarring joy to the otherwise still morning. That was the thing with music, Henry thought, a thing that Charlie Rocket had known all along – that you could call on it for an immediate effect; good or bad, but reliably immediate. It wasn't like that with films. For a film to have its proper way with you, you had to immerse yourself in it, to give yourself over to it in its entirety, from fade in to fade to black.

Henry showered, then shaved in the blue-and-green tiled bathroom, staring at the mirror, searching his face for the ways it had changed and become the thing that it was. There was gray on both temples, a little more jowl than before, and the color of his eyes, he saw, was best lit in confusion, wonder, doubt or concern; the deep and intricate lines around the milky-brown pools suggested that he'd spent far more time than he realized looking out at the world in this way. It wasn't the face he'd imagined for himself, and he didn't particularly like it – he would have chosen a surgical conflation of Cary Grant's firm jaw, Steve McQueen's despondent blue eyes and Jean-Paul Belmondo's thumbed, sensuous lips – but it was nonetheless his; and to Henry's mild surprise, he saw that it was the face of a man. A man who only had to shave every other day, who didn't know how – or why – to change spark plugs, but a man all the same. 'Between your knees,' he said at himself; he was no oil rigger and piano prodigy – no actor – but the words sounded all right. His face had at last reached a point where it could match a remark like that. He wondered whether his father would recognize this face. And he wondered what his father looked like; what sort of things his face could say.

It was still hot, and getting hotter, but Henry wanted to look like a serious person – a man – when he met his father, so he wore a light-gray suit and a wide red tie. Whether it was the dry air in the apartment or nervousness that made him breathless as he dressed, he wasn't sure. Maybe it was everything. Maybe as you grew older you just needed more air.

He hadn't driven in a while and the air inside his car – a Fedora-gray '63 Studebaker – was like the gas from a dead cow's gut. Henry opened all four doors, then stood back, gagging and gasping. He heard the music from the transistor radio wafting nearby and walked toward it. The sound came from a small shed in the rear of the apartment block. Henry pushed open the door and saw Shaker sitting at a desk, a paintbrush clenched between his teeth, another poked behind his right ear and a third in his left hand. It was dark and cool inside the shed and the place smelled of dust and oil paint. The walls were covered with color – silver robots fighting yellow robots; red-and-black Devil Girls riding rockets to the moon; a bug-eyed undertaker humping the knothole in a wooden casket; and a poster for the Jon Spencer Blues

Explosion, which showed a garishly toothy JFK losing the top of his head to a gouging bullet while Jackie, in a pink suit and matching pillbox hat, looked on ecstatically; the date of the band's performance, November 22nd, was written in blood-red letters below. Something almost clicked in Henry's head, but before it could Shaker looked up and said, 'Hey, there. What's the stink?'

'I think my car's dead,' Henry said. ''Cause of the heat. It's hot, huh?'

'Gets hotter, so get used to it. Lissen, you got yourself a nice vehicle out there, Henry P.' Shaker swapped his ear brush for his mouth brush. 'Oughtta show it a little more respect.'

'I know,' said Henry. 'I really do. So this is all your work, huh?' he said waving his hands vaguely at the walls.

'No, I bought 'em at a store and painted my signature on every one,' Shaker said, a drop of bright-blue sarcasm falling from the tip of the brush in his mouth. 'Of course they're mine. Don't they remind you of me?'

'Just making conversation. Just shootin' the old breeze.' Henry loosened the knot on his tie. 'So d'you have family, Shaker? Brothers and sisters and parents? Like that?'

'Rainey,' Shaker said with blunt certainty. 'Rainey's all I got and all I need.'

'Right.' Henry shuffled a bit, then made for the door. 'Well, I got some stuff to do, so I'll see you later.'

'Yeah.'

Henry stopped at the door and turned around. 'So d'you think the traffic will be okay? I mean from the earthquake and everything?'

'It'll be fine. This is L.A., Henry.' Shaker silenced the radio and jutted his goatee at Henry. 'We cope with stuff like that.'

'Yeah, I just thought maybe–'

'If you've got stuff to do, Henry P., go do it. Quit stalling.'

'Right,' said Henry. 'Okay. Well, I guess I'll talk to you later then.'

'Yeah.' Shaker turned the radio back up and began tapping two brushes against his teeth in time with the music. 'Hey, Henry.'

Henry turned. 'Yes?'

'Good luck.'

Henry was startled. 'With what?' he said, more dramatically than he meant to.

'The scripts. I saw 'em out front th'other day.'

'Oh, right. Thanks.'

Shaker began a paintbrush drum solo and Henry left, walking in step with the tiny, tinny tapping, the simple rhythm working its way into his head and carrying him hypnotically to his car.

After mailing the scripts, Henry drove slowly along Melrose Avenue, past the burger joints and auto-parts yards, the low, dry blocks of wan color – medical supply, real estate and insurance offices – and further, past the vintage clothes stores, art galleries, cafés and restaurants, which were quiet this early in the day and in the week. Ficus trees lined the grimy street. The light was dirty and diffuse, strangely unhealthy, as though Mother Nature herself was suffering from a mild hangover. Traffic was light and there were no collapsed buildings blocking his way. He made a slow left at Fairfax, just past the high school, wondering if maybe he gently ran over a schoolkid he'd have an excuse not to meet Jack Powdermaker. But all the kids were inside, learning whatever they taught students to get by in Los Angeles.

His escape routes were thinning out, and the corner of Fairfax and Wilshire was growing nearer. In a few blocks there would be no getting around it – he would have to see whether Jack the Body was his own flesh and blood.

43

Two shot. Henry took a booth and sat facing the entrance of Johnie's Coffee Shop. Air-conditioning brought the temperature down to tolerable, and he was glad to be able to leave his suit jacket on. In front of and behind him were very old people picking at large salads and difficult crosswords. The place smelled like burnt toast. He looked up to his right at the menu above the serving counter. The cuisine, like the décor, seemed to be authentically fifties – pork chops and eggs with mash, toast and jelly, and a row of pies that looked like those jobs that Joan Crawford cooked up in *Mildred Pierce*.

A waitress came by and Henry ordered a coffee and, momentarily forgetting what state he was in, asked for an ashtray. She tossed off a quick line about him having to whip over to Nevada if he wanted to have a cigarette with his coffee. He made some polite and feeble reply. She left and he wondered if living in California had turned him into an accommodating, acquiescent sort of fellow. The type of person who wasn't outraged when he wasn't allowed to have nicotine at the same time as caffeine; who didn't belt obnoxious copy-store clerks or smash into fire hydrants. Maybe it was an infection. Then again, he thought, maybe he'd always been like that and just thought he was otherwise. It was hard to keep track of who you were when you were always wishing you were someone else.

A deep voice barked. 'You Gondorf?'

Henry looked up and saw a handsome-but-gone-to-hell man who was enormously fat and round; whose sallow, gray-blue skin looked as though it did not belong to him, did not fit him – as though he'd climbed into it and was hiding, or pretending to be somebody else, somebody else's father.

'The hell are you staring at, pal?' the man said. There were leaves, small sticks and what looked like spots of mud and blood stuck to the fat man's jacket and water-stained shirt. His father would never have dressed like such an unabashed slob. This was a different Jack Powdermaker. Henry didn't know whether he felt disappointed or relieved.

He forced himself to look away. 'Uh, nothing. I'm sorry, I was thinking about something else.'

'Are you Gondorf?'

'Yes,' Henry said. 'Please, um, please sit down. I'm Gondorf.'

The man held out a pudgy hand. 'Jack the Body.' Henry shook it. 'I'm on a job, Mr Gondorf, a one-thirty call back in Burbank, so let's make this a useful meeting, all right?' Jack leaned forward and gave a slow, single nod of his head. 'I'm also somewhat testy from being in makeup since five, so how about a coffee?'

'Just so I know, Mr ... Jack ... So I know I'm talking to the right guy for what I require, what is it exactly that you do?'

The man pulled his head back in mildly outraged surprise. His mumpsy jowls and thyroidal neck should have wobbled, but didn't. 'Listen, Mr Gondorf, you're the one called me. I assumed you knew what it is I do.' The guy was coming across like a hit man, talking in shadowy, evasive circles. Maybe he crushed people to death. 'I do body work, is what I do.'

'Body work ... like on cars?' Henry offered tentatively.

The puffy, ashen face took on a hint of red. 'You kidding me? I'm a body.'

'Oh, I see,' Henry nodded. It was obvious that he didn't.

Jack spoke with florid forbearance, like a high school drama teacher. 'I'm a professional cadaver. Because of my great gifts in the areas of not breathing, not blinking, not twitching, not sniggering, not cramping and not moving for minutes at a time, I am the fifth-string, non-starring, unbilled movie corpse you barely notice: the rigid outline covered by a white sheet on a trolley in a morgue; the uncredited soldier lying on a battlefield. I'm the guy on the operating table after the septectomy gone wrong, the unsuccessful operation to transplant a heart or remove a tumor; the waxen, serene loved one lying in the casket, hands crossed upon my chest; I'm the bullet-riddled bodyguard in the back seat of a saloon car; the battered hit-and-run victim, the vomit-caked drug overdose, the flat-skulled suicide jumper. I'm a card-carrying, due-paying, SAG-certified dead person. I'm the Bernie you spend the weekend with. Understand? And today –' he paused and panted softly, the distended chest rising and falling stiffly – 'today I'm the bloated body of a guy who drowned in a lake, discovered by accident by some cops searching for a lost kid in a forest. Hence the pallid makeup and fat-suit, yeh?'

Yeh! Henry's glance snapped into the man's eyes. They were hard and bitter, hooded by sagging skin, pinched and secretive at the corners; the whites were a washed-out, jaundiced yellow, dotted with faint spots of pink. They were wet eyes: big and brown and wet, as though fluid – not tears necessarily, but some other mysterious leakage of the body or the soul – might spill from the raw, red lower lids at any moment. And Henry knew for certain that they belonged to Big Dad Jack.

'Jesus Christ,' Henry said quietly. 'It is you.'

'Actually, He's one I've never played. I'd more likely be cast as one of those guys flanking Him.' Jack Powdermaker pointed a finger at Henry. 'You want to tell me what's going on here, Mr Gondorf?'

From the corner of his eye Henry saw the waitress hovering beside the table, a cup and saucer in each hand. This would never be allowed to happen in a film, Henry thought, the moment would have to be played out smoothly, without interruption. She placed the cups in front of father and son and walked away, her heels squeaking slightly on the floor. Henry looked at his father, who was watching the woman's ass. 'It's me,' he said. 'Henry.'

Except for his mouth, which began opening and closing but making no noise, Jack Powdermaker was completely still. Henry stared at him, surprised that he felt nothing. Then he wondered if in fact he really did feel nothing, or whether he was hardening himself.

Something mumbled from the drowned man's lips. 'I'm sorry?' Henry said.

'You ought to be sorry, you little bastard.' There was venom in the low voice, and when Jack slowly looked up to face Henry, he saw it in his father's eyes as well. 'You ruined my life.'

Henry took a deep breath. He felt sickeningly light-headed, as though he might float away, transported by the shock and nausea of this moment, a scene he'd dreaded most of his life. What he said surprised him. 'No, *you* ruined your life. I had nothing to do with . . . what you did.'

'Nothing to do with it!?' Jack said through clenched teeth. There was sweat squeezing out from a thin, raised line of loosening rubber around his hairline. 'You humiliated me – and your mother – in front of . . . in front of . . .' Once again his mouth began silently gulping. Another great bead of sweat worked its way down the side of his face.

'You really believe it was me that humiliated her? Not what you were doing to her?'

'Nobody had to know. You showed everybody.' Jack shuddered inside his skin of rubber fat. 'Jesus!' He reached up, and with a horrific sucking noise, suddenly ripped off his hair together with a few inches of forehead, revealing a smooth, bald head and releasing a cascade of trapped sweat down his face. 'You showed everybody. That was the humiliation.'

There was silence between them for a long while. Henry lit a cigarette and ashed into the saucer. His coffee was cool. The waitress came over and mentioned Nevada again. 'Lady,' Jack said tiredly, 'this is my son. My son kills people. Many years ago, he took away my life. Let him smoke or he'll probably kill you too.' She walked away without a word.

'I *kill* people?' Henry said. 'Don't you think that's a little histrionic?'

Jack reached under his shirt and tore out more sweat-stained, white lumps of rubber fat, tossing them onto the seat by his side. Henry saw that his father was thin as well as bald. 'That's the way I see it. You took away my life.'

'I had to live with it as well. We all did.'

'You did it.'

'You *did* it – I just shot it. And believe me, I wish to God I never had.'

His voice choking with outrage, Jack said, 'Is that supposed to be of some comfort to me? That you regret it?' He stared and his brown eyes seemed to grow lighter with anger.

Henry's heart began a panicky hammering. He didn't know what to say. He wasn't sure what he wanted from his father, but it wasn't this. It wasn't simple hatred. An ashtray was slid in front of him. He looked up and saw the waitress give him a sly but nervous smile before shifting her eyes to Jack Powdermaker and flinging him a cold look. This small thing invested Henry with a strange equanimity, as though she'd pulled him back from an emotional eruption, or an abyss. He wondered if his father still had his model lobster boat; whether he looked at it and thought of his life back in Maine long ago. 'Don't you even want to know how Sandra and Daniel are?' Henry said. 'What they're doing? Who they are now?'

'Your mother spends most of her time talking to plants and your brother's shacked up with some piece of white trash named Shirley.'

Henry flinched. Jack was better informed than Henry had thought he would be. 'How do you know?'

'I keep in touch.'

'What about me?'

'I keep in touch with you, too.' He paused for a moment then said with slithering sarcasm, 'Son.'

'How?'

'The gifts,' Jack said. Something smug had crept into his face and voice. 'The gifts were all mine.'

'What gifts?'

'The hat, the rifle manual, the blood samples. And the bullet, of course. And the other things. The pictures. Didn't you ever wonder who sent them? And why?'

Henry felt wretchedly sick, stiflingly hot in his shirt, tie and jacket. He tightened the knot and forced himself to stay clear and calm. 'I . . . I didn't know who they were from. Or what they meant.'

'They were symbols. Elements of a metaphor.'

Henry's face was scalding, covered in sweat. It felt as if his skin might melt off. But he still wouldn't let himself remove his jacket. 'Symbols of what?'

'Of you assassinating my marriage. Ruining my life with that . . . with that repugnant stunt of yours on your parents' anniversary night. November 22nd.'

The date suddenly hit Henry and he remembered Shaker Townsend's cartoon Kennedy from that morning. He drew the sleeve of his jacket across his wet forehead and spoke slowly. 'Assassinating? That's a little . . . hysterical, don't you think? I mean, I know I helped end it, but assassinated it? If that metaphor is correct, then I also figuratively shot Mom and Daniel as well, then turned the gun on myself, because it screwed up all our lives, not just yours, y'know.'

Jack said nothing. Henry went on. 'Besides, while I admit to the stunt, the repugnant part was all yours.' Jack Powdermaker thinned his red-rimmed eyes at his son and breathed sharply through his nose. Henry wondered if he was drunk with the heat. 'Wasn't it? You did it to yourself, Dad. I was just the bystander with the Super 8. Little Henry Zapruder.' The word 'Dad', the way it had leapt out uncontrolled, rang dully and heavily in his ears. 'Anyway, your pathetic metaphor aside, why did you do it? Send me those things?'

'Because I didn't want you to forget.'

Henry spat out a single note of laughter, so sharp and dry that it caught in his throat. 'You thought I'd need help remembering?'

'I wanted you to suffer.'

'Yeah, well, I've suffered,' Henry said, his voice firm and clear. 'And I'll tell you what else, I'm sick of it. I've carried that thing with me in one way or another for my whole life and I'm done with it now.' He stood up and threw some bills on the table. 'I'm sorry it happened. I'm sorry for Mom and Daniel, and I'm even sorry for you, although God knows you probably deserve worse for what you did. But I'm finished with it now.'

Henry took a last look at his father, this old, bald, thin man who played corpses in movies, sitting there surrounded by lumps of prop fat. Then he walked away, leaving in his wake a resolved silence like the still moment immediately after a gunshot. And finally, just before he reached the exit and prepared to face the airless heat outside, Henry removed his jacket, loosened his tie and breathed deeply.

44

The heat stretched through all the days of the rest of that week and into the days of the next. Henry spent his time in contented, lazy wastefulness. In the mornings he trawled through his enormous collection of film magazines and books looking for pictures of writers at work. There were several that especially pleased him: a pencil hanging like a walrus tooth from Ben Hecht's drooping mouth, another on the opposite side of Charles MacArthur's mouth as they posed together; Robert Benton and David Newman searching each other's pained face for inspiration; Ruth Gordon and Garson Kanin on either side of a bottle of liquor, a blank yellow writing tablet sitting underneath it. Henry's favorite picture, one that he'd photocopied and enlarged, was of Billy Wilder and I. A. L. Diamond hard at it. In the foreground, facing the camera, was Izzy Diamond, staring forlornly down at a still, silent typewriter, while in the background, flat against a wall, Wilder lay on a couch staring blankly up at the ceiling, his feet up on the arm of the couch. In his right hand was a stick, with which he was tapping a small area of blank wall beneath a painting. Looking at that photograph, Henry could feel the heavy, expectant silence in the small office; could almost hear the steady, dry tapping of Wilder's stick against the wall. Henry loved that picture because he knew with absolute certainty that Izzy and Billy were, at the very moment the photo was taken, right on the verge of something – a scene from *The Apartment*, maybe. Or *One, Two, Three*. But definitely something, probably something great.

'Where's my partner?' he often said aloud to the photographs spread around him. Self-conscious even when he was his own and only audience, Henry was always careful not to make the question sound whiny. 'Who'll be my partner?'

In the slow afternoons, when the heat was most oppressive and draining, Henry slipped into the cool dark of a cinema and watched a film, sometimes two or three. He saw an awful lot of crap but forgave even the most dreadful movies their flaws because of the air-conditioning. Most difficult to forgive of the Henry Powdermaker Heatwave Film Festival (as he dubbed it) was Darla van Popje's follow-up to *The Magic Cocktail*. *Sunny Side Up* was the slender story of a lovably ditzy hooker – played by Bambi Yessno, who didn't so much chew the scenery as fellate it – who inherits a confectionery empire and sets about ridding the planet of prostitution by manufacturing and distributing chewing-gum-and-chocolate vaginas to desperate men around the world. In some quarters, mostly academic, the film was hailed as a breakthrough in feminist satire, the reasons for which entirely escaped Henry, who saw it as a collection of literally sugar-coated dick jokes. What didn't escape him was the fact that the chocolate whore was called Sunny and went around saying things like, 'Ease up on the wise', 'You're hurting my funny bone' and 'ixnay' (which she invariably pronounced 'iggsnay') – all elements lifted directly from his own film *Three Kinds o' Headache*. However, such was his high level of relaxed ambivalence that the two-bit plagiarism of a name and a couple of choice phrases didn't bother him too much. Cinema air-conditioning allowed him to forgive just about anything (except *Titanic*, of which he endured thirty-five minutes before rushing gratefully back out into the searing heat).

In the evenings Henry sat outside on his balcony wearing long shorts the color of sand and an ice-white, short-sleeved cotton shirt. He smoked cigarettes and listened to Burt Bacharach instrumentals gently rising in the heat from Shaker and Rainey's apartment downstairs. He smoked and thought about the fortunate lives of people in film, about how actors, directors, writers and even executives could reinvent themselves, their fortunes and their reputations from picture to picture. How one minute they're involved with some completely awful flop (Tom Hanks in *Bonfire of the Vanities*) and the next they're picking up a huge check and an Academy Award ('Tom' in *Forrest Gump*). These were lives replete with second chances. Out in the world, people had just one chance, or none.

Henry also thought about how his lust for success in film had begun to fade, like a dried drop of sweat that had once lain on his arm, or one of the pale, golden vapor trails of jet planes he watched disappear against the slowly darkening sky. A film truly worth making had almost no chance in this town. Every day the great pile of cinematic atrocities was added to, blighting both the form that Henry loved and the world in which he lived. Was there really room in the world for more than one Steven Seagal movie? What was the point of a cheaply made piece of crap about a talking, snowboarding, terrier in sunglasses? Or an orangutan doing anything? Why remake something already perfect like *Mr Deeds Goes to Town*? With Adam Sandler, for God's sake? How was Joel Schumacher allowed to direct a movie, ever? Who gave the green light to *Battlefield Earth*? And was that person still working or in prison? Who actually paid to watch something so awful? Why did people produce that sort of crap? They just wanted to make money, not films. And that, Henry felt, was an almost sinful motivation. He'd never been so acutely and brutally aware that film was less an artform than a business, and he hated this banal epiphany as much as his naivete.

When he became too bored and depressed thinking about the evils and idiocy of the film industry, Henry switched on the television and watched one of the many live broadcasts of people rebuilding the Hollywood sign on Mount Lee. On the first day Brad Pitt stepped on a nail and was rushed to Cedars Sinai under police escort for a tetanus shot. Henry was certain he saw tears plopping from Pitt's pinched eyes as he was helped, limping and grimacing, to the ambulance. Harrison Ford, resurrecting his former life as a studio carpenter and reprising his role in *Witness*, assumed control of all the other celebrity builders for the three hours he spent on site. Reports of the catering, provided free of charge by FilmFare, all proclaimed it excellent. The thing about the celebrity effort was that whenever a star came along to chip in, the site became a closed set. Ordinary citizens in the middle of measuring, painting, hoisting or panting were hustled away and made to wait behind LAPD-manned barricades, in case one of their number went crazy with a hammer or plumb bob. Of course this only applied to actors and a few high-profile directors – writers, producers and editors were for the most part unknown, therefore unthreatened, and as a result, uninterested and so, uninvolved. Henry did not see a single 'below the line' industry person working on the project, but often wondered if an uncredited Robert Towne or Bill Goldman had been secretly called in to rewrite the Hollywood sign.

Later, when it was dark but still too hot to sleep, Henry lay on the clingy clamminess of warm bed sheets and wrestled with the idea of telling his mother and brother about the fate of Jack the Body – the dead husband and father – but after long nights of lying awake, agonizing and charting the difficult course of likely conversations with Daniel and Sandra, he decided that he would absorb the burden himself. He decided that he owed it to them.

What Henry noticed, to his surprise, was that during these torpid dark hours his body seemed to be repairing itself – his heart was pumping forcefully and regularly, his lungs bloomed and his spine lost its stiffness and found its strength. His corporeality was returning and he was happy – probably happier than he'd ever been – but even so, even as he felt the growing absence of things he'd once thought defined him, and even as he rejoiced in the rejuvenation of his body, he knew that there was still something essential missing.

45

The great and powerful mechanism that is Hollywood can, on occasion, move with a bewildering and mysterious swiftness. When the machine wants something done – that injection of hype, that change of image, that reversal of fortune – it can get that thing done so quickly and completely it sometimes seems as if God himself is behind the operation, giving it the green light. This also works in reverse. When Hollywood doesn't want something to happen, the red light will appear suddenly and with a brightness almost blinding in its intensity. It had happened, deservingly, to Fatty Arbuckle. It had happened, undeservingly, to Hal Ashby. It should have happened, but inexplicably hadn't, to Joe Eszterhas. More recently, it had happened to David Caruso, Julia Phillips, Jane Hamsher and Don Simpson (although in the case of Simpson his death was held largely responsible). And now, or so he felt, surrounded by a blizzard of ripped-open envelopes, it was Henry's turn.

Just two weeks after he'd sent out his seventy-odd scripts, the letters of rejection had already passed twenty. There had also been about a dozen phone calls, but although more direct and personal, they hurt less because they left behind no physical evidence. In addition to the outright rejections were the numerous letters which told him, in varying tones of haughty condescension or snitty dismissiveness, that the company was not, nor would it ever be, in the habit of looking at 'unrepresented' scripts. A script was nothing in Hollywood without an agent; a writer even less.

'Dear Mr Poddermakker,' read the shortest of the responses from people who claimed to have read the script, '*Holen Cawffle* is pretty awffle.' Almost surprising himself, Henry had laughed out loud at the letter. It was so pithy and succinct he wished he'd written it himself, or at least had a job where he got to write letters like that to people like himself. The longest and most encouraging letter he received was from Jersey Films ('. . . while the premise is unusual and interesting and offers strong romantic/comic potential, you seem somewhat confused as to who the character actually is, and this severely weakens the overall dramatic structure of the entire script . . .'). There was also an expression of vague interest from a company called ArtKore, which he'd learned too late was a porno film production company. On the other hand, Henry reasoned, maybe if he removed most of the plot points and the characters' clothing, ArtKore might go for it.

But Henry's most promising lead – if only because he'd actually met the guy – was his appointment with H. M. Swansong.

High above Wilshire Boulevard, in a twentieth-floor suite, Henry exited an elevator as big as his bedroom and wandered down a quiet, carpeted hallway that smelled almost defiantly hygienic, as though it was patrolled by dentists. He found Swansong's office at the end of the hall, knocked and entered.

'Hello, ma'am,' he said to the young receptionist, as unnervously as he could. Like a lot of women in L.A. she was pretty, but in a way that suggested that, unlike a lot of women in L.A., she didn't think she should be given her own series or a recording contract within the next fifteen minutes. But she was still pretty enough to be considered beautiful if she became famous. She nodded and smiled at Henry as he cracked his shin on a magazine-scattered coffee table. Behind her was a door to another office. It was slightly ajar, and through the gap Henry could hear faint, but insistent murmuring.

'My name's Henry . . .' He stopped and let out a long sigh, smiling at the end of it. He raised his leg and rubbed his shin. 'Henry, ah . . . Powdermaker. I think I have an appointment with Mr Swansong.' And a broken tibia.

The quietly pretty receptionist opened her mouth and, in a tone that didn't match her face, shouted fiercely, 'Mr Swansong'll see you when he's damn good and ready!' Then with an urgent hand she beckoned Henry over to her small desk and handed him a card. 'Dear Sir or Madam, I apologize for what I just said and the way I said it. Mr Swansong pays me extra to do it and I need the money. I don't mean anything personal by it. Yours truly, Nathalie Reuter. P.S. Please do not verbally acknowledge receipt of this card and please destroy it when you leave.'

Henry laughed briefly but Nathalie gave him a pleading look. He stopped immediately but continued smiling widely, as he'd recently decided that exposed teeth were essential to Hollywood success on either side of the camera. He remembered William Goldman's line from his book *Adventures in the Screen Trade* about what he'd called 'audition meetings': that the proper note to strike was a mixture of shy, self-deprecating intelligence and wild, barely controllable enthusiasm.

Before Henry had time to sit down, rub his shin some more, flick through the day's edition of *Variety* and develop some wild, barely controllable enthusiasm, a telephone rang. He looked up. Nathalie had begun nodding even before she picked it up. 'Yes, H. M. Yessir. Uh-huh. Yessir, I'll tell him.' Not quite covering the mouthpiece with her hand, and with imploring eyes, she shouted, 'He's damn good and ready!!'

Swansong's office was enormous, dimly lit and quiet – despite the fact that there was a small film crew in there with the producer. Henry's pasted-on smile remained as he walked in, even though

Swansong was busy muttering into the camera trained on his face and didn't acknowledge Henry's presence. There were big, framed Wallace Ting and Gustav Klimt prints on one wall – spills of color in an otherwise beige room that somehow reminded Henry of 1987. Behind Swansong's huge desk was a floor-to-ceiling window, through which Henry saw the towers around Rodeo Drive, a few miles away; there was also a tall, mirrored wet bar with the words 'Fuck you' beveled into the glass. No awards, placards or photographs of H. M. with his arm flopped pallishly across celebrity shoulders.

Swansong finally finished his monologue for the camera and came around from his desk with an outstretched arm; his fingernails were coated in clear gloss and breath/lapel buffed to a high varnish. 'Good to see you, kid. Where's this agent of yours? He come with you?' He made a big show of looking behind Henry. 'No. No, I see you're alone. That I can see. I guess he had other business to attend to, am I right? No matter. You want a drink? A soda? Or something with a little kick in it? Scotch? Vodka? Rum? Gin? Brandy? Tequila? My booze is your booze, which I can tell you're thinking is a good sign that I like you already, isn't it, aren't you?' Henry shook his head. Swansong removed a heavy cut crystal goblet from the bar then filled it with milk from a refrigerator below, taking his time with a series of feminine, almost dainty movements. After his first sip the producer removed a white handkerchief from his jacket pocket and dabbed at his moistened lips then made smacking sounds of satisfaction that seemed to fly through the air with a physical presence, small dark gnats of noise.

The film crew – a furtive woman director, a fat, horribly dressed cameraman with an Arriflex and a hairy, horribly dressed sound guy holding a boom microphone – were close behind Swansong, making Henry very self-conscious. Even if he did drink during the day, which he practically never did, he certainly didn't want it recorded on film. Swansong caught Henry's nervous glance and said, 'Try to ignore these guys. They're doing a documentary about me for PBS. About the industry. Certain aspects of the business. Try not to take any notice of them. They won't get in your way.

You won't get in this kid's way, will you, fellas? C'mon, take a chair. Let's sit down.'

As he moved toward Swansong's desk, Henry looked warily over at the crew. 'Do I have to sign a release?'

'A release?' Swansong said, sinking into his leather armchair. '*You're* not gonna be in it, kid. It's about people in the business – you'll be cut out.' He turned back to the camera, which had moved to the side of his desk, and talked straight down the barrel, a smile trying vainly to take root around his mouth. 'Fucking kid takes one meeting and he's talking releases!' He changed his tone from faux comedy to sincere sincerity as he looked over at the director. 'Honey, you can edit that "fuck" out, right? I don't want to come across as some sorta blue-collar type.' He turned back to Henry and took another milk sip and lip dab before saying, 'Anyway, about this script of yours – I love it, I really do. It's really wonderful, it's fine. For a first draft, it's a quite nice piece of work, which, with some development –' Swansong held up an index finger and angled his head – 'I say again, with some development, could be really wonderful. That's the key word here – development. You hear me? But don't worry, I got some ideas, some really incredible ideas. It's a great story, kid, but I think we can lick it! What I said before about development: we need a construction man, a dialogue man, a polish man, and an additional dialogue man and ba da bing!bing!bing! we got a movie! Also, I hate the title. But I've got some notes. You ready? You ready for my notes?'

'I guess,' Henry said. 'Sure. Is it about nudity? Because–'

'We're no longer pursuing the nudity route. I got something new. I've got notes, some very good notes – three words,' Swansong said, holding up three fingers. 'He's a dog.'

'Who's a dog?' Henry asked. His shin was killing him.

'The main guy, whatsisname, Hampton. The kid pretending to be Hampton. What kind of a name is Hampton, anyway? Why d'you call him something stupid like that for?'

'It's Holden, not Hampton. And I didn't name him that, Salinger did.'

'Who's that, your partner? I didn't realize you were part of a team, which I have to say I never heard of the guy. Where is he? He coming along?'

'He didn't want to leave the house.' Henry noticed the director giggling and, beginning to enjoy himself, he smiled very slightly. 'So you're saying Holden Caulfield is a dog? I'm not too ... I mean, how would you get a dog to be all self-conscious and charmingly whiny?'

'Animation, you daffy bastard. It'll be an animated feature, a cartoon, a Disney-style cartoon. Tunes by Elton John, some piano jockey like that. Billy ... whatsisname. Coupla star voices for the leads and bang! we're in Hitsville. You ever see *Toy Story*, that 3-D thing? I'm talkin' something like that. *Hundred and One Dalmatians* meets *Cruel Intentions*.'

'About a singing dog who pretends to be a character out of a book?'

Swansong fluttered his fingers as he spoke. 'With a few creative tweaks here and there. Some finessing. Some improvements. Remember what I said was the key word here, development. Development. We'll log-line it as *White Fang* meets *The Lion King*. Maybe a little *Fritz the Cat* if there's any humping.'

'I don't think there should be any humping.'

Swansong raised his goblet. 'What you think doesn't matter. Way I'm thinking, Tom's a strong possibility.' The handkerchief reappeared.

Henry wondered if he meant Hanks or Cruise. Surely not Arnold?

'Maybe Bambi whatsername from that cunt movie for the love interest. She's hot right now.'

Oh God, Henry thought, this is too much. 'Is he any particular breed of dog?' he asked, not wanting to think about the fact that Bambi had become a desirable Hollywood property.

'Yeah, he's a whaddayacall, a German Shepherd. He's still got the red cap, though. He still wears that backwards cap on his head. I like that. It adds character, wearing that cap.'

'Between his pointed ears?'

'That's right! You're with me, you're seeing what I'm seeing, am I right?'

'Yeah, unfortunately I think I am, and, while I've got nothing against cartoons, per se, I think—'

'Hey! Don't get lippy with me, kid.' The tone of Swansong's voice changed, as though he'd become a whole other person. Somebody very mean and very angry.

'I'm sorry?'

'Don't start up with your per ses. Next it'll be to wit and ipso facto. I don't like that sorta talk. Keep it straight. Latin's for priests and homos.'

'Oh,' Henry said. 'Well, anyway, I think I'm gonna have to pass.'

'What?' Swansong's voice was loud and flat, like a dead piano key struck with a hammer. 'What?' he repeated on a lower note.

'I don't like the idea too much. I'm gonna pass on it.'

'You're gonna pass? *You're* gonna pass? Let me tell you something, you fucking little pisher – you don't pass. You're just the goddam writer. You do not pass. I do the passing. Understand?'

'I guess so, but what do I do if I don't like your idea?'

'Stand up,' Swansong said. He circled the great wooden desk, taking quick little steps that fell silently on the thick carpet. The film crew followed. 'I said, get up!' Glancing upward to ensure that he didn't hit his head on the microphone, Henry rose; Swansong was inches away, breathing harshly through tiny, flaring nostrils. 'What do you do if you don't like my idea?' the producer said quietly. 'That's what you want to know?'

Smiling nervously and, he hoped, appeasingly, Henry verbally shuffled. 'Well . . . well . . . well, I did, but now . . . y'know, now—'

'Bitch!' Swansong spat, his neck rising and thinning like a cobra's. 'You dirty little bitch. You are *nobody*. You are *nothing*. Your opinions count for precisely nothing. Do you understand that? I make movies. You pump gas or wait tables or hustle your cock or whatever the fuck it is you do, but you do not make movies. I make movies! I have produced four full-length animated features, each with a domestic gross in excess of eighty-six million, and I've personally poured the pork to three of the stars of those movies.'

Henry cleared his throat so his voice wouldn't catch. 'You . . . you sleep with cartoon characters?'

Swansong's open hand flew up and slapped Henry hard across the face. Henry almost fell down, spreading his legs to keep steady. He looked down and saw blood from his cut shin on his shoe, spreading onto the carpet in a glistening red pool.

'Just who the almighty *fuck* do you think you are, anyway!?' screamed the producer.

In the sudden quiet that followed, Henry could hear the faint whir of film rolling through the camera. He could hear the hum of the Nagra and Swansong's rough breathing and the hammering of his own heart and he could still feel the weight of the words spoken only moments ago: 'Who do you think you are?' Nobody moved. Nobody spoke. But the camera was still on him and Henry knew that this was his moment. He glanced into the mirror above the bar, then into the lens of the camera, opened his mouth and the words flowed; a clear, rushing stream.

Part 6

46

In the distance the black outline of a saw-toothed mountain range is faintly visible, its rough peaks dusted with snow catching light off the rising moon. It is the kind of mountain range on which, if we look hard enough, we might see – or imagine – a long row of tiny mules and prospectors, pickaxes slung across their silhouetted backs, slowly making their way across the dips and troughs. Swiftly pulling back from the mountains, in the sudden, looming foreground we see a flickering blue neon arrow on top of a slope-roofed building. The arrow points down to the word 'Motel', bright red against the darkening sky. Following the arrow down, we see that the gutter on the roof is overflowing with the brittle, bottle-green carcasses of dead insects, drawn to the light and extinguished by it. Beneath the gutter/graveyard hang loose, black electrical wires, thick as fingers, and below the wiring is a small window, flimsily covered by two thin lace curtains. Moving in through the window, past the curtains, we see a man lying on a bed in a cluttered, dingy room. His eyes are open, staring at nothing; somewhere in the room a clock is ticking. In a corner, a blank television screen buzzes white. We see the clock but do not notice the time, then return to the man's piercing blue eyes, still empty for a moment until the room is filled with the trilling of the alarm. The man's hand swipes the clock silent to the floor. Moments later he is in a tiny messy kitchen, wearing pants and an untucked shirt, a tie hanging loosely around his neck. There is water boiling on a dirty hotplate. He places a fresh filter in a Chemex-style coffee-maker, then reaches for a tin of coffee. We can tell by the look in his eyes that it is empty. He glances at a waste bin. He bends down and removes a used coffee filter from the bin, holds it up for inspection, sniffs it and, after a moment, with a look of heavy decision setting in his face, he plonks the soggy filter into the percolator.

Lying on the motel bed, the TV remote by his side, Henry laughs out loud. The film is *Harper*, and the man with the blue eyes is Paul Newman. He has never seen it before but knows the scene he is watching very well because he has read it many times in William Goldman's *Screen Trade*. Goldman describes it vividly, Henry remembers it vividly and here it is, precisely as he has imagined it, unfolding on the television right before his eyes: Newman's resigned expression as he stares at the lumpy brown filter, the slump of his shoulders, and his twisted mouth, almost gagging as he takes a sip of the brown muck. It is all exactly as Henry has pictured in his head. He laughs once more and the sound commingles with the clunking noise of two atonal bells outside his window. The bells ring whenever a car drives over a rubber hose in the gas station next door to the motel, and every time Henry hears them he catches a mental glimpse of the concrete driveway, the two grease-stained pumps and the signs advertising cold beer, ice and friendly service.

The motel room is small and dark, the furniture – two chairs, a dressing table and a double bed – little more than grim outlines which jump and shudder in the flickering light of the television screen. In that gray light Henry lies below the small window, on the soft bed, and thinks about all the things that have led to him ending up here in this small room, alone, waiting.

The deal. He had left Swansong's office in a stumbling daze, dragging his bleeding shin with him like a dead thing, caked blood spattered across the knuckles of his right hand. His unseeing eyes and stiff leg made him feel like the zombie he'd created that long-ago afternoon; the still-burning smack on his cheek the only thing that assured him he wasn't dead. When he got back to his apartment he sat on the couch staring at the walls, wondering what had happened to him, what he'd done. He sat there for three or four hours and he might have sat there forever – drowning in the inchoate thoughts of failure, success, humiliation, revenge, fate, death and destiny which swirled in and out of him, mixing with his blood and with the heat trapped in the small room – if the telephone hadn't rung.

'Hi,' she'd said. 'It's me.' Just like that; breezy almost.

'Hi,' he said, as casually as he could, even though his stomach was rolling. And as the conversation continued, Henry could almost feel the landscape of his life changing. It was like being in the earthquake all over again. He had to force himself to speak. 'Well . . . God, gosh, so . . . uh, well, yeah . . . so, uh, so how are you?'

'I got your letter,' she said.

'What letter?'

'Oh come on, Henry, don't be so disingenuous. It's oily. The letter you sent to the house.' Still breezy.

'I never sent any–'

'You owe my mother for the postage, by the way. There was no stamp on it.'

Stunned, Henry realized that the last letter he'd written Madeleine must have slipped in among the pile of scripts he'd mailed out. *I love you. That's all I have left to say, and all I've ever wanted to say.* 'Oh. What did it say?'

'God, Henry,' she said, the breeziness gone, replaced by a gust of exasperation. 'This wasn't an easy phone call to make, you know. And you're certainly making it a lot more difficult by acting all . . . amnesiac about everything.'

'I'm sorry, Maddy. It's . . . I can't explain. It's very complicated.' He loved saying 'Maddy' again; saying it to *her*.

'Yes, I suppose it must be,' she said drily. 'And you know what the real kicker was with that letter? You know what the worst part was, the thing that . . . Oh, never mind.' She sighed. 'I guess you forgot.'

'Forgot what?'

She became crisp, a cold snap. 'Never mind. What was all that Stefan and Vienna stuff about? Some film reference I'm sure, but I certainly didn't get it.'

'That's why it's quite complicated, Madeleine.' He liked saying 'Maddy' better. 'Where are you?'

'At home.'

'Where home?'

'*Home* home. My parents' place.'

'I remember it well. How's the old trampoline?'

'Had to be put down years ago.'

'Sad. So have you, uh, you got a job?'

'Yes, but I'm quitting because I hate the smell of the place. It stinks of affirmative action. And pity.'

Henry took a deep breath. 'Are you –' he forced the word out – 'married?' Madeleine said nothing. 'Well?'

'No.'

'Boyfriend?'

'God, you're unbelievable, Henry.'

'In a good way?'

'No, in a I-can't-believe-you're-being-so-quick-and-blunt way.'

'I know,' Henry said. 'Tell you the truth, I'm surprising myself. So have you?'

'Nope.'

Henry's heart thundered. 'How long're you gonna be home for?'

'A while.'

He could hear her tone thawing. 'A while as in hours or days?'

'Quite the interrogator aren't you, Hanky?' Melting.

'Hours or days, Maddy? C'mon, please.'

'I dunno. A few more days maybe.'

'Wait there,' he said quickly.

The next few hours were a blur. He felt enriched, uplifted, atomically energized. 'God, I feel so alive!!' he'd shouted, then laughed himself breathless at the B-movie hysteria of the sentiment. It was as though somebody had called and offered him a three-picture deal every day for the rest of his life, then called back when they realized he couldn't possibly fulfill the obligation and rescinded the offer, but paid him out in full anyway. A Jon Peters-

Peter Guber kind of feeling, he thought, again laughing out loud. His heart was suspended by a golden parachute.

He played just one three-minute song over and over again on his CD player: 'Reza' by Sergio Mendes and Brasil '65, a birthday gift from Charlie many years before. He sang along, even though he couldn't understand a word of the Portuguese lyrics – except *ave Maria* – but the piano, guitar and Wanda de Sah's lovely, husky voice singing the strange tune, a compelling combination of desperately yearning but deeply hopeful, calmed him as he worked. By the time he had boxed up and cleaned his apartment he knew every sound in the song by heart – every rimshot and guitar pluck, every angular stab of the piano and each meaningless Portuguese syllable – and he couldn't wait for Madeleine to hear it.

After he washed the blood off his swollen and blue-tinged knuckles, he'd called the copy center on Sierra Bonita and asked them to send Reyes over. An hour later Reyes was there, standing in the doorway with an expression of confused contemplation. The name 'Cesar' was stitched on his shirt front.

'Hi,' Henry said. 'I'm leaving town. You can have everything in here. Or nothing. Whatever you like. There's a good TV and a VCR, the stereo, the couch, a desk, a computer – the "p" sticks on it – some kitchen stuff and a bed which has seen no action whatsoever. So it's ... safe. You can have everything you see except the suitcase and that picture of the guy at the typewriter in front of the guy lying on the couch tapping the wall. I want that. There's also about two thousand movies on tape underneath a pile of movie books and magazines down in the back garden. You can have those too, if you're interested. I'm not really that interested anymore. They're good, but not that good.' Breathless, Henry put his hands on his knees and panted for a minute. 'Oh, I forgot,' he continued, straightening up. 'You can also live here if you want, for the next six months, anyway – the rent's paid up until then. I don't know if you're married or got kids or whatever, but if you can fit, you're welcome.'

Reyes lowered his eyelids and looked at Henry suspiciously.

'You sell your script for a million dollars? You a rich man now, that it? Getting rid of all your old things to start a new life?'

Henry shook his head emphatically, repeatedly. 'Oh God, no. Not at all. Well, I *am* starting a new life but . . . but not as a rich man. I just want to leave all this stuff behind. Come on in.'

Reyes' heavy left boot hit the wooden floor hard as he limped into the living room. 'You going after the girl?'

Henry smiled. 'From the script or in life?'

'Would be pretty stupid to go after some broad ain't even real, wouldn't it?'

'Yes, Reyes, it certainly would.' Henry nodded. 'In a way, I guess this is kind of like the wrap-up at the end of the third act. Tidying everything up. The loose ends and all that.'

'This not a film though, man. This what it is – la vida.'

'Oh, I know it Reyes, more than I ever did before. But it'd be nice if the old vida was a bit more like the way it is in films, wouldn't it?'

'Sure,' Reyes said. 'But it ain't.'

'Well, I know one way to find out.'

'Yeah, how?'

'D'you by any chance speak Portuguese?'

'No.'

Henry was quiet for a moment. 'Okay, well, I guess *that* exact moment would be different in a film – you'd be translating song lyrics for me right now. But everything else – you showing up here and my giving you all this stuff – that's pretty unexpected and . . . and . . . cinematic in a way, isn't it?'

Henry liked the way Reyes nodded unconsciously, with the corners of his mouth pulled down. 'If it the real thing, this a pretty kind offer you making. A pretty good deal.'

'Oh, it's real all right, don't worry about that.' Henry handed Reyes a set of house keys and pointed to Reyes' shirt. 'Who's Cesar?'

'Cousin.'

'D'you ever wear your own shirt?'

'If it's clean, I wear it.' Reyes gave a 'what the fuck' shrug of his shoulders. 'So why me, man? Why you want to give me your 'partment and all your things?'

'I like you.'

Reyes nodded once. 'Okay.' Then they shook hands, and Henry had liked that too.

Shaker and Rainey weren't home, so he'd written them a note.

Hey S & R,

I'm quittin' Hollywood. And, like a typical suicide, I'm wrapping things up before I go. Specifically, I'm willing my car to you. If you need to know how to change the spark plugs, there's an owner's manual in the glove compartment. Ha ha. Also feel free to chop, crop, French and/or shave as you see fit. Good luck with everything and say hello from me to the Burger Boy if they ever resurrect the fat bastard.

Henry 'Henry' Powdermaker (the guy from upstairs)

P.S. If you see a club-footed fella removing stuff from my apartment, don't call the cops. I gave it all to him. He's called Reyes but he sometimes travels under the names Sammy and Cesar. Also, he might be moving in. You'll like him.

Back upstairs, he pulled the picture of Billy Wilder and Izzy Diamond from the bare wall and threw it in his suitcase, along with the Brasil '65 disc. He thought about taking the picture of Sturges, but Sturges had not had a partner; he'd died alone.

Henry called a cab. There was just one more thing to do, one last element to take care of in order to make everything complete – closure, they'd call it in L.A.; or a 'payoff' in studio language – before he finally left.

A half-hour later the cab pulled up at the corner of La Brea and Sunset. Henry climbed out saying, 'Wait here a minute, will ya, Mac? I'll be back in a second.'

'The name's Vernon!' the cabby shouted, as Henry jogged toward the mouth of the alley where Toby Strong performed. Henry was surprised to see a big crowd spilling out of the alley and onto the street, standing in a mess of discarded greasy, yellow wrappers from the nearby El Pollo Loco. He muscled through and was even more surprised to see a large, busy film crew set up in the alley; Ken Burns, sitting in a director's chair, whispering closely to an eagerly nodding Toby, who was dressed in his performance rags. The wooden vegetable box he used to sit on was now a clearly branded plastic Pepsi crate. Henry caught a glimpse of the film slate: *A Whole Generation and Change – the Lives and Lies of Toby Strong*. He wished he'd had the picture of Preston Sturges with him, so that he could've wordlessly handed it to Toby, with something wry written on it. 'So they discovered you, without the flouncy shirt': that would've been perfect. But even though he was standing right on the verge of film, at the edge of the great world he'd once yearned so keenly to inhabit, this was still *la vida* and the beer-stained photograph of Sturges was lying in a pile of junk in a back yard in West Hollywood. Still, it was a pretty good moment.

Henry ran back to the cab. 'The airport,' he gasped. 'And–'

'If you tell me to step on it, I'll dump you right fuckin' here!' Vernon said.

Henry laughed. 'Actually I was gonna ask if you could take us via a view of Mount Lee.'

'Mount what!?' Vernon spat. 'Mount where!?'

'The Hollywood sign. I wondered if we could whip by the Hollywood sign.'

Vernon muttered, 'Fuckin' tourist,' and wrenched the cab around.

'Forget it. I changed my mind. Let's just go straight to the airport, huh?' Henry said, and the cab continued, making a full circle. Henry's right hand still hurt but he loved the pain.

'Wish you'd make up your fuckin' mind, bub.'

'I have made up my mind, Vernon.' Henry leaned on the name. 'Take me to LAX. I don't want to spend a minute longer than I have to in this stupid place – so step on it!!'

Hollywood. The plane flew out over the glittering Pacific, banked right at Catalina Island and headed back over sprawling Los Angeles. Henry had disliked being hemmed in next to a window, but what he saw just a few minutes into the flight made him glad of the discomfort. He'd been staring down at the brown mass of suburban L.A., which was intersected by black roads, ropy free-ways, sun-baked white buildings and a thousand shimmering swimming pools, trying to spot his apartment; wondering which of the tiny blocks his father called home, thinking abstractedly about the future he'd left behind, when all of a sudden the plane tilted and Mount Lee hove into view. Several hundred people, a mass of bobbing, colored specks, were gathered around the sign: HOLLYWOOD. An enormous crane lowered the D into place and there followed a flurry of fluttering white thrown up by the crowd, an instant storm of paper streamers which disappeared as quickly as it had been created, scattered and flattened by the wind. Hollywood was back in business.

Henry could have sworn he heard the eruption of a great cheer from the crowd as it greeted the marvelous moment. And he won-dered, too, if his own heart hadn't briefly beaten a little faster along with it.

47

In the motel room, many weeks later, Henry thinks about his flight from Hollywood, his sudden abandonment of film, and wonders whether perhaps the reasons for his being on the sagging, creaky bed at this moment go back further than that fate-hammered after-noon with Swansong. He changes the channel on the huge, teak-covered television and sees an anchorwoman named Suzi Wardrobe open her mouth, but before she can say something delightful or dreadful he changes channels again. William Bendix in a foxhole flickers and wobbles for a second before Henry changes again, not really sure what he's looking for but certain that Suzi and William aren't it.

Every little thing is connected to everything else – the words arrive out of nowhere, clear and sharp, as though projected white and bright from somewhere in his frontal lobe to just in front of his eyes. They are from a film, but for the moment Henry cannot recall which one. A few weeks ago, he feels sure, the name of the film, who spoke the lines, who wrote the lines and who directed the person speaking the lines would have come to him immediately. Now he is not so concerned. Or, he wonders, is it consumed? Every little thing is connected to everything else. It sounds like it could be Michael Moriarty via Waldo Salt and Robert Altman. Or maybe John Cazale on behalf of George Roy Hill and Ring Lardner Jr. Who knows, Henry thinks, and who cares? But at the same time, a part of him that refuses to go away knows for certain that neither of those trios were ever involved in a film together. Then, with a sad, deadening shock, he remembers that they are his own words, from his own film *Three Kinds o' Headache*. Written by Henry Powdermaker, delivered by Henry Powdermaker and directed by Henry Powdermaker. And he wonders whether if he hadn't made that film, hadn't hit Ethan Vaughan with the camera, if none of that had happened, would he still be here, right now, waiting for her? Or did all of it have to begin with his very first rejection from film school?

He picks up the letter on the bedside table – slightly grubby, soft and limp from being folded and unfolded so many times – and absorbs the strange, awful words once more.

'Dear Mr Powderkamer,' the letter begins (when he first read it, the typo made Henry wonder if it was intended for someone else; someone who was almost, but not quite, Henry Powdermaker). 'We are very pleased to offer you a place in History and Theory of Film at Syracuse University. To arrange enrolment please telephone our admissions office no later than . . .'

The deadline is the next day. He'll decide then. Maybe ask what Madeleine thinks he should do, although he's pretty sure he's made up his mind. Probably. But perhaps she'll make him re-think his decision. If he sticks to it. If he tells her. 'Where the devil is she?' he says aloud . . .

*

Long shot. The street was dark and deserted. It was late, after eleven o'clock, and he'd felt like a criminal; secretive and hunched over the phone, steaming up the glass with eager breath and anxious smoke. 'Hi,' he'd said, stamping his feet. 'It's me. Are your parents home?'

'Why?'

'I don't want anybody to know I'm here.'

'Where?'

'Corner of Seawall and Manley. In a phone box. It says to call 555–6273 for a good time. Ask for Rudy.'

'Oh, it does not. That five-five-five thing is only in movies.'

'True enough. But I really am just ten minutes away. Are they home?'

'No.' She sighed. 'Henry, what are you doing here?'

'I need to see you, Maddy.'

'Gee, how flattering. It's only been more than a decade.'

'What can I say? I'm pathologically latent. When'll they be back?'

'They're away. The house up in Macwahoc.'

'Can I come over?'

'If you're after a good time, fella, call Rudy.'

'Don't be so cheeky. You think I came all this way for a roll in the hay?'

'It's been a long time, Henry. How do I know what you want?'

'Y'know it's pretty uncomfortable in this booth, Madeleine. Smells quite awful too. Don't make me call Rudy. C'mon, you have to have a little faith in people.'

'Why do you think that you can just show up here after all this time and stroll back into my life? Oh Jesus, Henry, you bastard – now you're making me sound like something from a daytime soap.'

Henry laughed and stubbed his cigarette out on the concrete at his feet. 'I can't wait to see you, Maddy, you make me laugh. You really do. I've gotta see you. I came all this way.' He paused. 'Come on, you're killing me. Don't make me wait.'

'What's the sudden hurry?'

'The hurry is that I've wasted way too much time on the wrong things. Stupid stuff. I've got to get on with the things that matter. Real things. I've let too many people go who I shouldn't have. By which I mean you.'

'So go visit your mother. When's the last time you saw her?'

'I'll pay my respects to the widow Powdermaker after I'm done with you.'

'What the hell's *that* mean?'

'Nothing. Something s'posed to be rueful and witty. Never mind. Please, Maddy, I've come a long way. Really.'

'I hope you mean that figuratively as well as literally.' She sighed as Henry held his breath. 'Bring something to drink.'

He'd slammed down the phone and made a loud noise of joy that startled an owl in a nearby tree.

A short time later Henry was standing at the front door of Madeleine's parents' house, straightening his tie, patting down his hair and making sure that there was a nice, sharp crease in the trousers of his suit, convinced that women – especially slightly older women – appreciated that sort of thing. He tried not to think about the fact that his own mother's house was just a few hundred feet away and that she was probably in there boiling or pickling some vegetables she'd plucked from her garden. He decided that he would call her soon, but just then he had room in his heart and mind for only one person.

She answered the door. His throat dried, his brain numbed and his heart stopped. Madeleine Margaret Catherine Ford was more beautiful than anyone he had ever seen in his life. She wore no makeup, and against her dusty brown skin her green eyes shone, as though lit from within. Sounds – not even words – tried to escape from his mouth but nothing came. He blinked. He tried to clear his throat, his brain, but nothing happened – he was literally struck dumb by her beauty.

'Henry?' she said, looking somewhere past him. 'Is it you?'

He coughed, startling her, and his heart resumed its panic. 'Of course it's me, Maddy. Who else?' He thrust the bottle at her. 'See what I brought!'

Madeleine smiled . . .

*

'See what I brought!' Henry says out loud, viciously mocking his own voice. He lets himself fall backward on the bed and covers his eyes with his hands as he lies there, reliving the awful moment. 'See what I brought.'

The door to the motel room opens and Madeleine takes a tentative step inside the small room. 'See what I brought,' she says, holding up two cans of dripping soda. She is smiling and although she's teasing, the words are not said nastily.

With a quick and guilty glance at the letter on the table, Henry gets off the bed and comes toward Madeleine. 'Yes, I was just thinking about what a complete idiot I was that night.' When he is close to Madeleine he stops, to let her know from the warmth of his body, his breath on her neck, that he is there. Slowly, gently he reaches forward and takes the cold cans from her hands.

'I heard from outside,' she says, and puts a flat hand on his chest. 'What'd I get?'

'A Dr Pepper and an Orange Crush. Which one do you want?'

'Orange, please. We've been over this a thousand times before, Henry,' Madeleine says. 'Don't worry about it.'

He pulls the tab off the orange soda and wraps her fingers around it. 'I know, but it still bothers me. I once told that old girlfriend of mine, Audrey, about how if you don't keep in touch with people too much, they seem to stop growing in your mind. That they're stuck at the time when you last saw them, or maybe at the time when you liked them best. And, my innate stupidity aside, that's how it was with you. I mean obviously you looked very different, unbelievably beautiful and everything, but it just didn't occur to me that you'd ... y'know, that you were –' he swallows '– blind.'

'Quit doing the dramatic pause-and-swallow before you say the big bad word, Henry. I already know I'm blind. I know that you didn't know and that now you do, so just don't worry about it. You didn't make me any blinder.' She takes his hand and leads him to the bed and they sit on the edge. She laughs breathily. 'Remember that, the "getting blinder" crack?'

'Of course, Madeleine. Jesus. What are you trying to do, make me die of embarrassment?'

'This from a guy who's sleeping with me. Don't be so damned precious. You can assume a degree of relaxed familiarity with me if you like, Henry. Fake it even, if you have to.'

'I know I've ... we've ... y'know, had sex, Maddy. I know. I was there every time. But–'

She nudges him aside and lies down lengthwise on the bed. 'This is a bit like Pookie and whatever his name was from *The Sterile Cuckoo*, isn't it? All these motels. You wanna peel the old tomato?' Madeleine says, imitating Liza Minnelli circa 1969.

'Or *Lolita*.'

'Or *Paris, Texas*.'

'I never saw that, except for what you told me on the trampoline one night.'

She takes a sip of soda. 'You didn't miss much.'

'Anyway, I really wish you'd let me do stuff like that, Maddy. Getting the sodas and like that. You could hurt yourself. Break your nose or something.' He turns to her. There is a drop of orange sitting on her lip for a moment before she flicks it away with the tip of her tongue. 'God, you're so good-looking I can hardly stand it. Especially your nose. You don't want to break that nose, Madeleine Margaret. So let me get the sodas from now on, huh?'

'Listen to you. As though I haven't been tapping around for years already.'

Montage. Henry lies next to Madeleine and thinks about all the motels they have slept in over the past weeks. They have driven a long, long way, covered thousands of miles and dozens of motels. Madeleine loves to travel, the changing scents and smells, the shifts in air from dusty and dry to oppressively humid to wet with rain that has not yet fallen; the sounds of different cities, their distinct tastes and pulses.

One afternoon, he remembers, just a few days after they had bought the car and decided to take their long drive to anywhere, in a small roadside restaurant on the coast, Henry read the menu aloud to Madeleine. He advised her not to order the corn on the cob because it looked too much on the soft and brown side of crisp and yellow. 'That's a shame,' Madeleine said. 'Corn's a good food for the blind.' He'd wondered why, until a short while later when he watched her eat. He had never noticed before, because he was usually staring silently into her eyes, or describing the things around them, but on this afternoon he watched her hands. She would carefully move her left hand over the plate, searching for the location of her food, delicately touching whatever was there and bringing the fork over to it swiftly, but with an economy of movement that Henry knew was designed to make the least of her disability. Sometimes, however, a spot of cream or sauce would remain on her left hand. On that afternoon Henry had not known whether to say anything. These days, no more than a month since they'd set out, he would softly take her hand and remove the cream, sometimes wiping it off with a napkin, sometimes gently kissing it away.

While they drove, Henry told Madeleine everything that had happened since their last summer together but left until the very end the story of how he'd sat in the cinema watching her watch *Manhattan*. 'You know I always wondered about that,' Madeleine told him. 'It felt like someone was poking me in the back with their eyes. Especially at the end, when Mariel Hemingway leaves to study in London. I was getting poignancy hits from in front and behind. It was you. You and Woody Allen.'

In great, if sometimes painful, detail he described to her his film *Point of View*, its execution and origin. 'That business with the coins under the pillow – you doing it, I mean, not Alec,' Madeleine said. 'Did you get that from a film?'

'No, that was pure me.'

'Sweet. So you missed her while she was gone?'

'I did. But not as much as I missed you.'

'What did you hide under your pillow to remind you of me?'

'Nothing. You were on top of the pillow, Maddy. In my thoughts every night before I fell asleep and every morning when I woke.'

'You liar.'

'Yeah, you're right – the truth is I never gave you another thought since that summer.'

'Aw gee, honey, you're just as mean as can be,' she said.

He read aloud every letter he'd written her – mostly she nodded, but on one occasion she belted him angrily in the shoulder and once she silently cried.

'But enough about me,' he said, as they drove through flat, farm-country fields the color of spoiled food. 'I've had just about all of me I can take. The old me, anyway. I think there may be hope for a new model. But what about you, Maddy?'

And for the better part of the next five days, Henry listened.

'The odd thing is that when I think of it all now, telling it all to you,' Madeleine said at the end, 'it's like a montage, but without a visual element. It's all sounds and smells and odd, disjointed impressions. It's been very internal, my adult life. Composed almost entirely of thoughts and feelings and memories; no pictures.' He looked across at her as she spoke, softly playing her index finger across her lips. At her feet was a mound of ripped paper, torn takeout bags, napkins, cassette covers and magazine pages. 'I . . . I don't even know what I look like,' she said.

48

Lying next to her now in the motel room, lit only by the shimmering glow of the television, Henry wonders if everything really is connected to everything else. Did he have to be rejected from film school all those times for him and Madeleine to be together? Did he have to fail willfully and dismally in Los Angeles so they could end up here? What if something had gone right along the way – in either his or Madeleine's life? He hates to think.

'What are you thinking about?' Madeleine asks.

'Fate and destiny,' Henry answers.

'Oh, deep thoughts.'

'Actually, they're all pretty superficial and unsophisticated. I really should have opted for some sort of higher education other than watching fucking movies. It's made me into a very limited thinker. The only example I can employ to explain what I was thinking about is *An Affair to Remember*. No Shakespeare or Sophocles or Sartre or Steinbeck or anything, just the obvious, tearjerking plot devices from a corny old movie ... That's so pathetic.' And even as he says the last three words, they remind him of Donald Sutherland sighing the very same ones in *Klute*. 'God, I'm so ... bitched up by it.'

Madeleine kicks off her shoes and they drop onto the wooden floor with two small thumps. 'You're all right. A touch too self-indulgent, but I like you. Hell, I love you. You know why?'

'Of course I do. But tell me anyway, just in case.'

'Because underneath all that crap you like to put out, I think you're good, Henry. You're a poor, sad, confused, talented and annoyingly overanalytical man. But you're good. You're true. And I love the way you describe things around us. You use words ... not well, exactly, but ... properly. Truthfully.'

Henry rolls over and puts a hand on either side of Madeleine's face, his fingertips resting gently, lightly on her cheekbones. Then he leans down and kisses her. 'I love you too,' he says, wanting to bury the words deep in her heart.

'Good. Now that we've got that out of the way, what's on television?' Madeleine asks, slipping her hand under Henry's neck as he lies back down.

He reaches for the remote and flicks from channel to channel, explaining what he sees. 'Okay, we've got football players bashing into each other ... some actors pretending to be doctors ... different actors pretending to be lawyers ... Paul Newman sitting at his P.I. desk in *Harper* ... some guy building a birdcage out of beer cans ... Steve Zahn, the actor – I like that guy, he's pretty hilarious – driving a car and looking fiendish ... two women acting hostile about instant coffee ... a chainsaw commercial ... Nicky Katt, another actor I like ... he does impressive things with his hair ... the opening credits of some movie, Woody Allen I assume because Susan E. Morse is the editor and it's in that typeface ... a quiz show ... Paul Schofield in *Quiz Show* – there's a nice coincidence ... a commercial for women with big tits ...

William Devane's teeth ... a golfer ... a preacher ... Oh, good Lord!!'

Madeleine sits upright. 'What is it?'

'It's me! I'm looking at me. On the TV. I've just walked into the office of that idiot producer I told you about. Wow. This must be that documentary they were making. I totally –' He sees the PBS watermark in the corner of the screen. 'It is! I can't believe it ... this is ...'

'Calm down and tell me what's going on on the screen, Henry,' Madeleine says firmly. 'And put the sound on.'

Henry reaches for the remote control he has dropped on the floor. 'This is unbelievable.'

'Shut up and tell me what's happening!' Madeleine has grabbed Henry's left arm, pulling at it with excitement.

Henry speaks quickly. 'Okay, I'm limping toward his great big desk in this enormous office. I didn't realize I was limping so much, I'm really limping quite a bit from when I banged my shin on the coffee table just before. And I'm wearing – d'you really want to know what I'm wearing?'

'I want to know everything that I can't hear. I can't hear clothes.'

'Okay, I'm wearing a dark-blue suit with a bright purple, actually it's more of a cerise, shirt. The whole ensemble looks pretty foolish and there's a kind of matching stupid look on my face. My mouth is sort of hanging open and I'm listening to what that Swansong is saying about the horrors and joys of being a producer, about being in "the business". He keeps calling it "the business".'

A person is either in the business or they're not in the business. That's the nature of the business. I am in the business.

'Yeah, I hear him. What's he look like?'

It's a funny industry what I said before about the business.

'He's small, obnoxiously petite. And very thin. People like that are always really thin. I think they burn all their calories by maintaining a constant, high level of rage about ... everything. A lot of insane people have that same sort of shivery thinness. His face is thin, too. Thin and sharp and mean, and he has small, weak hands with this weirdo glossy manicure on the nails. I think he thinks it's cultured. European or something. Same with this milk-drinking affectation he's got going on. He's wearing a kind of hideous mobster sweater like the ones Dennis Farina wore in *Midnight Run*. Oh, sorry, you couldn't have seen that, I guess, because . . . Now I'm going red – here in real life, I mean, not on TV.' He moves his face close to Madeleine's, floating on her warm citrus scent. He takes her hand and says, 'Feel,' placing it against his hotly embarrassed cheek. Madeleine laughs and leaves her hand there. 'Anyway, it's a horrible gray and white and black sweater and he's got these–'

'All right, forget the fashion commentary, Henry. What's happening?'

Henry watches himself standing in the middle of the room looking confused. 'I'm just standing there looking confused. Mildly retarded almost. Now I'm bending down and rubbing my shin and making a kind of scrinched-up ouch face, but not mugging too much because the pain was genuine. Which is funny, because I didn't really feel it while it was happening, only afterward.' He shakes his head. 'You know those moments?'

'I know 'em.'

'I feel like my whole life's been one of them,' Henry says. 'Right up until when you called that afternoon – this afternoon on the TV right now. And everything since then.' He turns and looks at Madeleine, her long neck, her smooth throat, her bright green eyes. He is silent for a short while, looking at her. He pulls two Marlboros from a pack, lights them both, then places one between the first two fingers of Madeleine's left hand. On the television, Henry and Swansong are discussing the idea of Holden Caulfield as a German Shepherd. 'Well . . . you saved me, Maddy.'

She squeezes Henry's arm again and kisses his shoulder. 'Okay, shut up about that for now and tell me what's going on.'

'Okay, well he's coming toward me now, he's just told me to stand up. I already told you why when I told you about all this before. So I'm standing up now, looking quite nervous and a little worried because I have no idea what's coming next.'

I've personally poured the pork to three of the stars of those movies.

'That was me clearing my throat,' Henry says.

You . . . you sleep with cartoon characters!?

Madeleine laughs, then flinches at the sound of a sharp slap.

Henry tells Madeleine, 'They've zoomed in and there are some tears coming from my left eye, but only from when he slapped me just now. I'm not crying or anything. It stung like a bastard, though. I'm trying to stand up straight but my leg is throbbing. I'm looking down and the camera has followed and now you can see blood on the carpet all round my shoe. It's very dramatic.'

Just who the almighty fuck *do you think you are, anyway!?*

'Good Lord, what an unbelievable asshole,' Madeleine says, her voice pale with shock. There is silence in the room and from the television. 'What happens now?' she asks.

Henry looks at the television.

49

Spit has landed on Henry's chin, and in the sudden quiet he can hear the faint whir of film rolling through the camera and he can hear the hum of the Nagra and Swansong's rough breathing and the hammering of his own heart and he can still feel the weight of the words spoken only moments ago: 'Who do you think you are?' Nobody moves. Nobody speaks. The camera is still on him and Henry knows that this is his moment. He glances into the mirror above the bar, then into the lens of the camera (so that it appears to Henry, sitting on the bed in the motel room, that he is addressing himself), opens his mouth and the words flow; a clear, rushing stream.

'The more important question is, who do you think you are? I know who I am, at least well enough to know that I am not one of you. And that I'll never become a part of all this garbage you seem to think the world revolves around. But who the hell are you to have such an ego? You produce cartoons, for Christ's sake. Cartoons! And even if it wasn't cartoons, it'd be the same thing

– just more useless crap getting in the way of people's lives. That's all you do. You think because you make a ton of money it gives you the right to strut through life stepping on whoever and whatever you like. To slap people in the face if they disagree with you. Jesus Christ! Who do you think you are, Mr Swansong? You're not smart, you're not wise, you're not even decent. You're an arrogant, jumped-up little fascist psychopath, is what you are. You're a cliché. An actual live cliché. You'd be funny if you weren't real. And if there weren't hundreds of you all over this city. I mean, paying your secretary to talk the way she does to people – that's just demented. That's cancer of the ego, Swansong. Cancer of the soul. You equate loudness with power – raising your voice, shouting at people to get your way, to get your point across. That's not power, that's just . . . volume. Like . . . like that ear-blasting THX message before the movie starts – the audience is listening. Of course they're fucking listening, they've got no choice with all that goddamned noise coming at them. But are they paying attention? Are they really looking at and listening to what's up there? Do they actually see how completely fucking awful most of it is?

'Who are *you* – that's the question. And here's a clue – I know what the "H" in H. M. Swansong stands for. It stands for Hollywood, because you stand for everything that's rotten and sad and wrong about the whole idea of Hollywood. You're the reason people fuck their friends over to get ahead in this ridiculous industry. Any industry in fact – there are people like you everywhere, screwing things up for everybody else. But you idiots in movies are the worst. You're the reason people lie and cheat and steal and screw and yearn their guts out for something . . . for something so fucking fatuous. Ruin their whole lives for a fantasy. People like you believe that no sacrifice is too great for a chance at immortality, so you're sacrificing everything all over the place, jettisoning everything you think is unnecessary to your glorious ascension – and your humanity, your simple decency's the first thing to go. And the saddest thing is that you think immortality is all about seeing your face or your name up on a screen and you're wrong. Completely wrong – immortality is in your heart. Let me tell you something – David Selznick, who never produced a cartoon in his life, I should warn you, said that there might have been good movies if there hadn't been a movie industry. You're the movie industry, Mr Swansong. You're every bit of the degraded, pretentious, charmless, back-biting, conceited, incompetent, snide, sneaky, insecure, pathetic, phony, heartless fuck-fest you so lovingly call "the business". Well, you can keep your "business", it's all yours. I want nothing to do with it.

'Who do I think *I* am? I'll tell you who I am – my name is Henry goddam Powdermaker and I'm getting the hell out of here.'

There was silence.

'Anything you'd care to add to your little outburst?' Swansong said, smirking.

Henry knew that words could only say so much; that the first rule of cinema was not to merely tell what was happening but to show it. He needed something visual. Something cinematic. 'Yeah,' Henry said, raising and drawing back his right hand. 'This.'

Fade to black. Madeleine is confused by a crunching sound coming from the television. 'What was that?'

Henry tells her, 'I just broke Swansong's nose. I punched him. His eye's gone all puffy and pink. There's milk all over the carpet at his feet. Milk and blood and broken glass. That's him wailing and squealing and calling out for his secretary, Nathalie. It's all muffled because he's covering his face with his hands and staggering around as though he's been hit over the head with a shovel. He's like . . . he's like a cartoon, actually.'

'What are you doing?'

At the edge of the bed, Henry looks at himself on television, where he is looking at himself in a mirror. 'There's a large mirror in front of me, which Swansong had been blocking until I thumped him, and it says "Fuck you" on the glass. I'm looking at myself in it. Fucking myself, I guess. There's me in the room looking at my reflection in the mirror. Two of me. And I'm sort of smiling at myself, this very slight but sincere smile. It's . . . this sounds pretty corny, but it's as though I'm seeing myself – the real me – for the very first time. It's a good smile. It looks . . . right. Lean forward,' he says, delicately placing his hand in the middle of Madeleine's back and guiding her. 'Closer . . .' he says. 'Closer, bend down a little . . . perfect.' He tells her, 'Now I can see you reflected in the mirror on the television. You're right next to me in there.'

Henry looks at Madeleine for a moment, then back to the television. 'It's faded to black.' He turns the television off. 'Can you picture it, Maddy, in your head I mean? Everything I've told you? Can you see?'

'Yes, Henry,' says Madeleine, turning to him. In the dim room, lit by nothing more than a pallid spill of moonlight falling through the window, her bright green eyes seem to look right at him, into him. 'Yes,' she says. 'I see.'

Acknowledgements

My sincerest gratitude to the following people, all of whom contributed in some way to this book: my agent Pat Kavanagh; everyone at Fourth Estate, in particular my editor Nicholas Pearson; my wife Sally Van Es; my friends Sophie Cunningham, Lisa Bankoff, Michelle de Kretser, Ray Edgar, Rowan McKinnon, David Brown and Laen Sanches; Michael Chabon and Tobias Wolff for their writing; Curtis Mayfield, Jorge Ben and Bernard Edwards for their music. Thank you all.